*Once again Regina was acutely aware of
his strength—and of his reputation . . .*

Taskford was said to be totally lacking in scruples when it
came to women. Nothing she'd seen in his personality
would hinder him where the ladies were concerned. His behavior toward her in the parlor of *The Golden Boar* had
proven that.

She had been cool-headed then. He'd been an utter
stranger. Now things were very different, and she panicked
as her real fear arose and demanded recognition. Regina had
always been honest with herself. She was honest with herself now. She might be nervous about what Taskford intended to do, it was true, but she was afraid of something
else.

She was terribly afraid that she might help him do it.

Ride for the Roses

Christina Kingston

JOVE BOOKS, NEW YORK

RIDE FOR THE ROSES

A Jove Book / published by arrangement with
the author

PRINTING HISTORY
Jove edition / April 2000

All rights reserved.
Copyright © 2000 by Christina Strong.
This book may not be reproduced in whole or in part,
by mimeograph or any other means, without permission.
For information address: The Berkley Publishing Group,
a division of Penguin Putnam Inc.,
375 Hudson Street, New York, New York 10014.

The Penguin Putnam Inc. World Wide Web site address is
http://www.penguinputnam.com

ISBN: 0-515-12785-X

A JOVE BOOK®
Jove Books are published by The Berkley Publishing Group,
a division of Penguin Putnam Inc.,
375 Hudson Street, New York, New York 10014.
JOVE and the "J" design
are trademarks belonging to Penguin Putnam Inc.

PRINTED IN THE UNITED STATES OF AMERICA

10 9 8 7 6 5 4 3 2 1

For Gail Fortune. Only the best.

Prologue

London 1817

Cloaked in the night he waited, hunched down in the wind-blown bushes with a loaded pistol in his hand. He watched the lighted upper window of the narrow house across the street, an evil half smile on his lips.

He'd killed once to gain the fame he wanted, the fame he deserved. He wasn't about to flinch from killing a second time to guarantee that fame.

Soon his target would appear at the window. With the guests he was entertaining, it was inevitable. Cavalrymen were hearty drinkers. So, soon *he'd* go to the drink table to pick up some crystal decanter or other to pour for one of them. And that would bring him to the window.

The drinks table would be in front of the window. He always put it in front of the window. No matter how squalid the hovel in which they'd been quartered, his quarry had carefully removed it from its custom-made crate and put that table, the only thing he had left from his fool of a father, in front of a window to catch the light.

Tonight, that silly habit was going to cost Harry Wainwright his life.

• • •

"Ha! At last!" The stocky blond threw his cards faceup on the heavy, round table, jumped to his feet and whooped, "By heaven, I've got you for once, Harry Wainwright!" His glance swept the faces of the men around him. "You're my witnesses."

The slender man to his right looked pained. His ruffled cuff fell back as he raised his hand to shield his ear. "Please, MacLain. Contain yourself. You deafen me."

"Come now, Mathers." A dark, heavily built man settled back in his chair and said, "You know how seldom one of us bests Harry. Let the man gloat."

Mathers considered briefly. "You do have a point." He turned a languid smile toward the friend who'd won the hand. "Stone has won you my permission to gloat, MacLain."

The other five men in the candlelit room laughed.

Harry Wainwright, their host, rose and went to the table in front of one of the windows for the brandy. "Gloat well. I'll not let you best me again any time soon." He was grinning as he reached for the cut-crystal decanter.

In a sharp explosion of glass, one of the windowpanes in front of Wainwright disappeared. With a splintering crack, a pistol ball smashed into the heavy walnut paneling on the opposite side of the room. Clutching his head, Wainwright staggered backward, cursing.

More curses erupted from his guests. None panicked. Old friends from army days on the Peninsular, they were inured to the sound of gunshots. Their anxiety was all for the safety of their good friend. The heavily built man kicked his chair back and leapt forward to grab and drag their host away from the window.

One of the others carefully placed his cards on the table and rose calmly.

"Smythe!" Mathers's voice held a note of panic. "Stay away from that window!"

The rotund little man who'd just gotten up ignored his friend's order and, placing himself squarely in the middle of the expanse of glass panes, drew the drapes simultaneously from either side of the window frame, blocking out the night. "Thank you for your concern, Mathers," he said in a prim voice, "but I assure you I am in no danger. Who, after all, could ever mistake *me* for Harry?" The drapes carefully closed, he turned to the injured man and inquired quietly, "How bad is it, Harry?"

"I'm fine." Wainwright lowered a bloodied hand. As the corpulent man drew closer to see for himself, he growled irritably, "Let be."

Smythe brushed Harry's hands aside, unperturbed by his host's resistance. Pulling out a large white handkerchief, he reached up and wiped the blood from Wainwright's handsome face. Peering closely, he murmured, "Ah, good. Glass cuts. They're only glass cuts." He nodded with satisfaction.

Wainwright laughed and shrugged off the arm with which his taller friend had been supporting him. "Thanks, Stone. I'm *fine*." He clapped him on the shoulder and smiled, repeating, "Thanks." Taking out and folding his own handkerchief to hold against the worst cut, the one on his forehead, he offered his guests an easy explanation. "Some drunken fool heading home to his bed got careless with a pistol. Probably scared by a shadow. Nothing to get upset about."

Mathers laughed. "Some jealous husband, more like."

Wainwright's handsome face lit with wry good humor. "Hardly. I'm not that much of a threat. You'll have to settle for the fact that it was merely an accident." He brushed glittering bits of glass from his broad shoulders.

"Ha!" MacLain, the man who'd won the last hand, wasn't

going to let that pass. "That won't wash. We all know you're deadly with the ladies, Harry."

Shrugging as if he'd tired of that accusation long ago, Harry returned to the drink table in front of the now heavily draped window and brought back the brandy decanter. "Now. Who wants brandy?"

To a man, his guests enthusiastically accepted his offer.

Harry's long-fingered hand was rock-steady as he filled their glasses. His brow, however, was furrowed.

When he moved around the card table to the sardonic man who'd remained unmoved through it all, that man caught and held his gaze. "An accident, Harry?"

Wainwright was still for a long moment, his dark blue eyes intent. Then he filled the man's goblet. "An accident, Bly."

Chalfont Blysdale's light blue eyes bored into his host's. He spoke so softly that the others, deep in speculative conversation, couldn't hear. "An *accident*, Harry?" he repeated.

"Yes." His firm lips tightened.

"I don't think so."

An electric silence hung between them. Harry Wainwright ignored the thin trickle of blood that ran down the side of his face. His black brows drew down in a scowl.

Finally, very softly, he ordered, "Play cards, Bly."

One

Fog crept up off the Thames to blur the foundations of the nearest buildings and steal away the outlines of London's roofs and chimneys where they met the sky. It drifted around the shabby hackney cab and twisted up to hide the legs of the horse that stood resignedly in its shafts in front of it. Swirls of it eddied out of alleyways and into the streets like tributaries emptying into a river.

As the fog rose, the temperature dropped. Regina huddled in her wet cloak and gave thanks that she hadn't far to go. Her thoughts, like the weather, were dismal.

Philip was dead.

She searched her heart and found only a sweet, sad longing for what she wished could have been between them. Philip had died so young. Thirty-six was far too young to die, and the inn fire that had taken him and his wife, Lydia, had left her brother's children alone, a second tragedy.

It was the plight of the two orphans that had led Regina to abandon her career and come home again. Her own life and its hard-won successes could wait. The children and their needs must come first now.

Her lips twisted in a bitter smile. She doubted that Lady Lydia would be able to rest, knowing her despised sister-in-law would be taking over the care of her children. Well, there was no help for that. Regina was the only one left to rear her brother's orphans. To do it she had willingly left her very lucrative and satisfying post with Lady Sybella Dashwood in Ireland and come back home to England.

She couldn't mind. The children needed her. Her only regret was that reconciliation with Philip was now forever impossible.

A thump on the roof of the hackney cab told her her trunk was safely aboard. Tonight she'd sleep at *The Golden Boar*, the inn her parents had always frequented when their town house was closed and they were merely passing through London.

Pleasant memories of clean, crisp sheets and good food flowed through her. Such things would be doubly appreciated after the dreary days she'd just spent on the packet boat from Ireland.

The driver flicked his whip, and the horse ambled forward. The hollow tattoo of hoofbeats on the wooden wharf soon gave way to the ring of shod hooves against cobblestones. They and all other sounds became increasingly muffled by the thickening fog. Visibility dropped to nothing. Even so, in fewer than fifteen minutes, Regina was safely delivered to the welcoming, torch-lit innyard of *The Golden Boar.*

The fresh logs caught easily in the heat of the small fire that was always kept burning in the oak-paneled private parlor. The blaze leapt high for an instant, then settled to add its light to the warm glow of the room's candles and bring the cozy chamber alive with cheerfully dancing shadows.

"Will that be all, miss?" The innkeeper rose from his

knees and brushed his hands together. He stood gently smiling at the tall young woman in the plain, serviceable cloak.

She was, he thought, a rare treat for the eyes. She was dark and graceful, and lovely as they came, but that wasn't why he was attending to her personally. He'd not entrusted her to one of his employees because this quiet beauty was special. Though there was no "Lady" tacked in front of her name nor a maid to travel with her, she had that look of the Quality about her.

The regal way she held herself and her quiet air of command intrigued him. He was taken with her calm competence as well. Such confidence as hers was not usually found in a woman of any age, and he'd wager this one had not seen thirty yet. Indeed, he guessed she was at least five years shy of it. Titled or not, she was obviously a lady, and he was going to treat her as such.

She turned fine gray eyes on him. "It's '*Mrs.* Landry,' Innkeeper." Her voice was low and husky, her words holding none of the offhanded haste with which most patrons, eager for their wants to be seen to, usually addressed him. There followed a pause in which her eyes carefully appraised him. Then she told him, "I'm a widow."

The innkeeper, inordinately pleased that she'd gifted him with that extra bit of information, bowed and crossed the room to the door. "And I am John Halston. *The Golden Boar* is mine." He smiled at the note of pride he heard in his own voice. "I shall see to your supper, Madam." With that, he both astonished and amused himself by bowing again as he exited and closed the door.

Shaking his head at his own unusual behavior, he chuckled as he went down the worn stone steps to his spacious kitchen to see what he could offer Mrs. Landry that would be even better than the excellent meals he was serving in his public dining room. It had been quite a while since he'd had someone in whom he'd cared to take such a personal interest stop at his inn. It made for a nice change.

As he entered the overwarm kitchen, he fleetingly hoped that that devilish Harry Wainwright wouldn't come in and find he couldn't have his favorite private parlor this evening. Then there'd be hell to pay. Harry was one who was used to having his own way. He was a man, too, in whom disappointment wasn't met with graciousness. Ah, well. With any luck, Harry would be busy elsewhere this cold and foggy evening.

He chuckled. It certainly wouldn't be the first night the rake had spent in some warm and willing lady's bedchamber.

In the meanwhile, he told himself, *The Golden Boar* was *his* inn, and if he wished to pleasure himself by taking extra care of a special guest, he would. And he'd decided that Mrs. Landry was special.

Another chuckle escaped him. As an innkeeper, he had to be a good judge of character. That was why he put up with the shenanigans of Harry Wainwright. For, in spite of his reputation as rogue and rakehell, "Hard-hearted" Harry was an excellent fellow.

Alone in the parlor, Regina was still smiling. Being the daughter of a viscount had spoiled her, she supposed, but, oh, it felt good to be treated like a lady again. In her position as head trainer for the Dashwood Stud, she'd been more often treated like one of the men!

She walked to the fireplace and held her hands out to its flames. After a moment, her gloves dried and she drew them off, flexing her fingers in the welcome warmth. She let her cloak slip from her shoulders and draped it carefully over the back of a chair near the fire to dry. It wasn't a fashionable garment, but it had served her well on many a wind-blown pasture, paddock and training track and she was fond of it.

A yawn caught her by surprise. "My dear," she murmured, "*you* could do with some sleep." Crossing the handsome Oriental rug to a tapestry-covered settee, she sat and leaned back, nestled her head against the wing and curled her chilled feet under her.

She'd take a quick nap, she decided. That ability was a talent she'd picked up in the five hectic years she'd run the racing stable for Lady Sybella Dashwood. Frequent midnight visits to foaling mares in the breeding barns and a score of colics and lesser ills in the stables had taught her the value of snatching bits of sleep when she might. And here in this cozy parlor, she might right now. Closing her eyes, she sighed once and slipped down a long, blue velvet slide into dreams.

Fog swirled thigh-high on his tall, athletic frame as Harry Wainwright crossed the innyard of *The Golden Boar*. He muttered imprecations at the foul weather and the bad luck that had blighted his plans for the evening and brought him here in the first place.

Thanks to some letter Lucretia had seen her brother-in-law angrily penning, the henwit foolishly feared that her husband might return early from his country estate. Otherwise, he'd be snug in her bed right now.

Ah, well. Perhaps it was for the best. The threat—real or imagined—of a suspicious husband could be used to put a handy period to an affair with which he was becoming more than a little bored. Lately, Lucretia had become increasingly demanding, and if there was one thing he had no intention of tolerating, it was demands from a woman.

Any woman.

Especially a woman who was another man's wife.

His long strides took him to the door he preferred, a small one on the side of the inn toward the stables. It was the one that Halston's servants used when they took messages to the hostlers to ready carriages and bring horses to their riders. In all probability, Harry was the only member of the Quality ever to darken the little side door. Unlike the majority of his acquaintances, he preferred to come and go unnoticed— whether he was keeping an assignation, or merely coming for a needed rest from one of his adventures.

Tonight, though, he hadn't exactly been looking forward to a rest. He'd been anticipating something a little more strenuous—an ardent night spent in the perfumed arms of his current paramour.

That, however, was denied him thanks to her snooping, sanctimonious prig of a brother-in-law. So now, as a result of his disappointment and a little too much brandy, Harry's mood was at best what his close friends liked to call "uncertain."

He paused on the doorstep to swing his many-caped cloak from his shoulders. Shaking the worst of the moisture from it, he folded it over his arm, ducked his dark head to avoid knocking his hat off on the low lintel and headed down the narrow back hall toward what he considered *his* parlor.

More brandy, his feet up near a warm fire and a little conversation with his wise and interesting friend Halston, the innkeeper, and all would come right.

His rented rooms served their purpose. He kept his valet and his clothes there, entertained his friends there. But rented rooms and a single servant, no matter how devoted, didn't fill the gap left by the loss of the great town house in which he'd been reared.

So he cherished the peace he found at *The Golden Boar*. The competent and kind attendance of the servants of his innkeeper friend helped soothe the unconfessed empty ache in his heart—his legacy from his treacherous mother.

Opening the door to the parlor that was his personal retreat without ceremony, he was pleased to find a good fire already burning. John Halston must have expected him. The man was a wonder. He must remember to thank him for his thoughtfulness.

Smiling, he placed his hat on the small table just inside the door. A second glance as he dropped his damp cloak over the back of a chair wiped the smile from his face. There was already a cloak draped over the back of the chair.

Dammit! *His* parlor was occupied! How dare Halston let some other patron have *his* parlor? Where was the blasted innkeeper? He started to go look for him, seizing the doorknob with more than necessary force, rattling the door in its frame.

A soft sound from the direction of the fireplace stopped him. Turning to look, he saw a woman sleeping in the corner of the upholstered settee.

A woman alone. A slow grin spread across his face. *That* put a different complexion on the situation. Ladies didn't go about unattended. Things were looking up. He really *must* thank Halston for his thoughtfulness!

His brandy-dulled conscience stirred, suggesting this was not quite the thing.

Impatiently, Harry told it to mind its own business.

Without approaching the settee, he let his eyes roam over the figure curled up there. Even seated as she was, leaning into the corner of the settee with her feet drawn up under her skirt, he could tell she was tall. He frowned slightly. She was clearly taller than suited his taste. His taste ran to petite blondes, and compared to them, this was an Amazon of a woman—but even though her hair was dark it shone in the firelight.

She was beautiful, he decided, and there was a sadness about her that tugged at something deep within him. Drawn forward as if by an invisible hand, he went to stand over her.

She stirred, but didn't awaken, rubbing her cheek on the tapestry against which it lay. The gesture reminded him of a contented cat.

Suddenly he found himself wanting to touch that velvet cheek, wanting to know if the rosy blush there would be warm to his fingers. He grinned. He wanted to touch those soft lips, too. With his own.

Giving in to his own wishes, a practice he was very well used to, he sat down beside her. Slowly he leaned forward. As his face neared hers, he admired the fine texture of her skin, the natural color of her cheeks. With a slight quirk of his lips, he noted the faint freckles across the bridge of her nose.

He ceased smiling, however, as his lips touched hers. *Gently,* he told himself. Don't wake her. Her breath, deep and even, was sweet in his nostrils. Carefully, he fitted his lips over hers. Yes. They were as soft as they looked. Satin smooth and of a fullness that made him want to gather her in his arms and press his own lips more firmly against them.

Never one to deny himself, Harry slid his arms around her and did just that. When he did, the woman gave a sigh and reached her arms up around his neck, returning his kiss.

Wild desire slammed through him. *Damn Lucretia for failing to deliver the favors she'd so artfully aroused him to expect!* As his body tightened, the woman he held stirred in his embrace. Sleepily she murmured, "Brandon."

Harry Wainwright pulled away. He was totally unused to hearing any name but his own from lips he'd just kissed. He was frowning blackly when the object of his displeasure opened her eyes.

Now the fur would fly! He sat back and waited, totally unrepentant, a reckless grin replacing the scowl on his face.

Regina was startled by the proximity of the man staring down at her, but still too sleep-befuddled to leap up in protest. Besides, unless she was greatly mistaken, she'd just been kissed by him. Had also, she felt certain, kissed him back . . . rather enthusiastically as a matter of fact. That was an incontrovertible fact if she were to judge from the pleasant sensation in her lips. Maidenly outrage was therefore out of the question.

She supposed she should be alarmed, but she didn't feel in the least threatened—just intrigued. She took a deep, steadying breath. Having learned a little late in life not to rush her fences, she sat without moving a muscle, quietly regarding the intruder for a moment. He was a handsome devil. And a tall one, too. Most of the time, she looked the men she dealt with straight in the eye. This one she'd have to look up to.

Of course, she reminded herself, her mind still hazy with sleep, he could just be tall in the saddle. Many men had legs shorter than one would expect from their seated height. She hoped this one hadn't. She let her gaze travel the length of his body. Hmmmm. Very nice, long legs that were. Like her late husband's. She smiled slightly, remembering Brandon, still not completely awake.

"By Jupiter, you're a bold one." He reached for her.

She held out both hands to ward off her attacker. The man's movement had chased away the last vestiges of sleep. She wasn't dreaming. He was very real, and the situation was, to say the least, most unusual.

"No," she told him firmly. The word brought him up short. It was obvious he wasn't used to hearing it from women. That, and the ridiculousness of this present scene, made her laugh.

He grasped the hands she held toward him in both of his own.

A little tingle ran up her arms. From the startled expression on his handsome face, she knew the man had felt the shock as well. He attempted to draw her closer to him.

Regina resisted, deciding it was high time to put an end to this nonsense. His kiss had undoubtedly been pleasant, but had *certainly* been an impertinence. She was a lady, and the lazily smiling rogue before her was clearly a cad. "Enough, sir. Please let go of my hands." She gave him her coolest look.

He rose then, and towered over her. Deep blue eyes bored into her own. "My God, woman. Aren't you even a *little* afraid?" His low voice held a hint of incredulity.

She made no effort to yank her hands free. She knew she couldn't recover them if he persisted in holding them, and she had no desire to appear foolish. She had no desire to leave this man the victor in the matter, either. "No. Should I be?"

"We *are* alone."

"I have been alone with a man before."

"And you are aware of what might happen between a man and a woman in a closed room?" His voice was silky smooth, low and seductive.

Nicely done. She gave him full marks for the tone of his voice, the warm intimacy of his gaze. He was a devastatingly handsome man, and as sure of himself as any she'd ever met. From the crown of his fashionably cut, thick, dark hair to the toes of his highly polished Hessians, he was every maiden's dream . . . and every protective mamma's nightmare.

Thank heavens she was no green girl. In the years since she'd run away from her comfortable home to marry Brandon Landry, she'd learned a great deal about the ways of the world in general, and the ways of would-be seducers in particular. *And* she had learned how to take care of herself. So now she wasn't worried, in spite of his attempt to make her so.

She was strong for a woman. Stronger than many men of her acquaintance. She'd had to be when illness in her men had made it necessary for her to help with the stable chores at Lady Sybella Dashwood's estate. She was confident, too, that this rake was not the sort of man who engaged in undignified scuffles with unwilling partners.

So she smiled at him. "I am fully aware of what can happen between a man and a woman in a closed room, sir, but I am also perfectly aware that no such thing is going to happen here in this room between us." Rising as she did so, she pulled gently at her hands.

"Oh?" He kept his hold on them, but she refused to struggle.

"Yes. I know very well what a thoroughgoing cad might attempt when finding himself alone in a room with a defenseless woman." She looked him straight in the eye without so much as a blink. "You do not strike me as quite that depraved, however," she told him crisply. "You aren't one of those men who . . ." She left the sentence hanging, letting him finish it in his own mind.

His face flamed, and he straightened, offended. His voice was angry as he replied, "I do not force myself on women."

She gave the barest of glances at their linked hands. "But you *do* seem to hold on to them."

He looked down at their joined hands and laughed briefly. Damn, she was a cool one. He didn't let her go, though her manner had all but reduced him to a stammering schoolboy. What the devil was ailing him? He was never at a loss when it came to handling women. He hadn't ever been.

Frowning, he searched his brain for an answer. Then suddenly he knew what was ailing him. He wanted her. He wanted this cool Amazon of a woman as he hadn't wanted a woman in years.

That made matters simple. He threw back his head. His exultant laughter filled the little parlor. The mystery was solved, and a further solution was edging its way into his thoughts.

Regina saw the flash of strong, white teeth. He would, of course, have perfect teeth. Unfortunately, he had perfect gall as well. She wanted her hands back. Finally she gave a little tug.

"Ah, no." He kept his grip.

She saw the devil in his eyes, and before she could react, he had snatched her into his arms and brought his mouth down on hers. Her lips had been half open to protest, and she tasted the hint of a good cigar, the freshness of mint, more than a trace of fine brandy. *Ah, there was the explanation. The gentleman was drunk.*

She went giddy as he deepened his kiss. Sensing disaster, she called her scattered senses to order. The instant she'd marshalled them, she took the offensive. She kissed him as hard and as thoroughly as he'd kissed her. Then she shoved against the muscled wall of his chest with all her might.

Shocked by her response, the man let her go. The push staggered him.

Regina confronted him, head high, fighting to keep her breath even.

Harry was having a little trouble with his own breathing. He laughed again. "By God, woman, you're a wonder. You give as good as you get." A beatific smile lit his face. "What a mistress you'll make!" He reached for her.

Regina spun away from his grasp.

He dropped his hands and stood smiling lopsidedly at her. "Well, my Amazon? What say you?"

"About what, sir?" She watched him warily. The man was a force to be reckoned with.

"Be my mistress." His grin turned boyish. "I promise to pleasure you greatly."

She took a deep breath and willed herself not to blush. Willed herself not to consider his last statement. She'd no doubt he could live up to his boast. No doubt at all.

Finally she managed, "I'm sorry to disappoint you, sir, but I am not the material mistresses are made of. Though I enjoyed your kisses," she took great satisfaction in seeing the wild shock that statement put in his eyes, "I do not hold myself so cheaply that I would bed you simply for the pleasure you might afford me."

His brows snapped down. How the blasted hell did she dare to speak to him like that? Bed him, indeed! By all that he held holy, *he* was the one who'd do any bedding that was done!

Determination erupted in him. He'd teach the wench. He'd kiss her senseless. He moved forward to grab her.

The woman sidestepped him, putting a chair between them. She lowered her head and stared at him from under her winged brows. Her eyes narrowed and glittered dangerously.

Harry Wainwright was left clutching thin air. The expression on his face showed a fine balance between extreme irritation and frank disbelief.

A knock sounded.

Regina called out, "Enter!"

Immediately the door swung open. John Halston, the innkeeper, stood on the threshold with a dinner tray in his hands. The expression on his face was that of a man trying very hard not to smile.

"Mr. Halston," Regina Landry addressed him firmly. "Pray escort this gentleman to another parlor." She turned her gaze on the intruder. "I'm certain Mr. Halston will be able to make you comfortable in a room of your own, sir." She gestured her unwelcome guest toward the door.

To his own surprise, Harry actually moved in that direction.

Regina deftly administered the *coup de grace.* "Now, please excuse me. I have had a long journey and should like to eat my supper alone."

Two

"*Are you certain* I should apply for guardianship of my brother's children immediately?" Regina sat on the edge of the chair the solicitor had led her to.

"Indeed I am." Josiah P. Bagwell steepled his fingers and looked at her over them, nodding for emphasis.

"But you've just said that it will be very difficult for an unmarried woman to obtain guardianship."

"Yes." The solicitor nodded again, heaving a gusty sigh and shuffling papers into a neat stack. "Mrs. Landry, I'm afraid that it will be next to impossible for you to obtain it, but with Philip's finances at such a low ebb, and certain other things being as they are . . ." He frowned mightily over something. "I—and my partners, too, I might add—feel very strongly that you must try."

Regina looked at him, trying to read the purpose behind his words. What other things? She chose her own next words with great care. "I feel that you have a reason for urging me to attempt that which you say may be impossible for me to accomplish." She watched him bob his head emphatically again. "Would you please tell me why, Mr. Bagwell?"

He frowned slightly. "It is a matter of some delicacy, my dear." He cupped one hand around his chin and rubbed thoughtfully. "I should not wish to put myself in the position of seeming to slander a member of your family, you see."

"A member of my family?" She was surprised. "But there are only the three of us now. The children, Philydia and Thomas," she paused, "and me."

A sudden thought jolted through her, bringing her even more upright in her chair. "Oh! Oh, dear." Her eyes showed her deep distress. "And my detestable cousin Jasper."

Relief washed the frown from the solicitor's face. He wiped his forehead with a snow-white handkerchief, then used it to make certain his palms were dry. With a wide smile he queried Regina, "You do not then hold your cousin Jasper Ruddleston in high esteem?"

Regina let him see her exasperation. "Dear Mr. Bagwell. I cannot imagine that there exists *anyone* who holds Jasper Ruddleston in any esteem whatsoever. As for my part, I must tell you that I have always cordially detested the man."

"Ah! Good. Good. It is a pity—in this instance, at least, that the law of the land so favors the male. I have long thought that children should be the property of both parents, and not that of the husband alone. The law is very clear, nevertheless, and because the children born of a union are the exclusive property of the male parent it has always been very difficult in any case regarding children to gain guardianship for a female." He searched through the papers that littered the top of his desk. "Yes. Yes. Here we are." He shoved a long sheet of vellum toward her and handed her one of the new fountain pens that had recently been invented. "If you will just sign there at the bottom, I can get things moving with the courts. I hope they will consider his excessive gambling. At least that will win us some time."

It was Regina's turn to frown. "Time? Time for what?"

"For what?" His clear blue eyes were puzzled. "Why, don't you understand, my dear?" He cocked his head and peered across his vast desk at her. "Time for you to find a husband, of course."

Regina wasn't quite clear on how she'd gotten out of the office and into the street. She'd managed to sign the long impressive petition at the bottom where Bagwell pointed and to murmur something that served to get her gracefully out of his office, but she was still stunned by his calm assumption that she would go out and find a husband simply to satisfy the requirements of a stuffy court.

She fully intended to do her best to see to the welfare of her brother's children. Of course she did. Wasn't that why she had made seeing the family solicitor her first order of business when she hadn't been home in so very long? But marriage? Marriage, of all things. Why, marriage was a serious step. An irrevocable step. Marriage was sacred.

She took a deep breath and entered the hackney Bagwell's clerk had summoned for her. Common sense began to reassert itself and she told the clerk, "Would you please ask Mr. Bagwell to send me my cousin Jasper Ruddleston's direction at his earliest convenience?"

"Yes, Mrs. Landry. Certainly." He smiled broadly and stepped back to let the hackney drive on.

Regina spent the ride back to *The Golden Boar* planning her visit to Jasper. Somehow she must get him to tell the courts that he was willing for Regina to have guardianship of Philip's two children. But how?

At about the time Regina left the inn, bound for the solicitor's office, Harry Wainwright awoke—with a hangover. Pulling the bell cord with the hand that he wasn't using to hold his head, he summoned one of the inn servants and sent for John Halston.

"So," the innkeeper boomed as he breezed into the room. "You're back with the living are you, Harry?"

"For God's sake, John, stop shouting!" Harry clutched his head in both his hands.

Halston tried to moderate his laugh. "Too much brandy last night?"

"God, yes. And I seem to remember something . . ." His handsome face contorted. "Oh, no." He came out of his headache-pandering slouch. "Oh, no. Tell me there wasn't a woman here, too, John. A woman in my private parlor."

John's grin said he was enjoying this. "A woman, Harry? What sort of woman?"

"Tall, dark, beautiful." He smiled lopsidedly. "Strong."

Halston chuckled and handed his friend a cup of steaming tea. "Here. No sugar, just tea. It'll help you get your head back."

Wainwright's smile went wry. "If the damn thing doesn't stop pounding, I just may decide I don't want it back." He flexed his wide shoulders, stretching carefully. "Well?"

"Well what?"

Harry could see that his friend was enjoying this too much to make it easy.

"Damn you, Halston. *Was* there a woman?"

"Did you think you'd dreamed her?"

Wainwright groaned. "So it happened." He groaned again. "Dear God. I really accosted a gentlewoman." He sank gingerly to the seat of a nearby chair. Even distressed, he hadn't forgotten to allow for the unfortunate consequences of last night's overconsumption of brandy.

After a moment, he raised his head. Blue fire shot from under his brows. "Why the hell did you let me?"

"Let you! Let you?" John was flabbergasted. "How in Heaven's name do you think *I* could have stopped you."

"As my friend, you could at least have tried."

"Be reasonable, Harry. I didn't even know you were in the inn. I thought you'd planned to˙. . . errr . . . to . . . ah, spend the evening with Lady Lucretia."

Harry's scowl put an end to any discussion of Lady Lucretia.

Halston let a long minute slip by. "I don't think there was any *lasting* harm done, if that's any consolation."

Harry perked up. His left eyebrow rose, demanding more.

"She wasn't upset, you see. She wasn't . . . hmmmm . . . frightened by your . . . ah . . ." A hint of laughter slipped past Halston's guard. "Your rather strange behavior."

Wainwright paused in the act of pulling on his left boot. "What do you mean, 'my strange behavior'?"

"Well, kissing her went all right." He cocked his head, considering. "But I do believe that things might have gone more smoothly after that if you hadn't added your sweet inducement when you asked her to become your mistress."

"Become my mistress." His tone grim, he sat motionless, staring down at his other boot. "Oh, Lord. Surely not. Tell me I didn't."

"Can't, old boy. Be lying if I did. But if it's any comfort," Halston told him blandly, "I don't think she was truly angry until you promised to pleasure her greatly."

With a roar, the besieged Wainwright rose to his full height. An instant later, his right boot sailed through the air toward the head of his grinning host.

Regina's hackney, threading its careful way through London's heavy traffic, proved slower than Josiah P. Bagwell's extremely efficient messenger. A runner with her cousin

Jasper Ruddleston's address was waiting for her when she returned to *The Golden Boar*.

"Thank you." Accepting the envelope the man proffered, she gave the runner a shilling and walked into the inn. "I'd no idea this would get here so quickly."

The man behind the tall desk smiled. "Messengers often outpace vehicular traffic here in town, Mrs. Landry."

"Hmmmm." Regina's mind was on the matter of her visit to her cousin. Should she go now? Deciding her course of action with her usual quickness, she asked, "Could you catch my driver?"

"Certainly, Mrs. Landry." He signaled one of the inn's footmen to run and stop her hackney. Regina was on the man's heels to get back into it. She called, "Thank you" back over her shoulder.

As the door closed behind her, Harry Wainwright entered the lobby of the inn. He strode to the desk. "Albert. See to it that everyone knows I'm offering a reward to anyone who can identify the woman who rented my private parlor last evening, will you?"

The balding chief waiter who was spelling his employer at the front desk fought to keep his gaze from flicking toward the door. Mr. Halston had been most specific in his orders, and wild horses couldn't have dragged Mrs. Landry's name from him, much less the fact that she was just outside.

He cringed inside as he caught a glimpse over Mr. Wainwright's shoulder of her settling herself in the hansom as the footman came back in. Somehow, he managed to say, "Yes, sir, Mr. Wainwright."

"Thank you, Albert." Wainwright moved to the door with his usual powerful grace. There he hesitated. He had the strong suspicion that something was being kept from him. Scowling, he looked back at the man with whom he'd been speaking as if he wanted to add something.

Albert heard the rattle of wheels on the cobblestones of the street. Mrs. Landry's hackney was pulling away. He took a deep breath, and held it.

Harry Wainwright shook his head and opened the door. *Hell! He wanted to apologize to the woman for his crass behavior, but be damned if he intended to devote the rest of his life to it!*

As the door closed behind Wainwright, Albert let the breath he'd been holding explode in a massive sigh of relief.

The footman who'd put Mrs. Landry in her hackney nodded in agreement. "That was a close one."

Three

Shabby-genteel was the kindest description Regina could come up with for the neighborhood in which she found herself when her cab halted at her destination.

"'Ere we are, miss. This be the place." Her driver smiled cheerfully at her through the window cut high in the back wall of the hansom, his grin lifting the ends of his mustache.

"Thank you." Regina tucked the piece of paper with her cousin Jasper Ruddleston's direction on it back into her reticule.

The hackman let the trap fall back into place. Looping the driving reins around the butt of his whip, he climbed down from his perch.

Regina thanked the driver for helping her out and asked, "I wonder if you would mind waiting for me." Before he could object, she added, "I'd pay you for the wait just as if you spent the time driving me."

"Glad to do it, miss." He stroked his horse's neck. "Ole Bess here could do with a rest and a bit of grain. She's nice an' cool right now, so 't won't 'urt 'er to eat."

Regina was relieved that he'd agreed to wait for her.

There were no hackneys looking for fares along the streets they had just passed through, and she'd no idea how she'd get back to *The Golden Boar* if the cab left. Only after he'd fixed a nose bag to his horse's bridle did she look away to study the facade of Jasper's home.

The brick was in need of a little mortar replacement, but the proportions of the tall town house were pleasant. Its neighbors on both sides exhibited the same gentle decay. The shrubbery that lined the front walks and hugged the foundations of the buildings was sadly overgrown, but the grass was clipped in every yard. Clearly, this was a street that had seen better days but still had its pride. Wondering if the poor condition of the house was indicative of the state of Jasper's fortunes, Regina mounted the steps and knocked.

Almost immediately, the door opened. A pert maid in a mobcap peered out at her.

"I wish to see Mr. Jasper Ruddleston."

"Cooo. I'll go tell Mrs. Plumley." Then she shut the door in Regina's face.

Regina stepped back a little. If the next person to appear at this door was as rude as the mobcapped maid, she wanted more room between the blistered green paint of the tall door and the tip of her nose. Clearly, her cousin's household could do with a bit more training.

The door opened again. This time it framed a round face surmounted by a wild collection of blond sausage curls. Two curious, bright blue eyes appraised Regina. "I'm Mrs. Plumley. And just how may we help you?"

"I was told that my cousin, Jasper Ruddleston, lived at this address. Obviously I was misdirected. Please forgive the intrusion."

"Oh, no. No intrusion at all. Mr. Ruddleston does indeed live here. He has taken the first floor of my house." She swung the door wide, inviting Regina to enter. "Maggie, run up and see if Mr. Ruddleston is at home."

The little maid lifted her skirts and ran lightly up the staircase that rose along the right wall of the foyer.

Mrs. Plumley studied Regina frankly. "So you're his cousin?" She looked skeptical. "He's never spoken of a cousin."

Regina turned what she hoped was her chilliest smile on the rotund little woman. "I have been out of country for years. It is not surprising that he has not mentioned me."

"Oh, I suppose that explains it." Mrs. Plumley turned as she heard her maid returning.

"'E's home." Maggie was panting slightly from her run up and down the tall staircase. However, lack of breath did nothing to diminish her curiosity. She kept her gaze fastened on Regina.

"Thank you," Regina murmured, moving away from the door. At the foot of the stairs, she looked inquisitively back at the two women. "Which door, please?"

"Oh!" Flustered, the blond woman gave the maid a shove. "Maggie. What are you thinking of? Go."

Maggie ran over and preceded Regina up the stairs. At the top, she rushed to the second door on the left and knocked. Flapping her apron to cool her flushed face, she smiled brightly at Regina.

Regina returned the girl's smile and wondered what she'd gotten herself into. Certainly she'd never seen such a ramshackle household. Perhaps she would have been wiser to send a message to Jasper—a note inviting him to visit her at the inn. Perhaps . . .

The door opened abruptly. A man whose face clearly showed the dissipation that must rule his life glared out at the little maid. "What the devil do you want, Maggie?"

Maggie answered pertly. "It's not what I wants, Mr. Ruddleston. 'Tis this lady does the wanting." She gestured grandly toward Regina.

Regina stifled her exasperation. Obviously the girl had only checked to see if Jasper were in his residence, not if he were "at home" in the sense of being willing to receive a visitor.

"What?" He transferred his gaze to Regina. After a long moment, he smiled. It was a smile that did nothing to improve his appearance. He did, however, put one hand up to straighten his cravat. The other he smoothed over his thinning hair.

Regina didn't like the lecherous look that was coming over her cousin's face. To forestall its full development, she said briskly, "It is I, Cousin Jasper, Regina Ransome Landry."

"Regina!" His attitude changed instantly. "Good God, girl. I thought you were safely away in Ireland."

"And so I was until I received word of Philip's death."

"So." His eyes narrowly assessed her. Finally he stepped back and gestured her into the room.

Large and pleasingly portioned, the room had tall windows at the end facing the front of the house. They spilled abundant light into the room. It served only to show how faded the wallpaper and how worn the carpeting of the once elegant chamber had become.

"Maggie." Jasper glanced quickly at Regina to see if she was looking his way, erroneously decided she would not see, and pinched the maid's bottom. "Bring tea for Mrs. Landry."

The little maid stomped off down the steps, muttering, "Could 'ave said please, 'e could. Nasty old goat."

In the room behind her, there was a long silence during which the cousins studied each another. Finally, Jasper smiled and asked, "May I take your coat, cousin?"

Regina saw no need of divesting herself of the short Spencer she wore, especially since it would put her in closer proximity to Jasper. "No, thank you."

Jasper Ruddleston let his eyes roam his cousin's person. "What a beauty you've grown yourself into, my dear."

"Thank you." She made the words stiff. She didn't care for this man's compliments and she resented his stare. "I've come to talk with you . . ."

"Ah, but let us wait for the tea, shall we?"

"Very well." Regina wanted nothing so much as to get her talking over with and get out of this man's company. She'd never liked him when they were children. She liked him no better now. Jasper was the sort who made her skin crawl.

Her purpose would hardly be served by offending him, however. So she went to a chair and perched on the edge of it, folding her hands in her lap.

"I suppose I should offer you condolences on your brother Philip's death," Jasper said.

Regina's gaze met his. She waited, wary. She found she didn't trust this grown-up Jasper any better than she had trusted him when they were children.

"You were never close to your brother, though, were you?"

"Philip and I . . . ," she began.

"Philip never paid any attention to you, as I recall." He raised his voice slightly to speak over her, cutting off her response to his question. "I always thought it rather pathetic, the way you tried to attract his notice after your parents died. You only irritated him. So sad." His sympathetic smile was patently false. "Such a pity."

Regina fought to keep the heat from her cheeks. Jasper's words of sympathy were hollow, of course. He'd been purposefully hurtful when they were children, and time seemed to have done nothing to change that. She kept her gaze level and direct, hiding her anger behind a cool facade. She'd see him in hell before she let him know that his deliberately cruel words had wounded her.

He was, unfortunately, just beginning to warm to his subject. "And you'd no chance at all after he married Lady Lydia Graves. You were barely sixteen, as I recall. No sixteen-year-old ever born would have had a chance against Lydia Graves." He chuckled, but the sound held no mirth. "That was before Brandon Landry came to Charnwood as drawing master, wasn't it?"

Regina started to answer, but Jasper went on, "I assume the marriage drove another wedge between your brother Philip and you. After all, Lady Lydia had never approved of your horse-crazy, hoydenish ways." He held up a hand. "Her words, not mine, dear cousin." He smiled placatingly.

Regina was reminded of something unpleasant—something that oozed.

"Lydia was quick to sever all ties with you when you eloped, wasn't she, Regina?"

Regina still hurt when she remembered how she'd felt at being excluded from her own family. Even now, so many years after the fact, she had to take a deep breath to steady her emotions. But she'd die before she let Jasper know how she felt.

He belabored the point one more time. "And Philip obviously agreed with his wife." His voice was silky. "Philip severed his ties with you, too, didn't he?"

Suddenly she remembered that Jasper had been the sort of boy who liked to pull the wings off flies.

She didn't intend to let him know how much hurt his words caused her. "Things would have been simpler now if Philip and I had kept in touch," she answered with dignity, her chin high.

"Ah, but this is real life, Regina. Things are never that simple in real life."

Regina didn't need Jasper Ruddleston to tell her about real life. She'd lived a painfully real life ever since her young husband had been killed five years ago in a carriage accident. Until then, there had always been someone to stand between her and the world's harsh realities, but not since.

"You really shouldn't have married Landry, you know."

Regina merely looked at him with disdain. A poet as well as an artist, her young husband had made Regina happy in spite of their near penniless state. Laughter and love had filled their days, and she had never been sorry. Never.

"You could have come home when he died, you know. Your brother would have taken you in." Jasper smiled, but his eyes remained cold, watchful. "He and Lydia would not easily have forgiven you, naturally." When that barb seemed to have no effect on her, he laughed. "And, of course, our Regina was nothing if not prideful, eh? I'd wager you'd no desire to eat humble pie for the rest of your days, had you, dear cousin?"

Regina didn't owe him any answer. It was true that it had been her pride that had sustained her, and in the end, driven her. At that point, pride had been all she'd had. Without it she would surely have perished.

Pride rose in her now. Deciding she'd had enough of this verbal attack, Regina turned the tables. "Yes, you'd have won that wager. And I hear you are very good with wagers these days, cousin." Her eyes challenged him.

For the first time in their conversation, Jasper looked uncomfortable. He quickly changed the subject. "And just how did you manage to support yourself after Landry's carriage accident, Regina?"

His question stirred the past. She remembered how frightened she had been—and how reluctant she'd been to contact her family. Ah, but if only one of them had gotten in touch with her. What a difference that would have made. But they hadn't. All along she had hoped it was because they hadn't known. Now she knew that they had been aware of her circumstances. If Jasper knew, then they all had known somehow, even though she'd never written home, never told anyone in England that Brandon had been killed. So how had they known? Had her brother kept tabs on her to satisfy some need of his own without any intention of ever helping her? The notion was devastating.

She sat absorbing the blow, dealing with it. It amazed her how deeply it cut to find out that her family had realized she'd been widowed in Ireland and had made no move to contact her. Only pride kept her face impassive.

"Well?" Jasper persisted, clearly curious.

Regina thought back to the time she'd embraced the necessity of making her own way in the world. After much discouragement, she'd finally been hired as a companion by a difficult old woman. She hadn't enjoyed being a lady's companion to old Mrs. Entwhistle, but her time in that position had been thankfully short.

She would always be grateful to a merciful Providence for bringing Lady Sybella Dashwood—Mrs. Entwhistle's brother's friend's widow—into her life. The widowed Lady Sybella and her famous stables had been Regina's salvation.

As lady's companion to the irascible Mrs. Entwhistle, she'd met and chatted with Lady Sybella Dashwood. Their mutual interest in horses had drawn them together. In fact, it had been her increasingly frequent conversations with Lady Sybella that had brought matters to a head.

Mrs. Entwhistle's voice could have etched glass as she'd told Regina, "You are ignoring your employer to monopolize your employer's guest, Mrs. Landry. I will no longer tolerate such impertinence! You will leave my house at once." Mrs. Entwhistle had slammed her cane into the carpet for emphasis.

When she did, Lady Sybella had slapped a hand on her silk-clad knee and crowed, "Splendid, Elvira, my dear. You have done exactly the right thing. Your conscience is thus satisfied." Lady Sybella had smiled broadly. "Now I'll just tell you that if you don't want her anymore, I certainly do!"

While her soon-to-be former employer had gasped and gaped, Lady Sybella had risen, pulled Regina from her perch on the edge of a chair and given her shove toward the drawing-room door. "Don't just stand there, gel. Go pack your things. We're off!"

Regina smiled at that last memory, and absolutely refused to reveal to her cousin any part of the life that she had shared with the indomitable Lady Sybella. She would permit him a glimpse only of the part of her past that she had hated, and let the little slug make the most of it. Quietly she told him, "I worked as a lady's companion to a difficult old woman named Entwhistle." Her eyes brightened suddenly. "Perhaps you know her brother, Elwood. I hear that he, like you, is an inveterate gambler."

The statement was a direct hit. Jasper's irritation showed. His fake affability gave way to a scowl and his voice took on an edge. "Whether or not I gamble on occasion is no business of yours."

"I've made it my business, cousin, as guardianship of Philip's children must be a consideration now. Since rumor has it that you are in one of your . . . less successful stages with your pastime, I am in hopes that you will not wish to take on any new responsibilities at this time. Children can be quite expensive, you know."

"Ah, but, my dear Regina, I'm not certain that you are

aware that this is the most propitious of times to take over the responsibility of Philip's finances."

Regina rose abruptly. "The subject was not Philip's finances—which I hear are in rather precarious condition, by the way—the subject was his *children*. His children and their welfare, Jasper."

Jasper's consternation over his late cousin's financial reverses showed clearly. "What do you mean, Philip's finances are in precarious condition?"

Regina was angry. She'd hoped for better. Even from a man like Jasper. "You wouldn't use the children's money."

"Why not? Someone must manage their affairs. Besides, I'd repay them when my luck changed for the better. Handsomely."

Regina made a disgusted sound.

Just then, Maggie bustled in with the tea, took one look at the two glaring cousins, and turned and left with the tea tray.

Regina pulled her gloves on.

"You're leaving?"

She didn't trust herself to answer him. She nodded.

"Will you be trying for the guardianship of the children?"

"I certainly shall. I intend to see Bagwell, Philip's solicitor, in the morning."

Jasper's smile was oily, his reply overly confident. "Do what you will, Regina. I shall be there, myself. To press my own claim to guardianship. And I wager, my dear, that I'll win. I'll bet on it!"

Her angry voice floated back up to him from halfway down the stairs, "You would!"

At the foot of the long staircase, she encountered Jasper's landlady. The woman's suspiciously bright curls vibrated with indignation. Her childlike voice had overtones of fishwife. "Now see here, young lady. Cousin or no cousin, you can't come in here and upset dear Mr. Ruddleston this way!"

Regina looked at her in utter astonishment. The woman was serious. It seemed that there was, after all, one person living who held Jasper Ruddleston in high esteem.

Seething, Regina left the angry Mrs. Plumley's house.

As she settled herself on the worn bench of the hansom cab, she vowed she would do all in her power to keep Jasper from getting his hands on what was left of Philip's fortune, and most importantly, on Philip's children. She shuddered to think how the children would fare under the care of such a cruel and selfish beast as Jasper Ruddleston.

Four

Early the next morning, before the mist had even lifted off the Thames, Regina paced the walkway in front of the offices of Josiah P. Bagwell and Associates, Solicitors. She was hoping he would be able to squeeze a few moments out of his busy schedule to speak with her. She was anxious to see if there was any way he could stop Jasper.

When Bagwell arrived, he was clearly surprised to find her waiting there. "Mr. Bagwell, I need your help." As she explained her presence, Bagwell ushered her into the office. "Yes, yes. Of course we'll talk."

A startled clerk looked up from where he was coaxing back into life the fire he'd carefully banked the night before. Regina hadn't asked the clerk for admittance when she'd arrived, as she'd feared he'd have turned her away. The offices had certainly not been open for business then. They weren't yet.

"Sit down, my dear, sit down." Bagwell went around his desk and sank into his high-backed chair. Studying her face briefly, he announced, "So. I assume you have been to see your cousin, Jasper Ruddleston." He sighed and made little tsking noises. "So sad. So sad to see the sort of thing a man can become when he lacks ambition."

Regina answered with a hint of the anger her cousin inspired in her. "Ambition? Oh, Jasper has ambition, Mr. Bagwell. It is just not the sort one would hope to find in a member of one's own family. Jasper's ambition is to gain control of my brother's children so that he may use their fortune for his own gaming."

"Ah, yes. It is just as I suspected. How fortunate you have come home in time to foil his plans. So very fortunate for the children." He hesitated a moment, his gaze searching her face. "There is not, you know, much of a fortune just now . . . as I told you."

"I have savings. We shall manage," Regina told him firmly.

Her response brought a smile to his face, transforming it. Then he turned somber. "The situation was not an uncomfortable one when it began. The Charnwood racing stud was doing well—partly due, I think, to your brother's informal partnership with his neighbor, the elderly Earl of Taskford." He smiled at her. "Taskford was an unmarried gentleman with only distant family, and I think he rather enjoyed your niece and nephew. And they seemed to consider him almost a member of the family." His smile faded. "At any rate, your brother mortgaged his properties to his good friend, Taskford, to buy a promising stallion and a superior group of broodmares to breed him to."

Regina waited expectantly for him to go on.

"The former Earl of Taskford would never have pressed for the payment of that mortgage, and of course, the horses would have earned back the money. Philip had an excellent trainer. Unfortunately, the trainer and the old gentleman died in the same inn fire that killed your brother and his wife." He peered at her, willing her to understand. "We now find ourselves dealing with a new Earl of Taskford. . . ." He sighed. "And he is . . . a rather unpredictable young man."

Regina's breath caught. Did this mean Mr. Bagwell felt the new Earl might prove difficult? She leaned forward. "Surely he will give the children the opportunity—and a suitable period of time—to recover the mortgage?"

"My dear, I cannot answer that. I have not yet contacted the new Earl on the subject of his elevation. Though I have known him many years"—he shuffled papers and looked slightly embarrassed—"still I cannot predict how he will react in this situation. When you have lived on the fringes of the *Beau Monde*, admired and accepted for your abilities yet held at a distance because of your lack of prospects . . . well, you understand that he could be difficult to second-guess. And he is a . . . a *complicated* young man."

He sat back and chewed at his lower lip a moment, his brow furrowed. "I do, however, expect him at any moment. Perhaps after I have spoken with him I shall have a better idea of what he will—or won't—do." He smiled. "Of course, I shall do my best to urge him to be kindly disposed toward you and the children. And I want you to know, my dear, that I think you will be very good for them."

She smiled warmly at him, relieved to have him as an ally. "I . . ."

There was a commotion in the outer office. The murmur of the clerk's voice, and the rumble of a deeper, stronger one could be heard through the heavy door.

Mr. Bagwell stood, his expression apologetic. "My dear, I am so sorry, I fear I must ask you to excuse me for now. Would it be possible for you to wait here in my office, so that we may continue this discussion?"

Regina had gathered herself to rise. She sank gratefully back onto the chair. "Of course. Thank you."

Before Bagwell could leave her, the door from the outer

office burst open. "Baggy, old boy. Who in blazes would have guessed I'd—"

Regina almost dropped back off her chair. It was him! The man from her private parlor the other night. Larger than life he stood there, as thunderstruck as she herself felt. She shot bolt upright, staring back at him.

Harry was having trouble accepting the evidence of his senses. It was her! The very woman he'd spent so much time looking for. She stood straight as a sword blade, the expression on her beautiful face a perfect balance of surprise and disapproval. What fine eyes she had—gray and luminous in her perfect oval face. And her lips—set just now in a firm line—were soft and luscious. He knew from personal experience. He couldn't help himself—he fastened his gaze on those lips and grinned recklessly.

Regina didn't pretend to miss the fact that he was taunting her for her behavior the other night when she had kissed him. Incensed, she lifted her chin and glared at him.

Unaware of the little byplay, Mr. Bagwell said, "Mrs. Landry. Permit me to present Mr. Harry Wainwright." He was distracted by the search he was making through the papers on his desk. Finally, he found the file marked "Taskford" and looked up. He seemed surprised to find that all was not well between his two clients.

"Hmmm." He looked from one to the other, wondering if Mrs. Landry, in spite of having arrived in England only two days ago, was somehow aware of Harry's rakish reputation. That would be unfortunate, as they were to be neighbors.

It was unfortunate in other ways as well. Harry was one of his favorites. A good lad, in spite of his wild nature. Furthermore, Mrs. Landry seemed to him just the sort of young beauty to tame the wildness in Harry, to rid him of that dreadful soubriquet, "Hard-hearted Harry." And if she wanted to keep guardianship of her brother's children, she needed a husband. Surely, at his advanced age, the Good Lord might grant him just one wish? Perhaps . . .

He waved a hand vaguely at the new Earl. "I must ask you to excuse me for just one moment, Harry. There are a few things I want to tell Mrs. Landry." He smiled at Regina and gestured for her to sit again.

"Certainly, Baggy." Harry Wainwright grinned again and propped a shoulder against the doorjamb. He'd no intention of giving up his fine view.

Bagwell sighed to himself. Obviously, the lad was going to ogle the widow. What was one to do with Harry? He could see that the boy's arrogance was annoying the girl, but he knew that to challenge it would only make Harry worse. It always did. Bagwell *knew*.

He knew because he'd known the lad since his birth. Few knew Harry better. He'd managed Harry's family's affairs before the lad was born and throughout Harry's life. Helplessly, he'd watched the tragic circumstances that had shaped Harry, agonizing for the fine boy, powerless to stop them. Finally, he'd helped him through the scandal caused by his vicious mother and through the subsequent bankruptcy and suicide of his father.

Yes, he knew Harry, knew him very well. And he knew that Regina Ransome Landry might be the best thing that had ever happened to the man.

Regina sat again quietly erect and appeared to give all her attention to the solicitor. Her gaze was politely directed to his lined visage and she seemed ready to hang on his every word. In reality, however, her every sense was riveted on the broad-shouldered rogue leaning against the frame of the door.

Why was he here? How did he know Mr. Bagwell so well that he called him "Baggy" so disrespectfully?

Why was every nerve in her body set a-jangle by the mere presence of the man?

"Ah, yes. Here it is." The solicitor's voice broke the spell. He pulled a piece of foolscap from under a pile of papers and tendered it toward Regina. "These are the directions to Charnwood, and a list of the stages from which you can select to arrive there. I've added a few notes about those employed on the estate. I hope they'll be helpful."

Regina could feel her cheeks warming under Harry Wainwright's intent regard. She was careful to keep her voice steady in spite of the breathlessness she felt. "Thank you, Mr. Bagwell. I'm certain this will be of great help in uniting me with my niece and nephew."

"Yes, but wait, wait." Bagwell moved stiffly around the desk. "There may be something better." He turned toward Wainwright. "Are you going down to your estate any time soon, Harry?"

Harry caught on instantly. *She* must be heading in the direction of Taskford. Otherwise Bagwell wouldn't have asked him that question. "Yes. I shall be leaving . . ." Now he had to guess. When would she want to go? "Before long." That was vague enough. He watched Bagwell. He wasn't disappointed.

"Very good." Bagwell rubbed his hands together, pleased. "There, my dear." He beamed at her.

Regina was confused. Obviously she was missing a piece of the puzzle. "I don't understand."

"But I thought I had—"

"Not all of it, you didn't, Baggy." His voice was a soft drawl, caressing, directed at Regina. His gaze never left her.

"Oh." Bagwell turned to Regina. "I thought I had told you, my dear. When I said this is Harry Wainwright, I should have said the *former* Mr. Harry Wainwright. Mr. Wainwright is now the Earl of Taskford."

Regina's eyes went round with shock. "Oh. No."

"Oh, but I assure you it is so, Mrs. Landry. He is Taskford, your new neighbor."

Regina was horrified. Now she understood the solicitor's warning that the new Earl might be unpredictable. Unpredictable! That certainly put it mildly. Her only hope was that the rake wouldn't turn his attention to the matter of the mortgage on Charnwood before she could arrange to pay off the debt.

Harry's eyes showed intense interest. Something was up. He bowed sardonically, watching her. He hadn't missed the flash of acute distress that had crossed Regina Landry's face, and he found it extremely interesting.

From what he knew of her, she was too strong a woman to blanch merely at discovering she was going to have a neighbor she found distasteful. He'd learned a little about her strengths the other night. So there must be something else. Something of much greater moment than his thoroughly regretted drunken behavior in the private parlor at *The Golden Boar*. He wondered how long it would take him to find out from Baggy just what it might be?

The solicitor pursued his own agenda. "Perhaps you would not object to escorting Mrs. Landry to Charnwood, Harry. It's the property next to yours, you know."

"No, I didn't know." His gaze locked with the tall beauty's. "Nothing, however, could please me more than being of service to Mrs. Landry." His eyes laughed at her.

Regina's eyes blazed back at him. "Thank you," she lied, "but I have already made arrangements to get to Charnwood." She turned toward the solicitor. "I didn't want to mention it before in light of your kindness in having procured the stage coach schedules, Mr. Bagwell, but I am traveling with friends and must decline"—she returned her gaze to the new Earl's handsome face—"your kind offer."

God, Regina was certain, would be quicker to forgive her
for that blatant lie than He would be for what might happen
if she spent long hours in a closed coach with Harry Wainwright! In addition, the impropriety of traveling alone with
an unmarried man who was not a member of her family was
shocking enough to send her head reeling. Obviously Mr.
Bagwell had not given that problem his consideration.

"Oh, my. How forgetful I'm becoming in my old age!"
Bagwell interrupted her thoughts. "Regina, my dear. It completely slipped my mind that I had word from your friends
just this morning. A problem of some magnitude arose on
one of their other estates, and they will not be going in the
direction of Charnwood after all. They have sent their apologies and asked me to make arrangements to get you safely to
your home." His eyes twinkling at her, he gathered a neat
stack of papers to add to the file he'd already picked up, and
nodded Harry to the door. "I can think of no better way to do
that than to send you with his lordship, the Earl of Taskford.
Come, Harr . . . your lordship . . . we'll just adjourn to the
next room to take care of a few details." He turned back to
Regina, "Then I shall return to finish our discussion, my
dear." Softly he closed the door.

Appalled and astonished at the rasper Bagwell had just
told to counteract her own lie, Regina stared at the door as it
closed behind that erstwhile matchmaker and his client.
Without a doubt, Bagwell was thrusting her into Taskford's
company with an eye to settling the husband question. Certainly he had no idea of the man's character if he thought for
one instant that the new earl was the sort of man who'd give
up his freedom so easily. "Preposterous" was the only word
that came to mind for the solicitor's attempt to pair her with
the arrogant new Earl of Taskford.

Regina sat back and tried to come to grips with the news
that the libertine who had so recently kissed her was not

only going to be her neighbor, but was also the holder of the mortgage on Charnwood! She could think of no worse disaster that could befall her this day.

Then she heard the knob on the door behind her turn.

"So you are here, after all." Jasper Ruddleston made it an accusation. "I thought it must be you when the clerk finally described you."

"And just why should I not be here?"

"Because you're wasting Bagwell's time. There's no way you will be able to keep Philip's brats. You've no husband."

His smirk made her as angry as his rudeness. "I'll wager"—she loaded that word with sarcastic emphasis—"I have as good a chance with the court as you do, considering *your* reputation."

"My reputation!" His voice rose. "Well, my dear, at least I *have* a reputation." He spat the words at her as if they left a bad taste in his mouth. "*You* have been training horses for the past few years!"

She shot out of her chair to face him. He'd said "training horses" in a tone of voice he'd have used to say "running a brothel," and she had no intention of letting that stand. "I trained racers for the most respected woman breeder in Ireland. I have nothing to be ashamed of in that. Rather, I am proud of what I have accomplished."

"Ah, yes. You would be. As I recall, it was ever your preference to run around the countryside in boys' britches when we were children. You never were content to keep your place!"

"My place, as you call it, is my own to decide, not yours to dictate. It became what I could honorably make of it after my husband was killed." Righteous anger sharpened her tongue. "It gives me great satisfaction to inform you that I was a successful and well-respected member of my world. I'm sure you wish that you could say the same."

"How dare you!" Jasper was shouting. "How dare you act

as if I am in any way inferior to you!" He raised his cane to strike her.

The door was thrust open. The new Earl of Taskford seized Jasper by his coat collar. Hauling him backward away from his intended victim, he spun him around. Jaw jutting, he spoke straight into the squirming man's face, his voice hissing with suppressed fury. "How dare *you*, sirrah! How dare you shout at a lady?" He shook Jasper as a terrier might shake a rat.

Suddenly, his blazing blue eyes narrowed as he took in the significance of Jasper's upraised cane. "My God! Would you strike a defenseless woman?"

As Taskford prepared to deal Jasper a backhanded blow, Regina stepped close to him. Seizing his upraised arm, she cried, "No, please! He isn't worth it."

Taskford hesitated. His grip relaxed slightly as he looked down at her.

That was all Jasper Ruddleston needed. He twisted free and ran out of the office. Knocking aside one of the clerks who'd been drawn by the commotion, he made for the exit. The heavy front door of the law offices slammed back against the wall as he fled through it. Cracked plaster showered the floor.

Taskford stood looking down at Regina, his hand still poised to strike in her defense.

Regina stood gazing up at him, lips parted, her hands still gripping his muscular forearm.

Both held their breaths while lightning played between them.

Neither of them noticed the people around them until Mr. Bagwell cleared his throat noisily and said drily, "It's a pity you stopped Harry, my dear. A duel would have solved all our problems."

• • •

Late breakfast in Harry Wainwright's Spartan rooms was a gala affair. His five closest friends were in alt, overjoyed because of his good fortune, and brown ale flowed freely.

"Sorry about your relative sticking his spoon in the wall and all that, of course, Harry, but I'm deuced glad to see you elevated from the ranks of well-bred but less than well-heeled titleless bachelors." Cheerfully, MacLain swung his tankard of ale shoulder-high. Some sloshed on the tall, slender man to his right.

"I say, MacLain!" Mathers glared at him. "Have a care. This is my favorite riding coat, you know."

"How the devil should Mac know what coat you favor, old boy?" Stone was amused. "I certainly don't, and I know you as well as he does."

"Just be more careful, MacLain. We'd all appreciate it." Smythe sighed in loving memory of a coat he himself now lacked, thanks to MacLain, and watched as Harry's man, Williams, mopped the spilled ale from Mather's green-clad shoulder. When the valet had finished wiping the coat, he surreptitiously removed the pitcher of ale from the table and left the room, smug in the certainty that the master's friends had had quite enough.

"Well." Stone glared at the doorway through which Williams had gone with the ale. "There goes more gall than wisdom."

"You'd had enough, anyway, Stone," MacLain told him cheerfully.

"Who are you to say when I've had enough?"

Chalfont Blysdale's calm voice stopped the bickering. "Here, here, gentlemen. We've come to congratulate the new Earl of Taskford, not to get into a spitting match over a little slopped ale."

Harry looked at him assessingly, then spoke. "You're absolutely right, Bly. And I thank you all for your enthusiasm.

You're good friends and true. I can't imagine anyone—of our sex, that is"—his companions' laughter drowned him out. When it subsided, he went on, grinning—"*anyone* that I'd rather be with." He swept the group with a smile.

Sobering, he lifted a hand for silence and told them, "There's a fly in the ointment, however." He had their full attention. "According to my solicitor, my inheritance depends on my spending a year at Taskford Manor. I'll be an earl without a penny if I don't comply with the terms of my uncle's will." He was heartened by their sympathetic moans. "Therefore, I'd like to invite you to join me in a jaunt down to Taskford to stay as long as you'd like as my guests.'

"All five of us? Harry, are you sure?" Smythe was incredulous.

"Yes." The newly elevated Taskford smiled around the table. "All five of you. Why not?"

"Just seems like quite a gaggle, old man."

"The more the merrier, my friends." Harry lounged back in his chair. "I'm assured the estate will wine and dine me and any guests, though according to my uncle's will I'm to have no more than pocket change until I've stuck it out a year—or married. And we all know what the temperature in hell will be before I marry!"

"Hear, hear," went 'round the room.

"We've only to find ways in which to entertain ourselves." He lifted his long legs and propped booted feet on the edge of the table.

"Why, that's very kind of you, Harry. Very kind." Smythe's round face colored with pleasure.

"I'd be glad to accept, old boy, but I have to go placate my parents about my debts. My tailor, particularly, is getting impatient." The blond MacLain looked woeful. "I'm off to the family castle."

"If they tire of you, I'm glad to offer you a bed until

you're plump in the pocket again." Harry's expansive gesture slopped ale from his own tankard down his sleeve and he scowled at it. Maybe Williams had been right to remove the pitcher.

Stone laughed. "Don't you mean *when* they tire of him?"

"I say!" MacLain protested. "At the least you could say 'tire of *us*.'"

"True."

Harry chuckled and shifted his regard to Blysdale. "What about you, Bly? Will you come?"

Blysdale considered a moment, studying the carefully tended nails of his right hand. "I suppose I could see my way clear."

"See your way clear!" The heavyset man opposite him hooted. "As if you had any more to do than the rest of us."

"I'm sure, Stone, that *you* will join Harry's house party." Chalfont Blysdale could do the best sneer of all of them.

"Well, you're off for once, my supercilious friend. I'm pledged to bear Mac company. I'm to furnish courage for our impoverished comrade." He turned toward Harry. "Be glad to come after the senior MacLains throw us out, though."

"Good!" Harry's sleek muscles rippled under the snug doeskin of his breeches as he swung his feet back to the floor. The front legs of his tilted chair slammed back down. He grinned around the circle. "There. You see? With you lot in residence, I'll avoid perishing of boredom while I'm stuck out in the country."

"I see," Mac pretended offense. "We are no longer your bosom companions, we are now merely your physic."

Stone, joining in, grumbled, "Sounds deuced insulting to me."

Smythe didn't want to seem to oppose Mac, but he

thought it might be rather nice to be somebody's cure-all. He said very softly, "I should like very much for all of us to go."

"Come now," Mathers looked around the circle. "Harry meant it as a compliment. Besides, what are friends for? We must make plans to save the old boy from the doldrums."

Stone's voice took on a plaintive note. "I thought we *had* a plan to avoid being bored. I thought we were all going to that race that Belding is running Halidon in."

"Belding." Smythe gave a sniff to indicate his disapproval. "Never liked the fellow."

Stone frowned at him. "Has nothing to do with the fellow, Smythe. Has to do with the horse."

Mathers looked pensive. "Wasn't that the horse that was half brother to Cossack, Ashley Stoddard's stallion?" His brow furrowed.

"Cossack." Taskford smiled at the memory. "I knew him well. Friendly brute . . . for a stallion."

"Humph. You could say so. You'd sense enough to ride a gelding. Ash thought so much of your friendship with his brute that he left him to you in his will." Blysdale wore a crooked smile. "Whatever happened to Cossack after Ashley was killed?"

Pain flickered behind Harry's eyes. "Belding reported the horse was hit, too. He shot it to put it out of its misery."

They sat silent for a long moment, mourning the loss of a good friend and, because they were cavalrymen, mourning the death of a gallant charger.

Stone was the first to speak. "Remember the races we had?"

"Glory, yes," Mac said. "Harry always won at them, too. Just like at cards and with the ladies."

Everyone hooted.

"No, you block! Ashley always won," Harry corrected. "Ash and Cossack won 'em all."

"All right." Mac, face flushed, accused, "But you know very well we never counted Cossack. He was too good. And Harry was always second on Tammerlane."

In the general laughter, no one noticed that Harry's smile had died at the mention of his slain charger.

Mathers added, "And Belding on Halidon was always third. Halidon was almost as good as Cossack."

"Cossack and Halidon had the same sire," Blysdale mused. "Must have been the dam that gave Cossack so much more of the will to win." Then he declared, "Oh, hell. Forget racing. Harry only becomes an Earl once. Besides, knowing Belding, he'll run the legs off Halidon now he's going so well. We can watch him race another time." He looked around the circle for agreement.

Smythe said softly, "But I told Belding that we'd all be there."

Harry asked, "When did you tell him?"

"Two weeks ago. When he told me about the race. I ran into him on the way to your card party."

"Forget it. He'll never remember."

"True. A lot can happen in two weeks."

Mathers broke in. "Indeed. And a lot has, but what's of importance is this celebration." He saluted the new earl with his empty tankard. "Our Harry's been elevated to an earldom!"

Blysdale ended the discussion. "We'll go to Taskford. We can see Belding run Halidon another time."

There was a hearty chorus of "Ayes!" and "To Taskford." Then they were silent again, pointedly staring into their tankards.

Wainwright roared, "Williams! Ale!"

With a sigh, the much-tried valet reentered the room with the pitcher that he'd already refilled against his better judgement, and began pouring fresh ale.

Cheered by his comrades' good-natured support, Harry laughed and snatched up his own ale. "To fellowship!"

The others joined in the toast, and the room rang with their voices. "To fellowship!"

Blysdale added softly, "And to adventure!"

Five

John Halston looked up abruptly from his desk in the foyer of *The Golden Boar*. He smiled slightly and returned to his accounts.

Regina, who waited near the door beside her trunk, realized she must have sighed. She'd been doing that a lot lately. If she were to avoid disturbing others, she'd better get her mind off the seemingly insurmountable problem Mr. Bagwell had set for her—that of finding a husband.

To distract herself, she attempted to recall something, anything, that had nothing whatsoever to do with striving for the guardianship of her niece and nephew, or with loneliness and loss—especially the loss of her family. She strove to think of something amusing.

That task wasn't difficult. She had only to recall the scene the other evening here in the private parlor. She'd have to ignore the fact that the man involved was Taskford, of course. The evening's adventure would cease to be amusing if she once considered him in his role of being her new neighbor.

To lighten her somber mood, she set her mind to dwell only on the events of that particular evening, excluding everything else. Almost instantly, she felt the beginnings of a smile. What a ludicrous experience that had been! And she'd behaved in a ridiculous manner. Yesterday, at Bagwell's office, Taskford had made it perfectly clear he wasn't going to forget her actions. Nor let her forget them, either.

Without effort, she could call to mind the handsome, devil-may-care face of the man who'd boldly kissed her awake. It was a face *no* woman would have the least difficulty remembering. Not that firm-jawed visage lit by bold blue eyes framed in lashes too thick to belong to any man. She approved of the fact that his patrician nose was saved from perfection by a break at the bridge of it, but that reckless grin of his—that slash of white in a face tanned by hours spent out of doors—shouldn't be showing its perfect, even teeth in a fusty law office.

That grin belonged on the deck of a pirate ship!

Thinking of his sensuous mouth brought back the scandalous way in which *she* had behaved. With a blush, she remembered deliberately choosing to kiss those enticing lips. She fanned her hand in front of her face to cool her hot cheeks.

Suddenly a broad smile lit her features as she realized she didn't feel the least bit repentant. She knew she should, but she didn't. In fact, here in the safety of *The Golden Boar*, she could frankly admit that she'd enjoyed the man's kisses . . . and more than enjoyed returning them.

The new Earl had behaved like an absolute cad, of course. He'd have frightened a more sheltered woman out of her wits. Knowing help was merely a scream away, however, she'd held her own. Furthermore, she remembered with a little surge of pride, she'd given as good as she got, standing her ground in an arena from which ladies were expected to flee.

But she'd had no inclination to flee from the tall, dark

Taskford. No inclination at all. From that, she could draw only one conclusion . . . while *he* had been a cad, *she* had hardly been a lady.

Because of this, she was deeply concerned about having been forced by the cagey solicitor to accept the Earl of Taskford's offer to escort her to Charnwood. Her capricious behavior in the private parlor had opened her to insult, insult that would be more than encouraged by the impropriety of the current situation. It was a great relief, therefore, to see that Taskford was not alone when his traveling coach pulled up in front of the inn.

Introductions to the three men accompanying Taskford went smoothly. Regina particularly liked the self-effacing man called Smythe, and was pleased to learn that he would be riding inside the coach with her the whole way.

"I have no desire to tool the coach as Harry usually does, you see. And I'm not really comfortable in the saddle like my lean, athletic friends, either." He glanced over the other three men and a twinkle lit his blue eyes as he looked down at his own bulky frame. "The horse isn't very comfortable, either."

Taskford told her, "Smythe was a prisoner of the French for three months. When we got him back, it was too late. He'd already vowed to eat everything he'd missed while in captivity."

Bly looked at Harry as if he'd taken leave of his senses, shrugged and added, "Captivity? Correction. That he'd missed for the whole war."

Smythe blushed furiously. "And to make it worse, I'm bookish." He offered it as an excuse for not being as active as his companions.

Regina felt sorry for him. She gave him her most radiant smile. "I shall be happy to have you as my traveling companion, Mr. Smythe. I'm also an avid reader. To me, reading is one of life's greatest pleasures, and I'm sure we'll find a great many things to discuss."

Smythe looked like a puppy that had won unexpected praise. He offered Regina his arm, helped her into the coach, and followed her into it.

Harry scowled, and with unusual strength, slung her trunk into the boot of the coach one-handed. The footman who'd been about to hoist the trunk stepped back quickly to avoid getting bashed by it.

Blysdale thrust an elbow into Mathers's ribs as their host, the expression on his face thunderous, climbed up on to the box to sit beside his coachman.

"Interesting," he said.

"Interesting, indeed." Mathers grinned. "Rather a treat to see old Harry in a pet over a female, isn't it?"

"Maybe it isn't going to be quite as dull in the country as we'd thought."

Both men were laughing heartily as they mounted up.

By the time they stopped for lunch, Regina and Smythe had become good friends. The halt came in the middle of their discussion of Sir Walter Scott's latest book.

When Taskford leapt lightly down from the box to open the door of the coach, they hardly noticed him. They proceeded up the path to the inn door without breaking off their conversation.

Annoyed, Harry left his dismounted friends beating road dust from their shoulders and clothes with their riding gloves in preparation for going in to eat, and headed for the stables. After he'd instructed the hostlers to harness a fresh team to the coach in a half-hour, he followed his fellow travelers inside.

He found the others in the public dining room of the inn, seated at a battered, well-scrubbed round table. Bly was instructing the innkeeper to bring a cloth for it. Mathers was asking what there was to eat, and Regina and Smythe were now discussing the works of Mrs. Radcliffe.

Smythe sat on Regina Landry's left, eagerly leaning toward her. Mathers made haste to capture the chair on her other side the moment he saw Taskford enter. Blysdale shot Harry a grin and took the chair opposite the lady, gesturing him into the remaining one.

Harry snatched up his chair, turned its back to the table and straddled it. He watched, rather than listened to the discussion between Regina and Smythe. At the first pause in their conversation, he interjected, "The stagecoach passed through here just a little while ago, the hostlers tell me. They left London almost two hours before we did, so we're making excellent time."

Regina remembered the frequency with which she'd had to grab the safety strap on her side of the coach. "I'm certain that we are. No doubt we'll soon overtake them," she told him coolly. "You must have an exemplary coachman." She knew he'd handled the ribbons himself and she wanted to see how he'd answer her.

Without batting an eye, Taskford agreed. "Yes, he's most capable." His eyes met hers squarely.

Regina felt her lips twitch. The man was an unrepentant rogue. "I had thought you might drive us part of the way yourself."

"I'd thought I might." He didn't say any more.

She turned away to Smythe in an attempt to hide her smile.

Smythe asked, "What will you have, my dear?"

After a pleasant meal, they were on their way again, the fresh team eating up the miles under the competent hand of John Coachman. To Regina's surprise, Taskford had entered the coach for this leg of the journey. Though he simply sat opposite her and watched her, the power of the man's personality filled the luxurious interior.

Regina was glad Smythe was in the carriage with them as a chaperone. Then she heard him begin to snore! So much for help from that quarter.

Regina decided to set the tone of the conversation, almost fearful of the topic her host might choose. She looked at him squarely. "I must congratulate you on your elevation, your lordship."

He smiled. "Why is that? I suspect you might have found the old Earl a much more comfortable neighbor."

"Oh?" So they were to duel again. "And do you intend to make yourself less so than he?"

He laughed without giving her an answer to her question, then said, "Thank you for your congratulations, Mrs. Landry. Now that they are out of the way, I feel I must perform a task of my own. I must apologize for my behavior in the private parlor at *The Golden Boar*." He looked for all the world like a schoolboy expecting punishment as he added, "I fear I was a trifle . . . er . . . inebriated."

Several responses ran through Regina's mind. Most of them amusing, but none appropriate. Deciding it was safest to remain formally polite, she forgave him graciously, saying, "I understand completely, your lordship. Pray hold yourself forgiven." She then purposefully changed the subject by glancing out the window and exclaiming, "Oh, look. Isn't that a splendid chestnut!"

Taskford watched the horse bucking and running along its pasture fence in an attempt to get the team drawing their coach to pay attention to him. His hide gleamed red in the sunlight, his muscles played, supple and strong, under it, and his confirmation was near perfect. "Yes. He's a beauty."

Then he asked a question of his own. "Is it true that you used to train horses?"

"Yes." She answered with quiet pride. "I trained for Lady Sybella Dashwood outside Dublin for six years. Since the Charnwood trainer died in the same fire that killed my brother and your great uncle, I'll have to train again as soon as I get home. It's a blessing I'm so well prepared, as present necessity dictates that I continue the training of the horses at my family's stud."

"Necessity?"

The conversation was drawing too close to the matter of funds. It was only a step from there to the matter of the mortgage. She changed the subject. "Except for the sad circumstances, are you pleased to inherit such a fine racing stable?"

"I haven't seen it yet."

His blasé reply made her impatient with him. "Your late uncle's stud is famous in the racing world."

"Ah, yes. But I have my own standards."

"And what might they be?" She spoke with some asperity, offended by his attitude. Who did he think he was to reserve judgement on horses reputed to be some of the finest Thoroughbreds in England?

Unsmiling, Harry cocked an eyebrow at her. "Do you truly wish to know?"

She met his gaze openly. "I'm not in the habit of asking questions to which I don't want answers."

He smiled then, and began to tell her. "To please me, a horse must not only be fast, but intelligent. " His eyes glowed. "Not only intelligent, but good-natured—something you will admit is difficult to come by in a racing Thoroughbred."

"That depends on whether he's been properly trained to *want* to run, or been incited to panic to *make* him run, doesn't it?" Her statement was an indictment of inept trainers.

Admiration lit his eyes. "Your point's well taken." His gaze raked her figure, lingering on her breasts for a heartbeat. "Perhaps you *do* know how to train horses." Languidly he raised his gaze to her face. "In spite of the fact that you're a beautiful woman."

"I have trained several of the best runners in Ireland." She had to work to keep the heat out of her voice. Nothing would have kept her from saying it. Why was it that men always looked at . . . the exterior of a woman and jumped to their conclusions from that alone?

"Perhaps I've heard of some of them?" His eyes told her he doubted it.

Regina, more than a little annoyed that he doubted her ability because of her gender, drew a deep breath to begin.

She never had a chance to name the first horse. With a shuddering slam, the coach slewed to a halt. She was thrown across the interior to land in the Earl's lap, her hands against the squabs on either side of his head, their faces as close as a kiss.

Smythe was in a heap at their feet.

"Whoa! Whoa, there!" John Coachman roared from the box. They could hear horses screaming, people crying out.

Taskford lifted Regina to her former seat as if she were a feather. Throwing open the door, he leapt out, Regina on his heels. Behind them a groggy Smythe shook his head, pushed himself up off the carriage floor and followed.

The scene before them was sheer pandemonium. A stagecoach, the very one Regina had planned to be on, lay smashed on its side, its passengers strewn around it. The team lay or stood, eyes rolling, hopelessly tangled in their traces.

"Harry!" A man held his hand to his bleeding side, leaned against a tree and called again, "Harry!"

"My God! Haversham!"

Blysdale and Mathers dismounted and ran with Taskford to the aid of their wounded friend.

Regina took in the scene at a glance. The coachmen were seeing to the passengers. The frightened horses were unattended. She turned her attention to the team.

Striding toward the struggling horses, Regina called out an order to one of the passengers who'd escaped injury, "You there! Come! I shall need your help with the horses."

The clerk she'd pointed to squeaked in panic, "Who, me?"

"Yes, you. Come with me." Regina watched his pale face turn resolute, as she turned away and approached the horses cautiously.

The clerk squared his shoulders and followed her.

"Easy, boys. Easy." Regina kept her voice low, almost monotonous as she neared the thrashing team. The nearest horse, a big gelding who was down and tangled in his traces, stopped writhing and flicked an ear toward her.

"Easy, now." She began a soft whistling—tunelessly, as so many stable lads did when grooming the great, nervous beasts. Taking slow steps, she was careful to do nothing that would further disquiet the terrified animals. "There, there, boy. Easy." Another horse stopped struggling and wrenched its head around to look at her, its ears pricked toward her. The one harnessed to him bunched the muscles in his rump as if to kick at her, but didn't.

Now she was ankle-deep in the mud churned up by their flashing, iron-shod hooves. If the first horse resumed its fight to be free of the leather traces in which he was tangled, Regina knew there'd be no way she'd escape injury.

Quietly she ordered the clerk to come nearer. "I shall need a knife. A very sharp knife." The man rushed away to do her bidding.

Regina knew horses. Knew how threatened they felt to be

down or caught up in anything. Knew their tremendous strength . . . and how easily they panicked. Unfortunately, she was also aware of the practice of using unruly rogues for coaching teams. People who were unable to handle such horses often donated them to be rid of the problem.

Gently, she lay one hand on the twitching hide of the fear-filled gelding. He froze with the utter stillness of a wild thing about to bolt. "Easy, boy. Easy."

Some of the white disappeared from around his eyes. Too much remained to suit her.

"It's all right, I'm here. It's all right, now." The horse never blinked. She told him again, her voice warm honey. "I'm here."

The clerk returned with a wicked-looking knife and stared at her in awe as he handed it to her.

Regina never noticed his expression. The whole of her attention was on the fallen animal. She began to stroke him lightly until the horse relaxed and blew gently through his nostrils, surrendering his will to hers.

Regina began to work on the traces that bound him. As she did, his teammate, blood dripping from a gash just below his hock, moved uneasily.

Instinctively she said, "Whoa, boy."

Though they were already stationary, the familiar word worked to calm them. Only the large bay mare of the lead pair looked confused.

Regina used the knife to saw through one of the thick leather traces. Instantly, the horse under her hand started to rise. She put her knee on its shoulder, "No, boy." Then, less sharply, "Easy."

The gelding's eyes showed their whites again. She knew he hated, with all the primal fear of his ancestors, being down and held there, but he was listening to her. Regina was absolutely calm as she willed him to understand that she was helping him.

"I know, boy, I know." Regina recognized the trust his soft whicker offered her. Tears sprang to her eyes. "Hold tight, I'll have you out of this in a minute. Hang on."

A final slash, and the horse was free! Now she had only to get him up without startling the other horses. The last thing she wanted was to cause more injury by acting hastily.

Suddenly, across the way, Taskford looked up from where he stood over his wounded army acquaintance and saw what Regina was doing. Good God! There was the Amazon, *his* Amazon with a knee on the shoulder of a horse that was about to lunge up and destroy her. And she had a knife in her hands the size of a small sword! She was slashing through traces most men would have difficulty parting.

He ripped out an oath and whirled away from his friends. Every horse in the stagecoach's downed team reacted to his shout and sudden movement with an explosion of energy. Then he was swearing at his own stupidity. Silently.

Regina used words she'd learned in the stables of the Dashwood Stud as hooves flashed within inches of her head.

Her helpful clerk ran away to a safe distance.

Only the big bay mare remained motionless.

Panicked at the sight of his Amazon about to get her head kicked clear of her shoulders, Taskford raced toward the melee. He had to get her out of there.

"What the devil do you think you're doing!" He shouted the words at her in a rising crescendo as if they would return her to caution by their very force. He was wild with anxiety. The slender vision from his private parlor was standing against the muddy belly of a downed coach horse, one knee on its shoulder! Didn't the fool woman know she stood in mortal danger? Better than half a ton of horse was inches

from scrambling to its feet. When it did, it would cut her legs from under her and trample her into the churned earth!

Regina knew instantly that his words were meant only for her. She ignored him. Anyone with eyes in their head could tell what she was doing. It was no pleasure being cursed at, no matter what guise it took.

Taskford realized how stupid he'd been to rush at the horses because he was concerned for the woman, but he hadn't seemed able to help himself. "Dammit! What the blazes does that wench do to my common sense?" He forced himself to slow down and approach more quietly. His frame fairly creaked with the strain of not hurling himself at her, not tearing her away to safety.

After what seemed an eternity, he reached her side. Muscles jumped in his jaw with the effort to keep from shouting at her to get away, to get clear of the danger. His nerves stretched to the breaking point, he wrenched the knife from her hand and began systematically to cut more traces. He knew it would be useless to order her away. The quickest way to get her safe was to free the damned horses.

Regina had sensed his approach as surely as she felt wind rising. The two of them had been acutely aware of one another whenever they'd met previously—why should it be any different now?

Especially now, when her hair was straggling down around her hips and she was covered with mud and the blood of the off-wheeler?

She felt the pure animal strength that radiated from him. She smelled the crisp freshness of him—and resented it hardily. *She* stank of the horse she had cut free. And that horse, the horse she was urging quietly to his feet, came before petty resentment of pristine gentlemen and their unsolicited interference. "There, there, lad. Up you come." She tugged gently at the fallen animal's bridle, and he regained his feet with a lunge that sent the horses around them twitching and stamping—and the new Earl of Taskford cursing.

With a shuddering sigh, the gelding plopped his great head against Regina's chest. She scratched him behind the ears and under his chin and murmured, "Good boy. Oh, you are a *good* boy." She passed him to the clerk with a smile. "Walk him slowly, please."

Working shoulder to shoulder with the angry, muttering Earl of Taskford, Regina quickly sorted out the rest of the six-horse team. Once they were standing, they were less fractious.

"Here." The big bay mare she assigned to Smythe's care because it was the calmest and steadiest and would be careful of him. The mare promptly blew froth all over the perfectly attired Smythe, making Regina smile in spite of the situation.

Her concern shifted to the horse with the gashed leg, now that her way to him was cleared. She asked her gallant clerk to hold it for her, tore off a strip from her petticoat and temporarily bound the wound. Now she could leave him. She'd come back and do the wound up properly when the rest of the horses were safe.

Drawing two other horses forward as the Earl freed them, she assigned them to whomever was nearest, then turned back to help Taskford finish the job.

The mere sight of him stopped her where she stood. He was busy extricating the last horse from the tangled harness. His head was bent over his task and a lock of his heavy dark hair hung over his forehead. With his cheeks flushed and his lower lip thrust out a little in concentration, the Earl was . . . she sought for an apt phrase and settled on "rather appealing." She pressed a hand to her chest to still the flutter she felt there.

Then he looked up.

His gaze swept her from the top of her head to the tip of her toes. There was no doubt in her mind that he was repulsed by what he saw. She knew she looked as if she'd been dragged through a knothole backwards. She could almost feel the mud she wore, and she knew her hair was stringing down around her like some rag picker's tattered cloak. To be caught at such a disadvantage by the Earl of Taskford, of all people, was annoying in the extreme.

Neither was she pleased to see that Taskford was, except for his muddied boots, as clean as he'd been before he'd hurled himself from their coach. Odious man! She wasn't even going to notice how the muscles played across his back as he strove to release the final horse. "How the deuce did they get in such a tangle?" she heard him ask of no one in particular. "It's not as if they'd rolled down a cliff."

The last horse free, Regina dropped to one knee and began to examine the horse with the gash in its leg.

Harry started to grab her, to pull her up to safety. Then he registered that she was not kneeling completely. Grudgingly he admitted that she had put herself in a position from which she could instantly throw herself out of harm's way if the horse panicked. He watched in amazement as she expertly evaluated the leg wound. He was still staring when she looked up and demanded, "Get me some clean water, please."

"Bly," he growled, indicating his hat that he'd tossed out of harm's way earlier, "get the lady some water from that spring, will you." Not a request. More a royal command.

Blysdale saluted sarcastically, said, "It's your hat," and went off to where a spring gushed out of the hill on the other side of the road.

"Yes," Taskford said to Regina, "it *is* my hat. Is there any other article from my person that you require?" He hoped to shock her into noticing him.

He was doomed to disappointment. Cool gray eyes raked him from head to toe as Regina stood with her dress hiked almost to her knees, her hands ready to tear another strip of fabric from her tattered petticoat.

At the sight of her slender calves and trim ankles, Wainwright's pulse rate doubled. He frowned. This was ridiculous. It wasn't as if he'd never seen a woman's ankles before.

"Yes, actually I think I would." Regina's boldly speculative gaze settled on his throat. "I'd like your cravat, please. It will make a much better bandage than a piece of my petticoat." She lifted the torn hem of the abused undergarment toward him. "As you can see, the only fabric available to me is quite sullied."

Harry fought for equilibrium. Unaware of everything but the welfare of the horse he now held steady for her, she'd hiked her skirts up above her knees to show him her muddied petticoat was unserviceable as a bandage. His head spun at the sight of her slender legs, the glimpse of creamy thigh just above her knees. Even clad in mud-stained stockings, they were the loveliest legs he'd ever seen. And he considered himself something of a connoisseur.

With shaking fingers, Harry ripped off his cravat and held it out to her. Her smile as she received it made him weak in the knees.

Their fingers brushed under the crisp cravat. Regina gave a little gasp. *Why* was she reacting like a schoolroom miss? She didn't even like this man. Thank Heaven she had a wounded horse to concentrate on. Maybe the task would help her keep her head.

She cast a glance at the distant, scattered luggage of the coach passengers. Things were too chaotic there to ask for something to use for bandaging the gash in the coach horse's leg. With a hint of apology in her voice, she asked, "Might I have your shirt as well?"

At the question, Harry felt himself destroyed. At this moment, she could have asked anything of him. She'd just single-handedly saved six horses. She was no slip of a girl, it was true. She was as tall as many men of his acquaintance. Taller than Smythe. But she had the courage of any one of them. He'd never known such a woman.

Standing there straight as a young tree, totally unaware of how stunning she was with her glorious hair cascading around her and her dress clinging damply to her, she could have asked for the moon and he would have attempted to get it for her. Struggling out of his coat, he tossed it to Blysdale, and proceeded to pull his shirttail out of his breeches.

"I say. Taskford." Blysdale's pretended shock was underlaid with amusement.

"Stubble it," his friend snarled at him. He pulled his shirt over his head.

Regina was unaware she had caused the Earl's friend to laugh at him. She was too busy trying to catch her breath as she saw the broad, square shoulders and well-muscled chest the Earl had bared. Reaching out hands that seemed to belong to someone else, she accepted the shirt. Her gaze and her mind, however, were on the long scar along his ribs. She lifted distressed eyes to meet his. "How . . . ?"

He didn't pretend to misunderstand. "A French saber." Eyes hot, he scowled at her, daring her to ask more.

Regina was too busy with the turmoil of her emotions even to think of another question. Why was she so affected by the scar on this man? There were many men scarred from the war. Terribly scarred. Maimed, too. Why was this one man's long-healed wound tearing at her so that she felt ready to weep?

Resolutely, Regina tore her gaze from the Earl's bare

chest and turned her attention to the wounded horse. Using the clean sleeve of the Earl's fine linen shirt and the water the Earl's friend had brought her in his lordship's exquisite beaver hat, she applied herself to the task of cleaning the gash that marred the horse's hind leg. When the horse moved restively, she merely murmured, "Easy, boy," and her soft tone calmed him.

Harry watched her work. He was amazed to see the efficiency with which she cleaned the wound and the deftness with which she held its edges together as she bound the whole with his once-stylish cravat. Holding it in place with one hand, she withdrew from her shining mass of hair what was probably its last hairpin. While she thrust the pin through the pristine linen of his abused neckwear to secure it, he admired the glistening highlights in the dark, heavy fall of her tresses.

Harry's hands itched to run his fingers through that wealth. The urge rose in him to gather it into his hands and fist it firmly so that she would be helpless to move as he lowered his mouth to hers. Lowered his mouth to taste again the sweetness of her breath, to feel again the softness of her lips against his own.

Blysdale cleared his throat loudly.

Harry shot him a distracted glance. It changed to a scowl when he saw the open amusement in his friend's eyes.

Regina rose from securing her bandage. "There. That should do. He should be right as rain in a week or so." She smiled up at the Earl, expecting him to share in her relief for the welfare of the horse.

Harry saw only the clear gray honesty of her eyes. Glowing eyes. Glorious eyes. He couldn't remember a woman ever having looked at him that way. He stood staring down at her.

A sharp breeze arose, and Taskford's friend Mathers started forward with the Earl's coat.

Blysdale pushed away from the trunk of the tree on which he leaned, his gaze speculative. "Well, Mathers, it looks as if this may be a very interesting visit after all."

Mathers nodded, then walked up to Taskford. His face was carefully schooled to be expressionless, his voice to be bland. "I think it's time to put your coat back on, Harry."

Six

Regina, embarrassed to be caught gazing at the Earl like a mooncalf by Blysdale and Mathers, blushed to the roots of her hair, turned and hurried away from the three men.

Harry, halfheartedly cursing all tailors, gazed after her as he hastily shoved back into his coat with the aid of his two strong comrades. "Damn tight coat," he muttered. "How's a man to do anything but sit still in the blasted thing?" He buttoned it to the neck, the lack of his shirt and cravat giving him a raffish look.

All the while he was still acutely aware of the sensation caused by Regina Landry's gaze on his bare chest. His skin felt as if she'd stroked it with her fingers.

Mathers laughed. "Our saber-swinging days are over, Harry. This is the fashion. Better get used to it."

"Right, old boy," Blysdale told him. "A gentleman has no need of ease in a coat. You're not *supposed* to be able to do anything when you're a gentleman."

Harry's reply was a snort.

Smythe informed him seriously, "That's why we have servants, don't you know."

Harry gave him a tight half smile. His whole disposition seemed to have turned sour. No matter how irritated he was by this strange lack of control he was experiencing over his emotions where Regina Landry was concerned, however, snarling at Smythe wasn't an option. Snarling at Smythe ranked right up there with kicking puppies. Moreover, the quiet scholar was a good friend.

It was not Smythe of whom he was thinking, though. It was Regina Landry who occupied his mind. His gaze had followed her when she'd left him to struggle back into his coat. Now he watched her giving instructions to the stage coachman about the care of his battered team.

He frowned, annoyed. No woman should be so able—especially about the care of animals. It wasn't ladylike. It wasn't even feminine.

In long strides, he went to where she stood. Once there, he found something else to frown about. Mathers had beaten him to her side and was standing quietly, drinking in her every word as if the care of wounded horses was his dearest concern. Harry's teeth clenched. You'd have thought the blasted man was studying to be a stable lad!

Regina Landry was saying, ". . . and cold water the first twenty-four hours to reduce the swelling. After that, I don't think you'll have any problems with that fetlock. Should you, though, then warm wet compresses and flannel wraps should have him right as rain in no time. No work for a while. But you know all this, of course." She smiled kindly at the man. "And be sure to take care of that bump on your own head, too."

Grinning besottedly, the coachman gave her his word that he would do just that. He promised her he'd see the horse was cared for as she said, too.

Harry glared at his friend Mathers.

Mathers lifted an eyebrow at him, quirked his lips in an amused smile, then turned his full attention back to the woman at his side. Unflustered by his friend's disapproval, he walked with Regina Landry as she went to satisfy herself about the welfare of the stagecoach passengers.

Harry stationed himself at her other side, trying to come to grips with the ugly feeling that told him he was behaving like a dog with a bone. His self-deprecating thoughts were interrupted as, with a faint jingle of harness, a ramshackle carriage lumbered around the far curve in the road.

One of the coachmen called out, "'Ere's our ride to the next village, folks," and the battered passengers began to gather their things.

Regina was inspecting several of the travelers who'd been riding atop the coach and were a bit the worse for wear for having been thrown off it. At the sound of the coach arriving, she began dividing the group into those whom she deemed most in need of riding inside and those she felt could still climb to and ride safely on the top of the rescue vehicle.

As Harry watched, the blasted female began ordering people around! She personally escorted a blowzy farm woman to a seat in the vehicle. Hell, she even carried the woman's brat!

In very little time, the coach was filled, encumbered with luggage and ready to be on its way. Taskford was forced to admire Regina's ability to organize—unfeminine as he found it.

He walked up to the coach to enquire of his friend. "Haversham. Are you sure you won't join us in my carriage? We have room."

"Thank you, no, Wainwright." His glance indicated and lingered on a pretty young lady seated beside him who was obviously deeply concerned about his welfare. "I think I shall stay where I am."

Taskford laughed, closed and latched the door and called up to the box, "Hold hard until I'm gone. It will save you being overtaken and passed."

"Thankee, your lordship. My passengers have had enough excitement today without that."

Harry understood the implied criticism. He knew all about stagecoaches that were frequently forced off the road by young bucks in a hurry. Hadn't he done so himself when he was a callow youth with his first turn at the reins? He grinned up at the stagecoach driver, and turned to escort Regina back to his traveling carriage.

To his extreme irritation, he saw Mathers had beaten him to it again and was handing the widow into the coach, all smiles. When he joined them, Mathers offered, "Would you like to ride my hunter for a while, Harry? I'm certain you'd enjoy him."

Harry felt a stir of anger. What the deuce ailed him? What was this proprietary feeling about the woman that controlled his reactions? Well, he wasn't going to be ruled by it. Women weren't worth insulting a friend.

Outwardly pleasant, he answered, "Thank you, but no. I think I've had enough fresh air driving us to the inn for lunch. I'll ride inside for the rest of our journey."

Mathers saluted casually and turned away to mount his gelding.

Harry looked after him a moment and wondered why the devil he felt so blasted possessive about the Widow Landry. Before now, when one of his friends had shown an interest in a woman he'd pursued, he'd welcomed the competition. Always before, he'd stepped back and let his friend try his luck, too. Strange, he didn't seem to want to do so now. Hell, he didn't seem to be able to now. Mathers and he both knew how he loathed riding inside.

Unusually thoughtful, he climbed into his traveling coach and settled himself opposite Regina Landry, his back to the team.

Smythe and she were engaged in a lively conversation about the popularity of the horror novel, *The Castle of Otranto*. Regina was saying, ". . . I think the whole thing called for an inordinate amount of bravery on the part of that character."

Smythe made a derogatory sound and said, "I consider that it took an inordinate amount of bravery to pen the tom-foolery."

Regina's laughter made him smile, and he attempted to temper his criticism. "One does wonder how brave such imaginary characters would be in the face of a real enemy, don't you know."

Regina's smile faded and her expression grew grave. "You mean like the bravery our boys have to show in facing the French, don't you?"

Harry snorted. "They weren't all boys, madam." He spoke gruffly, irritated that the compassion in her face and voice had deeply touched him. Resentment at her having been able to move him rose.

"Indeed, not," Smythe agreed. "Harry was most certainly always in the thick of things, and he's no fresh-faced boy."

Taskford glared at him to be silent. Embarrassment would be worse than the resentment he was harboring.

Smythe smiled back at him and told Regina, "Harry was running over with bravery at Telavera . . . in fact at just about every battle on the Peninsula. But at Telavera, he led a charge that saved Wellington's staff from capture . . . and did it with his side laid open by a French saber."

"That's an exaggeration, David." Taskford's tone was menacing.

Smythe ignored it, however, warming to his subject. "At Baderjos, he sneaked over the wall into the enemy's lines and spiked one whole battery of their cannons. On foot. With the moon diving in and out of the clouds every time you blinked, by George!

"Why, the men would follow him anywhere! You should have seen their devotion to him. When he was shot, they all stood outside the surgeon's tent until they got word he'd live. Wouldn't even take care of their horses before they knew—and that would have gotten them a tongue lashing from Harry himself, had he been conscious to give 'em one. And well they knew it. But they had to see that he was going to be all right before they—"

"Smythe!" Taskford's voice was barely the civil side of a shout.

Smythe subsided, his face reddened with embarrassment at having said more about his friend than Taskford wanted told. "Sorry, old boy. Got carried away."

Taskford snarled, "Yes you did," then ignored him. His gaze was riveted to Regina Landry's face.

Regina, her heart hammering, was coming to grips with the turmoil David Smythe's words had raised in her.

Though Smythe had said nothing in any detail, Regina had pictured in her mind the battleground, the cannons in the moonlight, and had felt the danger pressing in all around. She could feel the concern of his men as if she had been there outside the surgeon's tent, waiting . . . waiting to know whether this valiant man was going to live or die.

"Mrs. Landry." Taskford's voice sounded far away.

It took her a moment to answer him. She had to compose her expression and regain control of her voice first. In no way was she going to let the man across the carriage know how moved she was to have learned of his bravery. "Yes, your lordship?"

"Before we came upon the wreck of the stagecoach, we were speaking of the horses you had trained."

His matter-of-fact tone completed her recovery. "Yes. You wanted to know the names of some of my trainees. There was Stardancer, Rainbow Chaser, and Rainbringer my first year. Then Kalispont and Going Lad the second. My third year, only Windmaiden did anything exceptional."

"By Jove, I'll say she was exceptional," Smythe broke in. "That filly won everything in sight according to . . . er, excuse me. I didn't mean to interrupt."

Taskford smiled at his friend. "I'm certain no one minds being interrupted by praise for an accomplishment."

"Quite so, Mr. Smythe," Regina agreed. "And thank you."

"You had three very successful years, Mrs. Landry," Harry said. "Congratulations."

Regina leveled a look at him. "I had *six* successful years, Lord Taskford." She proceeded to name off a list of very famous racers.

"You trained all of those horses?" His voice clearly showed his reluctance to believe that a woman could do what she'd accomplished.

"Every one," she told him firmly.

"Then I really must congratulate you. We were not totally without news of what was transpiring here at home while we were fighting the French. I've read of the victories of some of those horses you named. Quite impressive."

"Cossack would have done well, had he been raced here," Smythe said. "Oh, by the way, I told Belding we wouldn't be there to see Halidon race this time."

"Good."

"Cossack?" Regina was always interested in learning about extraordinary horses. "Who is Cossack?"

"A stallion who belonged to one of our fellow officers." Taskford answered her curtly, before his friend could reply. "An officer who might have been here to race him if I had been where I belonged—"

"Nonsense, Harry!" Smythe spoke with more authority than Regina would have expected from him. "Ashley Stoddard took your place because you were too badly wounded to go. Stop talking as if you had any choice in the matter. Stop blaming yourself for what happened. God knows it was bad enough that you chased after him. . . ." His voice trailed off as if he didn't want to go on. As if he feared he'd remind his friend of something best forgotten.

Regina couldn't help asking, "What *did* happen?"

Taskford's voice was like ice, grating. "Ashley led my men. Led my charge. I didn't get there in time. He was killed." His eyes bleak, he sat still a long moment. When he spoke again, his voice was nearer normal. "Ashley was killed, leaving a wife and three children to grieve. For them, it was as if the world ended. Even his horse was wounded and had to be destroyed."

"Anne Stoddard didn't mean the things she said to you, Harry." Smythe's eyes were full of sympathy. "That was her grief talking." He explained to Regina. "As soon as he'd recovered from his wounds—for he was hit again searching the battlefield for Ash—sufficiently to do so, Harry used his convalescent leave to go visit the Stoddards to express his condolences. Mrs. Stoddard was not herself. She said some harsh things. . . ."

"She put the blame exactly where it belongs. Ashley Stoddard is dead because he went into battle in my place."

"Harry, blast it! You were down. Wounded. You were ranting with fever. Somebody had to go, and you couldn't. It's as simple as that. When you dragged yourself out to go join them, you threw the whole camp into chaos."

"And all I did was get Tammerlane shot." His eyes filled with pain.

Clearly that was what Smythe had not wanted Taskford to recall. "And yourself again," Smythe reminded in a dull voice, knowing he'd not distract Taskford from his blunder.

With a heavy heart, Regina watched him change the subject.

"Remember, Harry. Anne Stoddard wrote and begged your forgiveness for the way she treated you when you went to see her. You forgave her."

Taskford's expression was stony.

Smythe cried out. "Oh, God, Harry! Isn't it time you forgave yourself?"

Taskford lunged for the door, threw it open and kicked down the iron step. Standing on it while he gripped the door frame, he shouted, "Hallo, Mathers. I'll take that ride on your hunter now!"

With a whoop, Mathers rode up to him and in a maneuver too rapid for those in the coach to follow, he and Taskford exchanged places. Taskford galloped off, and a slightly breathless Mathers threw himself down on the bench just quitted by his friend.

His laughter died as he looked at the two across from him. His gaze rested on Regina's face first, then went to Smythe's. Suddenly aware of their distress, he asked, "I say, is everything all right?"

Seven

Harry cantered his horse beside the carriage, sitting Mathers's hunter as if he were joined with it, bone to bone, sinew to sinew. He wasn't enjoying riding the fine Thoroughbred, however. Still lost in bitter self-recrimination, in remembering the wild grief of Ashley Stoddard's widow, he paid no attention to riding.

His mount shied at a squirrel that darted out to die under the wheels of the traveling coach, changed its mind and dashed back into the brush on the verge of the road. Harry swayed easily in the saddle without even noticing.

He didn't even have to close his eyes to see Anne Stoddard's strained face and her haunted, lost expression. And the children. Dear God, the children. Two handsome little boys and a girl barely able to walk yet. None of them understood that they no longer had a father. That their lives were forever changed.

And it was all *his* fault.

Black thoughts hung over him like a cloud, spoiling any pleasure Mathers had intended him to take in the fine piece of horseflesh under him. Burdened by guilt, he rode on.

Inside the luxurious traveling coach, Mathers and Smythe did their best to entertain Regina. After a while, she had no choice but to put the acute distress she'd seen in Taskford's face out of her mind and join in their conversation.

". . . and it seems the latest fashion among gentlemen is the shirtless look." Mathers was being absurd for her sake.

Refusing to feel chided for tearing up Taskford's shirt to bandage a horse's leg, she joined the teasing. "And mud is the latest for ladies. Only see how it causes the fabric of her gown to change subtlety and seem several colors." She spread her bedraggled skirts a bit. "And rips and tears have taken the place of lace flounces, for this trip, at least."

From outside the coach, Harry could hear laughter now and again. Mathers and Smythe were clearly enjoying the attractive widow's company. Knowing that did nothing to improve Harry's mood.

In a way, he was glad his friends appreciated the widow Landry. It would have taken the zest out of his pursuit of her if the others had decided she was in any way lacking. But it really wasn't necessary that they found her quite so engaging.

Regina Landry was a clear challenge to the sensibilities of any healthy male, but she was *his* challenge. And there was no way in hell he was going to permit Mathers—especially not Mathers—to steal the march on him. No way at all.

He wasn't worried about Smythe. Smythe, he knew, would not even attempt to take a woman from him. Neither would Bly. Mathers, however, would consider capturing Regina's affections a coup, and he'd never allow that.

Shaking off his unwelcome thoughts, Harry looked ahead and saw a familiar crossroads. Not far to go, now. Soon they would reach Taskford Manor, and a little after that, Charnwood.

The coach slowed to give the horses a breather, and he

rode close to the window to check on the focus of his musings. "Are you comfortable, Mrs. Landry?"

Regina answered him solemnly, "Of course. Your coach is very comfortable, your lordship." She looked down at herself with a rueful smile. "I only regret that my mud may be soiling your upholstery."

"Think nothing of it." His response was bland. Who cared about the upholstery? If it couldn't be brushed clean, it could be changed. He was only sorry that she was going to meet her brother's orphans for the first time looking like the wreck she'd made of herself saving the stagecoach team. Though *he* found her a charming picture with her hair in disarray and her gown plastered to her with mud, two gently-reared children probably would not.

Thrusting that concern to the back of his mind, he said, "I must ask you to excuse me. I shall ride on ahead and make myself known to the servants at Taskford. They will need some notice to prepare for my guests." With that, he touched his mount's side lightly with his heel and cantered away.

Regina watched him go until she would've had to crane out the window to see him any longer. The new Earl of Taskford cut an impressive figure on a horse. But then, he was a cavalry officer, after all.

By the time the coach, its latest team sadly worn by this last leg of their journey, arrived at Taskford Manor, Harry had already introduced himself as the new Earl, met his entire staff, and seen to it that hot baths would be ready for his three friends shortly after they arrived. That his own bath, due to his haste, had been a cold one was no novelty for a soldier.

Standing on the steps with his newly acquired butler just behind him, he watched the coach come up the long, curving drive.

With a jingle of harness and a chorus of soft whickers from animals only too glad to have returned home, the traveling coach halted at the foot of the broad stairway. A liveried footman opened the door of the traveling coach and let down the narrow iron steps.

Harry, standing at ease with his hands locked behind him, frowned as Mathers jumped lightly from the still-rocking vehicle and bid Regina Landry a perfectly charming farewell. "Until we meet again, Mrs. Landry." He turned and took the steps two at a time.

Smythe bade her farewell and made his way into the manor.

Bly handed his tired horse over to waiting grooms, and stopped at the window of the traveling coach to do the same. "Mrs. Landry. I shall look forward to the pleasure of seeing you frequently while I am here. That is, of course, if you will be so kind as to receive me."

Regina hesitated briefly. She hoped he wouldn't notice. How could she say she would be happy to receive calls from anyone when she had no idea whether she, herself, would find a welcome at her former home? Quickly deciding that the only sensible course was to leave that bridge to be crossed when she got to it, she smiled and graciously assured him, "You will be most welcome, Mr. Blysdale."

Bly bowed over her hand, turned away with one of his rare smiles and followed Smythe and Mathers.

Harry found himself unaccountably displeased with the genteel behavior of his friends. To insist on calling on Regina Landry was something he was *not* happy to see Bly do. He was glad he had the duties of host to carry him through his momentary displeasure.

"Hot baths for my guests, Helmsley. They'll want to be rid of their travel dirt." He turned his gaze to Regina, his eyes intent. "My housekeeper will see to you if you'd like to refresh yourself, Mrs. Landry."

"Thank you, no. I must be going on to Charnwood. If you could mount me, I'd prefer to ride." She smiled to remove any hint of criticism from her remark, "Your coach horses have earned their rest."

"I quite agree." Taskford raised a hand, and a lighter carriage drawn by a pair of perfectly matched grays came up the lane from around the mansion and halted behind the traveling coach. "I trust you won't mind if I accompany you?"

She could hardly refuse him. It was his carriage. "Not at all." It surprised her that he'd thought of his horses' welfare, then she was surprised that she'd not expected him to. Had she really thought him too self-centered to do so? Evidently. She was disgusted with herself for her harsh condemnation of the man. After all, his only demonstrated lack of sensibility seemed to be in his dealings with women. "Thank you. I must admit to a little fatigue, myself. Riding would have been tiring, as well as rather unseemly in my present garb."

Taskford handed her from the coach to the carriage and got in after her. As his traveling coach left for the stables, he tapped the roof of the carriage and the driver gave the grays the office to start. They followed the first coach toward the stables, but almost immediately turned off the manor's long driveway on to a well-traveled lane that Regina knew headed in the direction of Charnwood.

Charnwood. Home. Soon she would be home again. Soon she would see the niece and nephew she'd never laid eyes on. Would she like them? More importantly, would they like her? She was startled at the depth of the longing that swept over her. Oh, how she wanted them to like her. How she hungered to have what remained of her family want her as much as she wanted to be with them.

She made an effort to rein in her hopes. They were Lydia's children, after all, and while she was certain no mother would burden her child with unpleasant attitudes, she knew that Lydia had despised her.

Yes, soon she would be home again. Home at Charnwood, with all its memories, the bitter and the sweet. Home. Her heart felt as if it would burst with yearning. She was almost home again. But would she be welcome there?

From across the carriage, Taskford smiled. "I'm glad you don't object to my accompanying you."

She laughed at that, sweeping her gaze over him—noticing how handsome he looked. Even in the rush of their circumstances, he'd managed to bathe and change. She envied him.

He was diabolically handsome in evening clothes, his dark hair also black in the half-light. The black coat fit his broad shoulders to perfection, and the black trousers emphasized the length of his legs. The total effect was . . . devastating. Except that Regina, in spite of having once been highly curious about the length of those very same legs, was not about to be devastated.

Perusing her own bedraggled clothing, and striving for a light note, she told him, "I hardly think we are fairly matched."

"Mrs. Landry. " His eyes bored into her own, full of meaning, full of heat. "I think we are very well matched, indeed."

Regina blushed. Taskford clearly wasn't talking about the havoc the rescue of the stagecoach team had wreaked on her clothing.

He meant her to remember that night in the private parlor of *The Golden Boar*. That night when—thinking she would never see the man again—she had met him kiss for kiss, refusing to be judged the weaker in their strange encounter.

Very well. She preferred to remember that she had refused in any way to yield to him. "Yes, we are well matched." She spoke in a firm, clear voice, her eyes never wavering.

His glittered with sudden desire.

Regina took a deep breath and turned her head to look out the window.

The coach, a lighter one than the traveling coach in which she'd arrived at Taskford Manor, was, however, just as well sprung. Regina settled back, trying to appear totally relaxed. She wasn't relaxed, however. Her host was a large man, and in the confines of the silk-lined vehicle, seemed even larger.

For the first time, Regina was aware that he would be able to do as he pleased with her, should he be of a mind to indulge the desire she saw in his eyes. She admitted that with a little frisson of awareness.

"Are you cold, Mrs. Landry?"

"No," she said a little too hastily. "I'm fine." Belatedly, she added, "Thank you."

He smiled, his eyes hooded.

Regina felt her heartbeat accelerate.

"I should be glad to warm you." There was a faint undercurrent of amusement in his voice.

She drew a quick breath. She had no difficulty interpreting his remark. He had, after all, no cape with him to lend her. She lifted her chin and looked at him coldly. "I am quite comfortable, thank you."

"Ah."

What meaning did that have? She fought the impulse to draw her cloak closer as his eyes fastened on the swell of her breasts. Odious man. He had behaved himself while they were in the traveling coach with Smythe as chaperone. Now that they were alone, and she'd been lulled into a false sense of security, he was back to indulging his lecherous side again. He was deliberately trying to . . . She snapped her head around to look out the window again. She'd ignore him.

"Do you like the lake?"

Her emotions were in such turmoil that she'd been unaware she was staring out at a lake. "Yes," she said as if she'd looked it over carefully. "It is quite attractive."

"If I remember correctly, there is a small temple of love on its shore." He shifted to her side of the carriage. His head close to her own, he peered out the window. His right arm slid around the back of the seat as if he'd a need to brace himself.

Regina could feel the warmth of it behind her shoulders. She forced herself to breathe slowly. Casually she raised her left hand to her cheek to hide the pulse his proximity had sent fluttering just under her jaw. She could feel his breath on her cheek, feel his lips move against the hair near her ear as he told her, "There. Look there across the lake to the left. Aphrodite's temple, my great-uncle called it."

Harry breathed in the scent of her. Jasmine and roses. His blood began to burn through his veins. His voice husky, he said, "You are as lovely as any Aphrodite, Mrs. Landry."

Without thinking, she turned to chasten him for flattery. That was a mistake. The action put her face so close to his that their lips were almost touching. She saw fire ignite his eyes. His lips parted. He was going to kiss her! She knew a moment of panic. It was one thing to exchange challenging kisses in an inn where help was merely a shriek away, but out here there was no one to rescue her.

Once again Regina was acutely aware of his strength— and of his reputation. Taskford was said to be totally lacking in scruples when it came to women. Nothing she'd seen in his personality would hinder him where the ladies were concerned. His behavior toward her in the parlor of *The Golden Boar* had proven that.

She had been cool-headed then. He'd been an utter stranger. Now things were very different, and she panicked as her real fear arose and demanded recognition. Regina had always been honest with herself. She was honest with herself now. She might be nervous about what Taskford intended to do, it was true, but she was really afraid of something else.

She was terribly afraid that she might help him do it.

Eight

A change in the speed of the carriage alerted him. The horses were slowing as they came to the end of the private lane that connected Taskford and Charnwood. They turned right and the surface over which they traveled changed. Gravel crunched under the wheels of the carriage. They'd reached the long driveway to Charnwood Hall. With a muttered oath, Harry Wainwright, Earl of Taskford, straightened.

Regina felt a small sense of loss. Ridiculous. The man had come too close, and she should have rebuked him for it, not missed his nearness when he returned to the opposite bench. She'd better get, and keep, a firmer grip on her . . . imagination? *Had* he been about to kiss her?

Taskford said, "There's Charnwood up ahead." He made no move to shift his position to her side of the carriage as he had when he'd pointed out Aphrodite's temple. He remained sitting with his back to the horses.

They swept through the gate, past the gatekeeper's cottage, and went on up the drive at a spanking pace. When they drew up with a flourish at the foot of the terrace that fronted the comfortable sprawl of limestone that had long ago been her home, Regina had to blink back tears. Home. She was home at last.

Taskford saw the glitter she quickly veiled with her lashes and his chest tightened. He left the carriage as soon as it stopped, put down the steps himself and reached for her hand.

Afraid she might miss the step and fall on her face if she had another attack of tearful nostalgia, Regina accepted it gratefully. Her voice was husky as she said, "Thank you." Her gaze was locked on the facade of her birthplace.

Summoned by the sound of carriage wheels on the gravel of the drivepath, Charnwood's butler threw open the door. Tall and grave of manner, he moved out of the house and stood staring.

Regina took a hesitant step forward, then another. Then she was running toward him.

The old gentleman gasped, "Miss Reggie, is it truly you?"

She grasped both his hands. "Yes, Wentworth, it is I. And I am so glad to see you. I was afraid . . ." She bit off the rest of her sentence before she said something they might both regret.

She needn't have bothered. Wentworth said it for her.

"Afraid that Lady Lydia might have made changes in the staff? No, I'm happy to say, Lord Philip would not permit it. We are all still here." He held her at arm's length, amazed at the accumulation of mud and the general destruction of her clothing. "But what has happened to you?"

"There was a coach accident. I had to get the horses out of the tangled traces and see that they were all safe."

His smile was fond. "Horses. Yes, of course *you* would have to rescue the horses." He looked up then and saw the tall, elegant figure of the Earl. Immediately he dropped Regina's hands, straightened and became the perfect butler.

Regina turned in some frustration and said a little sharply, "You aren't coming in, are you?"

Wentworth's audible gasp recalled her to her duty. She sweetened her voice. "I mean, I must thank you for escorting me here, your lordship. And I would invite you to stay and visit, but this is no longer my home."

The note of sadness he heard in that admission kept Harry from misbehaving. He bowed. "It was my pleasure, I assure you, Mrs. Landry. Now, if you will excuse me, I must return to my guests."

Regina was so surprised at this tame response that she could only manage a stuttered, "Th-thank you for all your kindnesses, Lord Taskford."

He smiled, his eyes mischievous. "Until we meet again, Mrs. Landry."

He took her hand and pressed a kiss on the inside of her wrist just above her ruined glove. A ripple of deep awareness ran through her. Her eyes widened and she stared into his.

"And we *shall* meet again, Mrs. Landry. " His grin blossomed into wickedness. "I can assure you of that."

Caught in the tumult of too many emotions, Regina could only stare as he spun on his heel and sprinted lightly down the steps to his waiting carriage.

Wentworth called out, "Come in, Miss Reggie! Let me tell the young mistress and master that you've come home. They have not yet gone to their rooms for the night."

Regina, wrapped in the warmth that the old retainer's words generated in her spirit, entered Charnwood.

Taskford was spending the trip back to his palatial manor pleasantly planning his intended conquest of the luscious Mrs. Landry when his coach halted abruptly. "What the devil!"

"Stand and deliver!"

What utter rot! There were no highwaymen hereabouts. There were hardly any highwaymen, period, since most of the stagecoaches had become Royal Mails. Not with the armed guards they'd finally had enough sense to add to them.

Besides, that voice was familiar. Some fool was playing a joke. A very bad joke. Damned if he wasn't going to see who it was. Slamming open the door, he jumped to the ground, scowling.

Out in the twilight, a tall form swathed in a cloak that hid everything about him from knee to nose sat a rangy, dark brown horse. A mask covered the man's entire face. His eyes glittered malice through the holes in its black silk. Wainwright could see it clearly in spite of the shadow cast by the floppy brim of the hat pulled low over his brow. The rider had a pistol in each hand.

"Who the hell are you? I know that voice. I've heard it before. . . ."

The highwayman startled, then leveled his pistols at Taskford and fired.

". . . somewhere." A ball tore into the heavy muscle of his left upper arm, spinning him half around. Harry gasped and grabbed the wound with his right hand. Blood gushed between his fingers. He tightened his grip. As he did, the assailant's second shot sliced across the side of Taskford's head.

Blinding lights filled the sky from horizon to horizon. Searing pain scorched through him. "Damn you!" formed in his mind, but blackness was closing in and the words never left his tongue.

His knees buckled, leaving him kneeling. He struggled to rise, but his body refused to do his bidding. Desperately, he tried to raise his head to see if his murderer was reloading.

The effort failed. His sight dimmed and he pitched sideways into the grass of the verge.

The last thing he heard was the thunder of a blunderbuss.

His last thought was that he hoped it was his driver's.

At Charnwood, the housekeeper, summoned by an eager footman, crossed the spacious foyer to greet Regina. "Oh, Miss Regina. How wonderful it is to see you again!" She stopped just short of taking the woman she had known since babyhood into her arms.

Regina had no such hesitancy. She threw her arms around the plump little woman and gave her a bear hug. Her mud was dry, she could brush it off her friend later. "Winnie. Oh, how are you?"

"I'm just fine, my dear." She stood beaming at her former nursery charge. "I'm housekeeper here now. And I'm that glad that you've come home. Things are so difficult with no one to help the poor children. We are all at sixes and sevens without the master and mistress . . . Oh!" She slapped her hand to her mouth. "Oh, I'm that sorry, Miss Regina. About your loss. About your brother."

"Thank you, Mrs. Winstead." Regina lay a hand on the housekeeper's arm. "It . . ."

A large dog of questionable breeding tore in from the hallway. It lunged toward Regina and skidded across the last three feet of gleaming parquet to halt with its face inches from her hand.

Regina stood perfectly still.

Mrs. Winstead was frozen to fearful immobility.

Wentworth began a slow, cautious progress toward them.

"Why, hallo, pup." Regina presented her hand, palm down, for the huge apparition to sniff. From his shining black and brown coat, his hackles rose, making a ruff around his thick neck—also making clear his intentions.

Mrs. Winstead gasped, then held her breath.

Every line of the dog's body seemed to vibrate with tension.

Regina stood, calm and waiting.

After an instant's intense consideration, the dog relaxed and touched her hand with his cold, damp nose.

Regina laughed and scratched him behind the ears. "Good dog. Good boy."

Again that pause for consideration, then the dog gave a single wag of his tail and sat down, leaning against her. After a moment, his tongue lolled out of the side of his mouth.

Sighs came from both the housekeeper and the butler.

A small voice stated incredulously, "He *likes* you!"

Regina turned toward the speaker and her heart melted. He was eight, she knew, but he seemed younger, and he was beautiful. A mop of bright blond hair, just the color of her brother Philip's, topped the face of a cherub. A very sad cherub, with her brother's gray eyes. He hung back in the entry from the hall, neither retreating nor advancing.

"Yes," she said softly, "he does seem to like me, doesn't he? He's a splendid fellow. What have you named him?"

"My Papa named him."

"Oh?" She waited.

"He named him Caliban."

Regina took a deep breath, choosing her words. "Caliban was very powerful."

"Yes." The little face clouded. "But he was ugly, too. An' not very nice."

"Surely, then, you have another name for him."

"It's bad luck to change the name of a horse," he frowned mightily, "so I 'spose it's the same with a dog. I didn't change it."

"Then I'll wager you have something special you call him."

"Yes" His eyes brightened. "I do. I always call him Cal, and I—"

"Ladies do not wager." The cold, sharp remark came from a girl, not yet in her teens, who had come up behind her brother.

Regina studied the child. She was slight, and almost as beautiful as the boy. Again, there was Philip's silver-blond hair, but the cool azure eyes were those of her mother. The child's features were a blend of the best of both parents, and someday she would be a great beauty. Just now, the expression she wore spoiled any hint of it.

Mrs. Winstead started to speak, but Regina hushed her with a gesture.

Wentworth came to stand close behind Regina, and the dog circled her once and settled down again, pressing against her skirts on the other side. Regina answered the girl quietly, "Some ladies do wager, Philydia. Some very great ladies, in fact."

"You know my name because you are my Aunt Regina. I heard the servants making a fuss over you." She glowered. "My mother didn't like you."

"Yes, that is true." Regina didn't choose to add that the feeling had been mutual. "She thought I was too much of a tomboy, you see."

None of the hostility left the girl's face. "She said you were always in the stables."

Regina took another careful breath. "Yes, that's true, too." The stables had been her sanctuary.

The boy broke in. "Did you like horses?"

Regina turned to him with a smile. "Yes, indeed. I still do." At that instant, Caliban thrust his nose into her hand, demanding attention. She scratched him under his chin and he moaned in contentment. "I like dogs, too."

"So you wouldn't make me put—"

The girl interrupted. "And I suppose you still smell of horses, too."

Regina felt herself straightening, her chin lifting. Her voice was cooler as she answered, "When I first come in from the stables, yes, I imagine that I do." She spread her hands to indicate her dishevelled state. "I'm certain I do right now, too."

It was time she took charge of this conversation. If she left it to this child, she would no doubt be told to go away in the next few sentences. Her heart was heavy with the knowledge that she was not going to be easily accepted, not regain the family she had lost. Nevertheless, she'd come to help the children, and help them she would.

She was just taking yet another breath—and praying she'd be given the right words—when the boy stalked across the shining floor of the foyer. Staring up at her defiantly, he announced, "I don' care if Mama and Philydia don' like you. Cal likes you and I will, too!"

Regina smiled down at him.

After a moment, the child smiled back, and it was sunlight on clear water—Philip's long-ago smile, the smile from his boyhood. She yearned to snatch Thomas into her arms.

"That doesn't mean we need her here!" Philydia advanced from her position in the hall entry. "It doesn't matter if *you* do like her. You're only a child. *I* am almost grown up. I know how to manage the servants and what needs to be done, and I certainly do not"—she spun away from her brother and glared up at her aunt, her young voice rising to near hysteria—"need *you*!"

Suddenly a resounding crash filled the room. The huge front door was kicked open! Taskford's coachman stood framed in the doorway. His master's bleeding body sagged in his arms. Taskford's head wound had bled profusely, soaking the white front of his freshly donned shirt scarlet. More blood dripped steadily down his arm to his fingers.

In the stunned silence, they could hear the drops of it hitting the parquet floor. It sounded like gentle rain.

Then there was a soft plop as Philydia fainted dead away.

Nine

"*Merciful heavens!*" *Regina* rushed to the men in the doorway. Her frantic gaze fastened on Taskford's pale face. Gesturing to a spot on the bare floor, she ordered his coachman, "Quickly! Lay him down here."

The coachman looked startled, but complied, nevertheless.

Wentworth made a strangled sound and took a step forward.

Regina fell to her knees on the floor beside the wounded man. "Wentworth! A cravat. A belt. Something to stop the bleeding before we move him any further. We must hurry."

The stunned coachman stood back, twisting his hands, and staring at his new employer where he lay on the floor. "'Twas a highwayman." He repeated it softly, as if he couldn't quite take it in. "A highwayman. Right on the road between here and Taskford." He looked toward Wentworth, bewildered. "Did ever you hear of such a thing?"

Wentworth shook his head. "Not hereabouts," he replied vaguely, his attention riveted on Regina.

Regina reached out, desperate to stop the blood that was

flowing so freely from the Earl's arm. She was anxious to see how bad the head wound was, too, but she had to stop this awful bleeding first. As she worked, she glanced up and said, "How foolish!" Her voice was full of anger, anger aimed at this terrible deed, but her irritation was aimed at the unconscious Earl. "Why on earth didn't he do as the highwayman asked? A purse is hardly worth getting shot over!"

She tightened the cravat Wentworth had stripped from his own neck and watched intently to see if the pressure this exerted on the wound had slowed the bleeding. Satisfied that it had, she carefully pushed the Earl's hair aside and examined his profusely bleeding head wound.

"Thank God," she murmured fervently, "It's only a graze. But it will need stitching." She rose and looked toward Mrs. Winstead. "Winnie. Where shall we put him?"

The housekeeper looked up from where she knelt beside the unconscious Philydia and paused in her effort to revive the child. "I think the blue bedchamber would be the most convenient, Miss Regina." She turned back to her task and patted Philydia lightly on first one cheek, then the other.

"Very well." Regina signalled a pair of footmen to carry the wounded man to bed and turned to Wentworth. "Would you please send for the doct . . . ," she began, only to find him in the middle of doing so. She gave him a heartfelt smile and hurried after the men bearing the wounded Earl.

As she passed Philydia and Mrs. Winstead, she paused. "Is she all right, Winnie?"

Philydia moaned, and the housekeeper threw a quick smile at her former nursery charge. "She's only fainted," she told Regina. "She'll be as right as rain in a minute. Can you see to the gentleman without me?"

"Yes. I shall manage." Regina glanced at Wentworth. "Perhaps we should send to Taskford for the Earl's friends."

"I'll see to it, Miss Regina." He turned and gestured to a

footman. "Go back to Taskford with the Earl's coachman and explain to his lordship's guests why they must come at once."

The footman steered the dazed coachman out the door.

Taskford's driver kept shaking his head and muttering, "A highwayman. Who could have foreseen it?"

Regina, satisfied, hurried to the stairs. She paused with her foot on the first step as Mrs. Winstead called after her, "I'll be along as soon as I can."

Regina sped up the stairway. Her only thought now was for the Earl.

Behind her, on the floor near the foot of the stairs, Philydia was regaining consciousness. The girl's hands made vague, groping gestures. She opened her eyes. Her expression was as dazed as the coachman's had been. She stared at the housekeeper for an instant, puzzled. "What happened?" She frowned, trying to remember. "Oh!" Now her expression was horrified. "Oh, Mrs. Winstead, that man! All that blood!" Her own blood that had begun to return to her cheeks started to recede.

"Oh, no, missy." Winnie gave her a brisk shake. "You're not going to do that again. There'll be no fainting if you intend to be mistress of Charnwood. You must get up right now and take charge of this situation."

"I *can't*, Winnie. How can you ask it of me? I'm just a child, I can't cope with all this." She looked up through her tears and wailed, *"I can't."*

Mrs. Winstead was quiet for a long minute, looking steadily into her young mistress's eyes. Then she said with slow deliberation, each word dropping between them like pebbles in a pond. "Then are you not truly fortunate that your Aunt Regina has arrived back home at just this time." She made it a statement, not a question. Her face was set in lines of determination. There was no way Philydia was going to make Regina Ransome Landry unwelcome in her own home if Winnie Winstead had anything to do about it.

Philydia looked mulish.

"Are you not?" Mrs. Winstead sat back on her heels and watched Philydia where the girl lay, propped on her elbows on the polished parquet floor. "Well?"

Philydia glanced at her housekeeper's stern face. She wanted to rebel, wanted to be true to her mother. Really, she did. But there was all that blood. There was a wounded man somewhere in the house. There were things to be done that were quite beyond her. Things she didn't care if she *ever* gained the ability to do. She bowed her head and choked out, "Yes."

"Yes, what?" Winnie prompted.

Philydia needed another breath to finish. She took it and spoke the words she knew Mrs. Winstead wanted from her. "It is fortunate that Aunt Regina has come home."

Upstairs, Regina was stripping off her gloves and shrugging out of her ruined spencer. She tossed them onto a brocade-covered chair just inside the doorway of the blue bedchamber and moved to the bed.

He was so still! The blood that trickled down his face from the crease the bullet had made was the only sign of movement.

She couldn't even discern the rise and fall of his chest that would signal his breathing. Her heart clenched in her chest. He had to be alive! Surely, someone so vital could not have died so quickly? She almost panicked.

Taskford drew a deep, shuddering breath and moaned.

Regina almost cried with relief. Instantly she started giving orders. "Water. Boiled. Clean cloths. Quickly."

The footmen who had carried the Earl upstairs scurried off.

Regina heard Charnwood's butler enter the room. "Wentworth, we need to get his coat and shirt off. I think that will be more easily done while he is still unconscious."

"Easier for him, to be sure."

He moved to the side of the bed and lifted the Earl to a sitting position, piling pillows behind him. Taskford's head fell back, his arms hung limp.

Regina seized the end of a sleeve in one hand and slipped her other hand inside his coat at the shoulder—his good shoulder—and began to ease the first sleeve off.

Taskford groaned and rocked his dark head back and forth in pain against the crisp white linen of the pillow.

Regina felt her heart twist. Quick tears filled her eyes. Her hands stilled.

Wentworth's voice seemed far away. "Would you like me to do that, miss?"

Regina shook her head, not trusting herself to speak. Somehow her throat was too tight. She removed his sleeve as gently as she could and pulled it toward the center of his back so that it gave as much slack as it would to the rest of the coat. That was all she could do in preparation for taking the wounded arm from its sleeve, and she gritted her teeth, knowing it would not be enough to keep her from causing Taskford more pain. He was quiet now. Totally quiet. Slowly, she began to ease the coat off.

"Just . . . pull the . . . damn thing off!"

Startled, she looked him full in the face. He was conscious. Obviously that was why he was so still. Why he was not making a sound. His eyes dark with pain, he regarded her steadily. He was pale, so deathly pale. There were cold beads of perspiration on his upper lip and on his forehead, now, but his face was calm.

"What the devil are you waiting for?" The words grated from between his clenched teeth. He spoke them in stilted cadence, ashamed of the pain-inflicted breathlessness that had put gaps in his previous comment.

Regina took a deep breath and firmly pulled his wounded arm free of his coat. She felt him tense and knew he was fighting back a groan . . . or a curse. She hadn't time to worry about which, however. She was far too busy wiping away the blood that welled and welled from the hole the pistol ball had left in his arm. She must see if the projectile was still there. Her stomach tightened. She hoped the ball had passed through, hoped that she would not have to probe for it if the doctor did not arrive soon.

She'd taken care of more than her share of wounds on horses in the course of her career, but she'd never even seen a bullet hole before.

"Wait for the doctor." Taskford's voice was surprising gentle.

"I can't." She was surprised that he seemed to understand her feelings. Seemed to know she was momentarily faint of heart. "You're losing too much blood."

He laughed. It was a short bark of laughter that held no mirth. "I've bled before, Mrs. Landry." All the sympathy he'd seemed to be feeling was gone in an instant.

"This isn't a battlefield, your lordship." Her tone was firm. "I shan't let you lose any more blood."

Taskford grunted and stared straight ahead.

Putting him in his place seemed to give Regina strength of purpose. She cleaned the wound with the cloths and hot water Winnie had brought her. Ignoring the one jerk he gave when she touched the raw edges of the bullet hole, she dropped the bloodied cloth back into the bowl, and began to bind up his arm tightly.

Determined to get the best of her, Taskford murmured, "Surely you have stopped my circulation."

"I have stopped your bleeding, sir. In a few moments, I shall make the bandage a little looser."

"Ah, good. I should very much like to keep my hand."

"Don't express your relief too quickly, your lordship. If you begin to bleed again when I loosen the bandage, then I shall retighten it. I prefer to save your life, even at the cost of an extremity."

"Or two?" He gasped that out, and she watched him frown his displeasure over having done so.

She stroked his hair back from his sweat-damped forehead. Tenderness came from somewhere deep inside her and she told him softly, "Rest. Just rest. I shall be here with you until the doctor arrives."

There was a slight commotion at the door. Both Regina and Taskford looked that way. Philydia and Mrs. Winstead stood in the doorway, Winnie's arm around the girl. They heard Winnie inquire quietly, "Would you like to take over from your aunt, now, Miss Philydia? You are the lady of the house, after all."

"No, Winnie." Philydia was pale but her voice was firm. Her huge blue eyes took in the tableau before her. She saw every single detail—the bed with bloody streaks down its sheets, her aunt with gore all over her hands, and the bowl of reddened water with the blood-stained cloths hanging over its edge.

When she took a deep breath to steady herself, she could smell the scent of fresh blood. It smelled metallic, like copper pennies. Her stomach twisted and threatened to revolt. "No," she gasped, clutching at her midsection. She shook her head violently. "I see that I am not quite up to all the duties of the woman of the house, as yet."

"And . . . ?" Winnie looked at the girl with stern expectation.

"And I am . . ." Philydia had to force herself to go on.

Clearly she had no liking for the decision she had made. "And I am glad that my Aunt Regina has arrived at Charnwood to run the household."

Winnie gave the girl's waist a little squeeze and looked across the room to Regina. In her face there was pride and satisfaction that she and circumstances had brought about a change for the better in her young mistress. Warmly, she said, "Welcome home, Miss Regina." With gentle emphasis, she said, "We are *all* glad to have you here."

Ten

The doctor had only been gone a few minutes when Taskford's friends arrived in a crowd and surged up the staircase behind Wentworth like an invading hoard. Long-legged Blysdale was in the lead, Stone and MacLain—Taskford's two friends who'd gone to placate MacLain's parents—hard on his heels and Smythe trailing behind so badly that Mathers, forced by his excessive concern for good manners to keep the laggard a part of the group, hung back, bridging the gap.

"I don't like this." Blysdale's voice was tense.

"*None* of us like it, Bly." Stocky blond MacLain looked at him as if he'd fallen off a farm cart. "Harry's our friend and he's been shot."

"Oh, for—" Blysdale cut short his comment out of deference to the women within earshot. "I've often wondered how the devil Harry puts up with your lack of intelligence, but never more so than now."

"I say!" MacLain stopped and glared at Blysdale's back.

"Come on, Mac." His heavyset companion, Stone, gave

him a shove. "Harry's the thing. You can take offense at Bly later." He added, "Not that he'll care."

They turned the corner and stopped dead outside the door indicated by Wentworth's sentinel-like halt. The butler stood with upraised hand and a finger across his lips for a moment, then gently opened the door.

Wainwright was sitting up against a pile of goose down pillows. The grin that split his face when he saw them erased the lines of pain beside his mouth and told them how glad he was to see them.

They converged on the bed in a babble of greetings and concerned comments. "Where the devil did you two come from?"

MacLain, looking puzzled, told him, "M'parents' favorite coaching inn, Harry. You know we had to go sweeten 'em up. But we ran in to 'em on the road and did the job. Left us free to come stay with you."

"Yes," Taskford said, laughing with great care. "I remember you went to visit your parents. How fortunate you met with them on the road."

Blysdale rolled his eyes. It was evident he thought these two of his and Taskford's friends hopeless. Under his breath he said, "Fortunate for the parents. They had only to endure the company of their son for a single evening."

Mathers chuckled.

Stone and MacLain eyed the sling that cradled Taskford's left arm and Stone said, "Left arm, that's fortunate," at the same time that MacLain stated, "Lucky that it was your left arm."

Smythe's piercing study of Taskford's face under the bandage that encircled his head ended with a cautious, "You're pale, but otherwise you seem to be all right. No fever in the eyes, no lassitude in your attitude. I'd say—"

"Oh, do be still, Smythe." Stone was impatient. "I want to

hear Harry's story of the attack. You can play the frustrated doctor some other time."

"Yes, Harry. We want to know. How the devil did you get yourself shot?" MacLain frowned. "Your coachman said that you'd been set on by a highwayman."

Blysdale, narrow-eyed, spoke so softly that no one heard him. "There aren't any highwaymen way out here."

Mathers stood watching his stricken friend closely.

Taskford waited until they'd settled down and found places to sit, lean or perch, then told them, "It was the damnedest thing." His brow furrowed. "I was returning from delivering Mrs. Landry here to Charnwood, when there was a cry of 'stand and deliver.' When I jumped out of the carriage, I saw the bastard had a pistol in either fist, but I'd no idea he intended to use them." His scowl became fierce. This time it pulled the stitches the doctor had put in the gash along his skull. He stopped scowling.

Smythe inquired gently, "Why didn't you just give him your purse, Harry?"

Taskford's indignation exploded. "The blackguard never even asked for it!" He put his right hand to his head as he experienced another explosion—this one of pain. While he dealt with it, his friends dealt with this story.

"That's very odd." MacLain was scowling now.

"Damned strange, if you ask me." Stone was frowning hard, too.

"Perhaps it was not so strange." Blysdale's quiet comment carried clearly from where he was perched. All of them turned to stare at him as he added, "Just what did you see, Harry?"

Harry frowned again, felt his stitches pull and stopped. *Blast! When had he developed the habit of frowning so damned frequently?* "I saw a muffled figure on a horse. I'd

thought the man's voice familiar, so naturally I jumped out
to see who it was."

"Oh, yes." Bly's tone was as dry as autumn leaves. "Naturally."

Stone glared at the saturnine aristocrat.

Unruffled by his friend's implication that he'd been foolhardy, Taskford continued, "The fellow was masked and so
wrapped up in his cloak that I hadn't a prayer of telling who
the devil he was."

"But you thought he sounded familiar?" Mathers asked,
"Could it have been Perryman?"

"*Lucretia's* Perryman?" Harry's expression showed how
ludicrous he considered the suggestion that his former lover's
husband might be the highwayman. "Surely you jest."

"Now, Harry," Smythe was patient with the invalid,
"don't just cross him off the list of suspects without sufficient thought. After all, if he is entertaining any notion to demand satisfaction for your . . . er, hmmmmm . . . *friendship*
with his wife, it might have been in his mind to disable your
arm." He paused and added earnestly, "To make the duel
more favorable to him, you see."

"Harry, don't shoot with his *left* hand, you block." Stone
was disgusted.

MacLain laughed and told Stone, "Could. Shoots as good
with his left as Perryman does with his right."

Mathers added in a bored voice, "Harry shoots as well
with his left as most of us shoot at all."

Blysdale was getting impatient. "Gentlemen! And I use
that word loosely. We are trying to discover who shot
Harry." Blysdale's tone was acerbic.

"Yes," Smythe voiced their agreement, his tone firm.

While the others advanced theories, Blysdale moved to
the bed and asked quietly, "Could the voice have been that
of your cousin, Conway?"

Harry was startled. "Con? Lord, no! What made you think of such a thing?"

"Conway was seen in the vicinity. And he is next in line for the title."

"Well, it wasn't Con." He was careful not to scowl this time. "The voice was heavier."

Bly nodded and went back to his place.

Suddenly, Mathers smiled and walked to the door. Just outside it, he offered his arm to Regina Landry and drew her forward into the room.

Harry forgot, scowled—and winced again. It was positively uncanny how Mathers always knew when a lady was in the offing! Why the devil didn't the man get one of his own?

Regina, bathed free of Taskford's blood and freshly gowned, nodded graciously and greeted them. Smythe was absurdly pleased to see her again. She went straight to Taskford's bed, and placed her hand on his forehead.

His eyes burned mockingly up at her, full of suggestion. Before she moved away, he dropped his gaze to her breasts.

Regina wanted to slap him. Why must he always play the bold seducer? Didn't he realize by now that she had no intention of swooning into his arms? It must just be a habit with him. "You are better than I had thought you'd be. There's no sign of fever."

"Good. Then you will have no objection if I return to Taskford." He smiled crookedly and waited for her to beg him to stay just a while longer. Just a few more days—to regain his strength. He was used to women attempting to keep him by their sides with far lesser excuses.

"No. *I* have no objection at all. I am certain that you are eager to return to your friends, and I am just as certain that they would look after you." She smiled brightly around the group. "I'm certain you wouldn't have too much difficulty keeping him from scowling, at any rate. If he should, those stitches will pull like fury."

Harry was stunned into temporary silence.

Blysdale gave a crack of laughter.

The devil of merriment lurking in his eyes amused Regina. "I would like nothing better than to tell the doctor that you are in residence at Taskford." She turned to the men, centering on her friend, Smythe. "I'm certain that, being late of the army, you all know how to care for wounds, and really, there is nothing more to do but to keep the dressings fresh, so he wouldn't be much trouble."

Wouldn't be much trouble. Wouldn't be much trouble! She made him sound like some sick, old hound! Harry was seething. Never since he was thirteen years old had a member of the opposite sex dismissed him as "not much trouble." And if she used the word "certain" again, he was going to explode!

When she turned back to him, she said, "*However,* Doctor Phipps has left orders that you are not to be moved for at least a week. It is his opinion that you have lost too much blood, and that any exertion would put a strain on your heart. Therefore, Lord Taskford, you are, alas"—she spread her hands hopelessly and shrugged—"stuck here."

Regina turned to the waiting butler and said, "Wentworth, will you please see to it that every measure is taken to insure the Earl's comfort?"

Taskford's mouth dropped open. Wasn't she going to station herself at his side?

Regina ignored him completely to give instructions to Smythe—who was hovering protectively, as usual. Harry was not to overdo it while there were so many visitors and the others were to keep him quiet and amused.

Amused! As if he were some querulous child down with a

cold! Damn the wench! If he could just get her alone, he'd show her amused!

Blysdale bowed over Regina's hand, "Thank you for all you have done for our friend, Mrs. Landry." He let his gaze dwell an instant on the blue smudges under her eyes. "Please get some rest. Be assured that we will come inform you if there is any change in his condition."

She was about to speak when Bly continued, "We promise that we will call you and the doctor immediately if Harry should even look as if he might be taking a turn for the worse."

"And the moment he tires, we will leave quietly, so as not to disturb the family," Mathers assured her.

Regina smiled then, and told them all, "Very well. I'll wish you gentlemen a good night, then. I leave you to comfort your friend." She moved gracefully to the door, bestowed a final smile on them all and left the room.

Harry was steaming. *She'd treated him like an old retainer! Paid him no more attention than that she would have given some aging, ailing servant. Even less! Blast her!*

His ill humor evaporated a few seconds later, however, as his friends gathered close to try to discover who it was that was trying to kill the Earl of Taskford.

Regina's mind, too, as she prepared to go to bed, was on the same question. That being the case, she knew sleep would be impossible, even after such a crowded and active day. Instead of her bed, she sought the cool sanctity of the garden. There she paced and pondered the puzzle of the highwayman's attack. There was no doubt in her mind that the man had had every intention of putting a period to Harry Wainwright's life. No doubt at all. The attack had been vicious—and very nearly successful. Her heart quailed to think what would have happened if the bogus highwayman's aim had been a little surer.

The attack would have had to have been planned, as well. That was where her logic failed her. Who could possibly have known that he would be on the road to Charnwood?

She shook her head slowly. No. It had to be a coincidence, surely. All the people who knew he was going to take her home had been together. Except for Mr. Bagwell, and the thought of the aging solicitor desiring the demise of his favorite client was absurd.

Regina's thoughts spun. Who would have cause to kill the new Earl? Someone who would inherit the title should he be out of the way? Some enemy from his past?

He didn't seem the kind of man who made many enemies. Wasn't he, even now, surrounded by men who admired and liked him? No, Harry Wainwright, Earl of Taskford, was not one to make enemies of men. She paused, considering all she knew of the man, and had to add, *except husbands.*

Perhaps a jealous husband had been the attacker? *That* seemed a distinct possibility.

Suddenly Regina was exhausted. The events of the long day and her deep concern over Taskford combined with the trauma of returning home drained the last vestiges of strength from her. Though the hour was not yet late, she found herself wishing she could go to bed.

Regina turned to reenter the house.

Silhouetted in the doorway as if to block her entrance stood Philydia.

Sympathy for the child filled Regina. She, too, had had a trying day. "Are you feeling better, Philydia?"

"I'm fine, now."

Regina regarded the girl steadily for a long moment, silently reminding her that she should have said "thank you."

Philydia colored slightly. Then the hostility so carefully taught her by her mother came to her rescue. "I was just curious about when you would be going to the stables where you . . ." She let the sentence trail away.

"Belong?" Regina supplied without rancor.

The girl dropped her gaze.

With a very small smile, Regina brushed gently past the stiff figure of her niece. "Good night, Philydia." Her voice was soft and unruffled. She paused and turned back to let her gaze rest on the child for a moment, then said only, "Sleep well."

Eleven

Before Regina could "go where she belonged," as Philydia had wanted to put it, she had this long night to get through. Even as weary as she was after her arduous day, she had no intention of leaving Taskford unattended. She'd been told that fevers often developed after gunshot wounds—raging fevers that burned the life out of the wounded.

She was waiting to hear Taskford's friends depart so that she could check on him. Checking to see there were no bad effects from their visit was of paramount importance to her.

Regina smiled to think of the five stalwart companions who surrounded the new Earl. Not one of them would harm their friend, but they were all such forceful men that even being quiet and considerate they generated enough energy easily to exhaust an invalid, bless them.

She yawned. If she weren't careful, sleep would catch *her* before it took Taskford. After a while, when he'd had time to drop off, she'd go look in at their wounded houseguest.

Waiting would give her a little time to look over Philip's books. Regina crossed her room to the dainty lady's desk near the windows and looked down at the thick, heavy ledgers she'd lugged up from Philip's study while her bath had been readied. For a moment, she almost regretted having chosen now to go over her brother's records. They'd hardly be exciting enough to help her fight sleep.

It had to be done, however. If she was going to help the children, she must know what she was up against—in addition to her niece's open hostility. She sighed and settled to the task.

The ledgers were far from encouraging. From them, she learned—just as Mr. Bagwell had warned—that the Charnwood Stud was not yet operating at a profit. That was bad news with a mortgage to pay. Very bad news.

She sighed again and did some quick mental calculations. Her savings would certainly not stretch to the mortgage, but she could pay wages and the entry fees for the horses that she saw from Philip's neatly written notes were scheduled to race soon. With any luck, some of the runners would win enough to keep them going until the stables began to carry themselves and earn money toward the mortgage.

From the dates of the races, she saw that the sooner she got down to the stables, the better. She'd hoped to have a little time to win the children over, but saw that it was imperative that she begin training the runners immediately.

Due to their impending races, her most pressing job was to get to know Philip's horses. Get to know their strengths and weaknesses—and get them ready to win. Training, she knew, stood horses in much better stead than luck did on a racecourse.

The rattle of carriage wheels alerted her to the departure of Taskford's friends. Regina waited another half hour, poring over the ledgers one last time, then getting to the distasteful necessity of writing to her late husband's Cousin Edward.

Heaven knew it was a letter she would never write if there

were any other options open to her. Now, though, she had no choice. It was an urgent matter, thanks to her cousin Jasper Ruddleston's designs on the children's inheritance, and writing it would while away a bit more time. She wanted Taskford to be deeply asleep so that her visit wouldn't disturb him.

Sitting staring into the candles' flames, she pondered what she was going to write in this letter to Edward Overfield. Begging a man to marry her was a new and decidedly distasteful experience for her. She wished she could put it off until things were more settled. Putting it off was out of the question, though. Edward was far away in the wilds of Scotland pursuing something archaeological, and Heaven only knew how long it would take correspondence to reach him.

She'd written and rewritten the necessary letter many times and she had no doubt that by now Taskford would be sleeping deeply. Frustration was beginning to eat at her. The fuller the little basket beside her desk became with her attempts, the more fervently she wished she could just write, *"Edward, please come and marry me to save my brother Philip's children from our horrid Cousin Jasper,"* sign it, *"Hurry, Regina,"* and have that do the trick.

Life was not so simple, however, and an hour passed without the job being done to her satisfaction.

Relieved to have her concern for Taskford as an excuse to leave the onerous task, she put down her pen, snuffed the candles in the silver candelabra on the lady's desk and rose.

Quickly changing into more comfortable clothing—a loose shirt and a full skirt that wouldn't hinder her curling up in a chair—she tucked the last draft of her letter into her waistband and left her bedchamber.

Moving down the dimly lit hall, she approached the blue bedchamber quietly. Inside, the room was bathed in the light

of only a few candles, a soft glow meant to reassure someone awakening in a strange place rather than illumination by
which to accomplish anything. The low light did no more
than give luster to the rich damask hangings at the windows
and around the bed. If she hadn't known, Regina couldn't
even have told that they were blue.

Taskford lay as she had left him, propped up against his
bank of pillows. The golden candlelight that gilded the sun-
bronzed skin of his arms only emphasized the shadowed
pallor of his face.

Regina tiptoed to the bed and stood looking down at him.
His dark hair was tousled, so she knew he had tossed a bit in
his sleep. His cheeks were pale, their usual healthy color
gone. That, she told herself bracingly, was only to be expected with all the blood he'd lost. His firm lips were parted
slightly, and his breath came easily and regularly. All
seemed to be well.

Sleep had smoothed the lines beside his mouth, and he
looked oddly young. With his eyes closed, and his hands relaxed on the counterpane, fingers half-curled like a sleeping
child's, he also looked strangely vulnerable.

Seeing how well he slept, and reassured by the even
rhythm of his breathing, Regina pulled a chair from the
group in front of his fireplace over to the bed. Borrowing
two small, loose pillows from the settee, she settled herself
to keep watch over the wounded Earl.

Within minutes the trials of the day caught up with her,
and she dozed. Several times in the night she opened her
eyes to check on her patient, saw he was fine, and slept
again. Finally, exhausted, she slept soundly. When she
awoke, it was dawn.

The light of a rosy sunrise, coming feebly around the
edges of the heavy curtains at the tall windows, had awakened her. She got up quietly and stretched away the night's

stiffness. All the while, she accessed Taskford's condition. His thick, dark hair was even more tousled, his firm lips still slightly parted and relaxed, but there was a tiny cut on the lower one as if he had bitten it in pain. His chest rose and fell rhythmically, and there was no flush of fever on his cheeks. Stubble was beginning to show on them, though, shading his jaw.

She was smiling as she reached out to touch Taskford's brow. Before she'd even made contact with his broad forehead, his hand shot out and seized her wrist in a steely grip.

"Oh!" She was startled. Without the intenseness of his gaze, his face had seemed so peaceful that his glare took Regina by surprise.

Taskford told her, "Never, never sneak up on a sleeping soldier, Mrs. Landry." His eyes mocked her.

"I didn't realize that was what I was doing. I thought I was attempting to discover whether or not my patient was doing well." Recovered from her start, she tried again to touch his forehead. He didn't relinquish his grip. "I want to see if you have any sign of fever this morning." She looked at him expectantly. Her voice held a hint of amusement as she continued, "I shall need my arm free to do that."

"Hmmmm." He stretched without moving, a ripple of muscles that ran through his frame without changing his position. She saw him flinch when the movement went through his shoulders. He did not, however, let go of her arm.

Regina laughed. "Lord Taskford. I must ask you to return the use of my right hand to me. Not only do I need it to satisfy myself that you are doing well, but I must also have it to take it with me when I leave you to go to the stables to begin my work there."

He turned his head to look toward the windows. "It's barely dawn."

"Horses wake early." She gave her wrist a shake.

He lay looking up at her a moment longer, sighed and loosed her.

She put her hand against his forehead. "Good. You've no fever. We're fortunate."

"If you go to the stables, I shall be bored." His eyes filled with mischief. "I'm not accustomed to being bored in bed."

She made sure she didn't blush. Matching his stare for boldness, she said with deliberate huskiness, "Well, we certainly can't let that happen, now, can we?"

His eyes lit with interest. Behind it, however, Regina could see wariness. Perhaps he *was* getting to understand her. Sweetly she told him, "I'll send the children up to entertain you." She avoided his grasp this time and backed away from the bed.

"Thank you so much." His tone was dry.

Regina laughed and started for the door. "Since you're awake, I shall also send Wentworth. He'll see to your breakfast."

"No need."

She was about to ask why not when the door opened and a tall, spare man entered with a tray laden with things from the kitchen.

"This is my man, Williams. Williams, this is Mrs. Landry, the lady of the house." The two thus introduced nodded at one another, each appraising, then Regina went to the door. There she paused and looked back. It amazed her that even wounded and in a strange house, Taskford was still in command. She couldn't resist. "Williams?"

"Yes, madam?"

"Be certain the Earl has only bland food for a while, will you?"

Williams lifted the silver cover from his master's dish and exposed the steaming gruel in it. "As you say, madam." He bowed.

Regina inclined her head slightly in response and left just as a string of epithets directed at his man burst from the unhappy patient. "It is so satisfactory," she murmured to herself, smiling, "to meet a sensible man." She was laughing as she went to get her cloak to protect her against the early-morning chill.

Outside, Regina hurried to the stables. The bustle of getting the horses fed and led away to the various turnout paddocks was over. The stalls were cleaned of the night's refuse and their bedding was piled out in the sun, to be freshened and added to. The horses were working well at their warm-ups, and Regina was more than pleased at what she saw.

Now to the first hurdle. She straightened her shoulders and took a deep breath. These next few moments would decide whether or not she'd be able to run the Charnwood Stud successfully, and she knew it. Her stomach knotted.

It was imperative, with the race dates so near, that the horses be kept as closely as possible to the stable routine they were used to. Thoroughbreds were notorious for being the most nervous and difficult of all breeds, as well as the fastest. A wise trainer went to great lengths not to upset them. Changes in their stable routine would do just that.

Regina took a deep breath and approached the men. They had stopped their individual tasks, grouped themselves together, and stood waiting for her.

The confrontation was not unexpected. Men didn't like the idea of working for a woman—especially not in a field they thought of as exclusively a man's. Well, they could just get used to it or go. She'd do her best to win them over, but whether or not they stayed? That outcome was in the hands of the men.

Regina looked first at the obvious leader, a resistant mountain of a man, full of doubts and disapproval. She'd been briefed by Wentworth, and knew he was Tim Parson,

Philip's assistant trainer. She was going to have to convince him that she was fit to take over the reins of the Charnwood racing stable. It had to be done.

Fortunately, she knew his reputation for being reasonable and even-tempered. Otherwise, she had no doubt, he and most of the grooms would already have left last night when she'd sent word down that she'd be taking over the stables in the morning on behalf of her brother's children.

Now that she was here where they could ask her, the men had questions ready. Regina knew her answers to those questions would determine whether or not they remained to work under her. And it didn't look good.

The men looked upset and restless. She could hear snatches of their conversation. "She's too young to know what she's doing," and belligerently, "She's beautiful, what's she doin' muckin' about wif horses?"

Tim Parson's deep voice rose over and stilled the mutterings from the shocked stable crew. He thrust aside the amenities and went straight to the heart of the matter, all but growling his question at her. "What have you trained?"

She met his almost hostile, hazel-eyed gaze, accepting his challenge of her ability. "I've trained racehorses for the Dashwood Stud in Ireland for the past six years. If you'd like to know *who* I've trained . . ."

There was a perceptible lessening of tension at that. Any good horseman knew that horses were "who" not "what." As personable as humans and just as full of flaws and foibles, horses earned the right to their identities as surely as did bipeds, and the men who worked with the mighty beasts knew it.

With pride ringing in her voice, Regina called out the long list of winners she'd been privileged to train. After an awestruck pause and a series of speaking glances back and forth among them, every man nodded, turned, and went back to the tasks they'd deserted at her arrival.

There was a soft whicker from one of the occupied stalls as the horse there sensed the lessening of tension in his stable lad. Regina felt her own tension drain away.

Some of the men were clearly more than willing to work for her. Others, she knew, were going to watch her and decide—she was a female, after all. Regina prayed that they'd all stay in the end, for she'd a pretty good idea that she couldn't ask for a better crew.

Consulting the list she'd made from Philip's notes, she ordered Tim Parson to bring the horses she wanted to work with into the training paddock. Indicating some long poles piled near along a section of the fence, she told him, "I'd like these spaced regularly this far apart"—she glanced at the horses, then drew two lines in the dirt—"perpendicular to the rail, please."

"Why?"

"I need cavaletti over which to work the horses."

The huge man looked at her a long moment, then walked over to the heavy twelve-foot poles. He picked up four of the them, two in each hand, and laid them out as Regina had asked. Regina shook her head in amazement. One pole was heavy enough to require her full attention, and she was strong. Hadn't the Earl of Taskford called her an Amazon?

Having explained what she wanted done quietly and competently, Regina stood, wrapped in her trusty cloak, and simply watched the four three-year-olds milling about the paddock. After a minute or two of observation, she positioned Tim at the ends of the poles opposite the paddock fence and joined him there. Together, they formed that side of a lane down which the horses in training were expected to trot.

Regina saw that Tim was watching critically as she used

the long lounge whip to direct the young Thoroughbreds where she wanted them to go. Encouraging them with voice and patience, she got them to trot over the cavaletti. Regina praised each youngster lavishly.

When, at last, every one of the horses began trotting through at regular intervals, she smiled to see that Tim Parson's eyes held open admiration.

Regina continued to smile and praise, scolding only when the horses misbehaved over the cavaletti. She said nothing about their behavior when they were outside the lane. Their frisky bucks and the way they shook their heads, sending their manes whipping the air, told Regina they were enjoying the work, and she was pleased.

Tim's gaze was intent. "If I hadn't seen it, I wouldn't have believed it."

Regina grinned at him.

She called for the next group of horses, then Regina stepped away and gestured at Tim. "You take this next bunch. You can do it now." She made her way carefully from the paddock and went to sit in the shade of a nearby tree.

"Now" for Regina was the letter she could feel tucked into the belt at her waist. She could feel it as if it were a burning coal. She'd had to stuff her pride in her pocket, deny her hard-won independence and actually beg in writing it. And oh, how she loathed the whole idea!

But already she loved forlorn little Thomas, and her heart twisted when she thought of the turmoil she sensed beneath the cold hostility Philydia had shown her. Both of the children needed her so desperately. Thomas no more so than the resentful Philydia. So she'd done it. She'd begged. For them. She'd had no choice.

She pulled out the letter, a faintly crackling reproach to her self-respect. She'd brought it with her to look over one final time before she posted it. Could it be that some part of her hoped that she was thinking of retracting her plea? Or was she just going to torture herself by reading it one more time?

She put her head back against the tree trunk, and let her gaze roam over the clouds high in the sky, let her thoughts drift like them. What odd turns life took. She'd fought so hard to become her own person. Fought to make her own way, and by the grace of God, she'd done it even more successfully than she had dared hope. Now, that very success—success in a male occupation—had ruined her chances for a normal life. She'd become unacceptable as a marriage prospect, and now a malicious twist of fate had forced on her the necessity of finding a husband. Need dictated that she find a husband in spite of her proven ability to stand alone. What would she do if—

"Mrs. Landry!" Tim Parson drove all thoughts of niece and nephew from her mind. Regina looked up at the mountain of a man. He was glaring at her. "Yes, Tim?"

"These horses are getting tired."

"You're quite right." She watched the next three-year-old carefully. The muscles in his hindquarters were showing little quivers of fatigue. She should have noticed it before—would have if her mind hadn't been on the ghastly prospect of sacrificing her freedom forever. "Please stop them."

"Aye." Tim stepped forward and blocked access to the first caveletti with his bulk.

The horse approaching, a rangy bay gelding, sat back on his haunches and skidded to a halt. Tim went forward and caught him up. Snagging lead lines from the fence rail, he proceeded to gather the rest of the horses. Two in each hand, he passed through the gate Regina had risen to hold open for them.

She was disgusted with herself for having been inattentive. A mistake on her first day was inexcusable. Dispirited in spite of the knowledge that her charges were entirely safe with Tim, Regina headed up to the house. It was time to confer with Winnie.

The walk to the house took only a few minutes. She came out of the copse of trees that shielded the stables from the house and made straight for the kitchen garden. Letting herself in the ivy-shrouded side door nearest the stables, she walked down the long hall toward the kitchen.

There in its cozy warmth she found Winnie. The housekeeper deferred to her as if she were truly mistress of Charnwood. The feeling it gave her was bittersweet.

"Ah. There you are. 'Tis almost seven." Winnie was preparing tea. "Was there a problem with the horses?"

Regina swept off her cloak and hung it on a peg by the back door. She was well aware that Winnie was really asking if there had been a problem with the men. "No. And I think with Tim around, there is almost never going to be a problem with the horses."

"A help to you, is he?" Winnie's relief was obvious.

"A very great help. Philip chose well."

"Good. Sit." Steaming fragrance rose from the cups Mrs. Winstead placed on the long, well-scrubbed pine table. Regina remembered the many times she had come to the kitchen, just like this, to have tea with Winnie.

That memory triggered other, more recent memories. She recalled last evening when she'd arrived home. She shook her head, remembering.

"What is it, my dear?"

"I was recalling last night. My first evening home." A smile quirked the corner of her mouth. She would always think of Charnwood as home, she supposed.

"Och. And what a night last night was."

"Yes. It was certainly an exciting one. But the Earl is

doing well. It's Philydia who is foremost in my mind." Even though it had undoubtedly been the least exciting of the day's happenings, her confrontation with her niece still weighed heavily with her. "Philydia would have sent me away into the night if it hadn't been for the attack on Taskford." She smiled briefly at Winnie. "Or, I should probably say, his subsequent bloody arrival back here at Charnwood."

"Aye. It was what convinced Miss Philydia that she wasn't all as grown up as she liked to think she was. And a good thing, too. A very good thing."

Regina kept her gaze on her teacup, swirling the strong dark tea. "She'd still like to send me away, you know. Only your intervention stopped her in the first place."

Winnie was suddenly too busy at the oven to answer. God bless her.

Regina sighed. "Poor Philydia. Prejudices form easily enough without any help from outside sources. It's always a tragedy when an adult poisons a young mind, even when there's good reason." Her eyes sought Winnie's. "Which surely there wasn't in this case. I was only a tomboy, never worse than that."

Winnie twitched, tried to keep her tongue still in her head and gave it up. "Yes. And now thanks to her mother's thoughtlessness, Philydia is saddled with the burden of learning to accept . . ."

Regina put into words the rest to the sentence—an ending that wild horses could not have dragged out of Winnie. "Learning to accept an aunt she can't stand."

Winnie turned from the huge iron stove, her face filled with dismay. "Oh, my dear. I am so sorry."

Regina refused to feel pity for herself. She understood that Philydia was trying to keep faith with her dead mother. But the child was putting herself in an uncomfortable position. By continuing to throw barbs Regina's way, Philydia was alienating even the servants, and Regina's heart went out to her. "I'd so like to help the child."

"Of course you would. Anything else would be foreign to your nature."

"Well, we've made a truce, of sorts. Philydia has admitted that the arrival of a wounded Earl has shown her she isn't quite ready to take over the responsibility of being the lady of the house."

"Aye. That's what finally got her to agree to your being here. And I think she'll be mightily relieved to have you see what you can do with the horses. The size of them has always frightened her, so I'll wager she respects you for not being afraid to go near them."

"Yes. Well, at least that's an area in which I know I can help. But I so wish there was something more I could do to help her."

Winnie looked across the kitchen at her. "Stick to the horses, Miss Reggie, and let time take care of the rest."

"Yes. I know you're right." And she was set on doing just that. She was going to be of use, of service, to her family— but, oh, how she wished that she could feel as though she belonged. Feel that she was wanted, truly wanted. To belong, and to know that somebody cared.

She bit her lip, hard, to keep foolish tears from forming. It was pointless to cry for something she couldn't have. She closed her eyes against the pain.

Apple turnovers added their mouth-watering scent to the pleasing aroma of the tea. Everything always smelled better in the warmth of a kitchen, and the smell of the tarts was wonderful—and nostalgic. Bliss. "Apple turnovers." She opened her eyes again and smiled at her former nursery maid. "You haven't forgotten."

Winnie blinked quickly. "No. I remember well how very much you liked them as a child." She sniffed.

Regina was startled. "Winnie! Is anything wrong?"

"No. Nothing's wrong." The housekeeper dabbed at the corners of her eyes with her apron, then erupted. "Nothing's the matter unless somebody you care about has everything go wrong in their life and their family treats them just awful, like . . . like . . ." Words failing her, Winnie plopped down in her chair and began to weep in earnest.

Regina was transfixed. Winnie cared. Truly cared. Tears spilled down her own cheeks. "Ah, Winnie." The soft utterance was full of the pain of all those past years. "Dear Winnie. You *care*."

Mrs. Winstead's head snapped up. She stared at the stricken Regina. "Oh, my dear." Light glowed in her face. "Of course I care. I've always cared." She rose and went to the other woman to put her arms around her. "You were my baby, you know. My precious child. I have never forgotten you, and not a day has passed that you have not been in my prayers."

Her kindness was more than Regina could bear. Some dam deep inside her broke. From behind it spilled all the hurt her family's indifference had caused her. Somebody had cared. All that time when she had been struggling to make her own way, alone and frightened, someone had actually cared that she was safe and well. And that someone was Winnie. Winnie, who had guided her first steps and kissed her bruises to make them well . . . And all this time, certain that she had no value to anyone at Charnwood, she'd believed that even her beloved Winnie would have been so busy with Philip's children that she would have forgotten her.

Love, kept so long imprisoned by hopelessness, expanded and exploded in her. She held tightly to her cherished friend, weeping pain away.

Winnie patted her former nursery charge on the back and

murmured soothing nothings. They clung together until the worst of the storm was past, then they had a good cry.

After a few more minutes, Winnie hugged Regina hard and thrust her away. "Now just look at us." She made her voice brisk and businesslike. "The tea is getting cold."

Twelve

Upstairs in the blue bedchamber, the Earl of Taskford was finding that Regina Landry was a woman of her word. Just as she had threatened, she sent the Ransome children to his room. He lay still, eyeing them as he might have watched an enemy patrol.

The girl, a willowy blonde with the promise of great beauty, took charge of the introductions. "I am the Honorable Philydia Ramsome. I'm named after both my father and my mother. He was Philip, and she was Lydia." As if he were of no consequence, she gestured to the slender boy beside her and said, "This is my brother, Lord Thomas Ransome. He's the Viscount now that Papa has died."

If he hadn't seen the tightening of her hands into fists, Harry might have thought the death of her father a matter of no importance to her. What was the matter with the child?

She continued with her introductions. "And we know, of course, that you are the new Earl of Taskford." She dropped him a proper curtsy. "How do you do."

The boy murmured something, his gaze fixed on Taskford's face.

Harry said, "I'm very pleased to make your acquaintance." He wondered why it mattered to him that he wasn't telling the truth and decided it was because of the terrible vulnerability he saw in the face of the boy.

Thomas asked, "How are you feeling, your lordship?"

Harry started to say "fine" automatically, then caught himself. Obviously the lad had come to a sickroom to give comfort. It would hardly do to treat his earnest inquiry as if it were a mere social convention. So he said, instead, "As well as might be expected, thank you."

The boy moved closer, his gray eyes wide. "Does it hurt awfully to be shot, sir?"

The girl erupted at that. "Of course it hurts, stupid! Why else would men fall down and stop fighting their wars if it didn't hurt them to get shot?"

Harry watched the boy as he went from instant hurt to ready anger. Drawing himself up to his full height, the child roared at his sister. "It's impolite to call anyone 'stupid,' Philydia."

"Well, if it is, it shouldn't be when they are."

"I am *not* stupid!"

"But you *are* shouting, and that is more impolite than *I* could ever be."

The girl was so smug, Harry found himself cheering for the lad. The boy was clearly outgunned, however.

That was partly due to his age, which Harry guessed was around seven, and the rest due to the fact that he was a boy.

Why the devil was it that females held the advantage until males grew to the point that they could overpower them physically? There was something in that to ponder, but he was more interested in the children's quarrel just now.

"Aunt Regina says we must be kind to one another." The boy's voice was soft. Harry sensed real affection for the Amazon in it.

"Who cares what *she* says."

Harry answered before the boy could speak. "Well, I do, for one."

"You *do*?" Both children spoke at once. Their light voices held very different inflections. The girl's held incredulous scorn, the boy's grateful worship. Harry knew he'd just made one new friend, at any rate.

"Will it hurt you if I come sit on the foot of your bed?" Young Lord Thomas had evidently decided that the Earl of Taskford was an ally.

"Not at all. Please do."

Thomas ignored his sister's glare, kicked off his shoes and climbed carefully onto the high four-poster. His gaze never left Taskford's face, and if the boy's movements had caused him to suffer the tortures of the damned, Harry would have died before he'd have shown it.

Little Lord Thomas crossed his legs, tailor-fashion. "I have lots and lots of toy soldiers. I try to arrange them as I think Wellington would have done in the real war. I don't think I do it right, though." His eyes wide, he asked, "Were you in a great many battles?"

Where Harry would have turned off such a question from an adult with a frosty stare, he was powerless to resist the child. After a slight pause, he answered, "Yes, a great many."

"And did you always win them?"

Harry started to laugh at the absurdity of the question but caught himself. He could hardly tell a starry-eyed boy that no one ever really won battles. To explain to the child that every battle won cost so many lives that it made even a victory hollow was not the done thing in England.

In England, every boy wanted to be a hero, and it was the expected duty of every hero to encourage him to be. Until now, looking into the fine eyes and beautiful face of this lad, Harry had never questioned that duty.

His voice was tight as he answered, "We won our share."

"Was it exciting? Charging the enemy? Shooting your gun?"

For an instant, the roar of cannon, the screams of wounded horses and the cries of downed comrades filled Harry's mind. He could smell the fresh blood, the acrid scent of gunpowder. Then it was gone, drifting away like the smoke of battle. "There was excitement, yes." He smiled at the child, but the smile didn't warm his haunted eyes. "There was peril, too. And fear."

"Fear?" The boy startled as if he'd said something shocking.

"Did you think men in battle never felt fear?"

Thomas screwed up his face in deep thought. After a moment, he answered, "Yes. All right. I can see that you would be fearful you might get your charger hurt if you liked him a lot."

Harry's mind flashed to the mount he'd lost. Tammerlane, his big gray gelding. His faithful friend. The memory seared like a flame.

No more questions about war. He was too uncomfortable with them. Perhaps he was maudlin because he was wounded. Inactivity had never been good for him. It left too much time to think, to remember. Remembering was abhorrent to a soldier. He changed the subject. "Do you like horses?"

Thomas's face lit up. "Oh, yes!"

"Do you have one of your own?"

Philydia came nearer the bed. "He's too little to have a horse."

Harry refused to let his irritation show. "Oh, I should think he's big enough to have a mount of some sort, shouldn't you?"

"Mother said he was too irresponsible." She turned her gaze to her brother, accusing. "She said he didn't take enough care to keep his dog out of the house, so he couldn't expect to have a pony." She threw her brother a scathing look. "He sneaks, now, and *keeps* Caliban in the house with him."

"And just who is Caliban?" Harry watched the girl carefully, interested in her attitude. He could figure out who Caliban was without her help, but what made her so damned hostile to her little brother?

Thomas shot upright. "Cal is my dog." He turned hot eyes to his sister. "He's my friend and I love him and I want him here in the house with me."

"You know Mother never allowed it. And you are being dishonest not to tell Aunt Regina that he is supposed to be kept outside."

Thomas was close to tears.

Harry intervened. "Real friends belong at one's side, don't you think, Philydia?"

The question took her by surprise. "I . . . I don't know. I've never thought about it."

Harry kept his tone neutral. "Sometimes, we forget to give things sufficient thought. Sometimes, we just go along with what we've heard without deciding whether or not we really agree with it. Haven't you noticed that?"

"Philydia does." Thomas tried to be gentle.

"I do not!"

"Yes, you do. You never think for yourself. You just say all the things Mama used to say."

Philydia's face paled. With far less vigor, she repeated, "I do not."

Harry found that, as much as he disliked this girl, he couldn't let her suffer. He threw her a lifeline. "Do you have a horse, Philydia?"

"No. Not yet. Papa said I should learn to ride astride first and then on a sidesaddle. Mama said that I couldn't do that. That I'd always have to ride aside as she did."

Thomas took it up when she hesitated. "Papa made us leave the room then. He said that he and Mama would discuss it and let Phil know their decision."

Sensing that the issue had not been resolved before the death of the children's parents, Harry distracted them. "So how do you get about the countryside? Surely you don't walk everywhere."

The first signs of enthusiasm showed in Philydia's face. "Oh, no. We have a pony cart. And a wonderful pony to pull it."

With her eyes alight, she was a beautiful child. Harry smiled encouragingly, willing her to hold this mood.

Responding to his interest, the child said, "Our pony's name is Creampuff. He's a chestnut and he has a cream mane and tail." She smiled the first smile he'd seen from her. "He is splendid."

His own smile widened. "And which of you drives him? Or do you take turns?"

It was the wrong question. Philydia's face closed. The cold, haughty expression he'd seen before returned. "Why, I drive, of course. Mother said I should."

"Mama didn't think I was responsible enough because I kept trying to bring Cal in out of the cold."

"You see!" Philydia said it as if Taskford would agree that her brother was irresponsible.

Instead he said, "Why, I should think bringing a puppy in out of the cold was a very *responsible* thing to do, myself."

"Oh, thank you." Thomas barely breathed the remark.

"You mustn't do that, your lordship." Philydia's face was stern, her voice firm.

Harry's left eyebrow rose. He asked very quietly, "What must I not do?"

"You are encouraging him to believe he has done nothing wrong. Mother wouldn't like that."

Suddenly, Harry realized that these children had had a mother as cold as his own. His rising anger toward Philydia evaporated. The poor child was only following the only example she'd had—her mother.

What a pity. What a damnedable pity.

"When I am well," he offered, "you must drive Creampuff over to Taskford Manor to visit me."

"Oh, yes!" said Thomas.

At the same time, Philydia said, "Oh, no. Mother would never hear of it."

Harry was silent a long moment. He wanted to say, *Now that your mother is gone, perhaps you could ask permission from your father's sister. She is the adult in charge now, isn't she?* But he didn't. Discretion was indeed the better part of valor, and he sensed that Philydia might still be resistant to the thought of her aunt taking her mother's place. So he said calmly, "Well, the invitation stands. Come whenever you feel you might."

He turned his full attention to the boy. "Thomas, I think it is high time you learned to ride. If you can secure your aunt Regina's permission, I should be happy to teach you."

"My permission for what?" Regina stood smiling in the doorway. Her voice had been tender. When her gaze met Harry's, he was certain that she had been standing there for some time. He felt as if she had been . . . not spying on them, he cudgeled his mind for the right word and found it . . . *savoring* the children, drinking them in. He found that oddly endearing.

Thomas flung himself off the bed and went running to her. "To ride! To ride, Aunt Reggie. Lord Taskford has offered to teach me to ride horses!"

Regina looked from his shining face to the taciturn one of the man on the bed. The idea of Taskford with children seemed strange to her. His raised eyebrow told her he knew exactly what she was thinking. His mocking gaze challenged her.

"Well?" he said. "Have we your permission, Mrs. Landry?"

Regina felt a faint disappointment. She had hoped to teach Thomas to ride, herself. One look at the adulation on Thomas's face took care of that, though. There was no doubt the boy would consider her a poor substitute, indeed, for a much-decorated hero of the realm.

Remembering the way Taskford had ridden Mathers's chestnut hunter, his athletic body almost a part of the big horse, she knew that Thomas would come to no harm under his tutelage. So, with an inward sigh for having to yield space in their lives to the raffish Taskford, she replied, "Yes, of course you have my permission."

Thomas gave her a bear hug. "Thank you, Aunt Regina."

She looked down into his shining face and hugged him to her side. Her throat needed clearing before she could speak. "You two aren't tiring Lord Taskford, are you?"

"Of course he is," Philydia informed her aunt.

"No, they are not fatiguing me in the least. Thomas has been sitting very quietly at the foot of my bed, and Philydia has been kind enough to hold one of its four posts in place while we talked." Then Harry asked with a great show of innocence, "Won't you come into my bed, too?"

Regina laughed at him. "No. I think not. I shall just sit here in my chair and visit." She settled gracefully in the chair in which she'd spent the night, placing her pillows to give her the best support. She was amazed to find she was exhausted. The strain of her first day at the stables after an all but sleepless night was telling on her.

Harry looked at her closely and saw the faint blue smudges under her eyes. He knew better than to tell her she needed to go take a nap. She'd refuse, and he'd have put her at a disadvantage with the children. Instead, he decided to try to keep her here, sitting down and comfortable.

"The children and I were just discussing horses."

Philydia's eyebrows shot skyward.

Thomas wasn't going to have his hero proved wrong. "We were. We were talking about a horse for me." He glared at his sister.

"In a farm full of horses, it does seem that we could find one for you, doesn't it?" Regina smiled at Thomas. "The problem is, they are all bred for racing." She recalled a horse with a perfect temperament. "If only I had the big bay mare from the coach that wrecked. Except for size, she'd be perfect."

Harry asked, "You liked her that much?"

"Oh, yes. She was so calm, so sensible."

Harry saw her shining eyes and made a mental note. Then he said, "Race horses seldom have either of those traits."

"True. It's the breeding. I'm hard put, even among my brother's hack and hunters, to find one that doesn't lose patience when I ask it to sit still under me during training."

"Why is that?" Philydia's curiosity was natural. She was her father's daughter, after all. Regina was glad to hear her question.

"Well, all Thoroughbreds are descended from three foundation sires—Herod, Eclipse and Matchem. They are, in turn, all three descended from the Darley Arabian, Godolphin's Barb and the Byerly Turk—all what we call Arabians today. The addition of the Arab blood gave our English horses their speed."

"Also their high-strung nature," Harry added, preparing Thomas for disappointment.

"Were they really good horses?" Philydia wanted to know.

"Oh, yes. The Darley Arabian's great-great-grandson, Eclipse, was a fabulous horse. And he wasn't the last."

"That's true." Harry, to his amazement, could feel his own interest stirring. "He was totally undefeated."

Eyes bright, Regina leaned toward him. "Yes. He was never even challenged."

"Yes, he was." Harry's usually blasé voice was lively. "One race. The single opponent who made him extend to full gallop." He frowned. "Now who the devil was it?"

Regina grinned. "That's nice."

"What's nice?"

"You say 'who.'" She noticed he'd forgotten himself so far as to curse in front of her, too. She probably should have corrected him, for the children's sakes, but she liked this bright, interested Taskford. She'd had quite enough of the bored, insufferable rake he'd been.

"What?" He was puzzled.

"Never mind. Just a peculiarity of mine." She grinned again, recalling how the stablemen at Charnwood had tested her to see if she'd call horses "what." It gave her a warm feeling to find that Taskford didn't. "The other horse's name was Bucephalus. The owner's name was Wentworth—just like our own dear Wentworth." She squirmed forward to sit on the edge of her chair. Her elbows were on the edge of the bed now, to bring her closer to the discussion.

"That's right! It was the Beacon Course at Newmarket."

"Right! Four and a half miles." She frowned mightily. "How gruelling that must have been."

"Of course," Harry tried to sound casual again, "he never went up against the best horses of his day."

"He'd have beaten them."

He laughed at her certainty. "How do you know?"

"Because he distanced every horse he ran against except Bucephalus."

Philydia interrupted, eager to learn, "What does that mean? He 'distanced' them?"

Harry, who'd been sliding down in his bed to bring his face closer to Regina's, looked up at her. "To 'distance' means to be two hundred and forty yards ahead of the next closest horse when you get to the winner's post. That's quite a lead."

"Oh, my, yes." Philydia's eyes began to glow.

"And Eclipse sired three Derby winners." Regina was smiling to see her niece so animated.

"And he sired the mare, Annette." Harry was up on his elbow now, their noses inches apart. "She won the Oaks!" He'd forgotten to be casual. He was as enthused as the rest of them. "Do you remember that bet on Eclipse that some Irishman made?"

"Yes!" Regina's eyes were as bright as her niece's. "He bet a huge sum that he could place the winners in a race Eclipse was running in. Then he wagered Eclipse would be first and all the other horses nowhere."

"Nowhere?" Thomas frowned. "How could he do that? What did that mean? There were other horses in the race, weren't there?"

"That meant that the man who made the bet was counting on Eclipse to run as he usually did and distance the rest of the field," Harry explained to the boy. "And because Eclipse 'distanced' them all, they *won no places*. So the Irishman won the bet!"

Regina put out an index finger. Since he'd shifted down to meet her, it almost touched the tip of his nose. "It was O'Kelly. Captain something O'Kelly."

Harry frowned in concentration. "Later he bought Eclipse, didn't he?" He reached out and tucked a stray curl behind Regina's ear. Her cheek was like silk.

"Uh-huh." She nodded so vigorously that more of her hair slipped from its pins. "O'Kelly had already bought half ownership sometime before."

He tucked a second curl back in place and lightly traced her cheek from the tip of her ear to the corner of her mouth. He was beginning to be distracted from their conversation.

Regina shook her head at him and sat back in her chair.

Harry frowned his disappointment.

"Weren't any of the others great?" Thomas asked.

"What others?" Philydia really wanted to know what her brother was asking.

Regina smiled to see the absence of her usual scorn for him.

"The other Arab-sired English horses," Thomas told his sister.

Philydia looked to her aunt.

"Herod," Regina blurted.

"What about Herod?" Harry wanted to keep this conversation going, too. He was seeing Philydia act like a normal child for the first time, and he liked what he saw.

"Herod begot a mare, Aspasia, who was bred to Eclipse. Their lines joined in the resulting foal, Dungannon. Herod was descended from the Byerly Turk, and Eclipse from the Darley Arabian." She looked from Philydia to Thomas to see if they were both following her.

Harry was ready to help. "This blended the two lines. Then Dungannon sired a whole string of wonderful brood mares."

"Hmmmmm. Yes. But that was nothing. He also sired Pot'8'os, who—"

"I beg your pardon, Aunt Reggie. Did you say potatoes?" Thomas was bewildered. So was Philydia, but she was older, and hid it better.

Harry made his expression solemn. "She certainly did."

Regina laughed at them, her eyes brimful of merriment, her cheeks flushed. "Pot-eight-oh's," she enunciated carefully. "Pot'8'os, as well you know, Taskford!"

He laughed, too. "Yes, Dungannon sired Pot'8'os."

"No, no! Eclipse did." She wagged a finger at him. "You are deliberately trying to confuse the issue."

He laughed again at that. "The issue. Was that pun intended?"

She giggled, looked shocked and clapped a hand over her mouth. Heavens! Could she really have giggled?

Regina peered at Taskford. "Where were we?"

"You were telling us that Eclipse had sired Pot'8'os," he informed her gravely.

"Yes!" It was a cry of triumph. She gestured to him to go on with the line.

Harry grinned broadly and met the challenge. "Who sired Waxy, who sired Whalebone. . . ."

"Who carried the brilliance down the whole line. . . ." Regina was smiling her enjoyment. She couldn't remember when she'd had so much fun. This was the first time she had seen her brother's children relax.

"To the wonderful horses we have today." Harry finished for her, making their cooperation complete.

Regina's gaze met his and hung for one breathless moment. Something totally unexpected passed between them, something magical. She felt her heartbeat quicken and saw his eyes darken, his lips part.

Time stood still.

Thomas broke the spell. Almost wailing, he asked, "I'm very glad we have such wonderful horses. But isn't there just one *I* can ride?"

Thirteen

Time, Harry decided, passed slowly in the country. Very slowly, indeed. Ever since he'd been pronounced well enough to return to Taskford Manor, he'd been the victim of a strange restlessness.

He missed Charnwood and the sickroom visits he'd had from the Ransome children, missed most of all the even briefer glimpses he'd had of Regina Landry. He'd heard that she was busy with the work of training Charnwood's racers and he was, therefore, only mildly offended that she had no time for him.

Getting to know the inhabitants of Charnwood Hall had been worth the debilitating weakness and occasional twinges that lying in bed always brought him. Getting to know the fascinating Mrs. Landry would have been worth a lot more.

The only bad part of recuperating at the home of the Ransomes was that he'd had no desire to tease Regina Landry in his usual fashion under the roof shared by the children. His regard for them cramped his style. He looked forward to getting her on more neutral ground to see if he couldn't arouse the latent passion he'd discovered in her. So far, though, he'd been unable to think of a way to engage her interest.

His wound had healed nicely, but boredom was fast taking its place as his most pressing discomfort. He felt like a blasted layabout. Doing nothing but entertaining his houseguests—a pastime he equated with idleness—was driving him 'round the bend.

He was also constantly wondering what was going on at Charnwood that kept his Amazon from at least sending a note to inquire as to his well-being. His lips tightened. He wasn't used to women who failed to take up the flimsiest excuse to gain and hold his attention, and he was more than a little annoyed that the widow Landry showed such complete indifference toward him. She treated him like a *friend*, of all things. He shook his head and frowned. As each day passed, she became more of a challenge.

This morning, after a pointless afternoon, a boring evening and a restless night, Harry entered the breakfast room with a scowl on his face. Only Helmsley was present. Not one of his guests was in evidence to alleviate his boredom.

The sun streaming in through the tall windows did nothing to lift his mood. Nor did he care that the very air outside was green with spring and filled with birdsong. If anything, it made him all the more dismal.

He was restless, maddeningly restless. There just wasn't enough to do. His predecessor had left his estate in excellent order, and it was functioning like clockwork. The land steward was a gem—handling the tenants, their crops and their cattle expertly.

Harry knew he wouldn't have been any sort of help to the steward if the man hadn't been capable. He was a soldier, not a farmer.

The problem was simply that Harry had never expected to

inherit an estate and had made no effort to learn anything about farms and crops. He'd passed the whole of his life in the scintillating capitals of the world—or on a battlefield. So now he felt as useless as he had when he'd returned home from the war, and he didn't like it. Furthermore, the contrast between the bustle and rush of London and the long quiet days of the country was proving irksome to him.

He'd never found anything irksome about horses, though, and now that he was well again, he'd every intention of taking a hand in the management of the stables. He needed a good trainer to take up where Taskford's deceased trainer had left off. Never having trained racers, he wasn't about to risk upsetting the regime he was certain matched every other perfect aspect of his late uncle's empire.

He went to the side of the room, took up a warmed plate and perused the buffet. Such an array of food littered its surface that he couldn't help thinking of the days he and his men had starved on the Continent. Hunger had pinched at them night and day, stealing their sleep, draining strength from their sword arms.

God! What the blazes was the matter with him? What was this discontent that had seized him lately? Playing cards had become a bore days ago. Drinking was a crock. Not only did it fail to relieve his boredom, but it gave him a head the next morning that he could only wish were on his worst enemy. Besides the hangover, he'd heard somewhere that heavy drinking was liable to put period to the health of his liver!

He couldn't even take the edge off his irritability with a tumble in bed. Though he had a suspicion MacLain and Stone occasionally enjoyed the charms of two of the pretty, flirtatious milkmaids in the dairy, he found that *he* had a fastidious disinclination to trifle with women who were in his employ.

That discovery amazed, amused, and, oddly, rather

pleased him. Rarely was he "Hard-hearted Harry" Wain-wright, ever accused of finer feeling when it came to the pursuit of females. This newly discovered fastidiousness took care of any idea of dalliance with a dairy maid, however. The fact that he was their master made it impossible for them to refuse him even if they were inclined to do so. Therefore he'd be certain, in *his* mind at least, that his advances were nothing short of harassment on his part.

Thank God his friends seemed content enough. He'd expire of boredom if they deserted him. Why he couldn't join in their pursuits and be content mystified him.

Bly, Mathers and Smythe held long, involved—and often heated—discussions that seemed to keep them happy, but he was frankly not interested in sitting around talking philosophy. He enjoyed an occasional ride with Stone and MacLain, but not the avid hunt for willing females that now occupied the randy pair. So here he was this morning, a prey to restlessness on a scale he'd seldom experienced.

Finding himself still staring at the buffet, he piled more scrambled eggs on his plate than he'd eat in two sittings, skipped everything else but the bacon and went to his place at the head of the table.

The butler was at his elbow immediately with a cup of steaming black coffee and freshly ironed copies of the *London Gazette* and the *Times*.

Harry looked up at him. "Helmsley."

"Yes, your lordship?"

"How would one go about procuring a horse trainer?"

Helmsley gave the matter serious thought. "Ah, my lord. That is a tricky business indeed. All the good ones are kept busy, you see, and though there are persons that have trained with them, one can never be . . . ah, certain of their integrity. Horse trainers are rather . . . hmmmmm." He gave that up as a bad job and tried another approach. "There are some very fine people training horses, my lord, and I suppose there would be some who would give you an honest recommendation." His next words were almost blurted. "In spite of the fact that it might lessen their own chances to win, don't you see."

"Ah, yes. I see." And he did see. Why help train your competition? "Put that way, the problem is easily understood."

Helmsley nodded, relieved. "The estate next door, Charnwood, had an excellent trainer. Unfortunately, he, too, was staying at the inn that took so many lives when it burned." He refilled his employer's cup from a silver coffeepot, observing a respectful moment of silence. Then he continued. "I have heard it said that the assistant he trained is very good as well. If I remember correctly, his name is Tim Parson."

Helmsley cleared the plate that sat in front of Taskford, who had pushed it away and settled back with his coffee. He stood holding the plate, his brow furrowed. "I cannot say, however, whether or not he intends to stay on there now that the daughter of the house has returned from Ireland to take over the stables at Charnwood."

So she *was* going to take over the training of the horses on a permanent basis. Somehow, he'd thought that she'd just observe, then give her seal of approval to the man her brother had trained—that the days she'd spent at the stables while he convalesced had been her investigation and evaluation of the situation only. Now it seemed that that had been wishful thinking on his part.

But he understood men, and knew that while Irishmen might work for a woman, Englishmen would not. "How the deuce can *she* take over a stable!"

It really wasn't a question, but Helmsley, ever the perfect butler, answered it anyway. "One hears that Mrs. Landry worked for half a dozen years as a horse trainer at Lady

Sybella Dashwood's Stud in Ireland. It was necessary that she find employment after the death of her husband."

Taskford sat up straighter, his reaction to Helmsley's statement narrowing his eyes. So that was why she'd trained horses. He hadn't wondered about her reasons for having done so—had never thought that she might have *had* to, at any rate.

"The devil you say! Why should the sister of a Viscount have to support herself?"

Helmsley merely raised his eyebrows.

Harry didn't care that the man chose not to criticize his better. He was too angry about that having happened to *her*. It certainly explained why she hadn't expired of the vapors when he'd kissed her at *The Golden Boar*. The Amazon had held a post no lady would have taken for the simple reason that her family had not stepped forward to prevent her.

For six years she'd spent her days in a stable full of horses. Worked among the common sort of men who looked after them because her family had neglected to protect her.

He sat very still, letting his contempt for the late Viscount and his Lady Lydia subside. No wonder the child of that union was so unpalatable. With parents like hers, Philydia Ransome had never had a chance.

But why the deuce was he worrying about children? His real concern was their guardian. Their very attractive guardian. Wondering if he was getting soft in the head, he turned his thoughts to the luscious widow.

The fact that she'd worked among men, and among gambling men, at that, opened a great many possibilities that he hadn't really considered before. His interest was most definitely engaged. He filed this knowledge away for future consideration—then cursed himself for doing so. Then wondered why he had. "Blast!"

"I beg your pardon, sir?"

"Nothing." He relaxed his long frame against the back of his chair again. "Thank you, Helmsley. That information's very helpful."

He sat sipping his coffee and thinking about how he was going to hire this Tim Parson away from the Amazon . . . and wondered just how much that would anger or inconvenience her. She was a woman, after all. Would she be capable of understanding that his hiring the man away was a straightforward business transaction?

At Charnwood, Regina sat astride a big, dark-brown mare and watched the exercise boys breeze the young horses around the carefully prepared, broad circular pathway.

Turning to where her assistant stood, she said, "Mr. Parson, I'm not sure of the second bay colt. What do you think?" Regina wanted to include him, even though she'd already decided that the horse's strength wouldn't be enough to withstand the rigors of racing.

Tim Parson watched the Thoroughbred in question for a full minute, then sighed. "You're right, Mrs. Landry. He was fine unmounted, but the weight of the rider shows up weakness in his pasterns, all right."

"I'm afraid he won't do. Racing would break him down. He can enjoy a long and healthy life as someone's hack, however." Raising her hand, Regina held up two fingers.

Responding to her signal, the boy to whose horse she had assigned that number as it went on to the practice oval gradually pulled the horse up and left the track. "Yes, miss?"

Regina, in keeping with her policy of making her staff part of their mutual endeavor, was beginning to explain why she'd called him in when three riders appeared over the brow of the hill.

Instantly she knew, from the way her heartbeat picked up, that the man in the lead was Taskford. She watched him come, a supremely confident rider on a superb animal. But then he would be, of course.

She was relieved to see that he appeared fully recovered from his wounds and his subsequent loss of blood. There was color in his cheeks, and there were no signs of pain around his mouth.

Straightening her shoulders, she turned her horse to face the oncoming riders squarely. Not for the first time, she wished she knew why God had made this man, of all men, her next-door neighbor.

His long, tanned fingers brushed the brim of his hat. More a military salute than a civilian greeting. "Good morning, Mrs. Landry." He looked her over boldly, his eyes lingering on the britches she wore, his lifted eyebrow expressing his amused disapproval of the fact that she rode astride.

"Good morning, gentlemen." Her voice was calm and steady, her expression quietly inquiring. "How may I help you?"

The men with Taskford were Stone and MacLain, his newly arrived friends. She was neither as well acquainted nor as comfortable with them as she was with Taskford's other three houseguests.

Stone spoke first. "Good morning. We've come over to visit because we're curious about your horses, Mrs. Landry. Having seen the ones over at Taskford, we're hard put to believe there are any to touch them, but the head groom there tells us that you have a fine stable here at Charnwood, as well."

"Splendid animals at Taskford Manor, all of 'em," MacLain added. His gaze swept the group of three-year-olds she was training this morning. "Beat yours in a race anytime."

Regina could feel irritation rising. "Are you certain, Mr. MacLain? That is rather a broad statement, after all."

"Sure as sunrise." Oblivious, he cast another glance at the young horses on the practice oval.

Thinking him a bit dim, she told him, "These are our youngsters, Mr. MacLain, *not* our experienced racers." She was conscious of Taskford, sitting his horse, watching. Something goaded her. "Perhaps his lordship might like to have a race between our respective best horses." She turned her gaze on the Earl.

Taskford's eyes warmed. Devilment sprang to life in the depths of them. One corner of his mouth twisted upward. "Ah, but you would have to make such a race worth my while."

She lifted her chin at him. "Are you suggesting a wager, my lord?" Unbidden, Philydia's voice sounded in her mind, telling her that ladies didn't wager. She shook her head a little to clear away the nagging memory.

The Earl smiled.

Regina wasn't sure what was behind that smile.

Harry liked the way she stood her ground. He could see she was beginning to have doubts about the wisdom of betting against him, but her chin stayed high and her gaze level. Inwardly he grinned. Well she might have doubts! Little did she know the danger in which she'd placed herself. "I wager that my uncle's . . . that is to say, *my* horse, Talisman, can best any horse in your stable, Mrs. Landry."

Regina had to work not to look over at Tim Parson. Golden Sovereign, the fastest horse at Charnwood, was coming along *very* nicely. He was probably at his peak now. She'd found Sovereign already well-trained when she'd first worked with him, and she'd built on the schooling of his former trainer until she was certain he was the equal of any horse she'd heard of at Taskford. Therefore, it was with every confidence that she announced, "I think we can give you a race, Taskford."

"Excellent!" His smile broadened into a white slash of a grin. "Now we have only to settle on the terms of the wager."

A pair of horses neighed from the track. Hoofbeats slowed as the exercise boys pulled their eager young mounts carefully down to a walk.

"What do you suggest, your lordship?" Regina was distracted as the youngsters, having finished their requisite ten laps, came spilling off the practice track. Suddenly she called out to one of the exercise boys, "Have a care, Benson! I can see daylight between your horse's belly and your girth."

"Yes, miss!" The boy vaulted off and walked beside his prancing mount, steadying the saddle as he tightened the girth.

The Earl brought his horse up so close to Regina's that his knee touched hers. An electric current leapt between them. Regina's mount danced.

Taskford took deliberate advantage of her distraction. "I propose that if I lose, I will give you a year's free breeding to any stud or studs in my stable." He saw that his suggestion interested her—he had inherited some of the finest horseflesh in England, after all.

Taskford patiently waited for another distraction.

He knew one would come. They were frequent with young horses. It came almost immediately.

A chestnut gelding who resented his stablemates getting ahead of him shoved a shoulder into his rider, sending him stumbling. The boy didn't lose the reins, but his fall put him at risk from his horse's hooves.

Regina's mare spun in a circle and fought for her head. Her slender rider controlled her easily, but her mind was on the young horse and the exercise boy.

Harry seized his opportunity and called softly, "And if

you lose, I propose that you will accept my invitation to a very special dinner. Just the two of us."

The boy got up off the ground. Dust swirled. The boy ducked as the chestnut lashed out with his hind feet. Regina braced herself, praying quickly. It was so easy to ruin a young horse—and just as easy to be injured by one.

"Are we agreed, then?" Taskford was in real suspense now, his voice tense under the velvet caress he made it. Would she realize he'd not specified the intimate nature of the dinner he proposed? He held his breath.

"What? Oh, yes, very well." Regina's mind was on her horse and her exercise boy, not his words. Several of her young charges had been upset by the exercise boy's spill. Her first concern was getting her youngsters—equine and human—safely back to the stables. She started to marshall them in that direction.

Then Regina saw another problem. "John Pantey! Catspaw is limping. Have Mr. Parson check him out, please. If there's any heat, bathe it in cold water until it's gone."

"Aye, Miss Reggie."

She turned her mount, wishing she were not so aware of Taskford. Wishing his physical presence wouldn't disturb her so. She fought it by putting her back to him, putting mental as well as physical distance between them.

Flashing a glance over her shoulder at the Earl, Regina touched her heels to her mare's side and cantered away calling, "I know you'll excuse me, your lordship, I must see to my horses."

Fourteen

The weather had turned by the day of the private race. Heavy, dark clouds hung over the downs, their bellies sagging with the threat of rain. What rays of sunlight fell through or around them lacked their usual bold authority—like a fragmented army that joined a battle it knew it must lose. A wind had risen by the time Regina's stallion was tacked up and ready to compete in this contest between the best horses of Taskford and Charnwood.

Regina looked over her shoulder at the lowering sky. "Do you think the weather will hold long enough for the race, Tim?"

Tim Parson turned his gaze skyward. "Hard to tell." He shook his great head. "I don't like that wind."

A knot began to form in the pit of her stomach. "Doesn't Sovereign run well on windy days?"

"Yes." The word was heavy with caution. Tim turned solemn hazel eyes her way. "But he's a Thoroughbred, Miss Regina, and he can be skittish when things get to blowing around."

She regarded him levelly for a long moment. "Taskford's Talisman will no doubt have the same problem."

As if speaking the name of the opposing horse had conjured him up, Talisman, led by the Earl of Taskford himself, appeared around the last turning in the back lane from the adjoining estate. His two grooms followed, as well as his jockey on another horse. Behind them, chatting as they rode, were Taskford's houseguests.

Regina didn't look at Taskford. She didn't need to be distracted right now. Not with her stallion ready to race against his! Thank Heaven she'd given her instructions to her rider earlier this morning. She would never forgive herself if her orders were anything but clear, and she had no intention of losing this race. The prospect of free breedings to the stallions of her choice at Taskford Stud was too enticing.

Harry saw her as soon as he rounded the last bend in the lane. She was wearing that old cloak she affected, the one he'd been so surprised to find neatly laid over the back of the wing chair in his private parlor in Halston's *Golden Boar*. Today, under the darkening skies, her hair glowed with the same subtle, healthy gleam he'd so appreciated that evening—that evening when he'd given in to the desire to kiss a sleeping stranger and in doing so discovered a passionate woman who'd proven herself a match for him. With an effort, he tore his mind from the memory of that encounter and his gaze from the silken fall of hair that hung down Regina Landry's back to her hips. She'd worn it down and loosely held back by a ribbon in order to be able to ram that old, wide-brimmed hat down well enough to stay on in the wind, he guessed. It shaded her face and would keep off the impending rain.

Regretfully, as the last of the feeble sunlight disappeared, it also shadowed her hair. Still, he saw it in his mind's eye as it had been that night, dark with all the shades of brown and red in its blackness that made up the warmth of its rich sheen, and for an instant he could feel the weight of her in his arms, the long length of her against his own tall frame, and her lips against his own as she gave him kiss for kiss, meeting him boldly—as an equal partner in . . .

Blast and damn! What the devil ailed him? Never in his entire life had he felt as he did at this moment. Never in his life had he remembered the feel of a woman, the scent of a woman's skin, as he now remembered Regina Landry's. It was as if a capricious fate had embedded her in his mind, engraved her on his senses! He had held her in his arms for a brief interlude that had led to nothing, yet she haunted him like a brand burned into his spirit.

Other women he'd forgotten as soon as he'd had his way with them. Or, if he kept a relationship with them for longer than an evening's conquest, he forgot them the moment he left their beds.

What was there about this Regina Landry that she clung in his mind like the last leaf on an oak in winter? Devil take the wench!

Once he'd seduced her, no doubt he'd be able to forget her, too. Then surely he'd be over this foolish restlessness.

Sensing his inattention, Talisman neighed and reared. His forefeet slashed the air, threatening the puny human who held him earthbound.

Harry dismounted to prevent injury to the hunter he was riding and stepped to meet the huge stallion. Dodging the murderous hooves, he seized the horse's halter. He yanked the big animal back down by his own brute strength.

Talisman shook his mane in anger. He rolled his eyes, showing the whites, and swung his head toward his owner, baring his big yellow teeth. Harry laughed and punched the fractious stallion on the flat of his jaw. Shocked, Talisman sat back on his haunches and regarded him with a new respect.

Now that Talisman was calm, Harry handed him over to his two grooms and walked to where Regina Landry was standing. "Good morning, Miss Reggie. I see you're ready for our race."

Regina regarded him steadily for a moment, hoping to convey that she didn't appreciate his calling her by her Charnwood nickname. When he stared back, unabashed, she answered briskly, "I think Sovereign is ready for your Talisman, my lord."

"Very well. Shall we get on with it?"

Regina gave a curt nod and signalled her jockey forward to the roughly marked starting line. Golden Sovereign moved majestically to his place and stood pawing the ground. Talisman approached the line at a like signal given by Taskford, his jockey keeping his mount well away from the other stallion.

The signal to start was to be a handkerchief dropped by Chalfont Blysdale. All eyes were on him where he stood a few hundred feet down the course, straight and regal, a slim figure in a bottle-green riding coat.

Blysdale looked from Regina to Taskford, then at the two racers. Waiting for the second when the horses were evenly placed, he let the handkerchief go. The horses lunged forward. They were pounding past where he stood before the square of linen had fluttered halfway to the ground.

Dirt flew from under hooves digging at the ground for better purchase to hurl their big bodies forward. Great gouts of turf shot out behind the stallions as they raced, muscles straining, each fighting to outdistance the other. As they rounded the first turn, there was an ominous growl of thunder. Across the sky behind them, lightning flickered.

Regina was holding her breath. "Please let the weather hold," she murmured.

Above the race's course, restless clouds roiled, turning in on themselves, then spilling out wisps and tatters that were ever darker. Lightning glinted in their depths.

Both horses were giving their best effort. Each strained to pass his opponent. Muscles bunched and snapped taut under well-groomed chestnut and black hides. Sweat appeared on shining flanks. On they drove, flinging themselves heedlessly onward around the track. Lather flecked both chestnut and black briskets.

Whips flailed. Knee to knee the jockeys rode. Their cries frantically urged their charges on to greater effort.

On the sidelines, grooms shouted themselves hoarse. Taskford's friends cheered Talisman at the top of their lungs.

Tim Parson drowned them all out with his mighty shouts of "On, Sovereign! Move your lazy hide, horse! Run!"

They were mere yards from the finish line. Neither horse was in the lead! Neck and neck they came.

Then, suddenly, with a flash that all but blinded the tense watchers, lightning ripped the bottom out of the sky.

Startled, Golden Sovereign threw up his head. Talisman did not. And that was all it took to decide the winner. The race was over. Taskford's Talisman had won by a head.

The rain roared out of the gutted sky, soaking the thirsty ground, bathing the hot horses to steaming. Solicitous grooms quickly blanketed and led them away to drier, warmer quarters, running, heads down, beside their four-legged charges. The spectators ran for cover. The vast, rain-swept open space was deserted.

Except for a single pair.

Regina and Taskford stood facing each other in the downpour—Taskford with a twisted smile, Regina with her chin high and her hand held out to congratulate him. Somewhere in the wind and excitement, she had lost her hat.

He moved close to her. Instead of taking her hand, he reached out to bring the hood of her cloak forward to cover her hair, to keep the rain out of her up-turned face.

For a moment she stood in the circle of his arms, both of them still, not touching. She stared up at him from under the sheltering front edge of her hood. With an effort, she recalled what she had been about to say. "You have won. Congratulations."

He gazed down into her face for a long moment. Rain drummed on the tight fabric of his perfectly tailored coat where it stretched across his shoulders. Rain dripped from the brim of his beaver hat. He stood, drinking in the sight of her flushed cheeks, her solemn gray eyes.

Taskford's voice was husky as he told her, "It was a fluke. The horses were perfectly matched."

She smiled without humor. "Races are lost and won every day in just such a fashion."

"If you say so."

She sighed. "I'm afraid that I have forgotten our wager." A flashing smile lit her face. "I was so certain Golden Sovereign would win, you see."

"It was dinner. A special dinner." He added, very softly, "If you lost you were to come to a dinner of my choosing, in a place of my choosing."

For an instant, her eyes told him she thought of asking him something, then decided not to. He wondered what her question would have been. By leaving it unasked, she'd told him she believed in and trusted his sense of honor—of decency. For a split second, he experienced a sharp twist in the region of his heart. Instantly his mind quelled it.

Regina Landry had lost the race, by an unfortunate mischance perhaps, but she had lost. And he had every intention of letting her pay her wager. For it was by that payment that he intended to seduce the lovely widow, and that seduction was as necessary to him as his next breath of air.

He slid his hand into the warmth of the hood of her cloak. Into the warmth at the nape of her neck. He cupped his hand around the back of her neck. Her lips parted as she drew a quick breath, but she didn't move away. Languidly, he raised his other hand and removed his hat. The rain pelted down into his thick, dark hair, plastering it to his head.

Slowly, very slowly, he lowered his mouth to hers. His lips touched hers, cool with rain. He licked the water from them. She gasped, and he claimed her mouth with his own.

The world went spinning.

Taskford was amazed at the effort it took him to lift his head again. Taking a deep breath of the rain-washed air, he filled his lungs, hoping to steady himself. Looking down into Regina Landry's face, he saw she was as dazed as he. What was this strange current flowing between them? Feelings tore through him that he'd never experienced before.

He fought for balance. Solemnly, he said, "A victor's kiss," as if he had to explain away this thing that was happening between them. His voice was deep and breathless. He could tell she barely heard it. But she didn't pull away. Didn't tell him to remove his hand from the warm, dark place under her glorious hair. Didn't tell him he should not have and could no longer cup the nape of her neck in his palm. . . .

And then she did move away, seeming to think again.

Taskford made a great effort to gather his scattered wits. Desperate to secure her promise, before he let her go, he said, "Remember our wager. I shall send my carriage for you."

Regina, caught in his spell, isolated with him from all the rest of the world by the driving rain, could only nod.

Taskford caressed her cheek as he withdrew his hand and stepped back from her.

As he stood watching, his gaze locked with hers, Regina backed slowly away from him. Then a rolling crash of thunder rumbled across the land, shattering the spell.

Taskford stood unmoving in the rain as Regina turned and walked swiftly away.

Fifteen

"Look at you!" Winnie scolded Regina where she stood near the fireplace in her bedchamber. She walked around her as if she expected to find one side of Regina that was dry. "Wet clear through. You'll be lucky not to catch your death. Then where will everybody be? Who'll train the horses then? Who'll manage the children?"

Regina smiled at her old nursemaid. "Don't fuss, Winnie, I'm fine. I've been damp before. Many times. And the rain here in England isn't any wetter than the rain in Ireland."

Winnie wasn't going to give in that easily. "And the other considerations? The horses? The children? What about them?"

"Tim Parson is a fine trainer. The horses would fare well under his care." Regina's shoulders sagged. "The children. The children are another matter."

"Thomas loves you." She took Regina's rain-sodden cloak from her and draped it over a chair in front of the fire.

Regina smiled, remembering all the little things Thomas had done to make her feel welcome at Charnwood—showing her all of Caliban's tricks, sharing his collection of pretty stones, taking her down to the lake to show her his pet frog. Of course, when they'd arrived at the water's edge, he hadn't been quite certain which of the several frogs they'd found was his own special pet, but he'd offered to let her chose her favorite even at the risk that he might be giving up his own. "Oh, Winnie. He's such a dear child. I truly cherish him." As she spoke, she unbuttoned her tailored linen shirt, then peeled it away from her chilled skin.

"Yes, and because you do, he is growing more cheerful and secure every day." Winnie shook her head. "Before you came, he was always sad. So lost and lonely." Winnie took the shirt and dropped it with a damp plop on the green marble hearth.

"Do you really think he's glad I'm here?"

"Indeed I do." Winnie frowned. "How in the world did you get this wet?" She didn't ask who'd won the race. The house and the children were her responsibility. She let the men care about horses and such. Besides, from Regina's attitude, she had no doubt of the outcome, and her poor dear didn't need to be encouraged to dwell on defeat.

"It was raining." She began attempting to untangle the wet ties of her petticoat. "I wish I could see some sign that Philydia was glad to have me here, too."

"That may be crying for the moon, my dear." Winnie eyed her former nursery charge's chemise—so damp that it was transparent on her slender body. "Why did you stand so long in the rain?"

Why had she stood so long in rain? Regina felt warmth surge through her. She could feel a smile coming to hover about her lips. Ah, *how* she had stood in the rain. In her mind she could see it again, feel it again. The rain falling all around them. Just them.

She wanted to wrap her arms around herself, as if by doing so, she could hold the memory. Hold the memory of his hand on the nape of her neck. She could feel it there now, as if he still held her, feel the tingling thrill that had gone through her as his fingers stirred gently in her hair. Her own fingers stilled as she remembered, tangled in the damp ties of her petticoat.

Half closing her eyes, she could feel his lips—cool and rain-wet. The velvet touch of his tongue as he licked the rain away before he kissed her. The kiss itself, light and—

"What in the world is the matter with you, Reggie?" Winnie's voice was sharp. She brushed Regina's hands aside, untied her petticoat strings and jerked the garment down off her. "Has losing that horse race addled your wits?" *Och! There and I've gone and reminded her after all,* Winnie thought. Chiding herself, she shoved her young friend over to the copper bathtub full of steaming water and steadied her as she stepped in.

"No." Regina settled cautiously into the hot water. Against her chilled skin, it felt as if it were boiling at first. Then she relaxed with a deep sigh and rested her head against the high back of the tub. "I was sorry to see Golden Sovereign lose, of course, but that's all part of the game."

Winnie opened a heavy glass bottle and poured fragrant oil into the tub. The heat of the water released the heady scent of roses into the steam-filled air around them. Picking up a sponge, she rubbed it with the bar of fine, French-milled soap that matched the oil and soaped Regina's back. "I'm glad to see you so sensible about it."

There was a soft knock at the door. The two women exchanged glances. Winnie went to see who had knocked. When she opened the door and found her young mistress, she exclaimed, "Miss Philydia! Is everything all right?"

The girl plucked at the sides of her skirt with nervous fingers. She looked miserable. "I've come to tell my aunt how sorry I am about Golden Sovereign losing the race."

Regina saw the tension in the slight figure and her heart went out to her brother's child. "How kind of you, Philydia." She reached a hand toward the child in a gesture of welcome. "Won't you please come in?"

"No." Having abandoned her pose of haughty disapproval, Philydia didn't seem to know how to go on. The girl was letting her shyness show, and suddenly it overwhelmed her. She backed out of the door. "No, thank you. I must go see that Thomas washes his hands before we eat." She ducked away quickly, her courage gone. They could hear her rapid steps as she fled down the hall.

Winnie closed the door and leaned back against it, her eyes round with startled speculation. Maybe it wasn't hopeless to cry for the moon after all.

Regina's eyes were almost as wide as Winnie's. Tears filled them. Then a smile grew that threatened to split her face. "Oh, Winnie. *Prayers do get answered!* What a lovely surprise."

"Conway! This is a surprise!" Harry Wainwright walked into the parlor with his hand outstretched to greet his unexpected guest. "What brings you to Taskford Manor, Cousin?"

The tall, slender blond smiled a crooked smile. "Came to see what I'll inherit if you should decide to pass on to your just reward, of course."

Harry laughed. "Sorry to disappoint you, but I've no intention of dying anytime soon, Con." He wrung his cousin's hand with both his own. "It's good to see you. Can you stay long?"

"I'm hoping to saddle you with my company at least until the opening race is over. You're the nearest bed that I know of to Newmarket race meet."

"I'm flattered."

His cousin laughed at Harry's dry tone. "I hear it's to be a great race. Prinny says he's coming."

"Really." Harry's bored voice carried less than no enthusiasm.

Melvin Conway laughed. "Don't overwhelm me with your joy."

Harry laughed then, too.

Conway said, "This might be of more interest to you than the advent of our reigning Regent. Remember Ralph Belding?"

"Of course."

"Belding is racing Halidon."

Harry's interest was caught. "Good. Rumor has it that Halidon's speed has much improved since those racing days we put on between battles on the Continent. I've been wanting to see him run."

"He runs well. Very well indeed. He's the favorite."

Smythe sauntered into the parlor. "Oh. Conway. Glad to see you, old man." He crossed the room to shake the new arrival's hand. "Wondered when you'd turn up."

"Were you so certain I would, then?"

"Stands to reason. Racing nearby, you know."

"You really *were* expecting me?" Conway was astonished.

"Had to. Knew you'd not miss the first race of the season." Smythe turned his limpid gaze to Harry. "He never misses the first race of the season." He cocked his head. "Come to think of it, he never misses *any* race of the season. And of course, your place is close enough to save him the expense of an inn."

Conway had the good grace to blush. Then he grinned. "Yes, well, with any luck they won't all be held in your neck of the woods, Taskford."

Harry grinned. "Do you plan on being such an obnoxious guest that I won't want you back again?"

"I sincerely hope not!"

Harry threw an arm around his cousin's shoulders. "Come along. I'll take you around the stables."

"Good show!"

Harry threw back over his shoulder, "Coming, Smythe?"

"No, thank you, Harry," he called. Then, softly, "Smelly places, stables."

The two cousins left the parlor by the French doors into the garden, while Smythe stared thoughtfully after them.

"What are you thinking?"

Smythe jumped and spun around. "Blast it, Bly! Must you sneak around so? You startled me!"

"So I did. It's a rare treat to find you can move so quickly."

Smythe scowled. He opened his mouth to complain of his friend's unkindness, but Bly cut him off.

"I asked you what you were thinking."

"Before you scared me out of ten years growth?"

Bly merely stared at him.

"Oh, very well." Smythe's round face became grim. "I was wondering if Melvin Conway had come here for the race," he paused, "or for some other purpose."

"For instance?"

"Perhaps to play highwayman?"

"Ah. So you are convinced that the near-misses that Harry has been having are not precisely random events?"

"As are you."

"Hmmmm. Mathers, too."

There was a light step on the parquet just outside the parlor and Mathers entered. "Did I hear my name taken in vain?"

Smythe hastened to reassure him. "Nothing about you,

old boy. It's about Harry. Bly don't think the things that have been happening to Harry—that shot through the window at his place during the card party and the highwayman here—are coincidences."

Mathers looked at Bly, his expression bland. "Don't you, now?"

Bly met his gaze with a level one of his own.

"Interesting." Mathers murmured. He seemed to be debating something. Suddenly some of the tension in his shoulders eased and he said, "Especially in light of the fact that neither you nor Smythe know about the man that attacked him just after we landed back in England from the war."

"What the devil are you talking about?" Bly was as close to excited as they'd ever seen him.

"It was right after we had disembarked from that damnable ship that brought us home. Harry went down to see the horses being unloaded. It had been so bloody dark in the hold that none of us had been able to really check on their condition, and he was concerned even though his own charger wasn't among 'em. Before he got to the horses, though, someone struck him down."

Smythe's mouth dropped open.

Bly's set in a harsh, thin line.

Mathers watched his friends absorb the shock.

Finally Blysdale said, "You haven't told all of it."

"You're very astute." Mathers half smiled. "No, I haven't. There was more."

Smythe cried, "Well, tell it!"

"The attacker had a bandanna tied over the lower part of his face—and a knife in his hand." Mathers looked carefully from face to face. "I got the distinct impression that he was there to do Harry in. He ran off while I helped Harry."

Smythe gasped. "It was a lucky thing you happened by!"

Blysdale demanded, "Why haven't you told us this before?"

"I was sworn to silence by our host."

"But you're telling us now." Bly's voice held a question. Mathers wasn't a man to break his word.

"As they say, circumstances alter cases. Harry might think he has a better chance of trapping the felon by keeping everything quiet, but I'm not standing around keeping my mouth shut while our best friend gets his stubborn head blown off."

Smythe approved. "As he almost did by that highwayman."

"Exactly."

After a long moment, Blysdale said, "We must plan carefully how to guard him."

"What about Stone and MacLain?"

"We'll bring them into it when we need their muscle."

The other two nodded.

Sixteen

This was the evening that Regina was to pay her forfeit for Golden Sovereign's loss of the race. As she went to meet Taskford, she was possessed of a strange, breathless excitement. She was as nervous as a bride.

What was she afraid of? What did she think might happen? It was merely dinner, after all. And Taskford had five houseguests.

That gave her pause. Only that afternoon in the village shop in which she'd looked for ribbons to match her gown, she'd overheard the wives of two of her neighbors discussing her.

"I think she is the most exciting, admirable woman I've ever known. Just imagine having to support yourself like she did. And to do it so well. My husband says she has trained some really notable racehorses."

"Yes," the other unseen woman had answered. "It's quite sad."

"Sad! I think it's wonderful. What other woman do you know who has done so well?" Her voice had dropped to a whisper then. "She might have been forced to go on the streets. Destitute women sometimes are, you know."

"Yes, I do. But you shouldn't. You are barely more than a girl. At any rate, it doesn't make any difference."

"Why, whatever can you mean!"

Annoyed by the censure in her young friend's voice, the older woman had answered sharply, "Whore or horse trainer, you may be certain it's all the same in the eyes of the *ton*. In becoming a horse trainer, Regina Ransome Landry has, unfairly and unfortunately, placed herself beyond the pale socially. Much as we two personally might admire Regina, no decent man will ever marry her."

"That's so unfair."

"Didn't I just say so? And *who*, pray tell, ever told you that life was fair, Rose? Life is rarely fair. Especially to women." Her voice had faded as the women left the shop. "Why, I remember . . ."

Regina had to wonder if Taskford's friends held similar opinions. If so, she was not sure she was going to enjoy this dinner. Not sure at all.

But she needn't have worried. She wasn't going to Taskford Manor. The carriage he'd sent for her brought Regina to the Temple of Aphrodite, and Taskford alone was waiting for her. Her heart gave a lurch to see him standing there, statue-still, in his dark evening clothes. Silhouetted against the flaming sky, he waited, watching her approach.

The lake beyond the temple was as smooth as glass. Ribbons of the magnificent sunset, crimson and coral and burnished gold, were reflected in its calm surface. The white marble of the temple itself glowed warmly in the failing light.

As the carriage drew to a halt, the horses whickered to the team hitched to a fashionable phaeton parked under the nearby trees. It was a warm and friendly greeting between stablemates, and it added to the peaceful feeling of the scene.

Taskford came down to meet her. When the footman

opened the carriage door and let down the steps, the Earl reached out to her.

"Welcome, Mrs. Landry." Bowing over her hand, he turned it palm up and kissed the warm pulse at her wrist. He placed a kiss in her palm, as well, then folded her fingers over it and pressed her hand to his heart.

As he did, Regina's own heart began to beat as if it sought to leave her body. His gaze held her own. She wished she could deny her understanding of what she saw there. As clearly as if he had spoken his desire, she read it in his deep blue eyes.

Regina knew beyond any shadow of doubt that she was facing a difficult decision. She could relax, permit the small liberty he'd taken in kissing her palm, and set her mind to enjoying the evening, or she could object and remain on guard until she was safely home again.

Whatever she decided, she would have to be very careful—very careful, indeed, this night. It was clearly going to be a challenge to get through this dinner without having the Earl of Taskford discover how deeply he affected her. How his kindness to the children had touched her and softened her attitude toward him.

She hid her exasperation as she mentally chided herself. Why must this man be such a temptation for her? She had resisted the advances of handsomer men. Wealthier men. *Certainly*, if proper behavior was an intrinsic part of charm, more charming men! Why, then, did she feel as if she were in danger from her own heart here, with this particular one? Why, when it came to that, was she docilely allowing him to lead her to a white marble folly in the middle of nowhere? Faint alarms sounded in the recesses of her mind—but from those same recesses came the conversation of the two women in the village. The conversation that condemned her to a life of solitary loneliness.

Taskford tucked her hand into his arm and she walked beside him toward the entry of the circular folly. They rounded the side nearest the road, the side that had the most substance, in that it had a wall pierced only by narrow windows to protect the interior from the north winds. They stopped several yards short of the gentle steps on the open side that faced the lake.

The lake and its reflection of the sunset, purpling now, spread out before them. "Oh, how beautiful!" Regina could feel the restful magic of the scene working on her. It was as if Nature itself sought to make Regina forget her myriad cares in admiration of its handiwork.

"Yes, it is beautiful, isn't it." When Taskford spoke, Regina could feel the rumble of his words where her arm touched his side, was clasped to his side. There was nothing out of the ordinary in his words—but they, too, seemed magic.

"You're lovelier than ever this evening." He smiled down at her.

Regina accepted his compliment with a quiet, "Thank you, your lordship," and after a moment, permitted him to lead her across the last few feet of the close-cropped grass to the temple.

Inside the temple, where hundreds of candles burned, rainbows of color in the form of priceless Oriental rugs spilled across the snow-white floor. On a low, round table in its center, covered silver serving dishes, crystal wineglasses and fine china gleamed. A large, low arrangement of flowers sat in the middle of a pristine tablecloth, wafting subtle fragrance into the air. Around the table, the floor was strewn with dozens of silk-covered cushions for them to sit upon.

"Oh, how charming!" She looked up at him with genuine warmth in her eyes. She'd had no idea that he was the sort of man who could create such a mystical setting for a dinner. Somehow, she'd expected to be driven to Taskford Manor, shown to a stiffly formal—and slightly intimidating—dining room, and encouraged to be impressed by his show of recently acquired wealth. She was glad she'd misjudged him. Her smile of appreciation was as genuine as the warmth in her eyes.

Harry watched his guest sink gracefully to the cushions in the candlelit temple with as great an appreciation as that which she'd shown for his originality in planning their dinner. She had seated herself on the cushions with neither the requests for assistance nor the complaints he'd have had from every other woman of his acquaintance. Regina Landry was a lithe and lovely woman, and she stirred him as no woman had in years.

He poured her wine, then his own. Before touching the glass to his lips, he raised it in a toast. "To a . . . perfect . . . evening." He watched as she sipped her wine, her soft lips rosy against the glittering crystal, her eyes a bit wary, as if she had somehow guessed his intentions.

Ah, well. If she were alerted, it would only make her surrender that much sweeter. Hot wanting sang through his veins. The mere thought of the beautiful widow, drowned in passion and helpless in his arms, caused his breath to shorten. She was so beautiful, so totally desirable. The thought of this well-planned evening with her left him dizzy with desire.

"It's kind of you to invite me to dinner as a consolation for Sovereign having lost to Talisman."

He was startled. Not only was she thanking him for his consideration—where he knew very well there was none—she was graciously accepting her loss.

Looking around her, Regina said, "Whatever gave you the idea of a dinner here?"

He laughed. "The number of guests at Taskford, of course. I wanted to claim all your attention for myself."

"I see we are lacking a proper chaperone. You've not even brought your butler."

He started to speak, but she silenced him with an upraised hand and went on, "Since I am already beyond the pale, I suppose it doesn't signify and I shouldn't mind." Her eyes challenged him now.

He could feel the heat in his face. Dear Lord! He hadn't blushed since he was a schoolboy! Was he ashamed of having put her in such a position? The idea was ludicrous. Never had he felt shame in the pursuit of a female. It wasn't as if he preyed on helpless virgins. He avoided such women like the plague. Regina Landry was a widow, and was therefore fair game.

He was surprised to hear himself say, "I can assure you, I had no thought of how it might seem to you, Mrs. Landry. I had no intention of embarrassing you socially." He met her gaze directly. "After what passed between us at *The Golden Boar*, I had no idea we were still concerned with trivial social amenities."

That arrow hit the gold. It was Regina's turn to blush. She returned his level regard. "Indeed, things did seem to take on"—laughter crept into her voice—"an odd informality that evening. I suppose I'd hoped you'd been inebriated enough not to recall it."

"I don't think I've *ever* been that drunk."

An electric moment hung in the air between them. Then he smiled, and served her plate from the dishes before him.

They ate in silence for a few moments, his gaze on her mouth. "Your Golden Sovereign is an excellent horse. Under different circumstances, he might have won."

"Yes, he is wonderful." She smiled softly with pride in the big stallion. "It was just bad luck that the lightning startled him at the crucial moment."

Could he be hearing right? He could hardly believe his

ears. Certainly he felt surprise at having a woman accept defeat so calmly. The widow was actually reasonable.

He wasn't sure he liked that. Reasonable people weren't easily vanquished.

"Sovereign is in a direct line from the Darley Arabian, you know." She was proud of the fact. It showed that her brother Philip had been wise to purchase the young stallion even though he'd had to mortgage his estate to do so.

"Really? I understand Talisman is descended from the Darley Arabian, too."

"He couldn't be from a better line." Her eyes sparkled at him. "Just ask Philydia and Thomas."

He grinned back at her. "We taught them well, didn't we?"

"And, you will remember, they learned very quickly."

He nodded agreement and found himself enjoying her company, enjoying talking to her. Regina Landry's conversation was as interesting as that of his male friends. Respect for her was growing in him, rooted in the admiration that was already there.

He wasn't sure he liked that idea, either. Bent on seduction, the last thing he wanted was to admire and respect her as an equal. Never had he felt that for a woman. Certainly not for his unfaithful mother nor for the many women who had so eagerly welcomed him to their beds.

Blast! Why did he have to *like* her? With desire for her raging through him, the last thing he wanted from her was *friendship!*

The absurdity of his predicament hit him. Here, alone in an idyllic setting he had carefully selected for lovemaking, was the woman who haunted his dreams and caused his hungry body to torment sleep from his grasp, and he was thinking of her as a *friend? It was ridiculous!*

Laughter rose in him, then died in his throat. Regina

Landry was so damned beautiful, so desirable with her independence of spirit and her forthright nature. He wanted her so much it was painful, but how the hell could he be expected to seduce a woman who had just proven herself almost his equal—a companion at arms, so to speak.

Blast it! Why the devil couldn't she simper and flirt? Tell him about her newest ball gown or slyly mention some jewel she coveted? Why couldn't she say something catty about one of his former lovers—if, indeed, she even knew who any of them were. Then all this would have been simple. He could have slaked his desire and won peace for himself. But, no, she'd carried on like one of his men friends. Talking horses, *knowing* what she was talking about.

Now he'd found that she was even a good sport. What in Hades was a man to do with a woman like that? What the blazing, blasted hell! He was stymied.

It was going to be a night for a swim in cold water. Dammit!

He sighed deeply. Defeat lingered in the air. All his plans for her seduction were fading. In an expansive gesture, he refilled their wineglasses. "I suppose you'll be running Golden Sovereign in the Spring Meet at Newmarket?"

"Yes." She eyed her full glass, then pushed it aside. "I think I should eat something more now." She pondered a moment, then chose a bunch of grapes. "There's going to be a stakes race for stallions of any age. You'll be entering Talisman as well, won't you?"

"If I can find a trainer in time."

"That won't be easy."

"No, I don't suppose it will. You don't happen to know anybody, do you?"

She gave a regretful shake of her head. "I'm sorry. I haven't been here in England very long, you know."

Taskford watched the sensuous swing of an escaped curl.

She had such glorious hair. He'd give a great deal to really run his fingers through it just once. Really comb his hands through it—to spread it out on a pillow to bury his face in when he'd spent his passion and lay exhausted. . . .

He'd touched her hair the day of the race. Touched it as he'd clasped the nape of her neck in the dark warmth of her cloak's hood. Clasped her nape to hold her for his victor's kiss. Suddenly, he wondered if he could do it again. Then he wondered *why* he didn't do it again. A single kiss could do no harm.

Regina looked up at him inquiringly. "What are you thinking?"

"This." He rose from the cushions in a single fluid motion. Reaching across the table, he seized her shoulders and drew her toward him. He crushed his mouth down on hers and lifted her over the table to mold her against him. When he did, all his good intentions of a single kiss went flying.

Good sport or no good sport, his Amazon was a magnificently desirable woman. He deepened his kiss, demanding a response from her. And suddenly he knew that a single kiss would never have been enough between them.

As the fragrance of the crushed flowers in the centerpiece swirled around them, Regina twined her arms around his neck and pressed herself to him. Hunger as fierce as Taskford's shot through her. She curled her fingers in the crisp hair at his collar and held his mouth to her own. Desire thrummed through her. Her blood sang a siren's song. She had one brief warning from some far part of her brain, and then nothing. Nothing but the heated wanting that threatened to overwhelm her.

He was pulling the pins from her hair. She thought she ought to object. Certainly propriety demanded that she object, strenuously. But she did not, because she loved him.

When he groaned and lifted her to lie on the cushions, she

placed a hand against his chest to halt him and looked him directly in the eyes. "Are you thinking of seducing me, Taskford?"

"I've been thinking of nothing else since we met." He spread her hair out to cover the pillows, stroking it as he did. Revelling in finally having done so.

"At least you're honest."

He groaned again and grabbed up a double handful of her hair. He buried his face in it and inhaled the sweet fragrance of roses, the fragrance of the woman who lay under him. "You have such glorious hair," he murmured. "Your hair was the first thing I noticed about you. I think it was your hair that started this obsession I seem to feel for you."

With a little frisson of sorrow, Regina thought, *Obsession has very little to do with love.* Then she was beyond being able to think at all.

Taskford let her hair fall from his hands and smoothed it again against the pillows. Then he lowered his mouth to her throat and kissed the pulse that beat there. Then the sensitive skin just under her jaw. Then that under her ear.

By the time he traced her ear with the tip of his tongue, Regina was on fire. She breathed deeply and commanded her body to lie still—not to lift toward him, not to let him know how helplessly she wanted to respond to his caresses.

When she drew her steadying series of deep breaths, the movement of her chest drove Taskford to the edge. His own breath shortened as he lowered his mouth to the breast he'd slipped free of her bodice. Amazed, he saw he cupped it with an unsteady hand.

Regina placed her hand on his cheek. She forced herself to ignore the need building in her, the long-denied hunger threatening to send her out of control as she felt the evidence of his desire hard against her thigh. "Taskford." She gasped as his teeth teased her nipple. "Taskford!" It was command.

He raised his head and looked down at her. His eyes were glazed with passion. She could see the effort he had to make to control himself.

"Taskford. I must tell you something. You have to know that you are not seducing me. I desperately want you to know that no man will trick me or woo me into betraying myself. Not even you." She continued in a voice as soft as a sigh. "This night is my gift to you. A gift I make you of my own free will. Your possession of my body is *my* choice." And it *was* her choice. God forgive her, she would have this one night spent in the arms of the man she loved before she returned forever to her solitary life.

For a moment, Taskford was stunned. Then he understood, and a warmth rose in him that threatened to unman him. She was freely giving him the gift of herself.

When Regina saw comprehension dawn in his eyes, she lifted her arms to encircle his neck and kissed Harry Wainwright with a thoroughness he'd seldom experienced.

His breath caught, then expelled raggedly. She was, as she had been the evening that they had met in *The Golden Boar*, his equal partner—not just another woman to be tantalized and tormented to his will. His body blazed out of control.

Regina met him caress for caress.

When he took her, possessing her as his own with the first deep, powerful thrust, they fell, spiraling down the heights of passion like mating eagles, then soared together to the heavens. As one they exploded into release—Taskford and his Amazon, his beautiful comrade-in-arms.

Seventeen

Back in her own bedchamber after a dreamlike ride home in the early dawn, Regina sat down at her dressing table and made herself look her reflection straight in the eye. She wanted to gather her thoughts and to come to grips with what she had done.

Even though she knew she loved him, she'd had no intention of giving herself to Taskford. The mood, the wine, the lovely setting had all contributed to, but not been the reason for, her decision to do so. She sat quietly, looking into her own eyes, for a long while. She knew she'd made the decision to lie with Taskford because she'd wanted to. Because her love for him demanded it.

Outside her window, birds began to awaken and sing. Still she searched her heart. Had she regrets? Finally she was sure. She had no regrets. She had given him the gift of herself because she had wanted to. She'd have felt ashamed this morning in the clear light of day if she'd surrendered her honor to Taskford because of some mindless reaction to his skillful caresses, and she felt no shame. She felt only a soft elation that she had loved and been loved as she could never be loved again.

If circumstances had been different, if she had remained the proper daughter of her Viscount father, she would never have let Taskford make love to her. If she had still been an eligible party on the marriage market, she would have guarded her reputation with zeal, knowing she must not sully herself if she expected to find a husband, knowing that she owed her purity to a future fiancé. That was the duty expected of a girl born in her station of life. But her life had, with its unexpected exigencies, changed drastically from what was expected from her school days, and she was no longer socially acceptable.

It rankled, but she understood that she was ostracized from polite society because she worked for a living. Worse, because she worked for a living in a man's occupation. It would have been almost the same, of course, if she'd been a male. For, if one were Quality here in England, one simply did not earn one's bread by the sweat of one's own brow— or any other way—and remain in that exalted world called the *ton*.

She knew that she would have been just as unacceptable to the Gentry, the class into which she had been born, if she had chosen to be a *modiste* rather than a horse trainer. She found herself scorned all the more, however, for having entered a vocation that was considered—and indeed, she had to admit, was—far less ladylike than that of designing clothes for other women. It scarcely mattered. The fact that she was employed at all meant that she would never be accepted.

Determined to think about it no further, she picked up her hairbrush and drew it through her hair. Taskford loved her hair. He might not love the woman it adorned, but he was obsessed with her hair.

She looked at the heavy, dark mass of it and sighed. Her breath caught in her throat as she remembered the way Taskford had held it, tangled his hands in it. How he had buried his face in it and drawn deep breaths of it throughout the night.

With a smile, she remembered, too, how that had affected her, right down to her toes. She pulled her hair around her shoulder to brush the length of it, and it slid down her arm, twining itself around her forearm as she had twined herself around Taskford. Clinging, sliding, body to body, heat to heat.

She watched her face color and then go pale as she recalled the many breathless pleasures Taskford had led her to and through during the long moonlit night. Truly, he had kept the promise he'd offered her that evening at *The Golden Boar*. She was a widow, and had thought she'd known what it was to make love, but she had evidently been totally ignorant until he had . . . had "pleasured her greatly."

She could never let it happen again. She accepted the fact that she must guard her reputation and her heart. Necessity demanded that she marry to save Philip's children, and Taskford had not spoken of love even once . . . much less marriage.

She sat very still for another moment, then she rose and went to pull the bellpull that would summon Winnie or her maid. Suddenly, she didn't want to be alone any longer.

Taking a firm grip on her emotions, she told herself that this could not go on. She refused to let herself think any longer of the night that she had just passed with Taskford. No, she told herself, she mustn't think, now, of the wondrous night she had surrendered to him because she had fallen in love with him.

Now, she must think how to tell him good-bye.

Taskford had returned to the manor after driving Regina home just after dawn and fallen into his bed, fully clothed.

He'd slept the sleep of the exhausted, then risen, bathed and dressed without the aid of his valet. God knew he'd done it often enough on the Peninsular. He'd done it then out of necessity; he did it now because he wanted to be alone to savor for as long as possible the magic of the evening just past.

He was late going down to the breakfast room. Not surprised to find himself alone there, he served himself from the chafing dishes that kept his food warm, and seated himself at the table. Helmsley arrived an instant later, proffered the newspapers he'd re-ironed after the Earl's houseguests had made wrinkled shambles of them both, and poured coffee into his employer's waiting cup.

"Good morning, Helmsley. Thank you."

"Good morning, your lordship. I trust you spent a pleasant evening?"

Harry felt heat rising from under his pristine collar. Great God! Was he actually about to blush? What was happening to him? He sent his butler a frowning glance, then decided the bland Helmsley meant nothing more than polite inquiry, and told him simply, "Yes, thank you."

Helmsley seemed to hover, and the hovering finally got on Taskford's nerves. "Is there something you want to ask or to say?"

"Yes, your lordship."

"What the devil is it, then?"

"The mare you requested your head groom, McFeeters, to locate for you has arrived."

Taskford put down his fork. "Wonderful."

"McFeeters is grooming her even as we speak. He reports that she is thinner than he'd like her to be, but otherwise is in good condition."

Excellent. The mount he wanted for Regina Landry was down at his stables. Eagerness exploded in him. He didn't take time to analyze it. He half rose from his chair.

"Perhaps you should finish your breakfast, my lord. It would give McFeeters a little more time."

Taskford sat back down and applied himself to his breakfast. He intended to take the mare to Regina as an excuse to see her again, and there was, unhappily, no guarantee that she'd invite him to lunch.

Regina was working the third string of young horses when Taskford came into view. He was leading a second horse beside his own. The second horse moved well and calmly, head up, eyes and ears alert. Something about it seemed familiar. Her curiosity piqued, Regina called out, "That will be all for a while, men. Take them in, please. I'll be along later for the next string."

By the time she'd stopped speaking, Taskford was at her side. His own mount was acting up, resentful of the mare at his flank.

The men taking the horses back to their stalls cast curious glances at the Earl.

Tim Parson asked, "Would you like me to stay, Miss Regina?"

She gifted him with a warm smile. "Thank you, Tim. I'll be fine."

"Yes, miss." He shot a hard look at Taskford. "I'm certain you will be." It was more than a statement—it was a threat.

Taskford scowled at him.

Clearly Tim was reluctant to leave her. Regina thought he was a dear, but she knew better than to let him find that out.

She moved her horse to stand between the two men. "It's all right, Tim. Please see to the horses for me until I can get there."

Tim touched his forelock to Regina. His voice bordered on surly as he said, "As you wish." A final glare at Taskford, and he followed the other men and the horses.

Harry drew the big bay mare forward. "I've brought you a gift." His pride at having found the mare she'd wished for filled his voice. He held the mare's lead rope out to her.

"A gift?" Regina stiffened. Was she now to be repaid for the favors she had granted him the evening before?

Taskford let the lead rope fall to the ground between them when she wouldn't take it.

The mare moved to nearby grass, dropped her head and began to graze.

"Why should I not give you a gift?"

The word was the same one that she had used the night before when she had given him—freely given him—the "gift" of herself. Was he really so uncaring of her feelings that he would mock her this way?

Her eyes flashed. "I want no gift from you, Taskford. I expect no payment for what passed between us last evening."

He was struck dumb. What the devil was she trying to say? What payment? Surely not the mare. He'd sent his men to find the mare the day she'd mentioned admiring her. Hell, hadn't he sent Williams from his side as he lay in his sickbed recovering from his wounds? And Williams had left him to take to the head groom at Taskford Manor orders that he was to go get this blasted horse no matter what he had to do to get it!

At first, he'd wanted Regina to have the mare as a safe, quiet mount for the children. Then, when he's seen the unruly Thoroughbred she was mounted on when she observed the training of the horses, he'd wanted the mare for her . . . for Regina. God knew the one she was riding now was aching to break the woman's neck.

He'd wanted to do a good deed. Be a good neighbor. Be a friend! And all that was long before last night! She had no reason to be spitting at him like an angry cat, all fiery eyes and bared teeth.

"Dammit, Regina! What the blazes is the matter with you?" The day after he was shot, she'd mentioned that she admired the temperament of the bay mare in the team from the wrecked coach. He'd inquired for the mare, sent to purchase her. For Regina. It was a simple "thank you" for her having had him recuperate in her house. Now the blasted mare had arrived, and was proving to be a damned problem. Females!

Regina's chin went up. Her spine was stiff with wounded pride. Taskford had offered the ultimate insult. He was trying to pay her. Pay her as a man rewards a pleasing mistress . . . or a whore. It was unconscionable!

"Nothing is the matter with *me*, Taskford. The matter is with *us*! I think this incident clearly points out the necessity of saying a final and permanent good-bye to you, your lordship!"

Harry's face paled under his tan. He wasn't accustomed to being dismissed by a woman. "What do you mean, good-bye?"

"Exactly what I have said." Her eyes were calm, her expression implacable. "I shared an exquisite night with you. It was something you wanted from me that I took pleasure in giving you. But I am no man's whore, Taskford, and it will never be repeated. And I shall certainly not take payment from you for it!"

He was stunned. Not only was Regina misunderstanding everything—his innocent gift, his thoughtfulness in having found the mare, in even caring—she was taking umbrage over nothing. Hell! She wasn't even impressed that he'd noticed what the devil she'd said about the blasted horse, nor that he'd made a mental note that she wanted it! That he even gave a damn *what* she wanted.

She'd gotten everything all turned around, and now, she was giving *him* his walking papers. Him. Hard-hearted

Harry Wainwright. A man whom women begged merely to call on them. A man no woman had ever tired of, never had enough of. And certainly, damned well had never refused a gift from! He was incredulous.

Regina regarded him steadily for a moment. She saw the disbelief in his face. The denial that such a thing could be happening to him. She was almost sorry for him. Almost. If she weren't suffering so much herself, she might even have been amused. But she was suffering. She loved him.

If he'd been wise enough to guess that, perhaps things might have ended differently. But he wasn't that wise . . . and so it was over, and he would never know.

She, however, would remember. Remember and cling to the memory of their special night for every one of the rest of her days.

"Good-bye, your lordship." She bowed gracefully, her eyes hotly accusing. "I wish you a good day." She turned her mount to go.

Harry caught her arm in a crushing grip. "How dare you dismiss me as if there were nothing to be settled between us!"

She looked at him with that same devastating calm. "Matters between us *are* settled, your lordship. I have told you that I have no intention of becoming your mistress, and I deeply resent your attempt at payment 'for services rendered.'" Her voice was scathing. "I am no man's doxy."

With an inarticulate shout of outrage, Taskford yanked her from her horse and dragged her across his saddlebow.

Her mare, startled, shied away from them. Liquid brown eyes wide and rolling, she galloped off to the stables.

Taskford crushed his mouth down on Regina's.

Regina forced herself to remain unresponsive.

He thrust her away and shook her. "Damn you! Tell me that that didn't mean anything to you!"

She regarded him steadily. "It would be beside the point. I have told you good-bye. There can be no more between us."

His eyes blazed at her. He struggled for expression, but no words came.

Regina had all the words. "I mean it. I won't spend another moment alone in your company, Taskford." Tears formed on her lashes. "Now, please. Take what you've been given and make yourself satisfied. Please. Don't ruin—"

"My God, Regina. You can't mean this!"

"Oh, but I do." She turned her head to look toward the stables. Her men had seen her horse come in riderless and were boiling over the countryside toward them. "Go now, Taskford. Put me down and go. At least spare me a further scene. You owe me that."

With a strangled curse, he let her slip to the ground and spun his horse on its haunches. As he galloped away, he shouted, "You *will* see me again, Regina. Mark my words! I'll have you with me again, I swear it!"

Eighteen

Taskford had won! Regina looked down at the heavy sheet of vellum lying in her lap. She'd thought she had bested him, but he'd proved too clever in the end.

She glanced down at the square handwriting, as bold and arrogant as the man, and smiled a bitter travesty of a smile. His proposition, so carefully worded as a business offer, was aimed at her ultimate defeat. And in light of his offer, there was no way she was going to be able to avoid that defeat.

There was a diversion in the hall. Toenails clicked on the parquet floor, slipped, scrambled and moved onward. With a joyous "Woof!" Caliban, ears flying, ran into the study and threw himself at her, tongue ready to wash her face.

"Down, Cal, down." She fended the huge dog off as well as she could while laughing at his exuberant affection. When she turned her face toward the door, knowing the dog's master would be nearby, she got an ear washed. "Thomas! Please! If you can hear me, help! I'm in dire need of rescue!"

"Coming, Aunt Reggie!" Small boots clattered up to the

study doorway. Disheveled and panting, her nephew stormed into the room and threw himself on the dog.

Cal left his place half on top of Regina. Removing his front paws from her lap, he trampled her feet in their dainty slippers. He whirled and met his young master with an even more joyful bark than the one he'd given Regina, shoving the boy down to the rug. They wrestled there, growling and barking—the boy almost as convincingly as the dog—so fiercely that Regina, if she hadn't known better, would have thought Thomas in danger.

In the middle of the uproar, Philydia stuck her head around the doorjamb. She smiled first, then seemed belatedly to remember her mother's strictures about bestowing smiles too freely, and made her face straight. She came through the doorway with great dignity.

Regina had snatched Taskford's letter from her lap when she'd recognized that part of her anatomy as Caliban's destination. She still held the letter high over her head to protect it.

Curiosity seemed to get the best of Philydia, for she forgot her adult pose and ran to her aunt's side. "What is that you're holding up in the air, Aunt Regina?"

Regina's laughter died.

The instant it did, Thomas shot her a troubled look, gave Caliban a shove and told him firmly, "That's enough, Cal."

The huge dog flopped down quietly and watched them with interest.

Thomas sat up and asked, "Yes, Aunt Reggie. What is it that you have got?"

"It's a letter, children." She took a deep breath, her decision made. "And since it concerns you both, I think I want to share it with you."

"Who's it from?" Thomas's eyes were bright with interest. "I don' never get letters."

"It's from the Earl of Taskford."

"Oh." Thomas frowned slightly.

"What could the Earl want with us here at Charnwood?" Philydia looked puzzled.

What indeed! Regina snarled mentally. She still felt anger when she recalled the first paragraph of his letter. *My dear Amazon,* Taskford had written. *As two weeks have passed since our last meeting, I am finally convinced that you mean to keep your foolish vow that we shall not see one another. It is therefore necessary for me to resort to a stratagem that, I feel, will compel you to reconsider.*

As you know, Mrs. Landry, I stand in very real need of a trainer for my horses. By discreet inquiry, I have learned that you are finished with your duties at the Charnwood Stud by noon, leaving your afternoons free. I am proposing that you train my horses during those afternoon hours. The remuneration would be commensurate with what you were paid at the Dashwood Stud in Ireland, with an attractive added bonus.

I ask that you consider the position seriously, and that you give me your answer at your earliest opportunity.

Pray do not let the fact that I hold the mortgage on Charnwood influence your decision.

> *Your obedient servant,*
>
> *Geoffrey Harold Wainwright, Earl of Taskford*

Odious, arrogant man! That he would threaten her with the children's mortgage infuriated her. His postscript didn't do anything to soothe her, either.

Post Scriptum: The bonus I mentioned would be the mortgage on Charnwood, free and clear, at the end of a successful racing season.

The perfidious wretch. He knew very well that he had her. There was no way she could refuse his offer of a position as trainer for his racing stud. Not in light of the fact that Taskford held the mortgage papers on her niece and nephew's home.

Damn him! She should have known he wouldn't play fair. No doubt he was counting on the fact that all that time she would be forced to spend near him would undermine her will to resist his advances. After all, wasn't he one of London's most celebrated rakes?

She was in the classic trap, caught on the horns of a dilemma. She loved him, even as she despised him for these unfair tactics. She loved her young kinsmen and her home, even as she hated the thought that she might lose what little she had left of her honor in securing Charnwood for them.

In spite of her agony of spirit, there was nothing to be done. There was no way to save herself. She faced the fact that she had no choice. She couldn't allow herself one. Taskford had won!

Thomas put his elbows on her knees, and looked up into her face.

Philydia leaned against her side. Sensing Regina's emotional state, she slid an arm around Regina's tense shoulders.

Regina hugged the girl with one arm, lifting the vellum page in her other hand. She turned the letter so that there was no chance the child might see it, and read to them both only the parts she didn't mind them seeing. Clearing her throat she said, "Lord Taskford writes, *'As you know, I stand in need of a trainer for my horses. By discreet inquiry, I have learned that you are finished with your duties at Charnwood at noon'.*" Regina edited a bit more. "*'I am proposing that you train my horses in those afternoon hours.'*"

Thomas complained. "Then when would you play with us?"

Philydia's objection showed more maturity. "I say, Auntie, isn't that a rather gruelling schedule? When would you rest?" Then the hidden child peeked out of her eyes. "You do rest when you play with us, don't you?"

"Yes, my dears, I do rest when I play with you. And I shall miss that time very much. But it is only for a short while. As soon as the racing season is over—"

Thomas interrupted with a wail, "But that is ever so long!"

Regina stroked his hair. It was so like her brother's silver-blond hair, it tugged at her heart.

"Why are you wanting to do this, Aunt Reggie?" Philydia's eyes were grave, her manner cautious. Obviously the child sensed something.

"Because of the bonus he has offered at the end of the racing season." She turned sad eyes to her niece. "It is one I cannot resist."

"A bonus is just ol' money! That's no reason to give up your afternoons with us." Thomas was looking mulish.

"What can't you resist?" Philydia was watching her aunt carefully, her own eyes full of an unexpected maturity.

"The bonus is the mortgage to Charnwood. Free and clear."

"Free and clear?" Philydia was incredulous.

Regina nodded.

"Oh. That is hard to resist, isn't it."

"Indeed it is. It would mean that we wouldn't have to scrimp and save every penny to pay it off." Regina smiled at them.

"Or worry all the time that we'd be turned out." Thomas made his voice deep and dire.

Regina was shocked. "Why, Thomas. Where did you get such a notion?"

"From Mama." He acted positive that he'd gotten it right, and stood his ground. "From Mama when she and Papa were yelling"—he stopped dead and corrected himself loyally—

"when they were *dis-gussing* about the mortgage to buy Golden Sovereign and the new herd of broodmares."

Regina thought it best to let that go. "Well, at any rate, here is an opportunity to redeem the mortgage at no financial cost to us. I am afraid we can't refuse."

"Noooo," Philydia said. "I don't suppose we can refuse. If, that is, you are willing to work so hard, Aunt Regina."

"Of course I am."

"For Charnwood?" Philydia's gaze was riveted to her aunt's face.

Regina didn't miss the significance of that inspection. Quietly she said, "And for you. For both of you."

Her face glowing, Philydia straightened her shoulders. "Well then, how can *we* help?"

"Yes," Thomas stood up. "Yes. We can help. What can *I* do?" When Caliban leapt up with a hearty bark, the boy added, "Cal, too!"

Regina shook her head gently. "Oh, darlings, I'm afraid that there isn't anything you can do."

"Nothing?" Philydia's face was losing its glow.

"Well . . . ," Regina tried to soften the children's disappointment. "Soon, most of the work will be at the race meets. They will be at different locations, but all away from Charnwood."

Philydia looked at her brother. Thomas looked back. Silent communication leapt between them. Then Philydia said, "Why could we not go? We could do our studies in an inn as well as in the schoolroom here. And Mrs. Winstead could come to take care of us when you are busy."

"But we could be with you!" Thomas's eager eyes lit his small face. "We could be your chaperine."

"That's chaperone, Thomas." Philydia's tone was superior.

Regina stared at the children, thunderstruck. Since she'd

received the Earl's letter, she'd been visualizing the lonely nights at the racecourses. Been certain that Taskford would work some strategy that would assure them of procuring only adjoining rooms. Been positive that one night the connecting door would not—for some very good reason, of course—lock. Most of all she'd feared that when he came into her room—as she had no doubt he intended to do—she would lack the strength of character to send him away.

Now, thanks to the children, she had a very different picture in her mind as to how it would be. How wonderful it would be to see the shock on Taskford's face as he entered her bedchamber to find her sleeping with Winnie, while the two juvenile owners of the other string of horses she was racing lay tucked up in the trundle bed!

She burst out laughing. Clasping the children to her, she hugged them so hard they squeaked.

"Aunt Reggie! What is it?"

Thomas pushed himself free enough of her embrace to look into her face. "What's the matter, Auntie? Is this you being 'styrical?"

"No, darling. I'm not being hysterical." She laughed again. "At least, if I *am* hysterical, it's not the bad kind. It's from being so happy to have you two! Of course you may come. It's your right, after all. You *are* the owners of Golden Sovereign. When all is said and done, that does absolutely settle it."

"Why, Auntie. You just giggled." Philydia looked pleasantly surprised.

"Yes, dear. I think I did." Just to see how it felt, she did it again. Then she burst into her usual pleasant laughter. Maybe Taskford hadn't won after all!

Nineteen

Harry returned to the Taskford stables in a black mood. He'd ridden his horse into a lather, and brought him home with it only half-dried on his brisket. As a cavalryman, he certainly knew better, but he was too irritable and agitated to cool the beast properly on the last mile home. Not when he had an army of grooms to do it, he concluded, still upset.

The grooms would probably curse him for it the minute he was out of earshot. He didn't give a damn, he was still trying to rid himself of his unsettled feelings.

Regina Landry was to blame, of course. The blasted woman cut up his peace.

What was there about her that made it impossible to get her out of his mind? What witchcraft did she work on him that he couldn't just forget her? At least until he'd seduced her again.

He was used to making love to a woman, then simply putting her from his mind until he needed physical release again. No, that wasn't quite the case. Actually, he didn't *have* to dismiss them from his mind once he'd achieved their surrender. They simply slid from it. Like any other matter of no consequence.

Never before had any woman lingered on the edges of his consciousness and tormented his every waking thought. Never had one made his dreams blissful and blasted composites of Heaven and hell. Not one. Not ever.

Until now.

Blast the woman! What would it take to regain his peace? His easy mastery of his passions? He stalked up to the house, looking for something to do.

His friends saw him coming, and promptly made themselves scarce. Harry was in one of his moods, and friendship—even when one would give one's life for that friend—went only so far.

At Charnwood, Regina was instructing Tim Parson in how she wanted afternoons to go at the stables. It was simple. Tim was more than able to follow her orders perfectly. Indeed, he didn't even need them. She was giving him instructions simply because she didn't want to let go, didn't want to spend her afternoons training horses at Taskford Stud. If truth were told, she didn't like admitting that she'd been bested by Taskford.

Finished with her list, she said, "I guess that's it, Tim." She sighed.

"Why?" Tim always asked why.

She smiled at him, deliberately misunderstanding. "Because you're more than able to do the job. There isn't any more I need to tell you."

Tim looked at her, his hazel eyes full of reproach. She knew he meant to ask her why she had taken on the training of the Taskford horses.

"I really must go, Tim." She couldn't stand the look in his eyes, the reproach there cut her to the quick. Relenting, she told him, "My working for Taskford will buy back the mortgage on Charnwood."

"Oh." His face cleared. "Good luck, then, Miss Reggie." He was smiling for the first time since she'd arrived at the stables. "And I'll explain to the boys."

Regina was grateful. She'd noticed the way the stable-hands had looked at her askance ever since she'd told them she was going over to Taskford for the afternoons to train there. To train their competition. She could hardly expect them to be happy about that. Tim's explaining would help them feel a little better about, she hoped. "Thank you, Tim. I knew I could depend on you."

Her reception at the Taskford Stud was a duplicate of the one that she'd received when she'd first come home and taken over Charnwood Stud. The difference was that here, she didn't care.

She probably should have written a note to see to it that Taskford had come to the stables with her to give her his support, but she'd been reluctant to involve him. Better to fight it out on her own than to have the men see their employer leering at her.

She went to the same pains to establish her credentials that she had gone to with her own men. She was surprised to find the whole thing made much easier by the news of what she'd already accomplished at the Charnwood stables.

Within the hour, she had the first string of horses out so that she could evaluate them for herself. They were an impressive group.

"They've already worked today, miss." The head groom wasn't surly, just concerned for his charges.

Regina leveled a look at him. "Don't worry, Mr. McFeeters. I'm only going to send them around once so that I can see how they go. I won't overwork them."

He relaxed a bit, but she knew he wouldn't be content until his horses were safely back in their stalls. That pleased her. She much preferred working with a man who valued his horses over the good opinion of a stranger.

"Mount up, please." Regina rode her new bay mare out to the practice track. The mare carried her calmly and confidently in spite of the unfamiliar place and strange horses.

How she hated to give in and accept the horse from Taskford! It galled her to admit that he was right, and she wanted to refuse. Now, having to come here had taken the matter out of her hands. The necessity of having a steady mount under her made it impossible not to accept his gift. Firefly, the mare she'd been riding, was typically Thoroughbred—and totally unsuitable for her purposes. Today it mattered greatly that she have a mount that would sit patiently under her while she trained here. She realized that it was imperative that she make a strong first impression, and having Firefly dump her was hardly the way to do it.

The exercise boys followed Regina out to the track on their young mounts. One of them made a rude remark about a woman who rode astride like a man, but was quickly shushed to silence. Regina pretended she hadn't heard him.

She refused to worry. They'd get used to her soon enough. "I should like just three of you at a time. Once around the track, please. Just an easy gallop. I don't want them extended at all. Mr. McFeeters has told me they've already done their work for today."

Three of the six youngsters moved onto the track.

McFeeters raised his arm. The riders watched like young hawks.

Regina interrupted the proceedings. "Not a racing start, if you please."

McFeeters blushed hotly and called out, "All right, boys. Just take 'em around easy like." Instead of dropping his upraised arm, he gave a gentle wave of his hand, then brought his arm back to his side as if he didn't know quite what else to do with it.

The horses started off haphazardly, settled into an easy gallop after a few strides and circled the course. A bay with a tendency to fight the bit took the lead and held it the whole way around.

The second horse, a chestnut with a blaze and one white stocking, kept his nose level with the bay's shoulder. He stayed there with no apparent effort, flicking an ear backward every now and then to see if his exercise boy was happy with what he was doing.

The third horse kept his ears back, tucked close to his head. He was clearly annoyed to be brought out on the track again when it wasn't part of his usual routine.

Regina nodded and smiled as they finished the turn and exited the track. She turned to McFeeters. "We'll train the chestnut for the upcoming race at Newmarket."

McFeeters watched her closely as he said, "But the bay's in front."

"Are you testing me, Mr. McFeeters? The bay will wear himself out fighting his rider before he's gone a mile. He has a great deal more to learn."

"Yes, Miss Regina." McFeeters's face split in a grin. "We'll look forward to watching you train the chestnut."

"The last horse has a problem with this change in his schedule. We'll see if we can get him to adjust his attitude. Please remind me."

"Yes, miss." Respect was dawning behind his eyes. Maybe that bragging he'd had to listen to from the men from Charnwood about this woman wasn't hot air after all.

They were into the middle of the second string when Taskford rode up.

Regina's heart began to beat double time.

Taskford sat his horse thirty feet from her. He watched her for a few minutes, then touched the brim of his hat to her and rode away. Obviously he'd come only to assure himself that she had acceded to his bidding. He hadn't even done her the courtesy of speaking to her.

Regina had never come so close to hating him as she did at that moment.

At Taskford Manor, Blysdale and Mathers were in the study waiting for Smythe.

"Sorry!" He bustled in, round face reddened by his haste. "So sorry to be late. My valet couldn't seem to tie a cravat this afternoon to save his soul. Cravat from this morning was deucedly wilted, don't you know."

Bly and Mathers exchanged glances, then studied Smythe as if seeing him for the first time. To their mutual surprise, their plump friend was a picture of sartorial perfection. Strange they'd never noticed it before.

There was probably a lot they'd never noticed about him. Smythe's quiet nature seemed to efface him. Especially in the company of such a dashing out-and-outer as "Hard-hearted Harry" Wainwright.

Blysdale shrugged the observation aside and dove right in. "We have to give thought to our plans to keep Harry safe at the Newmarket Races."

"Indeed." Mathers's fine brow furrowed. "It's going to be difficult. Harry doesn't like you to hang on his sleeve, you know."

"True. And there will be such a press of people that we'll be hard put to see that nobody slips a knife into him."

Smythe shivered. "Oh, dear. Surely no one would do such a thing."

Mathers considered for a moment. "No. You're probably

right. The time I saw that assassin with the knife, he'd made damn sure Harry was off by himself."

"Of course," Bly mused, "if the shot through the window that night we were playing cards at his digs was part and parcel of this attempt to put period to Harry . . ."

"I thought it had been decided that that as just a jealous husband."

"Mayhap, Mathers. We must consider it among the attempts, anyway, just in case."

"Of course. Stupid of me."

"That makes three, then." Smythe was clearly distressed. "We must be very careful to guard him."

"There will be one complication." Bly wasn't happy.

Mathers frowned, "You're thinking of something specific, of course. I can see plenty of complications, thank you."

"Something very specific. A large complication. Harry is unpredictable at the best of times. Now he's going to be worse than ever."

"Why should he be?" Smythe's eyebrows dipped in perplexity, then rose in inquiry.

Mathers and Bly exchanged glances. Mathers answered for them both. "Because now he's in love with the Landry woman."

Smythe was astonished. "In love? Harry?" He turned it over in his mind. "With Regina Landry?" A smile dawned. "By Jove! That's splendid. She's a fine woman." He chuckled. "And I think she may be more than a match for our Harry."

"Oh, come, Smythe." Mathers was exasperated. "Harry's an Earl now. You know that makes such a match impossible."

"Eh? Why the devil should it?" Smythe was affronted for the beautiful widow.

Bly was even less patient than Mathers had been. He liked

the widow, too. "Because a woman who trains horses, no matter how well-bred she is, is simply not fit to be married by an earl."

Smythe opened his mouth instantly to protest, but the statement was working in his mind. His face turned red with resentment. Unfortunately, there was nothing he could say. It would indeed, as Mathers pointed out, be impossible for Harry ever to contemplate marriage with Regina Ransome Landry.

Suddenly he brightened. There was Harry to consider, after all, and Smythe had to say, "If Harry wants her, then he'll have her, and that's that."

Mathers nodded. "That's true." But he wasn't smiling.

"Yes." Bly didn't sound as if he liked what he was about to say. "But that doesn't mean marriage."

Smythe erupted. "But it must. She *has* to be married."

Both men looked at him, astonished.

Smythe plowed on. "She has to be married to keep her brother's children. That bounder Jasper Ruddleston will take them and milk Charnwood dry if she doesn't marry soon."

"How the blazes do you know a thing like that?" Bly was scowling.

Smythe's face reddened alarmingly this time. He thought of the confidential letter he'd received from his solicitor asking him to help Regina. Bagwell had broken all the rules when he'd asked him to keep an eye on Regina Landry for the sake of the children and charged him to help her find someone to marry so that she might retain her guardianship over them.

There was no way Smythe was going to break that confidence. Bagwells had been solicitors to his family for generations. He straightened in his chair. "I'm not at liberty to say."

Bly and Mathers were equally offended.

Smythe hated that. "Was told in confidence, don't you know."

"By the lovely Landry?" Bly's voice was heavy with sarcasm.

"No!" Smythe scowled, his soft mouth set in a hard line. "No, damn your eyes. It was certainly not the widow who told me, and it won't do any good to try to weasel it out of me, because I'm not going to tell. Just let it suffice that I've told you the truth of the matter."

For a moment there was silence in the room. Then Bly said softly, "I loathe Jasper Ruddleston."

Mathers, his mind on this new problem, tossed out carelessly, "Who doesn't?" Then he leaned forward in his chair and returned his full attention to Harry's safety. They had to make sure Harry stayed alive before they could trick him into marrying the beautiful Regina Landry. "All right. First things first. And first we have to protect Harry from whomever is trying to do him in."

"But we haven't any idea who that might be."

"True, Smythe. We'll just have to stick on his coattails to be sure nobody can get to him."

Bly steepled his fingers. "We can at least try to decide on a list of suspects."

"Well, we have the suspect who'll most benefit right here in this house. That's Melvin Conway. He's a more than obvious choice in that he's the next heir until Harry marries and gets himself a son." Mathers leaned back in his chair. "And, I don't have to add, he also appeared at Taskford Manor right after the attack by the bogus highwayman."

Bly grunted.

Smythe sighed. "If only there weren't so many jealous *husbands* in Harry's past."

Bly gave a short bark of a laugh. "Aye. But none of them were murderous about their wives' infidelities except Lucretia's jealous spouse. Except for Lucretia Perryman, Harry always chose well."

"Yes," Mathers wiggled his eyebrows and made his voice salacious. *"He just chose so often."*

Bly laughed with him.

"Oh, stop. Both of you! This is serious. Somebody is trying to murder Harry!"

If it had been in their natures, his companions would have looked sheepish. It wasn't, however, so they frowned at Smythe instead.

"Very well," Blysdale said. "Since we have now all agreed that the matter is serious"—he looked scathingly around at them—"I suggest we get on with our plans. Now, I think it would be a good idea if we . . ."

Twenty

The roads to Newmarket Heath were jammed. Traveling coaches, curricles, gigs, phaetons and more drove hub to hub. There was no chance at all for traffic to come from the other direction. If you were in Newmarket, you were going to stay in Newmarket.

Catching the excitement of their drivers, highly bred horses called nervously to one another. Choking clouds of dust from the many hooves and iron-tired wheels rose higher and heavier as they neared the town.

Corinthians scowled at ham-handed young bloods impatient to get to their lodgings at the meet. Tempers rising, older coachmen cursed them all under their breath and exchanged weary glances while their passengers checked pocket watches and wondered why the hands had barely changed their positions since the last time they had looked. The traffic moved, but progress was slow.

Regina had made provision for this impasse, however, and the time had come to implement her plan. She tapped on the tautly stretched and lacquered leather roof of the Charnwood coach, and their coachman pulled onto the shoulder of the road at the prearranged signal. Setting the brake under the shade of a mammoth oak, he sent the groom to the horses' heads, set his whip in its socket so that he could twist the driving lines around it for safekeeping and climbed down from his box. Opening the coach door himself, he let down the steps. "It's surely a mighty crush. Just like you said it would be, Miss Regina."

"Yes, Auntie," Thomas was wide-eyed. "I've never seen so many conbayences in one place before."

"That's 'conveyances,' Thomas." Philydia's voice was prim with superiority.

"All right. Con-*vay*-ances." Thomas looked as if he might have pouted at her, but he was too excited to bother. "I still never saw so many."

"There certainly are a great many, dear," Regina agreed with him.

Philydia craned out the window on her side, goggling at the spires of the town churches way up ahead. They barely rose above the pale dust cloud that the vehicles were causing. "Just look, Thomas. The church spires look as if they are floating. Like castles in the air."

"Ooooh, yes they do, don't they." Now he was craning out his side of the traveling coach to look toward their destination. "It looks so far away."

"I don't suppose it is, really"—Philydia made her voice very grown-up—"but in this press of vehicles, it will take hours for John Coachman to get to the inn!"

"His name's Mr. Ruffin," Thomas informed her. "Not John Coachman."

"I know that!"

"Then why—"

"Mama said that everybody calls their coachman John Coachman, no matter what their name is."

"That's silly."

Winnie put a hand on Thomas's knee, and he subsided. "I'm very glad I brought my knitting," she said firmly. "I shall pass those tedious hours getting to Newmarket quite profitably."

"Well, *I'm* very glad that Aunt Reggie brought our new ponies. We get to ride around this crowd." As if to give credence to his words, three horsemen cantered past the coach.

Regina drew back from the window hastily, not wanting to be seen. The men were Mathers, Blysdale . . . and Taskford. She closed her eyes. Taskford.

Merciful Heaven! How long would it be before she regained mastery of her emotions where Taskford was concerned? Rallying, she forced a cheerful tone and asked, "You're certain you'll be all right without us, Winnie?"

"Of course I will. I have Mr. Ruffin and O'Ryan, the groom, you know." Her eyes twinkled. "It's not as if you are leaving me alone in the wilderness."

Regina laughed. "We love you, Winnie." She darted forward and kissed her friend's cheek, then said briskly, "All right, children, let's get mounted."

She was sure Taskford was safely far ahead, but she took her time tightening girths and checking bridles anyway. Everything was fine, just as she'd expected, and she lifted Thomas into his saddle.

The boy looked at her with open admiration. "Glory, Aunt Regina. You sure are strong."

Regina laughed. "Thank you, I think." She touched his cheek lightly to keep any sting from her next words. "Being strong is not precisely a desirable thing in a lady, however, dear."

"Well, I am truly sorry to hear that, Aunt Reggie, because *I* think it's nice." He gathered his reins as his friend, Taskford, had been teaching him, and sat waiting, frowning only slightly when Regina fastened a lead rein to his pony's bridle.

Philydia looked as if she were about to quote her Mama on the subject of lead lines, evidently thought better of it and closed her mouth.

She was glad she wasn't put on a lead line. She'd been told by the Earl that she had a natural talent for horses. Like her Aunt Regina, he'd said, and Philydia had basked in the compliment. She had ridden a little more than her brother had, but was still the merest novice, and fortunately she knew it. Once up, she waited quietly for Regina to mount and lead the way.

Regina had had a sidesaddle put on her mare for propriety's sake. Once settled in it, she checked the children with a single, expert glance, smiled and moved her mare forward. Choosing, as Taskford had, the side of the road from which the light wind was blowing so as to be out of the dust, she led them toward the excitement that was Newmarket Race Meet.

Arriving at the stables without incident, she quickly dismounted and told the children, "I'll only be a few moments, dears." Then she looked them over for any signs of nervousness and asked, "Can you wait here on your ponies?"

They assured her that they could. Before she moved off, Regina gave her nephew his pony's lead line. She was very careful to give it into the boy's hand, even though Philydia was reaching for it. To have given charge of it to his sister would have ruined the day for him, she knew.

In response to her query, the children said, "Oh, yes, Aunt Reggie!" in perfect unison. Since Taskford had been coming to Charnwood several afternoons a week to teach them to ride, they had that one interest on which they were totally in agreement.

Regina gave them one last smile, then went to check her

four-legged charges. So great was the crowd that even after checking on the stable arrangements and making sure the horses she'd sent ahead three days ago were well settled in and rested, she still hadn't run into Taskford. She told herself she was only looking out for him because she wanted the presence of her young niece and nephew to be a complete surprise to him, but her heart told her she lied.

Blast everything! Why, of all the men in the world, did she have to fall in love with the Earl of Taskford? In the past, she had frequently thought that God had a wonderful sense of humor. She wished it weren't so in evidence now. Loving Taskford was anything but amusing from her point of view. She knew she was going to get her foolish heart broken.

At least, she told herself firmly, that would be what happened if she weren't such a strong-willed person. Then she sighed. Sometimes she wished that were not the case, either. She longed to be gentle and sweet. She'd been forced to become strong when her husband Brandon had died, and now she was stuck with the steel it had put in her backbone.

"Oh, look! There's Taskford!"

At Philydia's cry, Regina whipped out of sight around a corner. Looking back casually at the two children still sitting on their ponies, she remounted her mare and said, "You must be sure to greet him, *later*. I think it is time that we go to the inn and let them know we have arrived safely." She smiled to belie her next words. "It wouldn't do to get there later and find they had given our room away."

"Been bribed into giving it away, you mean."

Philydia had spoken softly, but Regina glanced at her sharply.

"That was something else Mama told us." Philydia looked as if she wished she hadn't remembered.

Regina leaned down to give her a hug and suppressed a sigh. Had Lydia *ever* told her daughter anything positive?

She certainly hadn't heard about it if she had. Out loud, she said, "Oh, I think that is unlikely, darling." She laughed and told the two children, "Of course, I shouldn't like to wait until *evening* to get to the inn. By then it might be a very different matter."

There. That might change Philydia's thinking without seeming a criticism of her mother. Regina hoped so. She so wanted to erase the negativity she saw in her niece, but she knew that correcting her wasn't the way. She prayed that the solicitor, Bagwell, would be able to keep for her the guardianship of her brother's children in spite of her loathsome cousin Jasper's best efforts to the contrary. She felt such a need to continue exerting a positive influence.

She knew that remaining their guardian would be difficult. Single, she wasn't considered able enough to raise children, and so far she'd had no answer from the urgent letter she'd sent to her cousin, Edward Overfield.

She thought again how dreadful it was that British law recognized children as belonging only to their fathers. Never mind that the wife was the one left to do the job of raising the offspring. Indeed, never mind that the men could hardly produce them by themselves! British law was British law, and women were the chattel first of their fathers and then of their husbands, and had no rights. And while widows seemed to be the only females to have any legal rights to speak of under the law, even so, raising children without a spouse wasn't one of them.

Custody of her young kinsmen was a matter that filled her prayers nightly. And she would have prayed just as hard for them if they hadn't become oh so very precious to her.

Harry had gone to check on his racers, and was a little disgruntled to hear that Regina Landry had already been there and done that to her own satisfaction. He'd hoped to en-

counter her as she went about her business in the stables
with his horses. He very much wanted to see her. There was
a hunger eating away at him, making him restless. And
Harry hated feeling restless. He was certain that contact with
Regina would help him come to grips with it.

He'd wasted time by trying to look up his old acquaintance, Ralph Belding, to ask where he had stabled Halidon,
his famous racer, but his efforts there had met with no success, either, and he'd given them up. Halidon had never been
close to his heart as had Ashley's stallion, Cossack, so it
didn't greatly matter to him. And, God knew, Belding mattered a whole lot less to him than Halidon.

He smiled to remember Cossack, the great beast that had
belonged to his friend and comrade-in-arms, Ashley Stoddard. But the shining memory brought another. His smile
died at recalling how man and horse had perished together
on the battlefield. If, he told himself, Cossack could have
been here to run at Newmarket, Halidon—and maybe even
his own Talisman, Harry realized with a shock—wouldn't
have a chance.

But Cossack wasn't alive to race anywhere. Belding had
put the great horse out of his misery when he'd found him
wounded beside his dead master.

Shaking off the blue devil that sought to settle on his
shoulder, he turned his thoughts to something that didn't tear
at his heart. It was an ability that every soldier acquired—if
he wanted to keep his sanity. He thought of something pleasant. Something a great deal more pleasant. His Amazon.
Regina Landry.

Planning for this trip to Newmarket, he'd been insistent
on procuring spacious, adjoining rooms for himself and his
friends. After his rapturous night in the folly with Regina,
he'd moved heaven and earth to get other rooms for his men
friends. Finally, thanks to a case of the measles keeping a

Duke and his family at home, he'd been able to make the switch. His friends were in excellent accommodations even closer to the track, and tonight, the spacious rooms he'd first booked would belong to him . . . and to the beautiful widow Landry.

He'd left nothing to chance. For a munificent bribe, he'd arranged for the key that locked the adjoining door between his and Regina's room to be lost. If he'd had to break down the door between them to see her alone, he would have, but this arrangement was more convenient—and a hell of a lot less noisy.

He *had* to be with her. Regina Landry was in his blood, and tonight he would hold her in his arms once again. Hold her in his arms and . . .

His breath shortened. His heart pounded. Suddenly, Harry couldn't wait to see her again. He'd prove to her they were not "finished." As soon as night fell, he'd go to her and convince her they could never stay apart. He'd transport her to inexpressible heights of pleasure in his arms and steal from her the strength to send him away.

He drew a deep breath. Then another.

How the blazes he was going to get through dinner with his friends while waiting for nightfall was beyond him. It had to be done, however. Not only were they his guests—they were his best friends, as well. But it wasn't going to be easy. He took a deep breath, straightened his shoulders and headed for the inn.

When the three from Charnwood arrived at the inn and dismounted, Regina sent their mounts back to the racing stables where her own staff could look after them. She breathed a sigh of relief. They'd made it through the crowds without encountering Taskford. Her secret defense remained a secret.

The innkeeper himself escorted them to their room immediately. That he would leave other people waiting to be accommodated and go himself rather than send a servant showed Regina that Taskford's consequence was working in their favor.

Philydia and Thomas had all they could do not to bounce with excitement when they saw the sunny chamber. The low-ceilinged room was spacious and well-appointed, but there were cotton, flower-printed curtains at the windows and light oak wood furnishing instead of the damasks and dark woods to which they were accustomed. It was such a contrast to the formal elegance of their home that they were delighted.

Thomas ran straight to one of the windows, knelt on the window seat, and hung out precariously, "Oh, Philydia! Come see! Just look at all the carriages on that road." He pointed back the way they had come.

Regina grabbed him by the seat of his britches and pulled him back in. "Careful, Thomas. You'll turn my hair gray."

Thomas laughed and ran over to jump up on the bed. Philydia flew after him.

"My heavens! You're as mad as March hares." Regina was laughing, too. "No bouncing, Thomas. A gentleman is even more careful of someone else's property than he is of his own," she scolded gently. "I can see that both of you are truly in holiday spirits."

To settle them down, Regina played spillikins with Thomas, then read the children stories from the books she'd brought in her saddlebags until Winnie finally arrived hours later.

The housekeeper slipped into the room like a conspirator in some spy plot. "You'll never guess what happened. I met Lord Taskford downstairs. He frowned as if he thought he should remember me from somewhere, but one of his friends interrupted his perusal, and I just looked at him quite blankly." Her eyes were so full of merriment that Regina decided this trip was good for everyone, not just the children. "Finally," Winnie went on, "he shrugged and walked off into the dining room." She cocked her head. "Isn't it interesting how people don't recognize you when you're not where they expect to find you?"

"Yes, it is, and I'm glad he didn't. I'd like to keep you a surprise." She looked around at them all. "Just listen to all that noise from downstairs."

The babble of excited men's voices could be heard even through the floor and thick, whitewashed walls of their room. Every now and again a particular man's laughter boomed out like a cannon.

Thomas and Philydia looked a little daunted by the hubbub. Life at Newmarket during the races was nothing like the quiet of the country.

Regina smiled at them and offered, "Would you like me to order dinner for us to eat here in our room?"

Another man's laughter carried up to them. It sounded very much like the braying of a donkey.

Thomas and Philydia exchanged glances, and Philydia wrinkled her nose. Together they answered their aunt. "Oh, yes, please." The children were in perfect agreement—as well as in perfect unison again.

Twenty-one

By nightfall, Newmarket had settled down. There was only a subdued murmur drifting up from the taproom where the few men who were unable to sleep for their excitement over the next day's race lingered in the inn. Except for an occasional burst of laughter, the noise could barely be heard in the rooms of the sleeping guests. Even so, it was enough to mask the sound of the door between Harry's and Regina's bedchambers quietly opening.

Clad only in a black silk banyan, Harry moved toward the bed as quietly as a great cat. As he glided out of the shadows, anticipation of possessing his beautiful Amazon once again shortened his breath. He smiled to feel the strength of the attraction the thought raised in him, the strength of the response she aroused in his body.

In the moonlight streaming in through the open window, he could see her head against the stark white linen cover of the down-filled pillow. Her dark hair across the pristine linen was a sable banner in the dimness. She was so heart-stirringly beautiful. How could she believe he would ever let her say, "Good-bye"?

Even if he'd be willing to permit it, how could she want to shatter the beauty of what had happened between them? That she even wanted to made him angry.

He took a deep, calming breath. This was neither the time nor the place for anger, he told himself firmly. He scowled. Why anger, anyway? He couldn't remember ever having been angry with any woman before. Why was it everything had to be different about this woman? Different, and more difficult.

His heart clenched in his chest at the memory of their last kiss. There had been anger there, too, in the kiss he had given her. He still didn't forgive the pain she'd caused him, nor the bruising his ego had sustained by her giving him his dismissal that day. But why the blazes did there have to be such animosity between them?

Now, this very night, he'd prove to her that she was wrong in attempting that dismissal. He'd convince her she was wrong by employing all the delightful ways he knew in which to drive a woman half out of her mind with wild desire. Then, when she was completely lost in passion, he would—

Suddenly he jumped back from the bed. The pile of pillows on the bed beside Regina had moved! As he watched, a plump arm covered by a sturdy flannel sleeve appeared and tossed the covers back to reveal the graying head of the woman he'd tried to place when he'd seen her downstairs earlier. The housekeeper! Now he remembered. She was the Charnwood housekeeper. Hell and damnation! What the royal blue blazes was *she* doing here?

It took no more than an instant for him to figure it out. The Amazon had brought a chaperone. He almost smiled. So that was the game she wanted to play, was it?

With determined stealth, he eased around the bed, his gaze fixed on his quarry. He'd simply pick Regina up and carry her out of this room to his own.

As he reached the other side of the bed, his toe touched something. Glancing down, he saw the trundle bed. With absolute astonishment, he saw the two children sleeping there.

Hastily withdrawing from that side of the room, he stood in the shadows regaining his equilibrium. As he did, the humor of the situation began to take hold in him. Obviously, his Amazon had marshalled her defenses. Regina Landry was evidently quite determined to keep her promise that they would never be alone together.

Well, she'd badly miscalculated the effect of this move. The beautiful widow had just made herself even more of a challenge. Harry thrived on challenges.

Smiling, he leaned across the "pile of pillows" he now recognized as the housekeeper from Charnwood and blew gently in Regina Landry's lovely ear.

Regina moaned softly and rubbed her cheek against her pillow. After a moment, she threw her arm up over her head. The full sleeve of her night rail slid down to her shoulder, leaving her arm bare.

Harry didn't even try to resist. He only regretted that he couldn't trail kisses over her bare skin instead of just his fingers, but there was Mrs. Winstead between them, after all. It would hardly be polite to lean on her!

His fingers feathered over the satin of the skin on the underside of Regina's upraised arm. He moved them from her wrist up to the bend of her elbow and circled them there. Regina moaned softly. He was gratified to see her arch her back in reaction to his chaste caress.

He grinned in the darkness, inordinately pleased. *Ah, Regina. I somehow don't think we've had our last and only night together, my dear.*

Winnie suddenly groaned and tossed to her other side. Harry leapt back just in time to avoid having her hit him with the arm she flung over—and discovering his presence by doing so.

He stood there in the shadows a few moments longer, enjoying the sight of his Amazon bathed in moonlight. Then he turned and padded silently back to the adjoining door. One last glance, a sigh for thwarted plans, and he was gone, the door closing quietly behind him.

The sun was hidden behind clouds the next day, Wednesday, the day of the first race, the Two Thousand Guineas. The weather was cooler than expected because of the overcast. Everyone was up early, vying for the best places to park their vehicles so as to give them the best view of the race. A light rain in the early hours of the morning had settled the dust without making the track muddy, and spirits were high with anticipation.

The only fly in the ointment of the men doing the heavy betting was the unexpected withdrawal from the race of Halidon, the favorite. Mr. Belding had removed his horse from the race because of a sprained pastern. Though there was major disappointment among those hoping to see the favorite run, several owners of competing horses were greatly rejoiced by the news.

Regina was not only glad to have cooler temperatures, she was even happier to have a day without sharp shadows. The three-year-olds she'd brought—two from Charnwood and four from Taskford—would fare better.

"Do you think one of *our* colts will win, Aunt Reggie?" Philydia's blue eyes were eager.

"No," Regina told her with reluctance, hating to dim that glow. "It would be wonderful, but you mustn't expect one of our youngsters to win. With the break in their training, the three-year-olds haven't had the experience that would give them the best chance."

She looked down and saw disappointment on Thomas's face. She smoothed his hair back from his forehead. Looking into his eyes, she sought to ease his mind. "We're getting them experience by bringing them here to Newmarket, though, so I think they will win a later race or two. Right now, we're accustoming them to the crowds and the excitement."

Thomas brightened. "What about Sovereign?"

"Golden Sovereign will be racing against stallions of all ages and experience, but he is ready to run, and"—she smiled broadly—"I wouldn't be surprised if *he* won."

"Oh." Philydia's eyes glowed. "That would be splendid! I shall keep my fingers crossed."

"Please do!" Regina was going to do the same. She was anxious that these, her first races in England, should go well. More than well. And above all, she wanted to win this owner-arranged one. To be truthful, she wanted Sovereign to win over Taskford's Talisman. To be more truthful still, *she* wanted to win over Taskford.

"Good morning, Mrs. Landry."

She spun around at the sound of his voice and found the object of her thoughts standing just behind her. She backed up a step, telling herself it was merely so that she could see him better. He looked splendid, of course, in a blue coat, a mustard suede vest, and doeskin breeches that clung to his muscular thighs like a second skin.

"Your lordship." She bowed her head in greeting and wondered why she felt so dowdy in the soft gray riding habit she'd made her uniform for track wear.

"How does it look for the 'Stallions of All Ages' Race to-morrow?"

"Talisman rested well. He settled in quietly and the work he's done was easy. He performed it satisfactorily."

"How do you know?" His gaze locked with hers. "You weren't here for any of it."

Ah, so the Earl was like so many other owners she had known. When it came right down to it, winning took precedence over everything—even good manners. She let him see just a touch of scorn in her eyes. "I know because Mr. McFeeters was here. He followed my instructions to the last period. I trust him implicitly to see to the welfare of your horses as well as to carry out my orders."

A little respect dawned behind his eyes. "How . . ."

Mathers pushed up beside Taskford and removed his hat. Courtesy demanded that he do no more than tip it when outdoors, but he wanted to show up the fact that Taskford had neglected to do even that. "If I may be allowed to finish my host's sentence . . ." he turned his head and directed his next words like darts at his friend "and mend his rotten manners." He turned back to Regina. "How do you do this morning, Mrs. Landry?"

Regina recognized the little byplay for what it was, and laughed. "I do very well, thank you. And you?"

"Except for my disappointment at not getting to see Halidon run, I do very well."

"So the rumor has been confirmed?" Regina was keenly interested. "Halidon has been withdrawn from the race?"

"'Fraid so. Belding is putting it about that he's sprained a pastern. Says he's not taking any chances with him."

Taskford said, "Pity. I haven't seen Halidon since we used to race in the army. I hear he's picked up quite a turn of speed. I was looking forward to watching him go."

"Ah, well. There's always next time."

"If you gentlemen will excuse me," Regina turned to leave, "I want to give my jockeys further orders."

"Efficient, isn't she?" Mathers watched Taskford carefully.

Harry stared after Regina. "What?" He looked distracted for no more than an instant. "Oh, yes. She is. That's why I wanted her as my trainer."

"She certainly left in a rush. Are you sure she wasn't made uncomfortable?"

"What do you mean?" Harry's hot gaze was narrow-eyed.

"Well, dear lad, you do have quite a tendency to leer at our Mrs. Landry." Blysdale strolled up to them as he finished speaking.

Mathers added, "You know, drool, slobber and so forth."

Harry laughed and ordered, "Be quiet, both of you. No doubt Mrs. Landry simply wants to change her race strategy now that she knows about the withdrawal of the favorite."

"So Belding really did pull Halidon?" Bly frowned. "I begin to wonder if we're ever going to see that horse run."

Smythe came up just then, his expression harried. "Gentlemen. Come. My groom is holding our spot, but without a member of the Quality in the rig, someone's liable to shove him out of line."

Harry frowned. "Why the blazes didn't you stay with it and send him for us?"

"Couldn't, Taskford. Have to go invite Mrs. Landry to grace us with her presence. That's why I had to be the one to come. Can't send a groom on an errand like that, you know." He spun on his heel and made off toward the stables.

The others shook their heads and started toward the choice spot in which Smythe had parked his phaeton. Just as Smythe had anticipated, two Corinthian bucks in a yellow-wheeled curricle were attempting to browbeat his groom into giving up his place to them.

"Sorry, gentlemen," Harry grinned at the sportsmen as he swung himself up into the phaeton. "Better luck next time."

Smythe, meanwhile, was hurrying to the stables. He passed the racehorses coming out. They were groomed to within an inch of their lives and all tacked up, jigging along with their personal grooms holding onto them for all they were worth. The six jockeys strolled along behind, discussing the way Mrs. Landry had instructed each and every one of them to do their best to win—to ride for the roses. They kept her special orders concerning their specific mounts to themselves.

Smythe went on past them, looking for the lovely trainer. He rounded a corner and saw her just ahead. She was opening a letter. Suddenly, before he got to her, she sat down on a tack box and put her face in her hands.

Seeing her obvious distress, Smythe hurried forward.

"Mrs. Landry! What is it?"

She looked up, her eyes full of tears, her expression that of a person whose mind is far away. "Oh, Mr. Smythe. It's you."

"Well. Hmmmm, yes, it is." He smiled shyly, his eyes still full of concern for her. "I came to invite you to sit in my phaeton with the lot of us from Taskford's. It's quite advantageously placed. You'll have the very best view of the race."

"Why, thank you." Her voice was husky with unshed tears, her polite smile was strained. "I should love to."

His voice became soft and gentle. "Won't you tell me what's the matter, Mrs. Landry. Is there any way I can help you?"

Regina started to give him a gentle reminder that she was not his concern. But his smile was so dear, and his eyes so completely kind, that it disarmed her. She blinked back more tears and took a shaky breath. Her voice quivered as she said, "Oh, Mr. Smythe, why is it that we can stand proof against ugliness but fall apart completely when offered friendship?"

"I have never known. But you needn't fall apart, my dear. A twofold cord is not easily broken. Together, friends can conquer anything. You've just admitted that you think of me as a friend. Won't you tell me what the trouble is?"

"There is nothing you can do, but it is sweet of you to offer to help."

"If I can do nothing else, I can share your burden. Sharing a burden makes it lighter, my mother always says. And I know that this must be a terrible burden, for you are a strong woman, and would not bend under less than a terrible load."

She sighed. "Yes. It is terrible. It's terrible because it's a burden that tears at my heart." She smiled at him tremulously and tried to turn his mind from her problem. "And you're just the sort of person who would have a dear mother like that."

His eyes told her he understood her attempt at diversion and that he refused to be diverted. "So what is our burden?"

She gave in to his gentle probing. "It's the children. Oh, not that they're the burden. They're wonderful. It's that my cousin, Jasper Ruddleston, wants to take them out of my custody so that he may use their inheritance to pay his gambling debts. I've been fighting him in the courts, of course." She made a despairing little gesture. "This letter from Mr. Bagwell, my solicitor, tells me that he has done all he can. Unless I marry before the month is out, Jasper will have won."

A horn sounded.

Smythe looked at her long and hard, his eyes grave. Finally he said only, "There's the call to the post. We must go now if we don't want to miss the race."

Regina swallowed her tears, lifted her chin and took his arm. Before she could go grieve in solitude, she must certainly watch the race. She was grateful she had someone as perceptive as her new friend, Smythe, to watch it with.

Twenty-two

The horses thundered toward the finish line, lathered necks outstretched, fighting for the lead. Regina's favorite colt from Charnwood, a feisty little gray, was in second place, straining to pass Taskford's leggy bay colt. Regina was thrilled! Her faith in him was justified. Warm satisfaction rose up under the excitement of the race.

On they came, legs flashing, hooves cutting through the moist earth left by the light rain of the night before. Great gouts of turf sailed through the air behind them as their iron-shod hooves sliced them from the earth. They galloped on in seeming silence, the sounds of their quick, labored breathing and the pounding of their hooves drowned out by the deafening roar of the crowd.

A last lunge, and the gray colt thrust ahead. The Charnwood entry had won! Regina had all that she could do to remain quiet, to hold to the dignity that no one expected to see in a female horse trainer—to remember, for the sake of driving that point home to others, that she was a lady.

Inside, her spirit was leaping with joy. When her host turned to congratulate her, she had to rein herself in tightly.

It wouldn't do to throw her arms around Taskford and give him a hug that would put a bear to shame! But she wanted to. Oh, how she wanted to!

She wanted to share with him the triumph she felt. She had won her first race as a trainer here in England! She felt as if she were fizzing—like champagne—with the sheer joy of her victory. Most important of all, it was the first race she had won for Charnwood—and for her brother's children.

Her mind was absolutely babbling! The Two Thousand Guineas! Open to all three-year-olds, both colts and fillies, the race was gaining prestige quickly with horsemen everywhere. And Charnwood's colt had won. She could actually feel her smile.

She could also feel Taskford's gaze on her. She turned to find him watching her, his deep blue eyes assessing. Daring her.

Suddenly, she was very glad that she hadn't hugged him when she'd had the urge.

That evening, with the running of the Two Thousand Guineas over, the atmosphere was calmer than it had been. Regina took the children down to the dining room for dinner. She meant it as a consolation for having insisted that they not attend the race. Winnie, of course, accompanied them. As a dinner it was passable. As a consolation it wasn't even that good.

"I still don't see why you couldn't take *me*." Thomas's beautiful little-boy face was sullen. "I, after all, am a man!"

Philydia fired up instantly. "A man? That's absurd! You're only a little boy! If girls can't go, then certainly little boys can't go, either."

Winnie glanced at Regina's face. She sensed what was coming.

Philydia looked at her aunt. "You said that children and

unmarried *ladies* never attended race meets because the gentlemen get so excited that they forget themselves with respect to their language."

"Yes, dear. They do." Regina braced herself. Lydia so often came to the surface in her daughter at moments like this. She wasn't mistaken. She recognized Lydia's haughty look of condemnation on Philydia's face.

"Then, am I to conclude you are not a lady?" Philydia challenged.

Regina put a hand out to still Thomas's indignant sputter. She rested it lovingly on his. Had anyone asked, she couldn't have told them whether she held his hand to comfort the child or to comfort herself.

After a long moment, she said, "Darling, I am a lady born and bred, and nothing can ever change that. Circumstances in life, however, do often change lesser things." She took a deep breath and continued in spite of her strong disinclination to share details of her earlier struggle. "When my husband, your Uncle Brandon, died—"

"You should have come home!" Philydia's eyes were hard.

Regina turned her face to the window. Though she looked at the sky with its lovely sunset, she saw nothing. She was seeing a frightened girl kneeling beside her young husband's deathbed and praying frantically that someone would come to take her home.

"Why didn't you come home?" Philydia all but flung the words at her. Her voice became a hiss. "Why did you have to go and take a job only suited for a man? Why did you have to sully our family name?"

Across the table from Regina, Winnie stood so abruptly her chair almost went over backwards. "That's it! That's absolutely it!" Deep anger marred her usually placid face. Fury simmered in the voice she attempted to hold to a whisper.

"I'll tell you why she didn't come home, Miss Philydia Ransome!"

Regina tried to interrupt, to stop her. "Please . . ."

Winnie gave her an impatient look and stormed at Philydia in a quiet voice not one whit less angry than a shout would have been. "She didn't come home because no one invited her. She couldn't come home on her own because she had no money to buy passage. She didn't come home because your Papa, God rest his soul, didn't go and get her. Her. His only family and his *baby* sister." She took a breath that rasped in her anger-constricted throat. "He didn't go get her because he was influenced by his wife—your mother—one of the meanest-spirited women it has ever been my misfortune to meet."

Regina gasped. "Winnie, I forbid—"

The usually imperturbable, sweet and motherly Mrs. Winstead turned on her like a snake. "You can forbid all you like, Miss Regina, but it is past time Philydia heard where she gets her unfailing ability to be so easily unkind!" She whipped back around to face the girl. "I've tended you all your life, Philydia Ransome, just as I did Miss Reggie before you. And I've always loved you. I always will. But as you grew more and more like your mother, I've not liked you. I've not liked you one bit. Not one little bit."

Philydia's face blanched.

Men closest to them were beginning to notice Winnie.

Winnie gave them a quelling glance, but did sit down again.

The men went back to their conversation, but watched from the corners of their eyes.

Thomas was squeezing Regina's hand almost as hard as she was squeezing his. Neither felt the discomfort.

Winnie was still all but whispering to Philydia. "I've held and held my tongue and tried to change you by love and good example, Philydia Ransome. But the time has come to tell you plainly that if you don't change your nasty ways, you can jolly well go on and grow up to be the viper your mother was. But you are going to do it without me!"

With that, Winnie stood up again, threw the napkin she'd held balled up in her hand onto the table, spun on her heel and stalked out of the dining room.

Absolute silence followed her exit.

Finally, in a very small, stunned voice, Thomas said into the deathly silence, "But they were *our* horses. Our very own Charnwood horses. We should have been able to go watch them race."

Regina hardly knew how she got the children up to bed. There was nothing she could say. Winnie had said it all.

Winnie had said too much. Regina hadn't wanted Philydia to know that her mother had been the major factor forcing Regina into her present socially unacceptable position.

When the children were tucked up, she kissed them both. She gave the now thoroughly repentant Philydia a hug. "It's all right, Philydia. Never mind."

"Will you ever forgive me?" Philydia sniffled.

"Of course, I've already forgiven you."

"But it's not all right. Winnie said that—"

Regina handed her a handkerchief and cut her off. "I think the point that Winnie was trying to make, dearest, is that you really should make a decision, right now, about what kind of a person you want to be." She looked deep into her Philydia's eyes, encouraging her. "You'll need the handkerchief for your tears, I'm afraid. Such decisions are never easy, you see, nor pleasant." She smoothed back the girl's hair and kissed her on her forehead. "I know you'll make the right choices. You just need to think about them for a while."

The lump in the bed beside and above them went, "Hrrrump!"

Regina fought down her smile. "I can't sleep yet, but I shall be back soon. Sleep well."

"I love you, Aunt Reggie!" Thomas blurted it as if he was afraid he'd never get another chance to tell her.

Regina smiled and told him softly, "I love you, too, Thomas. I always have."

Philydia began to sob.

Regina hesitated, then squared her shoulders and left the room. Some things one simply had to work out for oneself in growing up. Much as she would have liked to gather her niece in her arms to console her, she didn't. This battle was Philydia's alone.

As she slipped out the side door of the inn, she shook her head. There was nothing to be done. Winnie had been in rare form. The cat was, very definitely, out of the bag, and that was that. Philydia had been told the harsh truth about her mother. She, in her turn, however, had made it perfectly clear how she felt about her only aunt.

The aunt, Regina decided, would wait until tomorrow, after the big race, to ask herself how she felt about that. Right now, in spite of Philydia's contrite request for forgiveness, she was still a little numb.

She chuckled anyway. Who would have thought that her beloved Winnie could be such a termagant? No doubt by the time she returned to the room, Winnie would have softened and made everything all right.

As for right now, she was certainly far from sleeping. She might as well go down to the stables and check on the horses.

There was light at one end of the shed row, and men moving around a horse. Regina decided to check and see what that was about. After all, if there was a situation in which she could help, she certainly wanted to be of assistance.

It was only someone readying a horse for shipment home, however. The horsebox stood open and waiting, its floor deeply covered in fresh straw. She felt her shoulders relax, and realized that she'd been tense while approaching the light. One of her own men was there, so nothing untoward could be taking place, despite the lateness of the hour. She spoke to him softly. "Good evening, O'Ryan."

"Ah, Miss Reggie. Good evening." He gestured to where a powerful chestnut stallion stood in the cross-ties. "I was just having a look at the favorite here before he goes home."

"So this is Halidon. He *is* a handsome boy." Regina looked him over admiringly from the white star on his face to the tall white stocking on his right hind leg. "It's easy to see why he would have such a turn of speed. He's absolutely lovely."

"Why, thank you, pretty lady."

Regina turned to see a stocky man of medium height and military bearing. Proper etiquette dictated that she not speak to a man with whom she was unacquainted, but as a horse trainer, she laid no claim to good form for a lady. She made her voice cool. "You're welcome." She turned back to the horse, offended by the man's form of address. Mentally she shrugged. If she would walk alone to stables after dark, she must expect the occasional insult, after all.

O'Ryan placed his slender form between his superior and the strange man. "Mrs. Landry is the trainer for both the Charnwood Stud and the Taskford Stud." He added stiffly, "Sir."

The man laughed. "Forgive me. I see, Mrs. Landry, that I have offended your man. I hope I have not offended *you*. If I have, please, please forgive me."

Regina turned back to face him. Her gaze met his steadily

and she said with deliberation, "I forgive you. I'm sure you were misled by my presence here, unescorted."

Regina was pleased to see him redden at the inference that he was less of a gentleman to unescorted females than he would have been to one with an escort.

"May I introduce myself, Mrs. Landry?" At her regal nod, he continued. "I'm Sir Ralph Belding, from Essex. If I may be of any service to you, I hope you will call upon me."

Regina took his offer for the mere social convention that it was and focused on the horse. "Which leg did he strain?"

"The right hind. I've always believed that white on a horse's leg weakens it. Don't you think so?"

Regina supposed she didn't like the man because of his initial greeting to her. Whatever the case, she wasn't in the mood to avoid possibly offending him in turn. "No. Actually, I've never found anything to support the premise that white signifies weakness." Then she had to be fair. "Except that sometimes a white hoof is not as flinty as one could wish."

"Perhaps that is it." Annoyance underlaid his remark.

Regina watched with an expert's eye as the grooms led Halidon to the horsebox and loaded him into it. She saw no sign of lameness and was glad he'd recovered from whatever injury he'd done himself. His owner was being careful of him. That was good to see. Too many times she'd seen owners run horses who were unfit to race simply to satisfy their own vanity.

The Jockey Club, however, was making a great deal of difference, now. Soon, she hoped, they would have things so well in hand that bad owners wouldn't be able to put their horses at risk just to enjoy being able to tell their friends they had a runner in the race.

The fact that Belding was removing his horse for fear of possible injury cancelled out any irritation she had felt toward the man. It was with a genuine, if reserved, smile that she told him, "Have a pleasant journey home. I shall look forward to seeing your horse run at another meet."

Nodding her slight bow, she left him standing there. She wanted to go and check on her own charges.

She greeted the men from Charnwood and Taskford Stud, glad to see they were beginning to get along, putting aside their natural competitiveness, drawn together by the mutual bond of the horses they cared for. Finding all was well with her horses as well as with the men she had ordered to sleep near them, Regina returned to the inn.

O'Ryan walked with her.

Regina said, "Thank you, O'Ryan. I am truly appreciative of your escort. I shouldn't have been walking about alone here. It is not the same as being in one's own stable, is it?"

"Aw, miss. It's just that you're in the good habit of checking things at home, and forgot, like."

"Quite so." They had reached the inn. "Thank you."

The groom touched his forelock and hurried back off to the stable area.

Regina went into the inn and stood, irresolute. The upset earlier with Philydia continued to bother her. She had so hoped that things were improving between them.

Deciding she still wouldn't be able to sleep, she went out onto the little side terrace in the garden to sit awhile. A bout of sober thought seemed in order.

She was deeply distressed to find that she was an embarrassment to Philydia. Disappointed, too, that the girl refused to understand the necessity for her aunt's actions. But then, once the child admitted that she did understand, she would be tacitly expressing disapproval of her late father. Certainly that was the last thing Regina wanted her to do. It was hard enough for Philydia to admit—by not rising vehemently to her defense—that her sainted mother might have had a fault.

Like squirrels in a cage, her thoughts ran around. Her mind refused to quiet. She was far too restless to go to bed. Sighing, she leaned her head back against the stone wall behind her bench. Inhaling the sweet fragrance of an early rose, she began to relax.

Why must life always be so complicated? Why couldn't it be just a little more . . .

Suddenly she was listening to the low voices of two men at the other end of the garden. Had she really heard the name "Talisman"? Bolt upright on the bench, she strained to hear.

"Aye. We've nobbled him."

"How can you be sure?"

"Simple. Just pulled a hair from his tail and fixed him up good."

"How?"

"Yer wants to know all my secrets now?"

"I want to be certain you've done something that will work, you fool."

"Awright, Awright. We took the hair from his tail . . ." Wind rustled the leaves of the rosebushes, and Regina missed his next words. She was horrified to hear him finish his sentence. "It'll cut that big vein in his hind leg clean through when he goes to stretch out in tomorrow's race."

"Good enough. Go. Be sure you're nowhere to be found on the morrow."

The gate in the garden wall creaked. Regina sat perfectly still.

A minute later the gate creaked again, and she knew that she was now alone in the garden. Rising quickly, she glanced down at her pale blue dinner dress and made an impatient sound. If she were to go creeping out to the horses alone, she would need her cloak. In the pale blue gown, she'd look as luminous as a phantom. Changing it was out of the question. She'd be certain to wake Winnie if she tried.

Her cloak, she decided, would cover the gown completely, and render her one of the shadows.

She'd need a sharp knife, too, to cut the hair when she found it. She knew the trick, but how the devil they had managed to sew the tail hair around the large vein on Talisman's inner hind leg, she had no idea. Had they doped him? He wasn't the most tractable of stallions. In fact, it was a miracle they hadn't gotten their heads kicked off!

Hurrying up the stairs, she wondered if she should arouse Taskford. It was his horse, after all. He had put *her* in charge of the mighty stallion when he'd forced her to become his trainer, however. She'd die before she'd let him think that she was unequal to the task. Besides, she hadn't time. Every moment counted now!

She let herself into the bedchamber she shared with Winnie and the children and quietly crossed the room to get her cloak. Opening the door to the old armoire was a tedious process, as it creaked and she had no desire to awaken the sleepers. It seemed to take eons to open it, remove her trusty friend from its hook and quietly close the wardrobe again, but at last she was gone, letting herself out and closing the door with infinite care. She tiptoed to the stairs and hurried down them.

Twenty-three

Harry was just being helped from his coat when a sharp knock sounded at the door. He and Williams exchanged a glance. The hour was late. Before either man could move, the knock sounded again, sharper, more urgent.

"Let be." Harry shrugged his coat back up on his shoulders. Striding purposefully to the door, he yanked it open.

There was a quick movement at the end of the hall near the back stairs, and another closer to him. He lost all interest in the one near the stairs when he saw that the one right next door was made by Regina, swathed in her old campaign cloak, moving toward the other stairs leading to the front door of the inn.

Harry closed the door behind him to hide in the shadows of the hall. Jealousy hit him like a charging stallion. Why was she sneaking out of the inn so wrapped up that no one could identify her? What could possibly take her from the inn at this hour of the night? He corrected himself—morning. *Whom* was she rushing to meet?

He jumped back and pressed against the wall when she glanced over her shoulder, hoping she hadn't seen him in the shadows of the dimly lit hall. When she turned at the foot of the stairs and ghosted along the downstairs hall toward the back of the inn, Harry was puzzled. The kitchen? What the devil was she after in there?

The answer wasn't long in coming. Slipping up to the door, he looked into the still-warm, dark kitchen. He saw Regina peer around for a split second, her lovely face bronzed by the faint light from the small fire left burning in the huge cooking fireplace. An expression of satisfaction came over that lovely face. She went to the butcher's block to the right of the great table on which dinners were put together to be served to the inn's guests, and snatched up a knife.

While Harry looked on from the shadows behind the door she'd just entered, Regina tested the knife on her thumb, nodded slightly, and, hiding it under her cloak, left the inn through the door leading to the kitchen garden.

Harry followed at a safe distance. Had she stolen the knife for self-defense in an adventure she had no business attempting? What in blazes was she doing out at this time of night? What *was* the blasted woman up to?

He could feel his temper rising. And what the blazing hell was it about this woman that she could put him in such a pelter? Hitherto, no woman had ever been able to do that to him. They simply hadn't been that important.

He crossed the kitchen as soon as she'd left it and slipped out the door after her. Keeping a safe distance, he followed her through the kitchen garden, out the back gate, and down to the path leading toward the racing stables.

Fifty yards ahead of him, Regina hurried down the path in long, free strides. Her head was high, her cloak swinging to the rhythm of her graceful movements. With her mind on the safety of Taskford's stallion, Talisman, she had no idea she was being followed. Aware that stealth might be wise for her own safety, however, she slowed as she approached the line of stalls in which Talisman was housed.

She was instantly alarmed. The scene before her was devoid of a single person. Why were there no men on duty? She had been at great pains to see to it that there were men on watch. What had become of them? Made cautious by the fact that she saw no one, she put her back against the wall and slithered around the corner. Her toe struck something soft. The weight of the object staggered her.

She looked down. It was the Taskford head groom, McFeeters! "Oh, dear God!" The exclamation was jolted from her. Bending down to him, she whispered, "McFeeters!" Dropping to her knees beside his still form, she put her head to his chest. Oh, thank God! His heart was beating strongly.

The rhythm was strangely slowed, however. She peeled back one of his eyelids. In the light of the lantern just down the way, she saw that his pupils were wide. Only a narrow rim of blue iris showed around them.

Realization dawned. "Drugged!" She kept her voice barely a whisper. "Oh, heavens, McFeeters." She told him as if he could hear her, "You've been drugged!"

That explained how the men she'd overheard had gotten to Talisman. But who were they? Who had done this? And where were her other men?

Rising slowly, carefully, her gaze darting from shadow to shadow, she went in search of them. She had stationed three grooms from Charnwood down here with the horses, and two grooms in addition to O'Ryan and McFeeters from Taskford. "Dear Lord, please let them be safe," she murmured, taking comfort from the prayer.

Harry, unaware of her discovery, watched from his place of concealment as she reappeared. He couldn't get closer without her seeing him cross the open space to the shed row of stalls. He was pinned where he stood. From this vantage point he had a good view of the area. He could watch to see whom it was that his Amazon had stolen out to meet.

Back at the inn, Stone and MacLain were doing their own assigned watching. "There he goes!" Stone nudged MacLain awake.

"Wha'? Who?"

"Conway, you dolt."

Mac shook himself the rest of the way out of slumber. Blysdale's plan to keep Harry safe certainly played the very devil with a man's sleep. Stone and he had to trade off just like standing watches in the army. He might be used to it, but he sure as hell didn't like it.

Peering across the common at the door of the inn where Harry's cousin, Melvin Conway, was staying, MacLain could make out the man's slender form standing on the porch. As he watched, Conway threw a look back over his shoulder and glided down the steps. Taking long, loping strides, he headed in the direction of the stables.

"Stone! Hurry! He's on the move."

Stone cursed fluently. "Keep him in sight!"

"Hurry!"

Stone and MacLain slipped out of their own inn and followed Taskford's cousin Conway at a discreet distance.

In yet another inn, Blysdale awakened with a start. "What was that?"

Mathers moaned and asked, "Wh' waz wha'?"

Smythe bolted upright. "Someone is scratching at the door!"

Blysdale was out of the bed in a flash, his nightgown flapping about his long, hairy legs. Crossing the room, he threw open the door. Taskford's valet stood in the hall. "What news, Williams?"

"He's gone, Mr. Blysdale. Someone knocked at his door, and he was off like a shot. I followed just long enough to see that he was heading for the stables, then I came here for you."

"Good man!"

All three of the room's occupants began throwing on their clothes.

Williams's eyes rolled heavenward. Such shameful disregard for sartorial excellence caused his valet's heart actual pain. As proof of their concern for his master, however, nothing could have been more convincing.

As a man, the four of them rushed from the inn and headed for the stables.

Melvin Conway, unaware he was being followed, hurried to his objective. His heart was in his throat. Suppose the signal had been ignored? Or not given? The man he'd hired to knock at the door might have been intercepted. Might have been discovered and sent away. Might have been frightened off.

What if he got to the stables and his quarry hadn't come? Dear Lord, how would he handle that? He'd waited for weeks, ever since he'd been told that Harry had inherited the Taskford title and wealth. Now, finally his chance had come. His whole life hung on the events of the next half-hour.

Anxiety gave speed to his stride. The shed row of stalls that was his destination came into view. The stallion that insured the presence of the person he hunted was stabled there.

His nerves were aquiver. He was about to take the decisive step that would guarantee his future. For the rest of his life, he would live in blissful comfort if all went as he hoped it would. Conway put his hand inside his coat and drew courage from the feel of smooth metal. In just a few more moments . . .

Regina found the other two of her grooms before she got to Talisman's stall. She tried for a long minute to revive them, but to no avail. Heavy snores attested to the fact that they'd be unavailable for several more hours.

At least, the men were not injured. She sent a "thank you" skyward for that.

Now, though, she must see to the huge black stallion all by herself. Not the wisest policy. Especially in her present attire. In her slippers, she might as well have been barefoot, and the thought of having her toes mangled wasn't a pleasant one. She mentally chided herself for her foolishness in coming without having changed her footwear. But how was she to have known that there wouldn't be men to help her, experienced horse handlers to do her bidding? Heaven knew she'd brought enough of them to Newmarket with her! With a sigh of exasperation, she picked up a lead line and went into Talisman's stall.

Talisman moved to meet her quick as a snake, his movements abrupt, aggravated. Highlights on his well-groomed satin hide glinted with the speed of them.

Regina sighed with relief. No one had doped him, that was certain.

Seeing Regina enter the stall alone was more than Harry, ghosting along closer in the shadows now, was prepared to stand still for. He might have inadvertently let her discover his unconscious men unaided and uncomforted—even take a perverse pleasure in finding that she hadn't swooned on finding them, but he wasn't going to let her do this!

Having found that the first two men were only drugged, he'd assumed she'd encounter no worse with the next. He had let her hover over her two Charnwood grooms just to admire her courage.

Admiring her courage at finding unconscious men, however, was quite a different thing from letting her enter the stall of a fractious stallion alone. He'd be damned if he was going to let her try to handle Talisman without assistance. Abandoning all pretense of stealth, he rushed to help her.

Regina was just inside the stall. Talisman stood blowing down his nostrils and regarding her with hostile eyes.

"Stay back." Harry barked the order at her over the stall door.

Regina turned smoothly and quietly to face him. Her nerves had been tense to begin with, his unexpected appearance jolted them further. "What are *you* doing here!"

Harry moved into the stall. "This *is* my stallion, Mrs. Landry."

"Granted, but you know him no better than I do. You haven't had him that much longer!" It didn't matter that she wasn't making any sense. She was frantic that he would be hurt. He didn't know that Talisman had just recently been abused.

Taskford's tone was dry. "I spent ten years in His Majesty's cavalry, Amazon. I think I can manage not to get killed by my own blasted horse."

She didn't have time to argue with him. Any moment now the big horse might spraddle his legs and make the twine-strong horsehair taut enough to cut through the big vein it had been fastened around. Blood would spurt all over the place. Who knew how much of it Talisman would lose before they could quiet him enough to stop the bleeding? He'd be months recovering from the loss of blood!

"Hold his head, then." Regina was no stranger to giving orders, either. "I must see . . ." Regina handed him the lead line and eased down the side of the big black to his rump.

Talisman tensed and bunched his hindquarters.

"Take care! He's ready to kick!" Taskford forced the horse's head high, minimizing the chance of a full-powered kick in Regina's direction.

The stallion obliged by rising on his hind legs.

Regina cried, "Down. Down! Oh, do get him down!" For the first time, Harry heard fear in her voice. "He could be hurt. There's a . . ."

Harry, his body glued to the stallion's shoulder where he couldn't be struck at, shouted at her. "Damn the blasted horse. Take care of *you*!"

With a strength born of his fear for her safety, Harry yanked Talisman sideways. The stallion, caught by surprise, was momentarily off balance. Hauling him over, Harry snubbed him tight to the heavy iron ring set into one of the support posts. He leapt to Regina at the horse's rump. The two of them stood with their bodies inches from the horse's hindquarters so that any kick would be a hearty shove, not a pile-driving punch with a pair of iron shoes on the end of it!

Harry, his arms tight around her, turned so that his body was the one that would be hit if the stallion kicked. His tone flat, his voice a bored drawl, he asked, "Would you mind telling me what we are doing back here?"

She squirmed to free one hand.

Harry permitted her to do so before he remembered the knife. He tried to grab her hand the instant he remembered, but she twisted away and slashed down around him toward the horse's hind legs. "My God, woman! Are you trying to hamstring the beast?" Fury radiated from him.

His anger was nothing to her own. "No, you dunce!" she hissed at him. "I'm trying to save him! Let go!" She brought her heel down on his instep. At the same time, she punched back at him with her elbow.

Harry cursed roundly. What the devil had ever caused him

to think that this woman needed his protection? He used the breath she forced from him to good purpose. "Blazing hell!"

Talisman, eyes wide and nostrils distended, was twisting around, too. He was trying to see what was going on behind him. If he'd been less curious, he would have kicked the two humans to pieces and been done with it. He shifted restively.

Harry moved to a safer place and held a disheveled Regina at arm's length. "What the devil do you think you're doing?"

She struggled to win free of him, panting, "I'm . . . trying to get . . . the horse tail hair out of your stallion's flesh!" She pushed so hard that Taskford staggered.

He struck his elbow on the latch to the low door at the back of the stall that led to a space for hay storage for owners who wished to bring their own fodder from home. "Dammit!"

Regina attempted to finish her explanation of the danger to Talisman, ". . . hind leg before . . ."

Suddenly Harry comprehended. He released her so quickly that she fell against the stall wall. He grabbed the knife from her with one hand and Talisman's tail with his other. Twisting the stallion's tail in such a manner that the horse preferred not to move, he reached between the muscular hind legs with the glittering blade of the knife to sever the hair.

Talisman rewarded this attempted service by exploding into a buck that sent the knife flying one way and the Earl the other.

Regina ran to him. She put a supporting arm around him. "Are you all right?"

"Thank you. I'm fine." He regarded her quietly, a strange look in his eyes. "You really are a most unusual woman, Mrs. Landry."

She colored, but refrained from speaking. What in the world could she say to that?

"How did you know something had been done to Talisman?"

"I overheard two men talking in the garden."

"Could you identify them?"

"No. They were only voices. One sounded like a gentleman, one a common thug."

"And they drugged our grooms."

"Evidently." Her eyes were troubled. "I imagine that the drug was put in their tea."

Harry grinned. "Judging by the way they're snoring, it was probably in their ale. I'll bet they don't wake until morning."

She laughed and Talisman rolled an eye at her. "I'm certain you're right about that." She broke her gaze from Taskford's with an odd reluctance. She had to see to the welfare of the horse. He was her job, after all, not Taskford's.

She moved toward the stallion. "There, there, boy. It's me. Reggie." She laid her hand on his rump as gently as she could.

His muscles quivered.

She rubbed a small circle on his satin hide. Over and over. Until he relaxed. When he blew a gentle breath through his nostrils, she released him from the short rope Taskford had used to keep them both safe and led him to another corner of the huge stall. There she stroked his neck and talked to him until he was calm. Still he eyed her intently. Since that was certainly not unusual for a stallion, Regina relaxed.

Harry spoke from where he leaned against the wall. "You're very good with him."

"It's my job." She said it simply as she checked the horse. She was just reaching to feel down the insides of the stallion's hind legs for the needle holes she expected when she caught a movement out of the corner of her eye.

Terrified, she screamed, "Taskford! Look out!" And launched herself at him.

As she bowled him over, Harry caught a glimpse of a cloaked figure at the stall door with a gun in his hand. It was the highwayman!

Blysdale and his group met up with Stone and MacLain on the way to the stables. "Harry's down here somewhere," Bly informed them tersely.

Stone grunted to show he heard. His gaze remained pinned to the figure of Melvin Conway, the man he was stalking.

MacLain told Blysdale, "We're right behind Conway." He pointed up ahead to where his quarry was approaching the end of the stallion barn. They all saw Melvin Conway withdrawing something from his pocket as he rounded the corner of the stallion stalls.

A shot rang out!

Stone and MacLain stormed around the corner and fell on Conway.

A woman shrieked.

Conway shouted, "Blast you! What the devil are you trying to do? You've made me drop it!"

Blysdale saw that the object Conway had dropped was not a gun. Chagrinned, he ordered Smythe, who was just catching up to them, "Stay here and find out what the . . ." He stifled his expletive in deference to the woman standing silently with her hand to her throat, her face hidden in the shadow of her cape's hood. "Find out what's going on here." With that he rushed off to find Taskford, the rest at his heels.

Smythe blushed. "Sorry, miss. We've skulduggery afoot here at the stables tonight. My friends and I are just trying to protect the Earl of Taskford." He glanced at the irate Conway. "Sorry, old man, but somebody's trying to kill Harry, and you do have a capital motive, don't you know. Being next in line, and all that."

"Kill him! Devil take you, Smythe, it's his being the heir instead of me that guarantees me the chance of being the happiest man on earth."

Smythe stared at him. "What?"

The lady in the cape stepped forward. As she did, she let her hood fall back.

Smythe gasped. "Well, bless my soul. You're Lady Sylvia Steppleford—"

"Smythe! I won't have her name bandied about in a stable!"

Smythe gaped at the season's reigning debutante in open astonishment. "May I ask what you're doing here, my lady?"

She smiled, and he was dazzled. "I'm here to accept a betrothal ring from Mr. Conway."

Her proposed fiancé muttered, "If we can find it," and, bent double, began inspecting the ground, kicking bits of bedding straw around.

Seeing Smythe's bewilderment, the debutante explained. "I had to talk my uncle into letting me come down with his horse, because it was the only way to escape my suitors for long enough to accept Melvin's proposal. You have no idea how pursued you are when you are the wealthiest girl in England."

"Yes," Smythe shook his head. "I'm certain that what you say is accurate, but Conway isn't going to be the Earl of Taskford. Harry is."

"Precisely," she cried triumphantly. She looked at him expectantly.

Smythe just looked even more baffled.

The beauty explained. "I have been so hunted for my money, that I absolutely refuse to have it said that *I* married a man who had any. It is all very well for some women to be made out fortune hunters by the *ton* but utterly absurd for me to be accused of it. I won't have it.

"So I'm going to marry Conway. Now that it is clear that he isn't going to be a rich man, that is. Which is why we have had to sneak around like this. So! Do you see now?" She beamed at him expectantly.

Smythe thought she had attics to let. He could almost see the bats flying in her belfry. This girl was a candidate for Bedlam as far as he was concerned. He didn't "see" a blessed thing! "Hmmmm," he managed. It wasn't much of an answer, but it was the best he could do.

He looked at the besotted Conway and said brusquely, "Well, if your happiness depends on it, then I'd better go help see to it that you *don't* inherit after all!"

With a hasty bow to the heiress, he rushed off in the direction his friends had taken, deeply anxious about the single shot he'd heard.

Twenty-four

Regina felt herself snatched up and borne across Talisman's stall to the back wall.

In one powerful lunge, Harry slammed into it, his own body absorbing the impact, Regina held tight to him. He clawed for the latch to the storage space door, released it and pushed her through.

"Oh, no, you don't!" Regina grabbed him around the neck and reared back as hard as she could.

Harry, who'd been set to charge out to confront his assailant before the man could reload, twisted back to face her as he fell, thrusting out his arms in an effort to keep from slamming down on her. As he fell, the shot from the highwayman's second pistol tore a long furrow in the surface of the door beside them.

Harry yanked the door shut.

Suddenly, in the dim quiet of the storage room, time stopped. Vaguely they heard shouting, running footsteps and the clatter of a horse making a hasty departure, but none of that mattered to the two of them. Now that they knew they were safe, none of that was real to either of them.

Reality was the closeness of their bodies, his lying on hers, crushing her into the fresh, fragrant straw. Reality was Regina's arms around his neck, her wide eyes full of anxiety for his safety, her soft lips half-open and trembling.

Reality was the fact that he wanted to kiss her more than he wanted anything. Let the bastard go to have another crack at him at a later date. Right now, just right now, it was imperative that he kiss Regina Landry. He lowered his head and claimed her mouth.

Regina clung to his shoulders with a strength born of the knowledge that she had nearly lost him. She returned his kiss with more fervor than she'd ever felt before. Danger heightened every sense, multiplied every sensation.

She was so grateful. Grateful that he'd not been killed. Shaking in the aftermath of the flood of outright terror that had gripped her, she kissed him with desperation.

Harry was set aflame. Memories flooded his mind, filled it with the recollection of other kisses, with memories of even more intimate caresses, with the memory of having claimed her body over and over in the long, sweet night of unforgettable passion that they had shared.

Emotions more heady than the most potent brandy surged through him. An unwanted question thrust its way into his mind. How had he been able to withstand this driving need he felt for her for so long? He moved one hand to Regina's thigh and began to push up her skirt. Urgency rode him, hard.

She moaned and twisted beneath him, but she never broke their kiss. Her body arched to meet his. . . .

"Taskford!" The shout was from just outside their hiding place. "Where the hell are you, Harry?" It was Blysdale's voice.

Oh, hell! Harry struggled back to the harsh world outside the sweet enchantment that Regina Landry was for him. He would have to answer. But first, just one more kiss. Just one more. He lowered his head, felt her breath fan his lips—

"Here!" Someone thumped the door behind which they lay. "Look! This is a bullet's gouge, I'll wager."

Harry lifted his head.

Regina chuckled.

Quickly he put her clothing back in order. "Damn," he whispered. Then he kissed the tip of her nose, shoved up and put a hand against the door. "Ready?"

"As I'll ever be." She was picking straw out of her hair.

"Here we are!" He forced his voice to normalcy, fighting to keep the husky note of his passion out of it. "Thanks to Mrs. Landry's warning, we're safe."

Pushing open the door, he bent low to exit it, and turning back, offered Regina a hand. They emerged to find a crowd at the door of the stall. Great God! Even his valet was there! Talisman was looking from them to their rescuers with lively curiosity.

"Talisman! I forgot to look at his wounds." She started toward the stallion.

Harry grabbed her arm and hauled her back to him. "There are no wounds."

"But there must be!"

"There are not." He smiled grimly at her bewilderment. Softly he told her, "It was a ruse—a trick to get me down here so that I could be . . . shall we say . . . eliminated."

"I don't understand. How could anyone be certain you would come? I didn't go get you, after all." She regarded him with troubled eyes.

"They knocked at my door when you left your room." His eyes burned down at her, and he frowned in concentration. "I suppose somehow they knew that if I saw you leaving, I'd follow you to the stables." Hell, he'd follow her to the ends of the earth!

"How—"

A voice interrupted. "Will the two of you come out of there and tell us what you were doing in there in the first place?" Blysdale sounded as if he were fast losing his patience.

Harry looked down into Regina's eyes. "It seems that Bly thinks explanations are in order, my dear." He placed his hand on the small of her back and guided her past Talisman. "Shall we go and make them?"

After the events of the past night, the new day's race was almost going to be anticlimactic. Arranged by the owners of horses ineligible for the Two Thousand Guineas that had been run on Wednesday, and the One Thousand Guineas that was scheduled for Friday, as well, it now seemed almost inconsequential.

Regina, of course, completely immersed in the last-minute readying of the two stallions, Sovereign and Talisman, was unaware of anything else. She was particularly concerned with Talisman, worried that the excitement of the night before might have kept him from resting and, in spite of his superb conditioning, taken the edge off him. After a few minutes with the stallion and his two grooms, neither of whom seemed to be suffering too many ill effects from having been drugged, she was reassured.

"More up to the mark than ever, 'e is, Miss Regina. Bursting right outer 'is skin. He should run like the wind today."

McFeeters added, "Maybe we should have somebody disturb his rest the night before every race."

The grooms laughed, as expected.

Regina was hard put to smile. "I'm glad he's all right. I'm glad all of you are all right." She looked around at them and at the other grooms and thanked God that they had suffered no ill effects from their drugging.

Unlike her, they obviously had no thought of thanking their maker that the drug had been a harmless one. None of them seemed to realize that the perpetrator could just as easily have used something that would have left all of them debilitated . . . or dead.

It seemed the man in the highwayman's black silk mask only wanted to kill Taskford.

Regina stood absolutely still, powerless to move. She shivered. The enormity of those three words swept over her. *Only kill Taskford.* How would she live if the world no longer held the imperious, exasperating man?

"Mrs. Landry!"

She spun around to the groom who'd called her name and knew by the look on his face that it wasn't the first time he'd called to her. Pulling herself back from the brink of her terrible thoughts, she moved quickly in his direction. Dear Lord. She'd been woolgathering when she should have her mind completely on this race. That had never happened before. And she was never going to let it happen again. "Yes, Job," she told the man. "I'm coming."

With Talisman attended to, it was time to ready Golden Sovereign for the race. She called herself sharply to order and went to do it.

Excitement was high. Even though one of the two nationally important Newmarket races had been run, many of the men who had come eagerly to Suffolk in order to watch the three-year-old colts fight it out in the Two Thousand Guineas on Wednesday and to see the three-year-old fillies run tomorrow in the One Thousand Guineas felt they were even more fortunate to be here in Newmarket for this interim race. After all, word was that Taskford had entered his black stallion, Talisman, and where Hard-hearted Harry was, there was always that extra thrill attached to the event.

Some were even saying that he'd set up the race just so that his horse could win over the Charnwood Stud's Golden Sovereign. Sovereign was trained by the late Viscount Charnley's daughter—the one who had ruined herself when she was sixteen by running off to Gretna Green with her drawing master. Never mind that he was Baron Landry's youngest son, and that they'd married. Then, the gossip went, when her husband had died, she'd put the cap on her ruin by becoming a horse trainer.

The word was that she was very attractive. And everybody knew the reputation of the newly elevated Taskford when it came to pretty widows. Things had been dull for the gossipers in the *ton* since he'd dropped the beauteous Lucretia Perryman. It was past time for him to do something new to relieve the tedium of their days with yet another of his amorous escapades. Many wondered if this was the time. Was he pursuing the Landry widow?

They were all avid to know just what it was he was up to. To a man, they considered themselves lucky to be here to observe, firsthand, Hard-hearted Harry in action.

At the stables, Regina discussed first with one jockey, then, at a distance from him, the other, the way she wanted each of them to ride their stallion to his best advantage. She instructed both of them to ride to win, and sincerely wished each of them luck. It was of paramount importance to her that neither jockey detect in her a hope that one of the stallions win over the other.

Smiling at the knowledge that soon all her work would be put to the test—and confident that it would prove her ability—she left the men to hurry back to the inn to change her once crisp white shirt and black twill skirt for the well-tailored dove-gray riding habit that had become her trademark when at railside.

Taking the shortcut through the inn's kitchen garden, she apologized as she went past the cooks, and started up the hall to the stairs at the front of the inn. As she passed the door to the second private parlor, she heard Taskford's voice, then those of the children. Concerned that they might be bothering him, she stopped to listen.

"And then what?" Thomas's voice was full of excitement.

"Why, then Wellington brought the cavalry forward and overran the French."

"And that saved the day, didn't it?" Philydia's voice was as excited as her brother's.

Regina went on her way up to her room to change with a full heart and a fervent wish that someday Taskford would realize how good he was with children. That someday he'd marry and have his own.

With all her heart, she wished that things might have been different. That she might have been the mother of his children, and Taskford the means to save Philip's for her. Things weren't different, however, and life was no fairy tale. Society would never stand for an Earl marrying a female horse trainer, and Taskford owed it to future generations of his line to heed its strictures.

She went up the stairs blinded by tears for what could never be. She chided herself for her foolishness and told herself she must be sensible and get busy seeking a husband— one far less illustrious that the Earl, no doubt—in order to protect Philydia and Thomas.

Right now, though, she had a race to win.

Twenty-five

The day was magnificent. The sky was filled with gray-shadowed mountains of luminous white clouds. Sunlight glinted off every surface that would reflect it. The horses' coats shone, bits and stirrups sparkled. There was no pleasant, diffused light such as that they had had for the running of the Two Thousand Guineas. No, this light had a sharp brilliance, a harshness that picked out every flaw—and Regina felt as if most of the men present were using it to scrutinize her.

Well, God knew she'd survived such inspections before, and as a woman presumptuous enough to excel at a man's job, she would no doubt be called on to survive them again in the future.

When she'd been younger and more vulnerable, the resentment she'd felt at their resistance to the fact that she was good at what she did had been overwhelming. She'd hated the fact that people wouldn't accept her for her abilities, that they'd criticized her for even attempting to train horses, certain she'd fail. Then, to her utter astonishment, they'd criticized her for her success!

One didn't die of unjust criticism, however, and she'd lived through it and become a stronger person because of it. She may have lost her universal love of mankind, but she was wiser now because she was less innocent. *Or less ignorant,* she thought with a twisted smile.

She felt only mild resentment now, however. She'd been in the crucible far too many times for it to cause her to feel any more than that. Her only concern was the way her horses were going to run. Golden Sovereign had become closely attuned to her in the weeks she'd been training him. She feared he might sense she was on edge and be marginally effected by it. She wasn't as worried about Talisman. He was in fine fettle in spite of his exciting hour in the middle of the night.

Dressed in her "uniform" and with her face carefully composed, she watched the horses being led away down the straight mile of the course to the starting post. She might look a bit grim, but that was to be expected. After all, she was about to watch a race. And the outcome of this race would greatly influence her career.

If someone had asked her, and if she were honest, she'd have to say that she didn't really care what these men thought. The opinion of people who judged someone without knowing them or their abilities never had mattered to her. Those who were critical inevitably changed their tune when her horses won.

She lifted her chin and surveyed those of the race crowd who were nearest her—those privileged to be here with the trainers and owners at the finish post. The coolness of her gaze won the approval of some, caused others to turn away.

Blysdale and Mathers made a point of bowing to her when her regard rested on them, offering her their support openly. Beside them, Taskford pretended to be looking at the horses. His casual stance was a clear attempt at proof that there was nothing between them. Evidently he didn't want to start a rumor that might be embarrassing for her.

Stone and MacLain were arguing about the horses and didn't even see her.

Smythe lifted his hat, spoke a word to his companions and picked his way through the crowd to come to her.

Regina smiled at him in greeting. "Good day, Mr. Smythe."

His eyes full of excitement, he told her, "Well, this is the big day. Now all these curmudgeons will find out what a splendid trainer you are. We'll hope for first and second place, shall we?" He was about to add something else when the shout came that, a mile down the track, they were lining up the horses for the start of the race.

All attention went to the man further down the straight mile course who had the office of starting the race. Every eye was glued to him. Except Taskford's. Regina could feel his gaze touch her like a caress. She met his regard. Their gazes held, and Regina's heartbeat accelerated.

Taskford moved as if he were coming to her. To meet her—for she was about to move, too, inexorably drawn to him.

"They're off!" The cry broke the spell and drove the crowd to frenzy. Men shouted at the top of their lungs and shook their hats above their heads until the very air around them seemed to be in motion with the excitement they generated.

The horses were running hard, each striving to outdo the others, each driving toward the finish line, determined to be first. Golden Sovereign and Talisman were among the first four in the race. Golden Sovereign was running easily, hanging just behind the horse in front, his head even with its rump. Talisman ran on the other side, in much the same position. Sovereign was listening to his jockey, Talisman was arguing with his—fighting for the bit.

Sovereign began to gain. The field passed the half-mile post with Sovereign drawing even with the shoulder of the lead horse. Talisman shot forward to the same position on the leader's other side. At the three-quarter mile post, the leading horse began to tire. Sovereign and Talisman surged forward to pass him and run neck and neck. They were so well-matched, neither could pull away from the other. They were only three lengths from the winning post, and neither horse was ahead! The crowd was holding its breath.

Regina thought her heart would burst. Her nails cut into the palms of her hands. She bit back the shout that rose in her throat.

The stallions were ahead of the field by two lengths, but neither was going to win! Then Talisman's jockey took to the whip.

Regina's eyes flared wide. She almost called out, "No!" She bit her lip. And the horses pounded past. At the stroke of the whip, they reached the winning post . . . and Talisman threw up his head.

"Golden Sovereign wins!" The cry went round the crowd. Men pounded each other on the back, pummeled each other's arms and screamed the news. "Sovereign won! Golden Sovereign won!"

One moment, Regina was weak with relief, the next she turned and hugged Smythe so hard he begged for mercy.

Then Taskford was there, smiling and offering congratulations. "We are even now, Charnwood Hall and Taskford Manor. A winner each. Talisman at home, and Golden Sovereign here. Well done!

"I propose a gala dinner tonight to celebrate. You will come, of course, Mrs. Landry? You trained the winner, as well as Talisman, who placed. You should be guest of honor."

"In lieu of Golden Sovereign." She laughed up at him. Their gazes caught and held. They stood looking into each other's faces a moment too long. Then Regina tore her gaze away.

She had to take a deep breath before she could say, "And here come the owners of Golden Sovereign." She made it an announcement. Her arm swept out in a grand gesture that ushered a blushing Philydia, a bouncing Thomas and their self-effacing chaperone, Winnie, into the winners' enclosure.

But she had stood too long looking at Taskford with eyes that betrayed her deepest feelings. Far too long. And he too' long at her. From across the grassy space occupied by the winner and his elated owners, a man took careful note of that.

Regina went directly from the winner's enclosure to the stables to see to the care of Sovereign and Talisman. When everything was done to her satisfaction and her excited men had settled down to the point that she was certain they would forget none of her orders, she was ready to think of herself and the rest of the evening.

With a heart gladdened by victory, she headed back to the inn, thankful, not for the first time, that Taskford had chosen lodgings within easy walking distance of the stables. She thought that she saw two men up ahead on the path, but they had disappeared before she got to the spot at which she'd seen them, so she relaxed and went on.

She supposed she was just oversensitive. Or simply more aware of how often she walked about alone since she'd been addressed with such familiarity by the owner of Halidon.

Next time she came to Newmarket, she would bring Tim Parson instead of leaving him in charge of things at home.

She couldn't help smiling as she imagined a picture of someone accosting her with the mountain that was Tim at her side! That picture kept a smile on her face as she ran up the inn steps, full of happy anticipation about Taskford's celebration dinner.

Regina took special pains dressing. When she had packed the pale satin dinner dress, she'd thought she was being frivolous, but now she drew it from the back of the armoire with a sense of real satisfaction. It was only a year old, and fortunately fashions hadn't changed since she'd ordered it for one of Sybella Dashwood's formal affairs.

Crossing to the mirror, she held the gown up in front of her and watched the play of light over the ivory satin, noted how the color lit her face and brightened her eyes. She wondered how she'd wear her hair. Soon she was lost in feminine concerns, her comfortably bedded horses no longer the primary thing on her mind.

The races were over, and she had added such luster to her name by having won the Two Thousand Guineas in her first year as a trainer here in England that she could rest for a while on her laurels. To have had the gray colt from Charnwood win that race was enough, but to have had Sovereign win the race against Talisman . . . well, her cup was running over. She was doing well, very well indeed . . . at least where horses were concerned.

Harry stood, with a glass of brandy in his hand, near the door of the public dining room of the inn. He had engaged this room for this party when he'd thought Talisman would be the winner of the race run earlier. Now, he was busy accepting congratulations for being a good sport and holding the party in spite of his horse having been beaten.

"Well, Harry. Just look at it this way. No matter which of the two best horses won, you'd still have had to have wined and dined us in honor of your trainer."

Harry smiled, but there was a hint of warning in his eyes. It was perfectly clear to the man making the remark that he'd best have a care in making any further statements about Taskford's female horse trainer.

The man walked away, and Harry stepped to the doorway to look out. He'd done that more times than he cared to remember. Where the blazes was she? Didn't she know that, in the absence of the two owners—children too young to be here—she was the sole guest of honor?

Across the spacious room, Mathers was saying to Blysdale, "There he goes again."

"Poor Harry."

"Yes. Do you think he suspects?"

"That he's in love with her?"

"Of course." Mathers frowned at him.

"I doubt it. Probably wouldn't admit it if he did."

Mathers considered that a moment. "You're right. Probably tell us not to be absurd."

"Unless we were Smythe, of course. Then he'd no doubt tell us he was deeply in lust and think of something else to add to shock us."

"Why does he do that to old Smythe? I know he likes him."

It was Blysdale's turn to consider. "I really don't know." He frowned again. "Possibly it's because Smythe takes everything so damned seriously." He grinned like a wolf. "I know that's why *I* tease him."

Mathers said, "Look. See how Taskford's face is lighting up. She must be coming."

"Yes." Blysdale smiled naturally this time. "Yes, I think she must."

They looked on Taskford as proud parents might regard a child slow in gaining maturity.

Harry, completely unaware of his friends' scrutiny, stepped into the hallway to meet Regina.

She looked up at him, her eyes glowing. She had one arm around Philydia, the other around Thomas. Winnie followed. "I thought you might not mind them coming just to say hello."

"And to be toasted." Harry smiled at the children.

The children's faces lit up. Thomas asked breathlessly, "Oh, could we be?"

"I should think so." Harry grinned down at the boy. "It was your horse that won the race today, wasn't it?"

"Indeed it was," the boy assured him. He nodded so hard that his hair flopped into his eyes. Brushing it back impatiently, he said, "It was Golden Sovereign!"

Philydia added very softly, "He was the last horse that my Papa bought."

Harry and Regina exchanged a meaningful glance. The air between them filled with a current so strong that Regina wondered if it could be seen. Her lips parted. She drew a quick breath, then smiled.

Harry stared into her eyes. His own filled with light, as if he had just discovered something of infinite importance.

Thomas said, "Sir?" and looked from one of them to the other, bewildered.

Harry gave a hearty laugh and scooped the boy up. With Thomas sitting on his arm, and Philydia holding his hand, he strode to the center of the room. "Gentlemen!"

All heads turned in his direction.

"Here are the owners of today's winner, Golden Sovereign. Permit me to present Miss Philydia Ransome, and Thomas, Viscount Ransome."

"Hear, hear!"

"A toast!" The cries went 'round the room. Finally Mathers stepped to the center with Taskford. Holding both hands high for silence, he announced, "I propose a toast." The room quieted instantly.

Under Blysdale's able direction, waiters moved among them with trays filled with glasses of champagne. Each man took one.

When they were all served, Mathers lifted his glass to the two children clinging to Harry. "To the Ransomes, Miss Philydia and Lord Thomas. May this be the first of their many victories!"

"Hear, hear!" The men raised their glasses and drank the toast in solemn unison.

Regina looked at Taskford and thought how wonderful it would be if they were his own children who were so trustingly clinging to him. His children . . . and hers.

Then it was over. The toast was drunk, Harry was putting Thomas back on his feet and smiling at the boy and Philydia. "I am so glad you could come," he told them.

The magic moment was over.

Winnie left to take the children, surrounded by their happy glow, back up to their room. Regina looked after them, grateful that Taskford had so graciously given them their first taste of glory.

Harry cleared his throat lightly, and Regina looked back from the disappearing children to see him offering her his arm and smiling broadly at her.

She placed her hand on his forearm and entered the waiting crowd of men at the Earl of Taskford's party.

Twenty-six

The dishes had been removed, but as Regina's was the only feminine presence at the party, the gentlemen laughingly declined having her withdraw so they could have their port. They said if she would stay, they would promise, each of them, to limit themselves to one single glass.

Regina hated to leave them and miss the conversation. She admitted this and graciously accepted their offer.

Conversation was lively at all the tables. The food had been good, the wine had flowed freely, and everyone was in an expansive mood.

"Splendid party, Taskford."

"Grand party, Taskford."

"Hear, hear!"

Then from the general babble of congratulations on the quality of his party came, "Strange party, Taskford! You're supposed to be the victor to throw a party like this one."

The man's laughing comment was taken up by more of his friends. "Yes, Harry! What have you to say for yourself?"

Harry laughed and raised his glass. "Only that, in my

magnificent conceit, I expected *my* horse to win!" He spread his arms wide in a parody of a Gaelic shrug. "Imagine my shock when I remembered that I'd forgotten to cancel the arrangements."

The crowd of men filling the dining room, Harry's friends from his lean years, laughed uproariously, wishing him well, glad for his good fortune.

Regina looked around at their faces with a rush of joy for him. It was a great thing for a man to have so many friends who genuinely cared for him. She could understand caring for him. Too well. Never had she loved him more.

She put on a bright smile and applauded with the others as he bowed.

Across the table, Smythe watched her with sympathetic eyes. He could see she loved Harry. It was plain as could be to anyone with half an eye. No doubt others could see it, too. But Harry could be such a block about some things, and the one he was hands-down most obtuse about was women.

Regina Landry was the perfect woman for him, but Smythe doubted Harry would ever realize it—or admit it. He sighed heavily, feeling like the specter at the feast. He only hoped Harry would come to his senses and admit that the gallant widow was made for him before Jasper Ruddleston came to take the children away.

Nice little devils, those children. Regina loved 'em, too. Pity.

MacLain glared at him. As the general cheering died down and the tables returned to the quieter brouhaha of conversations, Mac demanded, "What the blazes is the matter with you? This is supposed to be a party, not a wake, Mr. Longface."

"What?" Smythe was jolted by the fact that Mac even noticed him. Thinking fast, he grabbed the first negative thought that came to him and offered it as his excuse. "Oh!

Apologies, of course. I was just thinking that I'd missed seeing Halidon run again. Wanted to, you know. Shame about him spraining a pastern and all that."

Regina spoke up. "I saw him being readied for the trip home. He seemed fine. I'm certain it was only a minor sprain. We'll no doubt see him run a race soon."

Harry turned his full attention to her. "So you saw Halidon?"

"Yes. On one of my trips to the stables that night of all the excitement."

Harry's loins tightened in instant response to the memory of the night he'd lain with Regina Landry in the warm darkness of the hay storage behind Talisman's stall.

Blysdale asked, "What did you think of him?"

She turned serious gray eyes to him. "I thought he was one of the most magnificent horses I'd ever seen."

The simple statement seemed to make the men at the table uncomfortable. Finally Stone said, "You should have seen his brother, Cossack. Now that was a horse. Put Halidon in the shade every time." He brightened suddenly, remembering. "Cossack would have been Harry's had he lived. Ashley Stoddard left him to Harry in his will."

Harry was watching Regina intently. "Was Belding there?" Ralph Belding had an unsavory reputation with the ladies. Harry didn't like the idea of her having met him on one of her visits to the stables. He knew how a man like Belding would interpret her walking out at night alone.

Regina nodded at Taskford to answer his question, but kept her regard on Stone.

"What did you think of him?" Harry asked, his voice tight.

Still looking at Stone, Regina answered with deliberate innocence, "I can't imagine a horse better than Halidon. You were fortunate to know him."

MacLain laughed. "It was Harry that knew him. Like old friends, they were. That's one reason Harry was hit so hard when Ashley was killed. The man who found Ash dead had to destroy Cossack."

Regina reproached him for the bad taste of his comment, "Oh, Mac!"

MacLain had the good grace to blush. "I didn't mean he didn't care more about Ash," he muttered.

Harry was still staring at Regina, steely-eyed. "I meant, what did you think of *Belding*."

"Oh." She turned her attention to her host. She was surprised to find him so grim. Then she remembered Belding's disrespectful greeting to her and assumed Taskford was aware of the man's proclivity for insulting unescorted females.

How dear of him! She was flattered that he worried about her, but wasted no time defusing the situation. "I'm afraid I didn't get along too well with your friend. I disagreed with him, and he didn't like it."

Harry felt rage rising. His eyes burned with a blue flame. If Belding had offered her an insult . . . Another idea entered his mind. His hands knotted into fists. If he had touched her! If Belding had laid a single filthy finger on Regina! He half rose from his chair. He'd hunt him down and kill him!

Regina's eyes widened. What possessed Taskford? She hastened on with her description of what had happened between her and Halidon's owner. Her first few words tumbled over each other. "I disagreed with him that Halidon's right hind leg was weak because it was white. I allowed that I'd never seen any defect in any horse"—she saw with relief that Taskford's angry color was receding—"that was attributable to any white marking." She made a little moue of ruefulness. "Then I had to admit that sometimes a white hoof was a little harder to keep a shoe on, and that quite ruined the effect."

There was general laughter.

Harry had to be certain. "He didn't insult you in any way, then?"

Regina remembered the leer in Belding's voice when he'd called her "Pretty Lady," but didn't think this was the best time to mention it. "Why, no, Taskford." She pretended to recollect something. "And of course one of our men, O'Ryan, was with me, so I was completely safe from insult in any case. Why?"

Smythe answered her. "None of us liked Belding in the army, Mrs. Landry." He informed her solemnly, quietly, "He always had such an avid hunger to be the best, to have the best . . . it rather put a man off, don't you see?" He colored slightly at having decided to criticize a fellow officer, but went on, needing Regina to understand. "Sometimes you got the uncomfortable feeling that his honor came second to his ambition. And without honor"—he spread his hands wide— "a fellow just ain't anything. You do understand, don't you?"

"Of course." Regina bestowed her sweetest smile on him. She was deeply sensible of the honor Smythe did her in being her friend. Of all Taskford's cronies, she valued him highest. Saturnine Blysdale was the most intelligent, Mathers the most courtly, and MacLain and Stone were certainly diamonds in the rough, but none of them meant as much to her as the sensitive Smythe. "I see," she told him. "Thank you for reassuring me that I wasn't just being unfair in taking such a dislike to him."

Smythe blinked at her. His shy smile thanked her for understanding why he'd had to speak so plainly.

Taskford relaxed visibly. She was glad to see he had, though she was still baffled by his odd behavior. Her gaze met his and she saw that the murderous blaze had faded from his eyes.

Suddenly, the excitement, the worry and the length of the day caught up with Regina. Weariness hit her like a ton of horseshoes. She stifled a yawn.

Looking around the room, she noticed a few of the male guests nodding and felt a lot better. She caught Taskford looking at her. Was that an indulgent smile? She could hardly believe it. It did give her the courage to ask permission of the gentlemen to retire. She smiled around the table. "Thank you for a lovely evening, gentleman. Taskford, it was a wonderful party." Her eyes warmed, her voice went husky. "And I especially thank you for making my niece and nephew feel so special." Her eyes grew moist. "I promise you they will remember your kindness for the rest of their lives."

Harry was the first man out of his chair. He attempted to answer her but found his throat had closed.

Mathers snatched up his wineglass. "To Regina Landry!"

Others grabbed glasses and joined in, "To Regina Landry!"

Regina smiled at them all, bowed and hastened from the room. By the time she had reached the stairs to go up to her room, she was blinded by tears.

Feeling a little foolish to have tears of joy streaming from her eyes, she averted her face as she passed the two cloaked men in the hallway near her room. She had just placed her hand on the knob to ease the door open quietly so as not to awaken the children when they grabbed her.

Downstairs, the last guest had departed and the five friends stood among ruins. Mathers said to Taskford, "I think your party was a huge success, Harry."

Blysdale added, "Indeed it was. So what's bothering you, Harry?"

Taskford shot him a glance. "Something that was said." He grinned. "It keeps running around the edge of my mind, but I can't catch the damn thing to see what it was."

"Aha!" Stone slapped a heavy hand on his shoulder. "Too much wine!"

MacLain nodded owlish confirmation. "Have had the same 'sperience. Many's the time. The trick is to drink less."

Smythe coolly added, "Might have been a good idea to stop drinking when the lovely Mrs. Landry left us."

"Hell, Smythe," Stone frowned at him, "that was our first opportunity to drink at all. Before that, had to be circ . . ."—he hiccupped—"cumspect, you know."

Smythe turned away from him murmuring. "*I* know. I wonder if you do."

Blysdale laughed. "Gentlemen! I propose that this might be a very good time for us all to go to our beds."

"I'll second that suggestion." Mathers smiled lopsidedly and held his hands against his temples. "Tomorrow, my head is going to hate every one of us."

MacLain began, "Aye. Taskford's the only one who—"

"Please," a tremulous voice from the doorway brought them around to face it. Mrs. Winstead, the housekeeper from Charnwood, stood there. She wore a simple woolen wrapper and a look of great anxiety.

Harry's heart plummeted as he registered the meaning of her presence here.

Tears started down Winnie's cheeks as she stretched her right hand toward them. It was trembling. In it, she held a single ivory satin slipper.

Twenty-seven

Regaining her senses, Regina strained against the bonds that held her. Every movement sent a searing pain through her head. She wasn't certain, now, that it had been worth it to fight her abductors so hard. Not when she'd been unable to cause enough of a commotion to draw anybody to her rescue. Especially not when it had apparently caused her attackers to knock her unconscious.

Where was she? The bed she was on smelled musty, and the walls of the room were covered with faded wallpaper that was peeling off in places near the ceiling. An abandoned house?

She turned her head to look at the window. The curtains were drawn, but she could see an edge of weak light around them. From that she deduced that, either the day outside was another overcast one or it was very early in the morning. From her unrested feeling, she decided it had to be dawn. Even knocked unconscious instead of drifting sleepily into that state, she reasoned, she would still have been more rested had it been later in the day.

She was on a bed. She didn't like that. Having her wrists

tied to the bedposts made her distinctly uneasy. Thank heavens her feet weren't tied in like fashion. If they had been, she might have panicked. She felt helpless enough, vulnerable enough, with them free.

She craned around to look at her bonds. On inspection, it looked as if the rope with which her hands were bound had not been cut into two pieces, but, after tying one of her hands, had been thrown behind the headboard to tie her other. If she could just flip the long end up over the post . . .

The door burst open without warning. Whipping her head around to look, she saw Halidon's owner, Sir Ralph Belding, framed in the doorway. Gathering all her courage, fighting to appear perfectly calm, Regina demanded, "What is the meaning of this outrage?"

She didn't really care what answer he might give. She knew from the fact that he'd let her see his face, that she was in deep trouble. It was entirely possible that he had no intention of letting her live.

Kidnapping was a capital offense, after all—though, she thought nastily, abduction of a woman was usually not considered such.

"Good morning to you, too, Mrs. Landry."

"Oh." Her temper got the better of her and her voice was heavy with sarcasm. "Oh, do forgive my poor manners. Certainly I should care more about your morning than about my having been abducted from my family and friends." She gave a yank at the cords that held her and succeeded only in hurting her wrists.

"I'd heard you had a way with insults, my dear. But I'd also heard you had good sense." He smiled. "Personally, I should think you'd do better to be nice to me."

The suggestion that she be nice to him made her flesh crawl. Regina didn't like the quality of his smile, either. She did, however, see that insulting a captor was hardly intelligent. Forcing her anger to the back of her mind, she said reasonably, "I'd like to sit up, please. It's not my habit to hold conversations while reclining." Deliberately she left out the "with gentlemen" that she'd almost added.

"Very well. I made provision for that." He walked over to her, looming over her as she lay there.

Regina had to make a real effort not to shrink away from him. She sensed it wouldn't be wise to let him see her true feelings. She knew instinctively that this was the sort of man who'd feed on a person's fear to that person's detriment. She made an equal effort to keep his eyes locked on her own. If he ran his gaze over her body, she'd feel as if a slug had crawled over her.

Belding flipped the rope over the tall wooden head of the bed and took a double loop around the single post nearest him.

Working to seem casual, Regina sat up and curled her feet up under her. She looked at him coolly and without expression. "Would it be too much trouble for you to tell me why you have brought me here?"

He regarded her thoughtfully for a moment, then seemed to reach some decision important to him—even, unless she'd read him wrong, pleasant to him.

"Yes," he said with satisfaction. "Yes." He smiled down at her. "You may hear it all. I imagine you will make a very good audience. Everyone likes to have an appreciative audience for his accomplishments, you know, and I have had to keep my cleverness a secret for far too long. I think I will enjoy telling you my secrets.

"In fact, you shall hear the story from the beginning. Yes, the whole story. From the very beginning. And when the tale is told, I shall answer your question."

The small hairs on the nape of Regina's neck rose. Her

common sense told her she was in the clutches of a madman, and she was sorry, very sorry, that she'd asked him why he'd brought her here. She had the distinct feeling that after he told her his story, she'd have even less chance of leaving this place alive.

Back at the inn, Blysdale led Winnie to a chair. "What is it, Mrs. Winstead?" He made his voice gentle. "What's happened to upset you?" It was a rhetorical question, one designed to put the older woman at ease. All five of them had already guessed what had upset her—the unexplained absence of her dear Regina.

Harry stood staring at the shoe the housekeeper clasped to her bosom. Hell blossomed slowly in his eyes.

All of them knew what the shoe meant. Regina had been abducted. If she'd gotten safely to her room, Mrs. Winstead would have known it.

And, if Regina were anywhere else that she ought to be, she would have been there with both shoes on her slender feet. The only way Regina Landry could have lost one of her shoes would have been in a struggle. And if she'd won the fight, she'd have put her shoe back on.

Every man of them was sick with that knowledge.

"It's . . . it's Miss Reggie," Winnie said, "I know something dreadful has happened to her. I just know it."

Mathers clasped her shoulder in a consoling gesture.

"I . . . I was coming down to peek to see why she was so late, and I found her shoe in the hallway just outside our door. Reggie would never go off and leave her shoe. Never."

Harry knelt in front of her and took her hand.

Winnie flinched a little from the expression in his eyes. Then she took a firm hold on herself and faced him resolutely.

"Did you hear anything, Winnie?"

"No, your lordship. Not a sound."

He looked away and was silent a long moment, just holding her hand. When he looked back, Winnie could see the misery in his eyes. And behind the misery, murder.

"We'll find her, Winnie, never fear." He gripped her hand a little tighter. "We'll find her and bring her back to you safely, I promise."

Winnie looked back at him, studying every line in his face. Finally she nodded, satisfied. "Yes, if it can be done, I believe you will do it." She stood. She looked as if she carried the weight of the Tower of London on her shoulders. "I must return to the children. It wouldn't do to have one of them awaken and find that Miss Reggie had disappeared. Thomas, particularly, is so dependent on her." She walked to the door slowly, as if she were reluctant to leave them. On the threshold she turned and said, "God grant you good fortune."

"Good hunting, more like!" Stone burst out as soon as she was out of earshot. He and MacLain were as taut as bowstrings, ready to go.

The only problem was that none of them knew *where* to go.

Regina tried not to press herself back against the heavily carved headboard of the bed. The last thing she wanted to do was to let Belding discover how repulsed she was by him. With every ounce of strength of purpose, she forced her body to appear relaxed, her face to assume an expression of interest. Anything less, and she would surely be in grave danger from him.

"I hated them all." Belding's very words seethed. His eyes burned. "Hated them for always being in the right place to be heroes, to be decorated. Hated them because they could do everything right, and I was always just a little wrong.

"They were the charmed seven—with no room for an eighth, you may be sure. Ashley, Blysdale, Mathers, MacLain, Stone and Wainwright. And, of course, their little tagalong member of the general's staff—Smythe."

He took an agitated turn about the room.

"We raced, you know. Raced our chargers every chance we got." His face turned ugly. "Ashley always won. That stallion of his, that Cossack, was the best anybody'd ever seen. People were always congratulating him and telling he'd make a fortune with him. Racing. After the war.

"Wainwright, the marvelous Harry Wainwright, always came in second. And I was third. Always third." Regina heard his teeth grate. "Only third." He fell to pacing again.

She carefully turned to keep her gaze constantly fastened on him. She recognized now that he was a person deranged by his own unrealized longing to be what he was never able to be. She knew such people could be dangerous. She gave him the thing he wanted most just at present. She gave him her full attention.

Then he was talking again. Telling her his story, striving to gain her approval for his cleverness. "I bided my time. I waited for my opportunity. When it finally came, I was ready. More than ready."

He stopped pacing. His face glowed with the memory of what he was about to tell her. He thrust his face at hers, then whirled and paced away. "I was so clever! When they made that last disastrous charge, I made certain I was well to the rear. Ashley went down, a ball in his left shoulder, and I saw my chance!

"Ashley was glad to see me stop. He thought I was his friend. He thought I'd stopped to bandage him and get him back into the fight. I knelt beside him while I shot Wainwright's charger out from under him. Harry, the fool, had come from a sickbed to be with his men. And with his friend Ashley." He laughed. "I remember the look of horror on Ashley's face about my shooting Harry's Tammerlane just before I shot him." He turned swiftly, darting her a piercing look. "Right between the eyes," he informed her cheerfully.

Though utterly revolted, utterly horrified, Regina kept her face expressionless. She could feel the tendons tighten in her neck with the effort.

He nodded his satisfaction at her apparent lack of censure.

He began walking the floor again. "Then, I had to shoot my own horse, Halidon, of course." He spun around to look at her again. "Do you know, I think he was surprised?"

Revulsion rose like bile in Regina's throat. Her breath stopped. She knew that she must keep her face noncommittal if she hoped to survive, but it was next to impossible.

"The cannon smoke was so thick I could have shot half the regiment and no one would've been the wiser!" He laughed as if the idea amused him.

Regina surreptitiously tried her bonds. Still she kept her face expressionless and her attention glued to the madman. She no longer had the faintest hope that he might release her. If he could murder a friend, he would murder her, too, with as little compunction as he would swat a fly.

"After that, the only close call I had was when Harry went to check on the horses on our return to England. He's always had a way with them, the stupid beasts, and a soft spot for them, as well. Idiot. He was concerned that they hadn't weathered the crossing well. When I heard he was going to inspect them, I nearly fainted!"

He peered at her closely again. "Would you like me to go on?"

Regina could only nod. She was of the strong opinion that

she wouldn't live long after it if she gave a negative shake of her head.

"I tried to kill Harry then, but Mathers came along before I could finish him." Belding pouted like a child. Then he walked over and sat down beside her on the bed. In a quiet voice, he said, "This is very nice. I've never had anybody listen to me so politely before."

Regina thought, *You probably didn't have enough rope!* She let none of her disgust show, however.

"Anyway. Now you see why I have to kill Harry, don't you? He was the only one who knew Cossack so well that he would always recognize him. Always remember Cossack. Hell! *He'd* even remember Halidon." He looked contrite. "Please forgive me. Shouldn't use profanity in the presence of a lady.

"Anyway, I've shot at him twice since. And," he giggled. He actually giggled. "I've *shot* him twice, too." He turned and touched her forearm. "That was in between the two times I missed. Remember when I played highwayman on Taskford land? I hit him then. Twice." A frown creased his forehead. "And you nursed him that time, didn't you?"

Regina couldn't help it, she flinched away from his touch.

"Ah, yes. Not proper to touch ladies. Forgot." He bounced off the bed.

She wondered if he were drunk. It certainly didn't bother him to confess murder to a lady!

"You pushed him out of the way when I shot at him in the stables here at Newmarket, too." He frowned mightily. "I should probably punish you for that." He appeared to be thinking hard.

Regina held her breath.

"Yes, I probably should," he decided. "First, though, I need to use you to trap Taskford. We'll do that in a day or

two. I want him to be confused and upset for a while, first."
Cocking his head to one side, Belding smiled winningly at
her. "So you're safe for a little while." He strode to the door.
Opening it, he turned and called out as he backed into the
hallway. "Sleep well!"

Twenty-eight

They'd spent the whole day searching. Harry had worn out four horses, Stone three, the others two apiece. They'd split the surrounding countryside into six parts and each of them had questioned every living soul in their assigned portion of it extensively—to no avail. No one had been able to give them any helpful information.

It was almost dark, now, the end of the first day. The men had only snatched a little sustenance between changes of horses—all but Taskford, who had eaten nothing all day. Now Blysdale, always the sensible one, had called a halt and demanded that they all eat a hearty supper.

"For God's sake, Harry! We won't do Mrs. Landry any good if we're weak and stupid from hunger. My mind is barely functioning at this point and I'm pretty damned sure yours isn't doing any better!"

"Where is she, Bly?" Taskford turned a haggard face toward his friend. "Who could have stolen her? And why?"

Even Blysdale couldn't think of a logical reason for abducting a race horse trainer *after* the race. Nor could he imagine any other reason for someone to have abducted

Mrs. Landry. He'd wracked his brain, but no explanation for her disappearance had come to him. She was gone. That was all they knew.

That and the fact that his friend Harry Wainwright, Earl of Taskford, was head over heels in love with the woman. Though he and Mathers had long suspected it, now they were positive. He wondered how long it would take Hard-hearted Harry to come to the same realization. And then, how long it would take him to admit it.

Finally, he answered his friend's question. "I don't know, Harry. None of us do." He let out a heavy sigh. "We're just all praying that, wherever she is, she's safe."

Harry stared out the window of the private dining room. Mindlessly, he watched a curricle coming back to the inn after a pleasant day's outing. The perfectly matched horses drawing it each had white stockings on their hind legs. The white of their back legs seemed to flash in the gathering dusk.

Smythe came over to him. "Time to eat. Come on, Harry. The food's ready."

Stone and MacLain sat at the table waiting for the others, staring at the food. Even they, usually hearty trenchermen, had no appetites. Neither one had even bothered to brush the dust off the shoulders of his riding coat. All of them had it on their boots. Even Smythe.

Everyone but Harry took up forks and began to force food down, sloshing ale after it. They ate like men eating in their sleep.

There was nothing to say. No information to share. There was no encouragement to be offered. Regina Landry was missing and they had not unearthed a single clue as to her possible whereabouts.

Across from each other, Mathers and Blysdale exchanged

glances, looked to where Harry sat slumped in his chair and then back at each other. Their eyes were bleak.

Harry brooded while the picture of the last thing he'd looked at ran over and over in his exhausted mind. The curricle. The matched team with the stockings gleaming white in the twilight. In and out they ran. In one side of his mind and out the other, only to return and flash through again, as if they ran around the back of his head to enter again from the side they had come in before.

The vision passed through again. He was too weary to stop it. The white stockings became more and more prominent each time they appeared. The one horse's on the right, the other horse's on the left. He passed a weary hand over his eyes, trying to rub the curious images away.

Mathers shook his head.

Blysdale's lips tightened. Both of them pitied Taskford. Neither of them knew what more they could do to help. Seeing him like this was torture for them both. Their eyes met again and they silently vowed revenge on whomever was causing their friend to suffer so.

"Great God!" Harry's shout rang through the room. He shot upright in his chair. Silverware clinked and jumped as he slammed his fist down on the table.

Stone spewed ale across it. Forks clattered to plates. Every eye fastened on Taskford.

Harry leapt from his chair. Toppling backward, it hit the floor with a sharp crack. "The stockings!" he crowed. "Damn me for a blind fool! The stockings!" His eyes blazing, his color high, he looked around the table at his companions.

They stared back at him as if he'd lost his mind.

"Don't you see?" He spun away from the table, then back again, agitated beyond the ability to stand still. "She *told* us.

Regina told us and I was too damned stupid to catch the significance of it! *She* didn't know, but *I* should have!"

Blysdale and Mathers rose and went to him. Gently they took hold of his arms. "Harry. Sit down again. Sit down and tell us what you're trying to say."

Harry shook them off. "Devil take you! Let go! Stop treating me as if I'd been too close to a cannon blast!"

Smythe came over and said quietly and firmly, "Then stop acting like it and begin at the beginning so that we can follow you, Harry."

For a moment it looked as if Harry would murder Smythe. Then he shook his head. Slowly he registered the fact that no one had the faintest idea what he had discovered.

He stood, legs apart, his head lowered like a bull about to charge, taking great breaths of air. He felt as if he'd been holding his breath since Regina Landry had been abducted.

Now, as he marshalled his thoughts, he thanked God for granting him the sight of the curricle he'd seen earlier and for haunting him with the vision of it until his exhausted wits had worked out the importance of the white stockings.

Slamming his chair back up on its legs, he plopped down on it and began to explain. "Listen! Remember the banquet in honor of Golden Sovereign's win?"

They all nodded.

"Remember Regina saying something about not having liked Belding and having argued about white signifying weakness in a horse's legs?"

They were all getting impatient with him. "Yes, dammit, Harry! So what?" Stone's face was beet red. Stone was not known as a patient man.

"Don't you see? She said that the stocking on Belding's Halidon *was on his right hind leg!*"

Puzzled frowns marred all but Smythe's face.

Smythe breathed softly, "Of course!"

MacLain turned on him, snarling. "Of course, *what*?"

Blysdale sat back in his chair, the light dawning. "Of course. The stocking was on the wrong foot."

"Yes!" Mathers came halfway out of his chair. "It was Cossack! Cossack had the stocking on the right foot. Halidon's was on his left hind leg!" It was his turn to slam the table. "Sweet Lord!"

MacLain was stunned. "No wonder 'Halidon' had developed such a turn of speed. It was Cossack that Belding brought back from the Continent. And we never guessed."

Mathers stated coldly, "But Harry would have known. Harry would have known right away. That was why Belding tried to kill him when he went to see how the horses had fared on the crossing home."

Blysdale's voice was deadly. "And that was no doubt why he couldn't run 'Halidon,' as he calls Cossack now, when there was any chance that Harry might show up to watch the race." His laugh was sinister. "That was costing him money."

"Harry's inheriting a string of racehorses was really bad luck for Belding," Stone added.

With an awful gasp, Smythe went pale. He fell back against his chair. "That means that *I* was the one responsible for the shot that barely missed killing Harry the night we were playing cards. *I* was the one who told Belding that Harry would be with the rest of us when we went to watch him run his horse."

Harry could afford to be generous. Now he knew where to begin looking for Regina. "Nonsense. That was an accident."

They all ignored him.

Blysdale voiced their certainty. "Harry has to end up dead so that he can't expose the fact that 'Halidon' is really 'Cossack.'"

"Not only that . . ." Smythe was recovering. His voice was excited. "Didn't Ash *bequeath* Cossack to Harry in his will?"

"Yes, by Jove! He did! And Belding wasn't about to part with a horse that could finally give him the glory we all knew he was so damned hungry for." Blysdale looked to Mathers for agreement.

Mathers didn't give it. Mathers sat still as a stone. His face was a blood-drained mask.

Bly looked from him to Harry.

"Oh, my God!" Harry, his gaze locked on the stricken Mathers, fell back in his chair, the blood draining from his own face. "Ashley."

Mathers nodded. Even his lips had gone pale. Ashley was not only his cousin. Ashley had been his closest friend.

Smythe's gentle voice put the horror that chilled them all into words. "Ashley." He spoke in a hush. "Musket ball in the shoulder, but pistol ball through the forehead. The center of his forehead."

They all knew the chances of that happening in the heat of battle—in the smoke and panic of a cavalry charge. Horror showed on every face. To a man, they knew with an awful certainty that Ralph Belding had foully murdered Ashley Stoddard.

And now Belding intended to murder Harry. God knew he'd tried time and again.

Further, they knew, now, that Belding had taken Regina Landry. There was no doubt in any of their minds that he had to be keeping her somewhere—keeping her as bait in the final, fatal trap that he intended to set for Harry.

In the dim room of the abandoned house in which she was being kept prisoner, Regina was trying to win free of the ropes that held her wrists. She was so thirsty. Her captor had neglected to leave her anything to drink. Her throat was so parched she had trouble swallowing.

She had suspected the man was mad early on. Now, she was convinced of it. Convinced that his mind was slipping even further from reality as time passed. Belding kept bursting into the room, each time with a plan wilder than the last for luring Taskford to his doom.

He'd started drinking.

Regina was beginning to be more and more afraid. Bravery to make her way in the world was not the same as bravery for facing a madman. Her wrists were raw with her efforts to escape her bonds. Her mind was weary with trying to think of a way to flee this house should she win free of them.

Studying the ivy-covered windows of the room had convinced her the house was sadly neglected, surely deserted and probably abandoned. If it were as well-hidden in greenery as the overgrown windows suggested, how would Taskford ever find her?

She steeled herself as she heard footsteps pounding down the hallway outside her door. Sitting up very straight, she composed her face for the entrance of her captor. She couldn't let him see that he frightened her.

Would she die now? She knew she was going to refuse to do anything that could be used to trap Taskford. That, in her captor's mental state, would constitute just cause for her murder.

A deep sadness filled her. Never to see those she loved again—to hold Thomas and Philydia, to hug Winnie. Never to see again the sun making cloud patterns and the horses sweeping through them across the downs. Not to see Charnwood, that she had missed so dreadfully for so long and reclaimed for such a short time, or Wentworth and all the old servants from her childhood that she'd hardly done more than greet again. Tears filled her eyes.

And Taskford. Taskford, who'd carried so long the pain of his father's suicide that it had become a part of him. The cruel knowledge that his mother's betrayal had caused his father's death had given him those mocking eyes behind which he hid his feelings. Her poor, beloved Taskford.

Never to share just once more the passion of the love she had for him—and wished with all her heart he could return—was almost more than she could bear. The tears spilled over. She turned her head to wipe them away with the satin sleeve of her gown. She'd not give Belding the sight of them!

The door burst violently inward. Its knob sent plaster flying out of the wall as it struck. Framed in the doorway, his face that of an avenging angel, stood Taskford.

Regina's head spun. Dizzy with relief, she sagged against her bonds. Oh, thank God! He was safe! Taskford was safe!

She could judge from Belding's curses echoing in the background that her captor was already in the hands of Taskford's friends. She could hear Blysdale matching him curse for curse, and smiled. Bly had always seemed so controlled. Her hands fell free as Taskford cut through the cords that had bound them.

He gathered her in his arms, "Don't faint on me now, Amazon." Relief flooded through him. The strength of the love he felt for her sent his senses reeling.

"I never faint," she countered. "I was listening."

He cocked his head and listened, too. His friends' vocabulary had suffered no loss of color in the time they'd been out of the cavalry. "Well, you shouldn't be."

She turned tragic gray eyes to him. "They know, don't they? *You* know. That he murdered your friend just to get his horse?"

"We've guessed." He closed his eyes for a moment as he held against an onslaught of memory and sorrow. After a moment, he said positively, "We know." His concern was all for Regina. "Are you all right?"

She nodded. She was glad for the strength of his embrace. For just this once being able to lean on someone stronger. "But I'm terribly thirsty."

He muttered a curse, drew a flask from his pocket and offered it. "I have only brandy."

She chuckled. "Thank you, no. Not on a dry throat and an empty stomach."

He grinned down at her, striving to hide the anger coursing through him to find her thirsty. "The results might be interesting."

"I'm not about to try it to see."

His eyes darkened. "Regina, I . . ."

Blysdale and Mathers walked into the room. "Is she all right?"

"Right as rain, now that you have all come." Regina smiled at them. Then she frowned. "I have to tell you all. He confessed to me that he murdered your friend, Ashley Stoddard. Halidon is really that friend's horse, Cossack."

Harry stood her on her feet, watching carefully to see that she was steady. Then he slipped an arm around her, scooped her up into his arms and walked out the door of her prison with her head cradled carefully against his chest. He strode out of the dark house Belding had rented for the race season and out into the fresh, clean air.

She asked to be put down and stood and breathed deeply, glad to be free, glad to be alive. Harry kept his arm around her as if he were afraid she would fall. She smiled up at him, rather enjoying the tender care he was taking of her.

Blysdale and Mathers exchanged glances. Then they shrugged. Right now, they had more important things on their minds than whether or not Taskford had come to his senses about Regina Landry. Right now, they had to see to the matter of getting a man formally charged with a murder he had committed two years before.

Harry led Regina to his horse. "I'm sorry I didn't bring a carriage. We were afraid the sound of its approach might alert Belding."

"I prefer the open air just now."

Harry lifted Regina to the saddle and mounted behind her. As his arms went around her, she leaned back against him and said softly, "Thank you for coming."

His love for this woman rose up and stopped his throat. How could he not have realized before how much she meant to him? How much he cherished her? He could think of nothing to say—not now. His only thought was to get her safely back to Mrs. Winstead. She needed to get home to rest from her ordeal.

Later. There would be time for them to talk later, when she'd recovered. Time then to tell her how the hell of the past few days had made him realize that he loved her. Loved her more than he'd ever known it was possible to love. More than anything, more than life.

For now, he just closed his arms tighter, more possessively, around her slender form, closed his eyes and pressed his cheek against her hair.

Twenty-nine

In spite of Harry's best intentions, there wasn't any rest for Regina once she was home. The horses were all safely back from Newmarket. They were being kept safe and in sound work by Tim Parson, her wonderful assistant trainer. Wentworth and Winnie had the house completely under control and running like the proverbial clock. The children were happily back in the schoolroom. And Regina had finally gotten over being thirsty.

Nevertheless, disaster struck.

Regina had slept late, dressed slowly and gone downstairs feeling as if she were walking through molasses. She was so relieved that the threat to Taskford had been removed that she was enervated. The excitement, danger and sheer terror of the past few days had taken their toll, and she felt as limp as a child's rag doll. Even the sun streaming into the bright breakfast room and the soft, fragrant breeze blowing in through the open windows did nothing to give her energy.

She'd just finished eating when Wentworth brought in the mail. He was smiling. "It looks as if you have a letter from Scotland, Miss Reggie."

"Oh. Good!" Now she had energy. "It must be the one I've been waiting for from my late husband's cousin, Edward Overfield." She picked up her fruit knife and broke the seal on the folded page. Suddenly she was still as an unwelcome thought hit her. If Brandon's cousin stood ready to marry her as she'd asked him to, then there would never again be any chance for Taskford and her to be together. Never again could she know the comfort of being held in his arms, know the wild ecstasy of his kisses. Never again.

It took her a moment to force herself to go on opening the letter. The children had to come first, never mind her own wishes. Her heart aching, she unfolded the missive. Quickly scanning it, she saw that it said, *"As sorry as I am to have to disappoint you, dear cousin, I must, for you see I was married last month. She is the most wonderful girl in the world, Reggie, and I cannot wait for you to meet her. You will . . ."* There was more, of course, but Regina couldn't deal with that now. Her head was spinning. Relief? Bitter disappointment? *What was she feeling?*

With an effort, she got a grip on her emotions. Edward was married. Later, she would write offering her congratulations and send an appropriate gift. Just now, she was scrambling for balance in her mind. She was glad for Edward, and glad that she was still free. She was sorry Edward was not able to help her rescue the children because lately she'd been haunted by such a strong sense of apprehension that it made her fearful of the sounds of anyone arriving at Charnwood Hall.

She put her hands up to the sides of her face. It had been years since she'd felt so beleaguered, so helpless. She didn't know how she was going to cope.

Winnie came in from the hall, concern in her eyes. "Have you had bad news, dear?"

Even in her distress, Regina could smile. So Wentworth

had gone to find Winnie and told the little housekeeper how she'd looked when she perused the letter from Edward. Well, the situation was their concern, too. Perhaps even more their concern, for surely Jasper would find some way to force her to leave Charnwood if he took over as the children's guardian, while Winnie and Wentworth would still be there. At least to begin with.

"Not bad news, precisely. Just a minor setback. Brandon's Cousin Edward has married. So I suppose, if I weren't so selfish, I'd call it good news."

"Oh, the dear boy. I never thought he would. How nice."

"Yes it is nice, but I had so hoped . . ."

"Yes, of course you did. We all did. Hope *is* the key, though. Now we shall just have to find you someone else to marry." Winnie put on a false cheeriness. "Aren't we fortunate that there is such a fine selection at Taskford Manor just now? I'm certain we shall have no difficulty. No difficulty at all." She turned away so that her young friend couldn't see that she was ready to weep for her.

Regina had to laugh. "I wonder how the gentlemen visiting Taskford Manor would react to your idea?"

"Why, they'd consider themselves most fortunate and rush to form a waiting line." In a whisper too soft for Regina to hear, she added, "And God grant that Taskford is at the head of it!"

Suddenly Wentworth appeared in the doorway of the breakfast room. Straight as a soldier, he waited for them to notice him.

Regina, amused by the mental picture Winnie's foolishness had conjured up of the gentlemen in question standing on Charnwood's front steps with bouquets in hand, glanced up at him with a sunny smile. The smile died at the sight of his face.

His expression was all the warning Regina needed. He'd

brought her a card on his silver salver. She was braced when she reached for it. As she held it up with a hand that had suddenly become unsteady, Wentworth intoned, "The *person* awaits your attention in the green parlor, Miss Regina."

She knew who it was for a certainty, then, even before she looked down to read the name on the card. Her blood ran cold. The card read, "Jasper Ruddleston, Esquire."

Jasper! Loathsome Cousin Jasper. Here! Now! Even with all the strain she'd been under for the past few days, how could she have forgotten that Bagwell had warned her it wouldn't be long before Jasper won—won the guardianship of the children. *Her* children.

The room was closing in on Regina. What was she to do? Her heart ached as if it were having a seizure. What *could* she do?

She dropped the card and rose stiffly from her chair. She felt a hundred years old. Turning to Wentworth, she looked at him with eyes that wouldn't focus. "I'll see him." Her voice sounded as if it belonged to someone else, distant, weak.

Wentworth warned her, "There is some sort of official with him, Miss Reggie," then drew her chair back and watched her leave the breakfast room. She moved as if she were going to her execution. The minute she turned the corner toward the green parlor, he dropped all pretense of dignity and hied himself off to the nursery schoolroom at a dead run.

Regina hesitated for a moment in front of the door to the green parlor. This was the parlor that the whole household detested. The walls were a dark Paris green that sometimes flaked off on the furniture in an annoying powder. The chimney smoked and the windows were draughty. The fact that Wentworth had put a visitor in this parlor they never used told her clearly what her butler thought of her cousin. She herself thought it a fitting place in which to meet the detestable Jasper Ruddleston.

She lifted her chin, squared her shoulders and flung open the double doors. With a great deal of satisfaction, she heard the smack of one of them hitting the wall.

"Ah. So there you are." Jasper was sprawled on the damask-covered chaise loungue, his dusty boots soiling the foot of it.

A self-effacing little man stood nearby, his hat in one hand. There were papers in the other. No doubt he was a representative of the court. Jasper had dragged the poor man here to tell her she must give Jasper the children soon, of course.

"Yes." Regina steeled herself and admitted to being present. "You have come to tell me you have won, no doubt?"

"Oh, yes." Jasper's eyes glittered with malicious triumph. His disappointment that she didn't react was palpable. After a moment, however, he rallied. "At any rate, I have come for the children." He grinned to see the pain on her face. "I intend to take them back to London with me today."

Regina forgot everything but the shock such haste would be to Philydia and Thomas. "Oh, but surely you will let me have a day or two to prepare them!"

"I'm afraid that will not be convenient for me. There is a house party at the Marquis of Hantcombe's next week that I don't want to miss."

"But surely you could wait until your return to take the children to London." Under her shock and agitation, Regina was well aware that Jasper would never have been invited to the notorious Hantcombe's house party unless he was assumed to have the money to gamble for the large sums that circle wagered. Already the vultures were gathering to strip Charnwood—gathering at Jasper's invitation.

She stared at him a moment longer, knowing it was hopeless to appeal to his better nature. Jasper Ruddleston didn't have a better nature. Anything she said or did would simply add to his enjoyment of having won. She didn't want to give him the pleasure. "If you will wait, I'll go get the children." Resignation was plain in her voice, but her mind was leaping from scheme to scheme in an effort to find one that would keep the children safe from this man.

"Thank you, but I think I shall come with you."

She could have murdered him at that moment. Not only did he not trust her . . . which she had to admit was perfectly sound of him . . . but he was going to make himself an unwelcome presence at what might well be the last moments she would have with Thomas and Philydia. Devil take the man!

She heard the rattle of wheels on the gravel of the courtyard and glanced out the window behind Jasper. Her heart soared! It was Philydia driving the pony cart for all she was worth, while Thomas clung to the side, cheering her on. As she watched, they took the lane toward Taskford Manor.

Regina's voice cheered in her mind, *Oh, clever, clever children!*

She was smiling as she led the way up the stairs to the nursery. The children had gone to Taskford for sanctuary. They would be safe from Jasper for the day. It wasn't a complete victory, but at least it was a skirmish that would prove an unpleasant surprise for their enemy.

It was four flights up to the nursery schoolroom, and behind her, Regina could hear Jasper beginning to puff. Her own steps quickened. Two flights to go. Perhaps he would have a heart attack before they reached their goal.

She could only hope.

They paused at the top of the last flight of stairs, Regina breathing easily, Jasper fighting to draw air into his lungs.

The little man who'd come with him was waiting quietly for the next development.

Regina watched Jasper and refrained from voicing any of the comforting excuses young ladies were taught to use when men of their acquaintance came up lacking. Far from wanting to offer a comforting excuse for his lack of fitness, she was enjoying his discomfort. With all her heart, she wished he would drop dead!

"The schoolroom is this way." She led the way down the hall with a light step. The children had to be halfway to Taskford Manor by now. They were safe, at least until tomorrow. She would have tonight in which to go to them to explain what was happening . . . to tell them good-bye.

The tears in her eyes as she grasped the knob of the schoolroom door were genuine.

It was not to her cousin's credit that the sight of them made him smile.

She opened the door wide. Sweet, fresh air blew across the spacious room from the windows. Sunlight spilled across the well-scrubbed floor. But the room was empty.

Books and toys lay scattered about. Two of the child-sized chairs at the battered round table had not been pushed back into place under it. One of them lay on its side on the nursery's braided rag rug. The room had the air of a place hastily deserted by its occupants.

"You bitch!" Jasper screamed. His hand connected with Regina's cheek in a blow that staggered her.

Fury burst through her like a rocket. Drawing her own hand back, she stepped forward to deliver a retaliatory blow.

Jasper scrambled backward out of range. "Murder! You'd murder me if you knocked me down these stairs!" He called out to the law clerk, "You're my witness! She's trying to kill me!" Jasper turned and plunged down a half-flight, screaming at Regina, "You'd kill me!"

Regina leaned over the banister and glared down at him. "What a perfectly marvelous idea!" She started running for the head of the stairway.

Thomas and Philydia hung on for dear life as their little golden-maned pony galloped down the lane off Charnwood and on to Taskford. The light wicker of the pony cart and the weight of the two slender children was not enough to keep the wheels on the ground over the bigger bumps. They seemed to proceed as much through the air as on the graveled lane.

Philydia had already lost the driving lines. Thomas had lost his cap. Both of them stared straight ahead, their faces set. Wentworth had told them to get to Lord Taskford, and they were going to get to Lord Taskford—whatever the cost to their courage.

Without warning, a horseman blocked their path. The pony skidded to a stop. The wicker cart bumped his rump in spite of the breeching strap, and he let out a startled whinny. Dust flew.

"Here, now! What's all this? Did your pony get away from you?"

Thomas defended his sister's driving ability. "No, sir! Creampuff did *not* get away from my sister," he said a little breathlessly. "Philydia just lost the reins, is all."

The rotund gentleman had leaned down from his tall Thoroughbred to stop Creampuff. Seeing that the panting pony showed no inclination to continue its mad dash, he straightened and looked at the children.

He could see they were highly agitated. To put them at ease, he said, "I'm Mr. Smythe, your aunt Regina's friend." He didn't want to have them afraid to answer him honestly, though, so he didn't ask what the trouble was. Instead, in his calmest voice, he inquired, "Is there something I can do to be of service?"

Philydia and Thomas looked at each other. Then they both burst into tears.

Smythe arrived at the great house at Charnwood in time to see Jasper Ruddleston dash out the front door as if pursued by all the demons of hell. A moment later a little man with solemn eyes and the demeanor of a clerk came out. When he and Smythe came within speaking distance, he said quietly, "I shall have to insist that she give him the children. I'm court appointed to do so, you know." He sounded as if he hated the whole business.

More concerned with Regina, Smythe let him go and entered the door Ruddleston had left standing open. "Hallo! Is anybody home?"

He was answered by the sound of a single, stifled sob. Hastening across the foyer, he bent to the figure seated on the bottom step of the curving staircase. It was Regina Landry, and she had her face buried in her hands. "My dear! What has happened? Are you all right?"

She hiccupped once and answered in a choked voice, "I'm fine, thank you. How are you?"

Smythe was distressed. To hear Regina voicing automatic social conventions while trying not to sob her heart out was nothing to be taken lightly.

He reached for her hands.

She gave him one, keeping the other on her left cheek.

Tucking the one he had under his arm, he drew her to and into the blue-and-white drawing room. There he sat beside her on the dark-blue damask sofa, and asked, "What's the matter, my dear? I met the children on their way to Taskford Manor, and came as soon as they told me that you had Jasper Ruddleston here."

She turned to him eagerly. "Have they reached Taskford safely?"

"Surely they have by now. They were . . ." His voice trailed off as he saw her face. Horror dawned on his own. He shot to his feet. Rage suffused his countenance. "Sweet Heaven!" He pulled down the hand she was raising again to cover the red hand print on her cheek. "Has Ruddleston done this?"

Regina could see violence in his eyes. "It's nothing." She tried to drag him down to sit beside her again. The usually tractable Smythe was unbendable. "It is nothing," she repeated. "Really! Oh, please, my dear friend. You know no mere physical hurt could cause me to cry like this. Forget my cheek!" Her voice took on an edge of hysteria. She reached out and grabbed his lapels. "Help me to cope with the loss of my children!"

Smythe regarded her quietly for an instant, then pulled her into his arms.

Regina resisted for a split second. She'd had to stand alone for so long, she was reluctant to lean on him, to lean on anyone. Then, suddenly, she broke and lay sobbing against his chest.

Smythe patted her back and held her tight, offering all the comfort he could through his embrace. He knew he was more sensitive than most men, and because he was, he knew she needed to cry this out. While she cried, he came to some important decisions.

After a while, Regina sat up and searched her sleeves for her handkerchief. Smythe handed her his own that he'd had waiting, and she mopped away the last of her tears.

He was astonished. Her eyes weren't pink, they were luminous—like skies washed clean by the rain. The tip of her nose was red from her weeping, however, and he found that very endearing. It caused him to smile.

Regina offered a tremulous smile in return. "I do apologize. I knew that I had to lose them. It was just the shock of Jasper arriving without warning." She frowned. "And gloating so. And demanding them right away." Her smile appeared briefly. "And I was frustrated, too, because I couldn't catch him to shove him down the stairs."

She burst into full-throated laughter. "Oh, glory! How I *wanted* to push him down the stairs! It would have made me feel so very much better!"

Smythe was looking at her a little fearfully.

"Oh, Smythe, you mustn't worry. I would never do *you* harm."

"Huh." It was a disparaging snort. "Wasn't afraid you would. Was afraid you were going to go all hysterical on me."

"Oh, my dear." She smiled radiantly at him. "How very brave you are to let me cry all over you when I could have 'gone hysterical' at any moment."

She frowned lightly. "Smythe, what *is* your Christian name? I simply can't go on calling you Smythe just because it is all I've heard the men do."

"My full name is Michael David Lawrence Smythington." He looked acutely embarrassed, started to add something and firmly closed his lips.

"Smythington? Then why do we all call you Smythe?"

He looked at her and said reasonably, "It's shorter."

"But it isn't accurate."

He shrugged. "Well, everybody knows. So it doesn't really matter. We all do it. Blysdale *is* really Blysdale, we just leave off the Earl of Blythingdale part. Mathers is Mathers, he's just the Viscount Kantford, too. Stone and McLain are both Baronets, so they're not such a bother, and Harry was plain Harry Wainwright until he got stuck with the Earldom."

He looked at her earnestly. "You see, in a title-toad-eating world, it's just a lot less bother to leave them at home, so to speak. The titles, I mean."

Regina was stunned. It was true that the world had a vast appreciation for titles, but she found it distinctly odd that there were men who preferred to hide theirs. She thought she found that rather admirable, but none of it mattered to her right now. She managed a soft, "Oh. I see," and let it go at that.

"My mother called me Michael David," Smythe was saying shyly. "You could do that, or you could chose just one. Whatever pleases you."

"Thank you. I shall call you David, if I may."

Regina was quite in possession of herself now, and could see that Smythe was wrestling with something. "What is it . . . David?"

"It's your children, Regina. I have a thought about how to keep them." He saw that Regina was about to speak. "No. Don't say anything until I have finished. Promise."

She nodded.

"I propose that we marry, you and I. With me as your husband, Ruddleston would be unable to take Philydia and Thomas from you."

"Oh, David." Her voice melted with affection. "You would do this for me?"

"It wouldn't be just for you, Regina. Nor just for the children." He dropped his gaze to his hands, now folded tightly in his lap, and said very softly, "I know that I'm not the sort of man who sends a woman's heart fluttering. I am neither handsome nor dashing. In fact, I am the most nondescript and unnoticeable of men.

"No woman has ever noticed me, other than you," he lifted his gaze to meet hers for an instant, "in friendship." He hushed her with a raised hand. "But I am honorable and honest and I try to be just. I think that I would not fall short of being a good influence on young minds. And perhaps I would prove a good enough companion to you."

Regina's eyes were growing moist.

"All of us know you love Taskford—except maybe Taskford, who's being terribly dim about it."

Regina started to speak, then realized she had nothing to say. It was true that she loved Taskford. It was also true that she had no idea whether or not Taskford loved her in return. It would take months, in all probability, to bring him around to the realization that he loved her, *if* he did love her. By that time it would be too late to save Charnwood for the children.

"Please seriously consider what I am saying," Smythe continued, "I know you could never love me, and I don't ask that. What I offer is a marriage in name only. One that will save the children's inheritance from Jasper Ruddleston, because you would be a married woman and their rightful guardian, as closer kin to them than he."

Regina raised a hand to stop him. He took it in both his own. "You are about to object that I would gain nothing from such an arrangement, but it is not so.

"I am not a man to raise passion in the feminine breast. If you marry me, I shall have at my side a woman I admire greatly, whose honor and integrity are not only above reproach, but would also guarantee that she be my friend, my faithful and kind companion for the rest of my days.

"You would be there to grace my table and to entertain my guests. To share my triumphs and my disappointments. That is much more than I have ever hoped for."

Tears were marking Regina's cheeks now. "Dear David. You deserve so very much more than that."

For just an instant his smile flashed. "No doubt I do, but chances are I shall never be granted it."

"Oh, David."

He reached up and gently brushed the tears from her cheeks. "I can promise you that you will have your brother's children, safe and sound."

She cautioned him. "I have fought for them once and lost, you know."

"You weren't my Duchess then."

"Oh, dear. Are you a Duke, then, David?"

He nodded. "Yes." He sighed heavily. "I'm the Duke of Smythington. So you see how it is. There are no end of females who would marry me in a heartbeat to be called 'Her Grace,' or to help me try to put a dent in the family fortune. But they would never be my friend. Every time I looked across the table at them, I'd be heartsick with doubt about their motives."

He slid to one knee in front of her. Clasping his hand to his heart, he said, "Marry me, Regina!"

Thirty

Philydia and Thomas relinquished the ribbons of the pony cart to a waiting groom and ran up the steps that led up to Taskford Manor. Here, they knew, they would find sanctuary.

Helmsley, Taskford's butler, had heard the sound of the pony cart approaching and was waiting at the open door. Seeing the way the children arrived full tilt, he gestured for a groom to take care of the poor little pony. The very fact that Philydia and Thomas Ransome had left their well-loved pony standing panting in its shafts told Helmsley how upset they were.

Thomas threw his head back to look up at the austere butler's face. "Could we please see the Earl, please."

"I'm sorry, Master Thomas, but the Earl is not . . ." He broke off and looked sharply down the drive to where a cloud of dust was boiling up toward the house. "Come in, children. I believe the Earl is just arriving."

The three of them stood in the doorway watching the approach of the rider on the great gray horse.

Harry saw the children and pushed his mount to the foot

of the steps. Making a flying dismount, he left his horse to the groom there. His momentum carried him up to them in a smooth run. "Thomas! Philydia! Welcome to Taskford."

"Thank you," they said in unison.

Then Harry saw the children were distressed. Obviously this wasn't just a visit in response to his standing invitation to come. "What is it? What's the matter?" His blood chilled. "Has something happened to your aunt?"

"No," Philydia answered, "Not yet."

Not yet! He resisted the urge to shake an explanation for that comment out of the girl.

Thomas offered, "Wentworth sent us over here when our awful cousin came to Charnwood. He said we were to rush to Taskford Manor and find you. He said you would keep us safe from him." He frowned. "From our cousin, that is. Not Wentworth."

Philydia put a silencing hand on her brother's shoulder. She raised tragic eyes to Taskford. "He's come for us, you know. Wentworth told us that Aunt Regina . . ." Tears came to her eyes. "That Auntie had lost her fight for us in the courts. Wentworth told us our awful Cousin Jasper Ruddleston was going to . . ." Her brittle facade was failing her, the tears spilled down her cheeks and choked her voice. "Was . . . going to take us away from Auntie to go live with him!"

Thomas tugged at his hand. "Please, your lordship. I don't want to go live with my Cousin Jasper. I *love* my Aunt Regina."

Philydia began to cry in earnest. "I love her, too, but she doesn't know it yet. And I may never get a chance to tell her," she wailed. "And I'm so afraid Cousin Jasper will hurt her when he finds we're not there. My Papa said Cousin Jasper is a man with a murderous temper."

Philydia was talking to empty air.

Harry hurled himself out of the huge double front doors like a man on fire. "Bring back that horse, Robinson!"

The groom was halfway down the long path to the stables, but he had no difficulty hearing his employer's bellow. Mounting the gray, he cantered him back to his waiting master.

Harry vaulted on as the groom jumped off. "Take care of the children, Helmsley!" and he was gone down the lane that led toward Charnwood before the groom had even caught his balance. "Sorry, old boy," Harry told the horse. He was glad he'd given the gelding an easy ride home from his last stop, because he was in a hell of a hurry now!

What if the children's fears *weren't* groundless? He'd heard some pretty unsavory tales about Ruddleston. Suppose he did offer Regina harm? His hands fisted on the reins. The horse threw his head in protest. "Sorry, lad." He softened his hands again. God, he must be out of his mind with worry to abuse his mount's mouth like that!

They rounded the curve from the lane to the main drive at Charnwood and galloped up the neatly edged gravel length of it to the broad steps at the front door. Harry made another flying dismount. This time he left his horse to its own devices.

Charging up the steps like a one-man invading army, he pounded on the door with his fist. It flew open, and he pushed past the startled footman as if he expected the man to try to stop him. "Where is she?" he demanded.

"M-Mrs. Landry is in the blue parlor, your lordship."

Wentworth came hurrying up. "The children, your lordship. Did they get safely to Taskford?"

"Yes, yes. They're safe and sound." Where was Regina? Where the blazing hell was the damned blue parlor! He rounded on Wentworth. "Take me to Mrs. Landry!"

"Of course, your lordship."

Wentworth hurried along, pushed by a sense of the Earl's urgency.

Harry caught a glimpse of blue through an open doorway up ahead. "Thank you, Wentworth. I can manage from here."

Alarmed by the steely tone of his lordship's voice, Wentworth followed him to the door of the blue and white parlor to be certain all was well. Reassured, he returned to his duties.

Behind him at the door to the parlor, Harry had stopped as if he'd run into a wall. Instead of Jasper Ruddleston, Regina was with *Smythe*. Harry's gaze flashed around the room looking for Ruddleston, murder in his eyes. Satisfied that only she and Smythe occupied the room, he plunged forward. "Thank Heaven you're safe!"

Regina saw the anxiety in his eyes and her heart leaped. This wasn't the blasé Taskford the world knew.

Smythe sighed, got up off his knee and stepped back from her. "Not deserting you, m'dear. Just don't want to get trampled."

Regina tried to pull her attention away from Taskford to tell Smythe how grateful she was, how appreciative she was of his offer to sacrifice himself to save the children. To tell him how very much she cherished him as a friend. It was useless. Taskford's eyes held her as surely as iron bands would have done.

Smythe smiled and backed out of the room. "I'll tell Wentworth you're not to be disturbed." As he pulled the double doors closed, Regina thought she heard him murmur, "Better luck next time, Smythe, old boy." Then the doors were firmly shut and she was alone with this man who had fire in his eyes.

"I . . . I am fine, Taskford."

He advanced on her purposefully. "What the devil were

you doing, letting Smythe be down on a knee in front of you like that?"

"David was . . . proposing."

"Marriage?" He sounded as if the idea astounded him.

Regina was annoyed. Did he think Smythe would propose anything else? "Yes. Marriage. *Gentlemen* rarely propose anything else."

"Are you trying to imply that I am not a gentleman, Mrs. Landry?"

Regina found herself backing away from him. This seemed a good time to change the subject. "The children are safe at Taskford Manor, are they not?" She backed into the arm of the sofa.

Taskford came on.

Her breath seemed impossible to catch. She heard herself taking short little gasps. She worked her way around the sofa without taking her eyes off Taskford's.

Harry didn't answer. He just kept coming at her.

"Jasper is gone." She held out a hand to stop him. "I'm quite safe." Still she backed away. Eyes wide, she watched him advance.

"Oh, no, my Amazon, you are far from safe." His eyes spoke volumes about the danger she faced. "Remember, you've just pointed out that I'm no gentleman."

For a moment, her woman's heart quailed. The man was obviously going to have her in his arms in the next moment. Then her head took over. Where, after all, would she rather be?

She fetched up against the back wall of the blue-and-white parlor so hard that her curls shook. Before she could move, before she could think, his hard body was against hers, pinning her there.

She could feel the muscles in his chest move as he slipped

his arms around her to bring her even closer, feel his breath on her cheek as he lowered his head to claim her mouth.

She slipped her arms up around his broad shoulders, and he moaned low in his throat. When she twined her fingers in the hair at the nape of his neck, his moan changed to a growl.

One of his hands dropped down to press her hips more closely to his lower body. That left no doubt of his intentions.

Suddenly, she was beyond thinking *what* she felt. She was lost in a whirlpool of sensation.

He lifted her and carried her to the sofa she had backed into a moment ago. Without breaking the kiss he was deepening, he lay her on the soft, blue satin.

His mouth demanded a response from her and she moaned softly in her turn. Desire burned along her limbs. She pulled him down to her, then placed her hands on his cheeks to hold his face away. Looking into his eyes she tried to read what she saw there. Was this simply lust? In return for the love she knew she had for Taskford, was she to receive no more than that? No better than that?

Harry let her push him away. Taking her now—much as he wanted to in his relief at finding her safe, much as his body clamored to possess her—wasn't what he had in mind.

Breathing hard, he rose and lifted her to her feet. Holding her still before him, he straightened her clothes and gently smoothed her hair. Stepping away from her, he watched for her reaction. He got a great deal of satisfaction from the surprise and disappointment he saw in her face.

"You love me." He made it a bald statement of fact.

She answered with a hint of anger. "Yes. I do." Her eyes glinted, her nostrils flared. She dared him to make something of her admission in much the way children at play dared one another.

He was all masculine ego. He grinned, making it a long, slow process. "Then why won't you be my mistress?"

She looked at him, her gaze level, steady. She had no intention of answering that question. She'd answered it before, and nothing had changed since. Nothing had changed except that now she had fallen in love with him. Deeply, helplessly, hopelessly in love with him. But she was still herself, and she still held herself in high esteem.

He moved a step closer.

She stood her ground.

"No?" He whispered the query.

"No." She answered quietly, firmly.

He reached for her.

She knew she should resist, knew he was toying with her, trying to break her will. She didn't.

He snatched her the last few inches so that when she landed against his chest she was as close as their bodies could fit. And suddenly she was angry. Angrier than she'd let herself be in a very long time.

So he wanted a mistress, did he? She'd show him mistress!

She grabbed the sides of his face and pulled it down to her own. If he'd pulled away, she'd have grabbed and yanked him back by the ears!

Harry, however, wasn't the least bit interested in pulling away. Her passionate attack on his mouth with her own suited him just fine. When she plastered her lithe body against his and moved seductively, his knees threatened to turn to jelly.

She pushed him into the nearest straight chair and sat in his lap.

Harry's head was so light that for the first time in his life he understood the word "swoon." When she wriggled in his lap like a netted trout, his passion exploded out of his much-vaunted control.

And Regina stood up. And back. And glared at him from under her brows, her disheveled hair falling into her eyes. "There, Lord Taskford. Now! How would you like to be *my* plaything! *My* mistress, if you will?"

One split second of sheer astounded masculine shock and Harry came out of the chair roaring. With a smooth rush he carried her down and pinned her on her back to the thick Oriental rug, the full weight of his big body holding her there.

His kisses rained on her like molten lava. His hands were rough and demanding. They met one another kiss for kiss, caress for caress, until they were both breathless—panting.

"Amazon," he accused.

"Libertine," she countered.

He burst out laughing.

After a second, she joined in. Was there ever such a man? Ever such a love? When did laughter follow hard on the heels of unrequited passion? Only with them! Only with him! Her laughter stilled.

Harry looked at her inquiringly.

Her eyes filled with tears. She felt fragmented inside. She mourned her love. So great a love. She'd never believed it possible for mere mortals to feel the ecstasy she felt, to soar to the heights she'd reached with Taskford. It was such a pity. Such a waste.

But to save the children, she must marry—she had no choice.

Harry rose from the floor and gently pulled her up after him. "What is it?" Concern deepened his already husky voice. "What's the matter, Regina?"

This was the moment. Now was the time for him to ask her to be his bride. Now, or never. He knew of her dilemma, understood her desperate need. This instant in time was the one in which he should—if he truly cared—ask her to marry him.

She waited. With her blood still pounding through her veins from their shared passion—with her heart in her eyes and her soul crying out to him, she waited.

And Taskford did not speak.

Regina felt her world crumple and dissolve around her where she stood. It was over. She resigned her great love to that place where dreams go to die.

Now she was left with but one duty to perform. She was faced with the task of telling Taskford she was going to marry Smythe.

Taking a deep breath, she marshalled her courage.

Harry frowned slightly, recognized that she was about to say something he wasn't going to like, and sat on the arm of nearby chair. Repressing a deep sigh, he prompted her. "What is it?"

She followed his example and sat. Finally, she said, "As you know, I must marry to keep my brother Philip's children."

He nodded.

Regina went on. He had failed her one last time. "So I am going to marry Smythe."

Harry shot off the arm of the chair. He took two turns of the hearth rug, biting his tongue, then sat down again, the muscle in his jaw jumping. "No."

She laughed. Her laughter had an edge.

Harry didn't care for it.

"Smythe," Regina informed him, "is a person of honor and integrity, someone who will be good for the children. Someone who . . ."

She stopped as realization of what she was doing hit her. Why was she trying to justify her proposed action? What did it matter to Taskford? She wasn't going to be his mistress, and that was all *he* cared about. She went on anyway. ". . . has offered to be my husband so that I may keep Philydia and Thomas."

He asked in a voice as cold and still as death, "Have you told him you're going to marry him?"

"Not yet, but I shall." The hint of a smile brushed her lips. "You interrupted us before I could give him my answer."

Hearing that, Harry rose and stared at her long and hard, his eyes blazing. Then he spun on his heel and stalked majestically from the room.

Thirty-one

On the day of Regina Ransome Landry's necessarily rushed wedding, long garlands of fragrant flowers festooned the little village church. Their perfume filled the air, wafting over the assembled crowd of those who had come to watch the late Viscount's sister marry her nobleman.

Never had the ancient stone edifice looked so festive, not even for the wedding of the late Viscount to his lady. Never had enthusiasm run so high. For, now, young Viscount Thomas and his sister, Philydia, were safe. Safe from the greediness of the awful Jasper Ruddleston, who would have ruined the estate and impoverished the village.

No praise was high enough for their savior, the man who was about to wed their Miss Regina. And he was doing it by a special license that he'd driven all the other night to bring back in time for the wedding.

Every nook and cranny of the old Norman church was splendidly decorated for the wedding. Winnie and Wentworth had marshalled half the residents of the hamlet, commandeering every able body to gather flowers for the great day.

The greenhouses of both Charnwood and Taskford Manor had been stripped of every bloom . . . in spite of the fact that they had not been able to ask permission from the absent master of the manor. Excitement was high.

Everyone rejoiced.

Except the bride.

In her bedchamber at Charnwood, Regina stood in front of her pier glass and carefully studied her reflection. She wanted to look her absolute best for a very good reason. This wedding was the only one that dear Smythe would have. He was sacrificing his chance at finding and marrying his true love in order to save Philydia and Thomas. Regina felt that the least she could do was to make herself as beautiful a bride as she could be.

The dress, which had been her own mother's wedding dress, was lovely. Of cream satin, with an overdress of antique lace, it had been altered to fit the current style by a host of seamstresses working through the night. Now, falling in soft folds from the high waistline to the floor, it accented her unusual height as it skimmed her slender figure.

The veil that went with it, also of antique lace, had been her mother's as well. Regina turned to look behind her at the yards and yards of it that would trail down the aisle after her, and sighed. Looking again at the figure in the tall mirror, she noticed that her cheeks were pale. She wondered if she would be sighing and pale-cheeked if it were her true love she was going to meet at the altar . . . and knew that she would not.

If she were going to walk down the aisle to meet Taskford to be joined to him forever, her eyes would be shining with a light that would cause the whole church to glow. Her cheeks would be flying flags of bright, eager color, and her heart would be singing.

But she wasn't meeting Taskford. As much as she loved

him, she was going to marry his friend instead. She lifted her chin at her reflection and told it firmly, "Yes, my girl. You are going to marry Smythe." Her breath caught. "David," she corrected herself. "And you are going to smile for him, and be beautiful for him. Because if anyone deserves the best you can give, it's David."

Winnie came in, then, with Regina's bouquet. White roses and daisies and several tiny flowers she couldn't name were all made misty by the abundance of gypsophila tucked in between them. Baby's breath. Such a sweet name. Regina had always loved it.

"Are you ready, dear?" Winnie tried hard not to sound sad.

Not trusting herself to speak, Regina nodded.

"Come, then, the carriage is waiting."

In the vaulted vestibule of the church, four of Taskford's friends were gathered. As the hour for the ceremony drew near, they glanced out the tall, nail-studded oak doors more and more frequently.

"Where is he? Where the hell is Taskford?" Mathers's agitation drew the attention of the sexton.

"May I be of service?"

"Not unless you know where the Earl of Taskford is."

"I'm afraid not." He smiled apologetically, and said, "Isn't the church lovely? It is such a rare thing to have all these decorations when couples are married by special license. There is usually not enough time to do things up so well." He looked around the church, beaming, then nodded to them, and went on his way to the narrow stairs that led up to the choir loft and beyond. Soon mellow notes rang softly down from the bell tower, as he quietly practiced the combinations he'd chosen to sound for the recessional that would follow the approaching nuptials.

"What the deuce will we do if Harry doesn't show?" Mathers ran a finger around inside his cravat.

"Ah," Bly told him. "Then the fat will be in the fire, indeed."

MacLain ran a hand through his thick, blond mane and demanded, "Well, which one of you knows where he went?"

"None of us, fool!" Bly was getting short-tempered under pressure.

There was a distant sound of horses' hooves and the jingle of harness. All four men leapt to the doorway to peer out.

"Oh, Lord!" Mathers was tearing at his cravat again.

Stone said, "It's her."

Bly and Mathers glared at him. Bly grabbed Stone's shoulder. "Go. Warn Smythe."

"Warn him about what?"

"Tell him Mrs. Landry's almost here."

"Why warn him about that? She'd have to be here if they're to be wed."

Bly turned on him with murder in his eyes. "Just go tell him!"

"All right! No need to snarl." Stone shook his head and started around the side of the church to find the groom.

Mathers said, "Maybe we should have told him and Mac what's going on."

MacLain demanded, "What *is* going on?"

"Never mind!" Bly almost shouted at him. Just this once, he almost wished that he and Mathers and Smythe *had* told MacLain and Stone what was going on.

Mathers pasted a smile on his face, tugged at his vest and started down the steps to meet Regina's flower-filled barouche.

Bly followed, but his eyes were focused on the farthest curve in the road.

The sight of Regina drove everything else from Mathers's

mind. "You are exquisite, my dear." He kissed the hand she extended to him to help her from the low-slung barouche. Then escorted her to the church vestibule.

"Thank you." Regina's voice was just the least bit shaky. Hearing that, she took a steadying breath, smiled at a puzzled, frowning MacLain and looked up at Bly. "You, I believe, have offered to give me away, Lord Blythingdale. I must thank you." She put her arm through his and was surprised to feel that he was as shaky as she was. Darting a glance at his face, she saw that it was as set as a granite statue's, his eyes troubled.

Before she could ask him what the matter was, the organ began the music to which she was to proceed up the aisle. Bly lunged forward like a whipped horse, then steadied and shot her a rueful half smile. "Sorry. Bit nervous."

Regina could understand that. She looked ahead to the altar. The vicar stood there, his white robes tinted with a multitude of colors carried by the shaft of sunlight that spilled down from the rose window. Smythe stood beside him. He looked as nervous as Bly.

She arrived at the altar.

"Dearly beloved, we are gathered together here in the sight of God and in the face of His congregation to join this man and this woman in holy matrimony, which is an honorable estate . . ." The sonorous words rolled out over the assembled well-wishers, and Regina's heart ached. She flinched inside when the vicar intoned, "honorable among all men, and therefore not to be enterprised nor taken in hand unadvisedly . . ."—Regina wanted to cringe—"lightly"—Regina's eyes closed as he said—"or wantonly. . . ."

Surely, she prayed, her reason for marrying would serve as her excuse in the hereafter.

When the vicar asked, "Who gives this woman?" Bly

stepped forward and handed Regina to Smythe. A look of such intent questioning shot from Smythe to Bly that Regina was startled.

"Well?" Regina could barely hear Smythe's single-word question.

Bly heard it, though. "Not yet."

Smythe let Bly have a scowling, bug-eyed look.

"Stall!" Bly hissed.

The vicar had had enough. "Gentlemen!" he said sharply.

Bly spun around and marched to the seat reserved for him beside Mathers.

The vicar continued the ceremony. His practiced tones carried every clearly enunciated word throughout the church. After what seemed an eternity to Regina, he finally got to the part where he asked, "If anyone can show just cause that these two . . ."

Smythe was twisting around, craning his neck to see the door of the church.

Regina wondered what in the world he was looking for. Was he worried Jasper would appear with the court bailiffs?

"should not be joined in the bonds of holy matrimony . . ."

Bly got up from the front pew and stalked to the back of the church.

Mathers let out an explosive sigh, jumped up, and followed him.

Regina was hard put to preserve the calm attitude of sweet acceptance she had fought so hard to achieve during her carriage ride to the church. Truth to tell, she was feeling just the tiniest bit annoyed.

The vicar's face was reddening. His voice took on a distinct edge. "let him speak now or forever hold his peace. . . ."

"He's here!" Bly's shout shook the rafters.

Over the startled murmur of the guests, Regina heard Smythe breathe a heartfelt, "Thank God!"

At the far end of the church aisle, iron-shod hooves shot sparks from the stone-flagged floor of the church. Mathers yelled, "Look out!" and dodged aside to keep from being knocked down by the horse. "Blast it, Harry! This is a church!"

In response, Taskford vaulted off the horse he'd ridden into the sanctuary and tossed him the reins. He thrust a fist skyward. "I do!" He declared in ringing tones. "*I* declare an impediment!"

He strode halfway up the aisle, his shoulders and boots covered with the dust of the road. Stopping there, he announced, "She can't marry Smythe! There's an impediment!"

Regina's eyes opened in shock. What could there possibly be? She was a widow.

"State the impediment, Lord Taskford," the vicar commanded.

"Me! *I* am the impediment!" Harry continued deliberately up the aisle, one sure, slow step at a time. His gaze locked with Regina's startled one. "I am the man she loves."

Regina closed her eyes.

"And I love her." He had almost reached the altar.

Regina's eyes flew open. Her heart bounded.

"I rode all night when I left her to get the family ring from the London vault. I was on the Archbishop's doorstep to procure a special license early the next morning. I was denied it." He shot a fulminating glare at Smythe where he stood half hiding behind the vicar. "I rode two horses into the ground to arrive back here from Canterbury in time." He lowered his head and glowered even more intently at his friend.

Smythe murmured, "Oh, Lord. He knows."

Harry transferred his fierce regard to the clergyman. Forcefully, he pronounced, "And, by God, if Regina Landry is going to marry anyone here today, it is going to be me!" With those words, he leapt lightly up the steps of the altar to where she stood and snatched Regina down into his arms.

The vicar said, "Well! I never!" and that carried to the back of the church as well as the sonorous beginning words of the marriage ceremony had.

Harry and Regina didn't even hear him, they were lost in each other. Taskford murmured, "I love you, Regina Landry. Will you marry me?"

Regina, tears blurring her vision, could only nod.

The clergyman, however, wasn't lost in anything. "This is highly irregular!"

Smythe touched his arm lightly. "Actually, it's not *quite* so bad as you think, vicar."

The man spun around to glare at Smythe.

"You see, old boy, the reason I was squirming so during the ceremony was that I was worried that Harry might not arrive in time."

The vicar was approaching a state of shock.

"He had to, you see, if we were going to go much further with the service."

"What the dev—" Wide-eyed, the churchman slapped a hand over his mouth and began again. "What is going on here?"

"Well, we all knew that Harry loved Regina. It was plain to everybody but him. We just had to jolt him into realizing it."

"This is a travesty! How dare you so misuse the sacraments of the church!"

"Well, I didn't really misuse 'em *too* badly. And you must," Smythe said, nodding to where Regina and Taskford stood staring hungrily at one another, "admit that it was all for a good cause."

The vicar looked to where the two lovers stood, and his attitude softened. "But what if he hadn't come! My God, man, would you have married her? Knowing she loved another?"

Smythe answered him quietly. "Yes. I'd have married her. But it would have had to have been at a later date."

"What?"

"Couldn't have married her today, vicar. You see, it's this way. The names I got put on my on my special license are, Regina Ransome Landry—"

"Well? That's perfectly proper," the clergyman snapped. "We all know no special license can be granted unless the names of both parties appear on it."

"Yes, that's true. But as I was trying to tell you, the other name I had the Bishop put on the license was not mine."

"Not yours!" the vicar exploded. "This is most, most irregular, sir! Not your name on the license?"

"No. The name I had put on the license was 'Geoffrey Harold Wainwright, Earl of Taskford.'"

Below them on the steps of the altar, Taskford, with a great shout of laughter, crushed Regina to him and claimed her mouth in a lingering kiss.

Behind them, those who had come to wish Regina well, and to politely thank the nice man who'd so gallantly stepped forward to marry her and save them all, erupted in waves of fervent cheers that were most, most unchurchlike!

Epilogue

Amber firelight played over them as they relaxed on the settee in front of the fireplace. Harry sat holding Regina in his arms, and she nestled her head on his shoulder. Both of them smiled fondly down on the scene at their feet.

There on the warm hearth rug, Philydia and Thomas played with Regina and Harry's twins, their golden heads bent over the tiny, dark-haired ones.

"No!" Thomas reached for the nearest boy's hand, saying, "You can't put that in your mouth."

"He's teething," Philydia informed him from the height of superior knowledge.

"That doesn't mean he can chew on any old thing he picks up." He lifted the object for her to look at. "See. It's Mother's riding glove."

Regina held her breath, waiting for Philydia to correct her brother.

Harry tightened his embrace, cherishing her, wanting to guard her against hurt.

Regina could feel his jaw clench. He cared so fiercely, but they'd agreed never to chasten Philydia for correcting

Thomas, never to transgress against the loyalty the girl had for her dead mother.

Philydia stared at her brother for a long moment, but her usual objection to his naming their Aunt Regina "Mother" remained unvoiced. She looked from Thomas to her baby cousins smiling up at her, then she looked over to where her aunt and her uncle by marriage sat.

Regina tightened her grip on Harry's hand.

Bending his dark head to kiss Regina's forehead, Harry murmured, "So, my intrepid Amazon, there *is* something that you're afraid of."

"Yes," she admitted, "but now I have you." She turned her gaze back to her niece and nephew, and whispered for him alone, "I was afraid of having nowhere to belong."

From his place on the hearth rug, Thomas was announcing in his clear, high voice, "Caliban brought the glove from the hall table." He reached out to pet the huge dog.

Caliban's tail thumped the floor.

Staring at her hands where they lay clasped tightly in her lap, Philydia sat considering for a long moment. Suddenly her eyes filled with tears, but she bit her lip and blinked them away. Evidently she had come to some important decision, for she raised her chin in a gesture reminiscent of Regina and stared meaningfully at her brother. Then she said firmly, "Thomas, stop petting Caliban. You don't reward an animal for stealing things off the hall table. You should teach Caliban to leave"—she took a deep breath—"*Mother's* gloves alone."

Regina's own breath caught.

Taskford drew air into his lungs, surprised that he'd been holding *his* breath.

They were interrupted by a soft sound from the hall just as the tall clock between the windows of the garden wall chimed the hour. It was eight o'clock, and Wentworth was opening the double doors to the family drawing room.

Winnie entered the room with a pair of nursemaids close behind her. "Time for bed, children."

The nurserymaids curtsied to their employers, scooped up the twins and started across the vast expanse of Oriental carpet toward the door, murmuring endearments to them. Unaware of the tension in the room, Winnie waited for the two older children, her hand outstretched. "Come, please."

Rising obediently from the hearth rug, Philydia called after the babies, "Good night, twins." She looked younger, happier than Regina had ever seen her—as if a tremendous weight had been lifted from her.

The girl's courage seemed to fail her when she must address Regina directly, though. With a shy glance toward the adults who were now her very own family, she softly breathed, "Good night."

Thomas and Caliban followed her from the room, and the double doors closed softly behind them.

For the next few minutes, there was no sound but the crackle of the flames in the fireplace. Then a log shifted and fell, sending sparks flying up the chimney like a cloud of ruby fireflies.

Regina sat quietly, basking in the knowledge that Philydia had finally won through her long bitterness and accepted her. After a silent moment, she said in an unsteady voice, "It would seem that I've just been made welcome here in my home." Her eyes alight, she smiled up at her husband. "Now, I have two places to belong."

Harry rose and gathered her close.

Standing in the safe circle of his embrace, Regina let her head fall back against her husband's arm, and looked up at him. Never would she tire of gazing into his face.

As she perused it, firelight glinted on his strong white

teeth. He was smiling down at her with that special smile she had never seen before their wedding—the loving smile that told her he had finally found his happiness in her and in their marriage. It made her feel as if her bones would melt.

How could she ever have thought that she could live without him?

Harry tipped her face up and claimed her lips with his own.

After the long moment of their kiss, he spoke. Quietly, but firmly, he told her, "Just don't ever forget, my darling Amazon, that the place you *most* belong is right here in my arms." He paused and looked deep into her eyes as he told her, "Because I *always* ride for the roses."

Author's Note

I have taken great liberties with the physical layout of New-market in order to enhance the story. I hope my readers will forgive them in the interest of the Romance.